Q...
the...
Ha...
Sp...
be...

Pr...

'A...
on...

'Re...

'The perfect mix for a highly charged, fast-moving crime thriller' *Glasgow Herald*

'There is a whole world here, the tense narratives all come to the boil at the same time in a spectacular climax' *Shots* magazine

'[Quintin Jardine] sells more crime fiction in Scotland than John Grisham and people queue around the block to buy his latest book' *The Australian*

'Engrossing, believable characters ... captures Edinburgh beautifully ... It all adds up to a very good read' *Edinburgh Evening News*

'A complex story combined with robust characterisation; a murder/mystery novel of our time that will keep you hooked to the very last page' *The Scots Magazine*

By Quintin Jardine and available from Headline

Quintin
Jardine

STAY OF
EXECUTION

headline

First published in 2004
by HEADLINE PUBLISHING GROUP

First published in paperback in 2005
by HEADLINE PUBLISHING GROUP

First published in this paperback edition in 2011
by HEADLINE PUBLISHING GROUP

6

Cataloguing in Publication Data is available from the British Library

ISBN 978 0 7553 5871 7

Typeset in Electra by Avon DataSet Ltd, Bidford-on-Avon, Warwickshire

Printed in the UK by CPI Group (UK), Croydon, CR0 4YY

Headline's policy is to use papers that are natural, renewable and
recyclable products and made from wood grown in sustainable forests.
The logging and manufacturing processes are expected to conform to the
environmental regulations of the country of origin.

HEADLINE PUBLISHING GROUP
An Hachette UK Company
338 Euston Road
London NW1 3BH

www.headline.co.uk
www.hachette.co.uk

Finally, too long delayed, this book is dedicated to the ladies and gentlemen of Lothian and Borders Police, for their inspiration, their public service, and for tolerating the existence of a wholly fictional force in their midst without complaining too much. (Or even at all.)

Acknowledgements

The author's thanks go to . . .

The Central Intelligence Agency, for publishing its
World Factbook on the Internet.

Les Marcheurs Belges, who have to be seen to be
believed . . . and even then, it's difficult.

Carme Rivera Caballero, for lending me her dog.

Eddie Bell and Pat Lomax, for helping me carry this
off . . . and on.

Martin Fletcher, for his unfailing support.

Kim Hardie, for hers.

Mira and Nurmi, for giving me such stiff competition.

And . . .

Eileen, for putting up with all the writing months when
she finds herself living with a grizzly.

One

The big Scots detective stood in silence, because there was nothing to say. He was a mature man, over the crest of the hill that leads into middle age, and he had known his share of life's inevitable sadness; indeed, if truth be told, more than his share. Yet the place in which he stood affected him in a way that he had not experienced before. He had seen it on television, and he had read of it, from the awful beginning and through the grim weeks and months that had followed, but nothing had prepared him for the actuality of it. It was vast, yet no greater than he had expected. There was no sepulchral silence about it: even on a Saturday the traffic rushed past nearby. And yet there was a sense of something all around, something that with very little imagination could have been the echoes of the screams of three thousand souls.

A voice broke into his meditation. 'By sheer evil chance, I was on my way here when it began to go down,' his companion said, quietly. 'After the first plane had hit, I saw people standing, staring at it, like they didn't believe it. Some of them even had camcorders. They stood there filming, like it was some movie special effect or whatever, and they'd got lucky. They were the tourists, though. Our guys, the New Yorkers, most of them were running for their very lives.'

Mario McGuire looked to his right, towards his host rather than at him, for the man seemed to be staring at a point in the distance, an imaginary screen on which the scene was being re-run. He wondered how often he had seen that movie, in the light of day and in the dark of night, and how many more times he would see it in the rest of his life to come.

'Not you though,' he said, respectfully. 'Not your people; they ran into it.'

'And twenty-three of them didn't walk out. I knew every one of them, from John d'Allara to Walter Weaver: four sergeants, two detectives and seventeen patrol officers. But, aah, the fire-fighters . . .' He looked down, then up, then away, as if he was composing himself. 'New York Fire Department lost three hundred and forty-seven people, of all ranks. Twenty-three fire chiefs died here, you know. Those people even killed the Department chaplain.' When, finally, he glanced at McGuire, the look in his eye seemed to say that however well he knew the facts, however often he recited the names of the dead, aloud and in his head, he was still having trouble making himself believe in its raw, terrible truth.

Inspector Colin Mawhinney, commander of the 1st Precinct, New York Police Department, which takes in Manhattan Island's financial district, looked to be in his early forties. He and his guest were of equivalent rank in their respective forces, and although the Scot surmised that he was the younger by a few years, he wondered how quickly he would have risen through the ranks in a body almost twenty times larger than his own.

Everything about the New Yorker looked classy. His hair, more grey than black, was cut close, to fit neatly inside the uniform cap that he held respectfully in his hand. His uniform was immaculate, and his shoes shone as brightly as its badges. McGuire, on the other hand, was in plain clothes, and more specifically, a lightweight Italian suit: he was glad that he had packed it, since New York was much warmer in October than it had been in April on his last visit, ten years before.

He had expected to be taken to the site of the World Trade Center, although privately he had hoped that it would not happen. He had been there before, as a brash young tourist, and had taken the elevator to the top, accompanied by his trembling girlfriend of the time, a nurse called Rachel. Her face had become a blur in his past, but the rest of that day had not. It had left him with the belief that the WTC was one of the genuine wonders of the modern world, and despite the warning shot of the first terrorist attack on the edifice, or perhaps because of it, that it was invulnerable. And so he recognised the look that he had seen in Mawhinney's eyes; for he suspected that it had been in his own.

The visit had been obligatory, though, right there on the programme for the first day of his official visit. Before September Eleven, one or two of his hosts might have called him, jokingly, a visiting fireman, but not since. That term had gone from the lexicon of Americana, and instead he had been received as plain Detective Superintendent McGuire, divisional CID commander. The formalities had been completed at the

3

beginning, on his arrival a day earlier: the Scot had been received at One Police Plaza by the head of the Patrol Bureau. There had been a photo-call, at which he had handed over a cheque for eighty-one thousand dollars, the proceeds of a series of fund-raisers run by the Edinburgh police force's NYPD Friendship Committee, in aid of fallen officers' families. Then, after a tour of the headquarters building, he had been turned over to Inspector Mawhinney for the rest of his stay.

That morning, they had followed a parade up to Ground Zero from Battery Park, where the patrol car had dropped them. The procession formed itself into ranks behind a red fire tender, decorated on either side by hand-painted banners asking God to bless America. The people themselves, young women and children just outnumbering the elderly, wore no mourning clothes. They were casually dressed, and many carried placards displaying the names and images of their loved ones. They were led by an Irish band of drums and bagpipes, its members wearing green kilts and feather-plumed bonnets. It played no laments along the way; the tunes were stirring. There were no tears among the marchers, no overt displays of grief; instead they smiled and held their heads high. Their message was one of defiance, and more, of pride in what they had given overcoming the sorrow for what they had lost.

At first McGuire had hung back, fearful of being taken for a ghoulish intruder, but Mawhinney had drawn him forward, joining the tail of the parade. 'We're both cops, Superintendent,' he had said. 'We're welcome here, I assure you.'

'I'm in plain clothes, though.'

The American had released what was almost his first smile

since their introduction. 'You could be wearing a Sioux war-bonnet and you'd still look like a cop.'

They had processed in silence, the precinct commander drawing salutes from the patrol officers who lined the route, and returning them with military sharpness and with a nod of recognition. McGuire had served in uniform long enough to be able to judge a senior officer's popularity from the body language of those under his command, and he read more than respect among Mawhinney's men and women: he read a degree of reverence.

The route was short, less than a mile; it reached an assembly point. The band played 'Amazing Grace', and photographs were taken by the marchers, of the site and of each other. Then they dispersed, drifting back towards the southern tip of Manhattan, to the point from which they had set out, leaving the two policemen to make their way down into the great crater.

'How long have you been precinct commander, Inspector Mawhinney?' McGuire asked, as they stood, looking up and around, aware that high above, several dozen people were looking at them from a roughly built viewing gallery. He thought that, as a survivor of the horror, the man might be having difficulty just being there, and he sought to change the mood.

'I've been down here for almost five years now,' the American replied. 'And let's drop the formality, uh, before we run into a problem over who should be calling who "sir". I moved here from the 34th Precinct, up at the north end of the island.'

'Was it a big contrast?'

'It's not far in mileage terms . . . this isn't a big island . . . but yeah, it was quite a change, from an ethnically mixed community, with a strong academic core, to the heart of the global economy . . . although since you're British, you'd probably say that's in London.'

McGuire shook his head. 'I may be only a simple detective, but I can count.' He nodded to the east. 'I know the value of shares traded along there on Wall Street, compared to any other stock exchange on the planet. Besides, I may have been born in Scotland, but my dad was from Dublin and my mother's the daughter of two Italian immigrants.'

Mawhinney chuckled softly. 'What does that make you?'

'My bosses back in Edinburgh would say it makes me unmanageable; I prefer to think that it makes me broad-minded.'

'Your bosses must rate you, or they wouldn't have sent you on this trip.'

'Nah. Bob Skinner, my DCC, put a dozen names in a hat and drew mine out. Mind you,' he added, 'it helped that I was prepared to pay my own expenses.'

'DCC?'

'Deputy chief constable.'

'Does that mean that your boss isn't a detective?'

McGuire laughed. 'Sure, and if he isn't, then as like as not, the next time I go to church I'll see Ian Paisley coming out of the confessional. Big Bob may be on the executive floor at headquarters . . . some would say he runs the force, but God help them if he hears them . . . but he'll always be a detective.

We have a head of Criminal Investigation, that's Dan Pringle, my one-up boss. He's supposed to be in command on a day-to-day basis. The DCC's role is way up there, doing crime strategy and all that stuff, and deputising for Proud Jimmy . . .'

'Who?' exclaimed Mawhinney.

'Sorry. Our chief constable's name is James Proud. Sir James Proud, in fact; hence his nickname. The DCC's his number two and stands in for him as necessary, but Pringle reports to him directly; the big guy's the bane of Dan's life, for he just can't keep his hands off. There's a legend about him once taking his three-year-old son on a stake-out, long after he'd left the active line.'

'A legend? Is it true?'

'Not quite. As I understand it, Master James Andrew Skinner was only two at the time.' He paused. 'He's kept hold of Special Branch too; that's outside the normal CID loop. I reported to him when I ran it.'

'Special Branch?'

'Our semi-secret police. They tie into the security services, which really do stay secret despite the best efforts of our government.'

'Something like our National Security Agency, then. You've heard of that?'

'The NSA . . . isn't it also known as No Such Agency? Sure, I've heard of it; and the stories about it.'

Mawhinney gave a grim, humourless smile. 'I read somewhere that a famous person said, "There are powers at work in this country" . . . meaning yours . . . "of which we know nothing." The vast majority of Americans could say the same thing.' He glanced round, and slightly up, at McGuire. 'You mentioned your boss's son. Do you have kids?'

'No.'

'Married?'

'Yes, but we're separated. It's amicable and all that; we're just sitting out the two-year period, before we can apply for a simple divorce.'

'You'll still have lawyers' bills, though, I'll bet.'

'You'd lose. Where there are no kids involved, you can do it all yourselves: and we will.'

'That sounds like a good system you have in Scotland. It can be anything but simple here.'

'It is, and I'm thankful. The last thing either Maggie or I would want would be to set out the breakdown of our relationship in open court.' He shrugged. 'Not that there's anything scandalous about it, but with us both being senior police officers . . .' He saw the inspector's eyebrows rise. 'She's a detective too,' he explained. 'Superintendent like me, CID divisional commander, like me, only she's in the city and I'm in Borders.'

'Borders?'

'Yeah. It's a rural area; bit of a fucking backwater, if truth be told, but it's okay for a first command posting. I don't think I'll be there much longer, though. There's changes in the wind, and they could blow me somewhere else. Things could be happening right now, for all I know.'

'Does that mean you can't wait to get back?' asked Mawhinney.

'You're kidding!' McGuire exclaimed. 'I love your city,

man. I hope you like mine half as much when we all go back next week on your half of the exchange visit.'

'I'm sure I will. I've always wanted to visit Edinburgh.' The American frowned. 'But what did you mean, "we all"? Is there another cop coming with us, or were you just trying to talk like a Southern Gentleman?'

His guest grinned. 'Neither of those things. Sorry again, I should have told you earlier, but I'm not here on my own. Since Maggie and I split I'm in a new relationship, and Paula came with me on the trip.'

'Will you remarry when you can?'

The Scot shook his head. 'No.'

'That sounds very definite.'

'It is. Paula's my cousin.'

'Is that a bar to marriage in your country? It isn't in New York.'

'No, but . . . there's the Italian thing, the family, and of course the Church; not that I could remarry there anyway, but you know what I mean. On top of that, neither of us wants to get hitched. We don't even live together: close to, but not in the same house. We've just fallen into this thing, it suits us, and we're both happy with the way it's working.'

'She isn't a cop too, is she?'

'Hell no. She runs the family enterprises; that's one reason why she's here with me, to do some research into the deli business, New York style. I'm a trustee too, but most of my involvement is through a lawyer with power to act, to keep things square with the day job.'

'Is it a big company?'

'Big enough, and bigger since Paulie took over.' He stopped abruptly. 'But how about you, Colin?' he asked. 'Do you have a working wife?'

There was a pause. 'I did.'

'Don't tell me. She's a cop and you're divorced.'

'No,' said Mawhinney, quietly. 'She wasn't a cop, and she's dead.'

McGuire threw his head back. 'Ah, shit. Me and my mouth. I'm sorry. When did it happen?'

'September eleven, two thousand and one.'

The Scot gasped. 'She . . .'

'Margery was an account manager with an investment house called Garamond and Stretch. She worked in the second tower to be hit, just at the point of impact. I had decided to go in early that morning. I like to let all my officers see the boss,' he said in explanation, 'round the clock, not just during the day shift. She usually started at eight o'clock, and so that morning we arranged that we would meet for breakfast at nine. That's how I came to be here. I had just started the walk from my office . . . I don't like using cars for private appointments . . . when the first plane hit. I called in on my cell phone and ordered all available officers to the scene, then I ran the rest of the way, to take command, but first to find my wife and get her out of there. I called her on her cell phone as I was running, to find out where she was. She was still in her office: she told me they had been advised to stay put, so as not to hamper the evacuation from the other tower. I told her that as soon as I got to the scene, as ranking police officer I would order complete evacuation of the area, and would she please get the hell out of there. She said she would talk to her boss and tell him what I had said. A few minutes later I was there, giving that very order and hoping to find her coming out of the entrance door. But she never did. And then the second plane hit.'

He reached out his right foot, in its brightly shining shoe, and touched the ground: it was as if he was caressing it. 'They never found her body, Mario,' he murmured. 'In a sense, we're standing on her grave.'

'Man, why didn't you say?' exclaimed McGuire. 'I'd never have . . .' He stopped, abruptly. 'Come on, let's get out of here.'

'No, no,' Mawhinney retorted. 'Really, it's all right. I come here often, and not just in uniform. Sometimes, like a lot of people, like those we saw earlier, I bring flowers. Maybe it'll change in time, but right now, like many of the bereaved, I just don't have anywhere else to go.'

Two

They assembled in the centre of Brussels, all thirty-seven of them. All of the squad were men; even in the twenty-first century there were no women allowed among the ranks. Whenever they were challenged about this their stock excuse was that the uniforms just did not fit women properly. As they lined up for the photographers they stood smartly at attention, twelve of them with heavy ancient weapons shouldered.

The troop carrier, as they called it, stood ready and waiting, its engine running in the evening chill to charge the heating system. There was only one bus, for on this special journey there would be no camp followers; no wives, no lovers, and especially, no children. After all, as the colonel put it, they were setting out on a symbolic invasion.

'They won't know what hit them,' said the commander, confidently, to the newspaper, radio and television reporters gathered in a group, looking across at his company, displaying them with pride in his eyes, and an outstretched arm.

'How many stops will you make?' asked a young woman, holding a microphone.

'Five,' replied the officer, a short man with white hair, a

clipped moustache, and a slight paunch that pressed against the buttons of his heavily braided blue tunic, on each shoulder of which three crowns and a bar shone. 'First in Hull, where we land tomorrow. Then we are on to Manchester, then Newcastle. But those are just training runs, you might say. The real invasion will begin at a town called Haddington. We complete our preparation there. And then,' he paused, eyebrow raised dramatically, as if he had seen Robert Newton's Long John Silver . . . and he looked almost old enough to have been at its première, 'the final assault: Edinburgh itself. It's an honour, a great honour.'

'Indeed, Colonel. I imagine it's the greatest honour you've ever had,' the reporter ventured.

The other eyebrow rose, the forehead ridged, and the nose seemed to go a deeper shade of red. 'I meant, young lady,' the colonel boomed, theatrically, 'that it is a great honour for the Scots. It's time those brigands were taught a few lessons in the finer military arts.'

He turned his back on her, dismissed his troops and waved them towards the waiting bus.

The reporters watched, as the various implements were cased and loaded into the cavernous luggage space beneath the cabins of the long coaches. 'He really means it, doesn't he?' the woman murmured to the man next to her.

'Oh yes. He means it.' The other reporter, old enough still to be using a notebook rather than a tape, scratched his chin with the end of his pen. He looked at his colleague. 'You think he's as mad as a wasp, don't you?'

'As a nestful,' she said agreeably.

'Maybe he is now, but he wasn't always. Auguste Malou was a real soldier once, in the Royal Belgian Army.'

'Do we have real soldiers in the Royal Belgian Army?'

'Come on, girl, you know we have; though not like him, not any more. When our boys go abroad these days they're usually wearing the blue UN cap. Malou's from another era, forty years back. I believe he may have been infantry at one point, but he told me that the later part of his career was spent in the administration of the band of the First Guides Regiment. That's no joke either; it's world famous. When he retired, fifteen years ago now, he came upon this lot and decided to put a bit of discipline into them.'

'What went wrong?'

'Don't be so bloody cynical, nothing went wrong . . . other than age, at both ends of the spectrum. A marching band has to be sharp. When Malou took over, he brought in some new faces, guys he had known in his army days. And he formed the Musket Platoon, to give them a bit of extra pizzazz. The Bastogne Drummers . . .'

'Why are they called that?' the woman interrupted. 'They're from Brussels, not Bastogne.'

'They were named in honour of the fallen in the great siege of World War Two. They were famous at first, but they had fallen away, until Malou revitalised them.'

'Revitalised? They look a little shop soiled to me.'

'He could only do it once. The men he brought in are in their forties now, and beyond, some of them; their crispness has gone, and the youngsters . . . some of them haven't found theirs yet. But don't be too hard on them; they're still not bad, not when they're fresh at any rate. They were invited to Edinburgh, remember.'

'They were? I thought they volunteered.'

'No, the trip is official. It may just be too long, though.'

'Why? Won't they get better with all these stops?'

The journalist grinned. 'That's the problem. Them getting better, that's not how it works. You take a few dozen old soldiers, free of their wives and their fancy women, you put them on buses and you send them away for ten days; before you know it, well, they're not as fresh as they might be.'

The woman looked puzzled. 'Why?'

The veteran shook his head. 'I have to spell it out? The baggage compartments on those buses are very large. There's room for all the luggage, and the instruments, and the muskets, and for still more; so they fill it up with as many cases of Stella as they can get in.'

'You mean they get drunk?'

'They're Belgians, aren't they? Our country is proud of two things above all others: its chocolate and its beer. Those boys aren't too keen on chocolate, that's all.'

'But can't the colonel keep discipline?'

Her fellow journalist frowned. 'He'll try, I suppose, for a couple of days: this is an important trip, and it will reflect on Belgium, and on the army. But old Auguste isn't in the army any more, and besides . . . Did you see the colour of his nose?'

Three

Deputy Chief Constable Robert Morgan Skinner peered into the goblet that he held cupped in his big hands, swirling the sweet sticky Amaretto around the sides, then watching as it settled back at the foot. Finally, he took a sip, nodded and smiled at his hostess.

'I like this stuff,' he said. 'I'm not a great one for liqueurs: your VSOP and your Armagnac would be wasted on me, and I positively dislike whisky, but I do like this.'

Louise McIlhenney, née Bankier, laughed. 'You could have fooled me. You didn't have any aversion to the hard stuff when I knew you at university. Whisky and dry ginger ale as I remember it.'

'I was young then, though,' he countered. 'My dad took a nip now and again, so I did too, till it came to me that it didn't make me a better person. When I realised that, I stopped.'

She looked across the space between them, her mind transporting them back twenty years and more. 'You used to talk about your father all the time. You don't any more. What happened?'

Bob sighed and let his head fall against the high back of the armchair. 'He died,' he said softly. 'And I haven't passed a day since then without missing him. It hurts too much to talk about him.'

'It shouldn't. You were so obviously proud of him.'

'Still am. I'll talk about him when it's right, don't worry. James Andrew and Seonaid . . . and Mark; even though he's adopted and has a living granddad of his own . . . should know about him, about who he was and what he was. It concerns me when I hear of sections of family history dying with successive generations. Did I ever tell you I had an ancestor who was press-ganged to fight against Napoleon? That story was given to me by an aunt, but she never wrote it down, so now even if I was inclined to try to trace him, I would have trouble.'

'Come on, man,' Neil McIlhenney chuckled. 'You're a detective.'

'Maybe so, but you know as well as I do . . . or you bloody should, Inspector . . . that every investigation has to start somewhere. I don't even have a name I can be sure of, never mind a place and year of birth.' He grinned, laugh-lines crinkling round his eyes. 'I might still write a book about him one day, though.'

'How can you, if you can't trace him?'

'I might do what a few unscrupulous coppers have done before now: falsify the evidence.'

'Eh?'

'Make it up. I'm talking about fiction, Neil. It's a long way off, though; writing's one of my retirement dreams.'

McIlhenney frowned. 'You're not thinking about writing your memoirs, are you?'

'No way! I'd have to leave too much out.'

'How's Sarah?' Louise asked suddenly. 'You haven't mentioned her all evening.'

'Fine,' Bob replied absently. 'She's fine. So are the kids; the bold boy Jazz has started school now, God help them.'

'Fine she may seem,' his hostess interrupted, 'but she must still be feeling the loss of her parents.'

'Of course. It's been a lousy year for her: for both of us, for that matter, with my health scare as well. We'll be glad to see the back of it.'

She smiled. 'Well, here's something that might cheer you up. This old lady's pregnant.'

Bob sat bolt upright in his chair. He stared at her, mouth agape, then at Neil. 'You what?' he exclaimed. 'Congratulations. Nah, that doesn't go far enough, at . . .' He stopped abruptly.

'At my age, were you going to say?' Louise teased.

'No, of course not!'

'Of course yes, but it doesn't matter. We've taken medical advice, I've had every physical you could imagine and we've been assured that everything's fine. I've been told not to run any marathons this winter, but that wasn't on my game plan anyway.'

'Well, that's just great. What do Lauren and Spence think of it?' Neil's children from his first marriage were watching television in the room that Lauren insisted on calling 'the study'.

'I suspect that my daughter thinks it's disgusting,' said her father. 'Kids her age think that people our age are supposed to stop all that stuff, but they're both acting pleased.'

'Too right. Does anyone else know?'

Louise shook her head. 'You're the first other than them through the wall. We're going to tell Mario once he gets back from his New York trip.'

'I hope you ask him to be godfather. He'll be great.'

'He is,' Neil reminded him. 'He's Spencer's god-dad. But if he's to do it again, we might need to put a word in for him with Jim Gainer. I don't imagine he's his Church's favourite son at the moment, being separated and everything else.'

Bob shrugged. 'That's between him and his conscience . . . and Maggie to an extent, although I've spoken to both of them and their separation does seem amicable.' He looked his friend in the eye. 'Between you and me, is she involved with anyone else?'

McIlhenney hesitated. 'She's been out with Stevie Steele a couple of times, but just for dinner; no afters. They're friends, and that's all. Stevie's got a girlfriend on the go just now, anyway.'

Skinner gave a snorting laugh. 'Steele's always got a girlfriend on the go: and I doubt if that would stop him.'

'It won't arise in this case.'

'What won't?' Bob's right eyebrow rose.

His friend caught his meaning. 'Not that or anything else. Like I said, they're pals, and that's as far as it'll go.'

'You seem sure.'

'I am. I know the whole story behind the split.'

'Is it something I should know?'

McIlhenney smiled 'No. It won't be a problem for you.

19

Maggie isn't into men right now, and that's all there is to it. She's fully focused on her career.'

'Okay,' said Skinner. 'That's good enough for me.' He finished his Amaretto, pushed himself out of his chair and peered through the curtains into the impenetrable murk. 'Ouch!' he murmured. 'What a night. Thanks again, you two, for giving me a bed.'

'That's all right,' Louise replied. 'You have an important meeting tomorrow, I'm told. It would never do if you got lost in the fog on the way there!'

Four

If wee Moash Glazier had been possessed of a slightly larger vocabulary than the one that he had picked up on his short, sad and furtive journey through life's shady valleys, and across its rain-drenched plains, then he might well have agreed with the prosecutor who had once described him in the Sheriff Court as 'an opportunist thief'.

As it was, he had understood the woman to have called him 'an awfy stupid thief', and had shouted, 'Ah'm no'!' across the room, to the immense displeasure of the Sheriff and at a consequent cost of a further thirty days for contempt, added to his six-month sentence for various offences.

Moash regarded himself as a working man. He supported himself, his greyhound, and his ferret, by stealing any everyday item that had been left unsecured and in his path by a negligent owner, and by selling it on at a knock-down price to unfussy buyers in the pubs that he frequented. He kept on the move; the speed with which he disposed of his haul, and the type of customer he found, meant that his arrest rate was relatively low.

He had a genuine dislike for the unemployed, or at least for those who made no attempt to find work, and he stole from them as readily as from anyone else within his field of vision. Moash applied a simple principle to his business life. He never lifted anything that was sufficiently unusual to attract attention, or so valuable that its owner became seriously excited about its loss. He was also circumspect about those from whom he stole, never forgetting a housebreaker acquaintance who had been unwise enough to have burgled the house of one Dougie 'The Comedian' Terry, and who had been the victim of a fatal fall from his own fourth-floor living-room window less than a week later.

His cautious approach did not always keep him out of trouble. Occasionally he would be caught in the act, or with goods still in his hands; he was familiar with the inside of the Sheriff Court and with the hotel accommodation in Saughton Prison. However, since he was never worth jailing for too long, he took such minor blips in his stride. His most serious and most embarrassing mistake came one evening in a bar in Newhaven where he attempted to sell a plumber the tools of which he had relieved him two hours earlier. That had earned him a kicking which he had found much harder to take than a few weeks' jail time and which had kept him out of action for even longer.

He had not been deterred, though, and had continued to ply his trade, without further serious mishap.

Where others might have been reluctant to go to work in severe weather conditions, wee Moash regarded them as windows of opportunity. People were distracted and tended to be even more careless than usual. Frost made them bundle up in thick overcoats, which could be easily nicked from restaurant waiting rooms, while rain made them keep their heads down, and much less likely to notice him as he went about his business.

Where the sudden fog that had clamped down was nothing short of a public emergency to others, to him it was a gift from above. He had always been able to steal successfully in broad daylight, and a city where nobody could see him was a laden vine waiting to be stripped of its grapes.

Marchmont and its environs had always been one of his favourite pitches. Many of the tall grey terraces still lacked secure entrance doors, and people, especially those idle bloody students that seemed to inhabit the place like rabbits in a warren, were daft enough to think that if something was out of sight in a stairwell or back court, then it was out of the mind of someone like him. Wrong.

He had a girlfriend in Lochview . . . Moash Glazier had no permanent address, but he had two lady acquaintances and split his nights between them, when not enjoying free board and lodging elsewhere. He crept from her house just after six a.m., made his way up across the Pleasance, being careful to give St Leonards police station a wide berth even in the fog, and made his way up Nicolson Street and Clerk Street towards his hunting ground.

He did not like to hang about: 'in and out quick' was his motto, in all things. That morning, he was especially lucky. In the first building he visited, he found a pair of almost new, if muddy, boots on a front step . . . 'Thanks very much, yah daft radge' . . . a case of tools . . . 'Aye, that'll be right' . . . and an unsecured mountain bike . . . 'Lady's tae go by the size, even if it dis hae a crossbar.'

Sixty seconds later, wee Moash Glazier was pedalling along Warrender Park Road, the boots hung round his neck, with their laces knotted together. He knew better than to touch the tools. In any event what he had was easily saleable, and enough to keep his elbow on the bar top for a while. There was no need to hurry. No one was going anywhere that morning, so as soon as he was out of sight of the building . . . after a couple of seconds . . . he was safe. It was only when he started drawing deeper draughts of air that he realised how cold it was. The temperature was around freezing, but seemed much colder in the thick greyness. The roadway was treacherous too, so he took extra care, and went even more steadily than at the outset.

He stuck to the middle of the carriageway, since there was more danger of hitting a parked car than being hit by a moving one; he was almost across Marchmont Road before he knew it, and turned left.

The traffic lights at the junction with Melville Drive shone dim red through the fog; he laughed as he rode through them and crossed over into the Meadows. There was a pathway at the entrance to the broad fields; even if he had known that it was called Jawbone Walk, it would never have occurred to him to wonder why. It was white with frost, and so rather than risk his limbs on it, he used it as a guide and cycled on the grass alongside it.

Moash had stolen more than a few bikes in his time, and as a result was a good cyclist. He could handle the gears on the most complicated modern machine, and on occasion kept one that he had nicked for a few days as a getaway vehicle. For all the cold, as he rode across the Meadows, he was actually enjoying himself. He laughed maniacally in the gloom, then threw back his head, slapped his saddlebag with his right hand, and cried out, 'Hi ho, Silver! Awa . . .'

He was in mid-yell when something hard hit him full in the chest. He was knocked backwards off his faithful steed, landing on his shoulders on the cold, hard, wet ground and turning a full somersault before coming to rest face down.

Wee Moash was not a fighting man; he knew the basics, but experience had taught him that flight was usually more expedient. But he was so taken aback by his involuntary dismount that he jumped to his feet, fists raised and ready to square up to his attacker.

'Ya bass!' he shouted, advancing on the dark figure, stopping in his tracks only when he realised that it seemed to be hovering in mid-air. In an instant his natural caution returned. He took a closer look, the figure was dark indeed, and as he drew closer he realised that this was due in part at least to the fact that it was wearing a heavy Crombie overcoat. It was also wearing black leather shoes.

Moash advanced until he could reach out and touch the thing; he did, and as it swung slowly round, he looked up and into its face.

'OhmyGoad!' he screamed. He backed away in panic, tripping over something that lay on the ground and landing heavily on his backside, jumping up again as he felt the wetness soak through his jeans, thinking for a moment that he had pissed himself, until he recognised to his relief that it was only the hoary frost on the ground.

'OhmyGoad!' A whisper this time, tinged with awe as his fear evaporated.

And then three instincts kicked into action. The first was one he rarely used: common decency. He took from his jacket pocket the mobile phone that he had stolen the day before, but had been unable to sell, and dialled nine, three times. 'Emergency services,' an operator answered. 'Which service do you require?'

'Nane,' he answered, 'but ye need the police in the Meadows. Fit o' the walkway, ahent the old Royal.'

He ended the call and responded to his second instinct: opportunism. He retrieved his fallen bike and leaned it against the trunk of the tree from which the dead man hung. Then he used it to clamber high enough to reach the body, unbutton the overcoat, and ease it off the shoulders until it fell to the ground. He jumped down, retrieved it and slipped it on. It was at least a couple of sizes too big for him even over the jacket that he was wearing, but he knew a couple of guys who might part with fifty quid for it.

Finally, self-preservation took its turn. Moash slipped the boots round his neck, seized the only other saleable item that he saw around, remounted the bike and pedalled along Meadow Walk where it turned left, away from any road by which the police might approach. This time, he pedalled as fast as he could.

Five

Sir James Proud's uniform had never fitted him better. The extra girth that once he had carried had disappeared under a regime of diet and exercise; Lady Proud had even said to him that he looked as if he had lost years in age as well as pounds in weight.

Appearances can deceive, though, Chrissie. The thought ran through his mind as he looked around the conference table. He estimated that he was the oldest person there by around fifteen years, and the thought chilled him, more than a little. For the first time in his police career, he wondered whether he should get up from his chair and tell Bob Skinner, 'You do it, son. It's your turn now.'

His deputy was there, and so was the assistant chief constable, Willie Haggerty, the rough-edged Glaswegian who had shaken up the uniformed side of the force since his arrival. They flanked him, as he coughed quietly, to clear his throat, and to end the quiet chatter and set the meeting going.

They were gathered together at eight a.m., an hour that the veteran chief constable regarded as ridiculously early, but it had been forced on him by the politicians, or, to be fair, their managers. He knew from decades of experience that civil servants never had regard for anyone's diary or convenience other than those of their masters.

'Good morning, ladies and gentlemen,' he began. 'I suggest we begin by introducing ourselves. You know me, and, I think, DCC Skinner on my right and ACC Haggerty, who's responsible for all operations in the city of Edinburgh, on my left. We also have the honour . . .' He was sure that his deputy twitched in his seat, for a split second, at his use of the word. '. . . to welcome Scotland's deputy justice minister, Ms Aileen de Marco, MSP. She's sitting next to Willie, and beyond her is her private secretary, Ms Lena McElhone. Next to Bob Skinner is Chief Superintendent Brian Mackie: he heads a specialist team that we've set up to take executive control of major state and public events, operating across our divisional structure. His people will have a key role on the day.' The dome-headed man on Skinner's right was wearing a uniform that was almost as sharp as that of the chief constable: he nodded and threw a diffident smile to the table.

'Beyond Brian, there's DI Neil McIlhenney, head of Special Branch.' The big detective, whose private views on the early scheduling of the meeting mirrored those of the chief, raised a hand.

'Now,' Sir James continued, 'I suggest that we go round the table, with everyone else introducing himself. Let's go clockwise.' He looked at the man seated next to Lena McElhone.

'Thank you,' said the bearded, bespectacled visitor. 'My name is Godfrey Rennie; I'm in charge of the part of the Justice Department that deals with the police.'

The man on his left, slight, owlish: 'Mike Munro, head of the division responsible for Edinburgh.'

A stocky figure in a dark suit, expensive, but worn over the collar of a priest. 'Monsignor Eduardo di Matteo: I represent the External Relations Division of the administration of the Vatican State.'

Another priest, his suit dark also, but more worn. 'Father Angelo Collins, private secretary to His Holiness.'

Gold-rimmed spectacles, silver hair cut in military fashion. 'Giovanni Rossi: Vatican logistics.'

Angular, patrician, sandy hair swept back from his forehead, eyeing the rest through Gucci spectacles perched on the bridge of a long nose. Skinner knew the type and liked them even less than he liked politicians. 'Miles Stringfellow, Her Majesty's Foreign and Commonwealth Office.'

And finally, black leather jacket, open-necked white shirt. 'Jim Gainer, Archbishop of St Andrews and Edinburgh.' Across the table, Lena McElhone blinked; her mouth fell open slightly. His Grace smiled at her, and winked. 'I like to go incognito, sometimes,' he said.

The chief constable turned to de Marco. 'Aileen,' he said, 'I know that you have to be off fairly soon, so would you like to begin by addressing us.'

'Thank you, Sir James.' The deputy justice minister laid down the pen with which she had noted every name on the pad in front of her. At first sight, Bob Skinner thought as he looked at her, she was a typical member of the new Scottish parliament, and of its executive. Not only was she female, she was blonde, perfectly groomed and attractive, somewhere around thirty-five, politically correct, a Glasgow councillor who had stepped up to the national stage, and smart enough to know that her idealism was nothing unless it was harnessed by realism. He might have been inclined to distrust her, but Willie Haggerty knew her from his Strathclyde days; he rated her too, and that was recommendation enough for him. There was something else the ACC had said about her; now, meeting her for the first time, Skinner saw what he had meant. She had that indefinable extra spark, not the charisma of a pop star, or even of a Jim Gainer, but a quiet sense of her own ability that communicated itself to those she met.

She had very attractive pale blue eyes, too, and they made contact with everyone as she began to speak, passing a little personal warmth each time. In spite of himself, Skinner returned her soft smile. 'I'm not here to issue any orders, or even make any requests,' she said. 'I promise you that; I've come simply to give you a message. The visit which we're gathered here to discuss is the most important this country has had in many years, maybe the most significant ever.

'We are welcoming home . . . and I say this as a practising atheist . . . the greatest living Scotsman. Be sure that the executive will give you all the support you need, of whatever kind, to ensure that everything goes smoothly. This will be a great, emotional occasion.' She paused. 'But it will be even more than that. It's true to say that the election of Cardinal Gilbert White as Pope was as big a surprise in Scotland as it was everywhere else in the world. It was greeted with a spontaneous public celebration, the like of which I have never seen. Now, beyond that, the reign of John the Twenty-fifth offers us a unique opportunity. Religious intolerance has been the curse of Scotland for four hundred years, but here, for the first time, we have an event that can draw divided communities together, and heal all those old wounds. We in government will be doing our damnedest to make sure that happens. As far as we're concerned . . . and this is the personal message that I bring from Crichton Griffiths, the justice minister, endorsed by Tommy Murtagh, the First Minister himself . . . that means that people must have open access to His Holiness, so that they can see him for the man that he is, and so that he in turn can reach out to them. That's all I have to say.'

The ageing chief constable nodded to the young minister. 'Thank you, Aileen. As always, the executive's support is welcomed. It's good to hear that we're being watched from on high too.' An attentive listener might have picked up a trace of sarcasm in his tone. 'Yet as always, there's a counter side. Bob, would you like to continue?'

Every eye in the room, save those of his colleagues, turned towards Skinner. The big DCC leaned forward slightly, his big hands flat on the table in front of him. A lock of steel grey hair fell across his forehead; he frowned, only for a second, but the gesture caused the scar above his nose to deepen suddenly into a trench-like feature. But then he looked up at the minister and smiled, his clear blue eyes catching hers.

'Yes, thanks, Ms de Marco. You're right, as Jimmy says, and I'll be among the first to sign up for your vision. The papal visit is an opportunity, if not to bring about love-ins at every Rangers–Celtic game, because there will always be ultras at either end of those grounds, but at least to create a new climate, and to isolate them as far as we can. But it's an opportunity for other people too. I've been in this job for a few years now: until a couple of years ago my principle was, if it can happen, plan for it as if it will. That's all changed, though. Now we have to think the unthinkable, we have to use our imagination in ways we've never really used it before. We cannot underestimate the determination of those who see us, our institutions, and our people, from our leaders to our very babes in arms, as mortal enemies. I will do everything I can to ensure that those who want to see the Pope get to see him, but there have to be limits. I'd be grateful if you would thank the First Minister and your boss for their interest in us, but I'd be even more grateful if you'd tell them from me not to use the phrase "open access" in public.'

'And from me,' Gio Rossi interrupted. He had introduced himself as logistics officer, but the police at the table knew that his real function was security.

'I'm not in a position to tell them anything, Mr Skinner,' said Aileen de Marco, quietly. 'That's how they want it to be.'

'Okay, I'll tell them myself, if I have to. Pope John the Twenty-fifth is indeed the greatest living Scotsman, and it's my job and the job of my colleagues to see that he stays that way. He's also among the leading living targets in the world, and probably, because of his style, the most vulnerable. Don't worry, the public will see him and they'll hear him, but they're not going to be touching the hem of his robes. This will be the tightest security operation you have ever seen. Your bosses might get to kiss his ring, but only after they've been through the metal detectors.'

The minister smiled. 'Do you really see them as potential assassins?'

Skinner nodded. 'Absolutely.' He did not smile.

'Oh, come on.'

He leaned further forward. 'Remember what I was saying about thinking the unthinkable? There's a scenario: it was found among some al Qaeda papers in Afghanistan, and circulated throughout the intelligence community by the CIA. A deep-cover terrorist gets close to someone in the moments leading up to a major event, someone who's going to be in proximity to the target. He slips something into his pocket. The explosives available these days mean that it doesn't need to be very big to do the job. It could be no bigger than a cigarette case, a calculator, or even a fountain pen. Once it's done, the innocent First Minister, or Mrs First Minister . . . her handbag's an obvious place to stash a device . . . has become a walking bomb. As soon as he's next to the target, it's detonated remotely and, boom, it's raining sticky bits of President, or Queen, or even bits of you. Get the picture? Everyone is searched.'

'Even the Pope himself?' Godfrey Rennie asked, a hint of outrage in his voice.

'No one will get near his person, but yes, his robes will be searched.'

'You're kidding!' the civil servant protested.

Skinner threw him a long, cold look. 'And why on earth would I do that?' he asked quietly. He knew Rennie from crime-prevention committee meetings in St Andrews House, and blamed his nit-picking for their seemingly interminable length.

'That's standard practice,' Monsignor di Matteo interrupted. 'We take security very seriously, even if that means that we have to do things that in the past would never have occurred to us. His Holiness understands, and leaves such matters entirely in the hands of Signor Rossi and his logistics department.'

'And their qualifications are . . . ?'

The chief constable blinked at Miles Stringfellow's interruption. He made to reply, but Skinner beat him to the retort. '. . . are not to be discussed around this table, sir,' he snapped. 'You should know better than to ask a question like that.'

'Her Majesty's Foreign Secretary tends to ask whatever questions he likes,' the man countered. His voice was as smug and unctuous as his smile.

Almost in unison, as if on cue, Willie Haggerty, Neil McIlhenney and Brian Mackie leaned back in their chairs. They were waiting for the DCC to explode, but for once Sir James Proud was able to head off the storm before it burst upon the head of the visitor from Whitehall.

'That may be so,' he said calmly, 'but I think that in this case he would be prepared to receive his reply from Signor Rossi and Monsignor di Matteo in private. So, if you don't mind, we won't pursue that line of discussion. However,' the old chief went on, 'it might be helpful to us all if you explained the reason for your presence at this meeting. Our friend Mr Munro didn't go into that when he advised me that you would be joining us.'

Stringfellow ran his fingers through his immaculately groomed hair. 'I'd have thought that was obvious,' he exclaimed archly. 'You could say that I am here to ensure that your natural enthusiasm does not get out of hand, and to represent, and if necessary safeguard, the interest of Her Majesty's government . . . Ms de Marco's parent company, as it were . . . in this visit. It should not be forgotten that Pope John the Twenty-fifth is not only the head of the Roman Catholic Church, he is also the head of an independent state, and of its government. As such, this is a state visit. The fact that it's happening in Scotland is neither here nor there. It's a matter for the Foreign and Commonwealth Office, none of whose responsibilities, as far as I am aware, were devolved under the Scotland Act.'

'And what does that mean, exactly?' asked Proud.

'It means that any proposals you make here are subject to approval by the FCO.'

'Now wait just a minute!' Aileen de Marco exclaimed. 'My department is responsible for policing in Scotland; that is absolutely clear. We don't report to you or anywhere else.'

'I repeat, madam,' Stringfellow replied, 'that this visit is a British rather than a Scottish matter. We should have oversight and we intend to have it.'

The chief constable tapped the table. 'Now just hold on there, sir,' he said, as visibly annoyed as most of his colleagues had ever known him. 'You seem to have forgotten something. A state visit is a royal event. It's the Palace that has to be satisfied. As a deputy lord lieutenant for this area, I'm better qualified as a representative of Her Majesty than you are. There's another thing, too: I've policed five state visits during my time as chief constable of this city.'

'With respect, Sir James, your role is ceremonial and it

counts for nothing; and while your previous experience is invaluable, your security plan must still be subject to our oversight.'

'Excuse me!' The words were barked from Stringfellow's left, as the Archbishop of St Andrews and Edinburgh shouldered his way into the argument. James Gainer was six feet tall, and had a neck like a tree-trunk. Any newcomer walking into the room would have taken him for a police officer, rather than a prince of the Church. His appointment to succeed the elevated Cardinal White had taken many non-Catholics by surprise. However, those who could see beyond his unorthodox approach to the priesthood, his rough-and-tumble dynamism and his youth . . . he was forty-four . . . knew the effect they had on thousands of people and knew that he was the outstanding candidate. He had been described as 'a dangerous choice' by one conservative cleric, but most saw the wisdom of selecting someone who was radically different from his predecessor.

'Am I sitting here listening to you guys fighting a turf war over my boss?' he asked.

Stringfellow looked round; his smile was patronising. 'That's rather simplistic, Your Grace. This is a state occasion, and it must be treated with all the ceremony appropriate.'

'Crap.' Across the table Lena McElhone let out an audible gasp. 'This is a man,' he snapped, 'an old man at that, coming home to his people. We will look after him, thank you very much; we will protect him and we will deliver him back safe to Rome. I'm the Pope's representative here, and I'm answerable to him for the success of this visit: not to you or anyone else, only to him; the Bishop of Rome. I know Signor Rossi's qualifications for the task, and I know Bob Skinner's as well. But I know sod all about you, my son, and that I don't like. With all due deference to your master, the Foreign Secretary, the reality of the situation is that unless I'm satisfied with the security arrangements, we don't have a show. That means that Bob and Gio are in charge. If that's simplistic, fine.'

The Foreign Office representative drew in a breath and stared frostily at the table-top. Aileen de Marco put her pad and her pen into her briefcase and pushed her chair back from the table. 'I have to go.' She looked at the deputy chief constable. 'Mr Skinner, you'll copy me into everything?'

'Yes, Minister.'

She smiled. 'You make me sound like a TV series; every time someone says that I want to laugh. The name's Aileen; I'm a New Labour minister, remember. To save time, if you could copy my private office directly, please, rather than through the department.'

Skinner saw Godfrey Rennie's involuntary frown as she rose, everyone else standing with her.

'Sure.' He paused, then nodded towards Stringfellow. 'Aileen, you do know what all this is about, don't you?'

She looked puzzled. 'No. What?'

'His boss . . . I don't mean the Foreign Secretary; I mean everybody's boss, the one with the smile . . . wants to be front and centre, alongside the Pope at all the events. With his wife, of course; especially with his wife. Best seats in the house.'

'It's news to me.'

'And to Tommy Murtagh, I'll bet. I don't hear any outraged denials from along the table, though.' He looked at Stringfellow again; the man was tight-lipped, angry, but the look in his eyes confirmed the truth of the DCC's guess.

'I'm sure they'll sort it out between them,' said the deputy justice minister, cautiously. 'But what will that do to your security planning?'

'Nothing. I'm used to working in tandem with the close-protection teams. We protect the area, they protect the individual, just as Giovanni and his logistics team protect the Pope. I'll let you have a copy of the final programme for the visit, and a summary of the security plan, once Jim's cleared it.'

'Thanks. Give Lena a call when it's ready.' She turned to her private secretary. 'You got a card?' The woman nodded, fished in her handbag for a business card, and handed it to Skinner. Then she turned and left the room, escorted by the chief constable, with her assistant in their wake.

As the DCC went back to his seat, it seemed to him that with her absence the room was just a little more drab, a little more dull. He glanced out of the window and saw that the fog was still thick outside, encircling the Fettes headquarters building like a wall. Daylight seemed to be fighting a battle with the enveloping darkness, one in which it was no more than holding its own.

The summer had been blazing, unnaturally hot, and autumn balmy until, as if to complete the cycle, October had brought a sudden cold snap, culminating in a fog which the *Evening News* swore . . . and no one was about to argue . . . was the worst seen in Edinburgh for forty-seven years. It had arrived halfway through the previous afternoon; it had not been unannounced, but its density had taken the weather forecasters by surprise. Since early morning, as soon as it had become clear that it would not lift with the dawn, television and radio stations across central Scotland had been broadcasting emergency messages announcing school closures and bus, rail and flight cancellations, and advising everyone to stay indoors, until they could venture out in relative safety. Skinner had been grateful for Neil McIlhenney's offer of his spare bedroom rather than driving the twenty miles to Gullane at no more than walking pace, then having to leave home before six to reach the office in time. Sarah had understood when he had phoned her; in truth she had sounded indifferent.

'Gentlemen,' he called out as he sat, bringing the meeting back to order, 'the chief has to prepare for a board meeting this morning. He won't be back, so I'll take over the chair.' He looked at Stringfellow. 'Let's tie up any loose ends. This visit has been arranged from the start in association with the Executive rather than Westminster. If . . . and it wouldn't be the first time . . . there are tensions between Downing Street and the First Minister's office because of it, I don't want to know. All I want is a final guest list. For what it's worth I think that having two of the world's highest profile targets side by side on a series of public platforms is a fucking horrible idea.' He threw a glance at the Archbishop. 'If I was wearing your mitre, Jim, I'd advise against it. That said, I do remember His Holiness as a man who doesn't like to say no. So, if it happens, I'll protect them. But Mr Rossi and I need to know, and damn soon, because until we do, we can't finalise our plans.'

He leaned back, feeling suddenly irritable, and uncomfortable in yesterday's shirt. 'In fact,' he said heavily, 'it's pointless going on here.' He pointed at the Foreign Office man. 'You,' he pointed at Rennie, 'and you. Go away and speak to your respective ministers and get this sorted out. I want a final decision on the VIP list, and I want it by close of play today.'

He reached across Willie Haggerty and picked a document off the top of a pile that lay in front of McIlhenney. 'We've spent valuable time preparing this,' he exclaimed, waving it in the air. 'If any of it's going to be knocked on the head, I need to know.' He felt a final burst of exasperation. 'And I need to know *now*!'

Six

The high screens that had been erected were, for that moment, mostly unnecessary. Nobody could have seen the thing they were hiding, unless they were less than twenty yards away, and the police had cordoned off an area one hundred yards in diameter to keep the casually curious public and the professionally curious media at a safe distance.

Police Constable Harold 'Sauce' Haddock was not a happy young man. He had been on patrol duties for no more than a few months and all of them had been purgatory. For all that older officers assured him that everyone had unlucky runs, it seemed to him that whenever the brown stuff... Sauce's grandfather had been a policeman, and a Free Presbyterian, and he had been forcibly discouraged from swearing... hit the fan, it always seemed to splatter on him.

Two days into his time on the panda cars there had been a rail incident, a jumper on to the line from the small footbridge behind the castle: technically it had been one for the transport police, but Sauce and Charlie Johnston, his mate, had picked up the call. Barely a week after that, he had been called to a house in Dalry where a man had been found dead. The unusual difficulty had arisen from the fact that he had been dead for a fortnight. Not long after that there had been a drunk who'd fallen out of a window during a party and impaled himself on railings below. Then there had been those two kids . . . but he didn't like to think about that.

When they had taken the call, five minutes into the start of their shift, he had known that whatever it was, it would not be the high point of his day. All that the control room had told them was that there had been a call from an agitated but anonymous member of the public asking for police to come to Meadow Walk. The caller had been asked to wait at the scene, but even Sauce was experienced enough to know that there was little chance of that.

For a while, they thought that the call might have been a hoax. They had been edging along George IV Bridge when the shout had come in: it had taken Sauce ten minutes to drive the short distance to George Square, adjacent to Meadow Walk and relatively safe to park in the darkness. They had checked the stretch up to Lauriston Place, but found nothing; they had retraced their steps, going carefully, one on either side of the cycle path and walkway, torches lit as they searched, yard by yard, all the way down to the Meadows.

'A comedian,' Charlie had exclaimed at the foot of the walk. 'Just what we did not fucking need on a morning like this.' PC Johnston's grandfather had been a miner and a Communist, given to intemperance in all things, including language. He had been on his way back up to the car when Sauce had called him back, his voice hoarse, not from the fog but from fright.

It had almost been out of his vision, the heavy fruit of the tree: almost but not quite. They approached it inch by inch, almost comically, as if there was a chance of the dark shape leaping down on them. Their torches were useless until they were up against it, or rather him. When he had shone his beam directly into the purple face, with its bulging eyes and its swollen, protruding tongue, he had realised in that same instant that he was adding one more image to his private catalogue of things never to be forgotten as long as he lived.

The body was still hanging from the thick bough as Chief Superintendent Manny English and Detective Inspector Stevie Steele looked up at it, but two constables on ladders were supporting it, one on either side, while a third used a screwdriver as a lever to untie the thick belt that suspended it. The senior officers were close enough to see what was happening, but not directly under the tree, keeping disturbance of the immediate area to a minimum.

They watched as the PCs took the weight, and carefully lowered the burden to the ground, beside the pathway. As soon as they were finished, the on-call medical examiner stepped forward, and knelt beside the stiff, still form. He shone a light into each eyeball, loosened the leather noose and drew it over the head, then tested each of the limbs. Within a minute he jumped to his feet, nodding emphatically to himself.

'He's been up there since last night,' he announced. 'Rigor mortis is fully established; that indicates that he's been dead for around twelve hours . . . or more, of course.'

'It's feasible,' said Steele. 'In the darkness of last night you

43

could have walked past within a couple of yards of him and never have known he was there.'

'Aye,' muttered English, 'but who was he, and why didn't anyone come looking for him?'

'Maybe they did, sir. Have you checked missing persons information?'

The divisional commander bristled in his uniform, and Steele knew that he had made a mistake. Manny English was a notorious book operator: his question was one that could, and should, have gone without the asking.

'There haven't been any,' he replied tersely. 'Not in the past week at any rate, and you've just heard what the MO has to say. Do you want him photographed again?' he asked.

'No sir. There's no point.'

'Very well. Let's get him into a plastic coffin and off to the mortuary where they can thaw the poor bugger out.' He waved through the slightly thinned fog to two uniformed men, who were waiting beside a blue van with a ventilator on top.

'One thing first,' said Steele. He bent over the body and felt around the chest area, then opened the dark grey suit, and from an inside pocket produced a wallet. He opened it and, from a compartment within, drew out a business card. 'Ivor Whetstone, MCIBS,' he read. 'Director of Business . . .' He glanced up at English. 'He's a banker, sir.'

The chief superintendent nodded sagely. 'I could tell by his suit that he was some sort of a business type; banker, lawyer, accountant, something like that.'

Steele could tell in his turn why his senior officer had not prospered in CID. 'I once arrested a bank robber who wore the same brand of suit as this,' he said.

'I wonder what drove him to do it?' English murmured.

'Drove whom to do what?'

The uniformed commander looked at the detective in exasperation. 'Him.' He pointed at Whetstone's body. 'That.' He pointed at the tree.

Steele sighed. 'At the very best, sir,' he said, 'this has to be a suspicious death; maybe even a homicide.'

'Ohh, really?' English exclaimed. 'Honest to God, that's CID all over, rushing to judgement.'

'I'm judging bugger all, sir.'

'You're ruling out suicide, though.'

'I'm not ruling out anything, but I don't see this as suicide.'

'Why not?'

'Where's his support?'

'What?'

'Whatever it was he climbed to top himself: the guy's feet were about a metre off the ground.'

The chief superintendent frowned, and thought for a few moments. 'He could have climbed the tree, then out along the branch and jumped off.'

Steele could not restrain himself: he laughed. 'I'll tell you what, sir. You're about the same age, size and build as that bloke, and your shoes are much like his. You show me how he did it. You climb up that wet, slippery, thick tree-trunk, with not a single foothold, and then you climb out along that limb.'

'Maybe he did,' English persisted.

'Listen, sir. If we'd found him lying under the tree with his fucking neck broken, then I might just have agreed with you. The way things are, I'm calling a full scene-of-crime team here, and I'm calling Detective Superintendent Rose.'

'If you must, you must.' The divisional commander stalked off.

'I must, sir,' the inspector called after him. 'There's one other thing too.' English stopped. 'Where's his coat?' The chief superintendent frowned but said nothing.

'If this guy came out here last night to end his life, he wouldn't have needed to string himself up if he wasn't wearing a coat. All he'd have had to do was lie down and go to sleep. Nobody would have found him and he'd have been dead of hypothermia by morning.'

Seven

Skinner was in his office in the early afternoon, working his way through the day's paperwork, when Detective Sergeant Jack McGurk, his executive assistant, came in to tell him that Archbishop Gainer and Signor Rossi had returned unexpectedly. He frowned. 'Don't keep them waiting outside, man,' he snapped. 'Show them in at once.'

The DCC and McGurk were still new to each other. When Neil McIlhenney had left the exec post for Special Branch, he had been given the job, in Skinner's absence, of choosing his own successor. That absence had been longer than anticipated, and the young sergeant had spent the time cooling his heels and reporting to the rough-hewn Willie Haggerty. It was not an ideal situation: McGurk could have exercised the option of going back to divisional duties, but he had been assured that a stint in Bob Skinner's office would be a career springboard, as it had been for the likes of Brian Mackie, Maggie Rose and especially for Andy Martin, who had made it in his mid-thirties to an ACC's uniform in the Tayside force. So he had stayed, and he had waited for the return of the Big Man.

When, finally, it had happened, McGurk found himself wondering about the wisdom of that decision. He did not know Bob Skinner well but, like everyone else in the force, he knew of his legend as a crime-fighter, and as a leader who earned respect and loyalty rather than demanding it. The reality turned out to be a short-tempered, menacing figure, intolerant of the slightest error, delay or omission.

He had taken the job in the belief that if the DCC liked you, you were made, and with the assurance of Neil McIlhenney that there was no better man in the force for whom an officer could work. With every day that passed, the less secure the sergeant felt in his job, the more he wondered how he had displeased Skinner, and the more he missed his former boss, the dour, quirky, but likeable head of CID, Chief Superintendent Dan Pringle.

After a few weeks of rockets and reprimands he had gone to Pringle and had asked what he could be doing wrong. 'I can't help you there, son,' the veteran had told him. 'If it's any consolation, you're not alone. I got a right bollocking the other day because Greg Jay's clear-up rate had gone down. I even heard him shouting at McIlhenney one day, and he's his best pal in this place now that Andy Martin's gone.'

'He yelled at Neil? How did he take that?'

'Oh, he yelled back, because he was right. But don't you try it, son: you're not McIlhenney, not yet at any rate. The best thing to do is make allowances for him. He's been ill, although he tries to pretend it never happened, and on top of that his brother died. Big Bob's human just like the rest of us; if he's no' himself, maybe it's not that surprising.'

McGurk had taken his advice, but he had come close to forgetting it on a couple of occasions. With the Archbishop and his colleague at the door, and within earshot, he swallowed the latest rebuke impassively, stood aside and ushered them in. He made to leave, as the guests sat on the soft leather couch, opposite the window, but the DCC called after him: 'No, Sergeant, you stay here. I may need a note of this meeting.'

Grateful of the recognition, McGurk took a pad from the desk and a pen from his pocket, and pulled across an upright chair. He was almost six and a half feet tall, and he had found that he could not fit comfortably into the DCC's reception seating.

'Anyone want coffee?' Skinner asked. The Archbishop shook his head; Rossi, the Italian, looked across at the filter machine on a table in the corner and made a face.

'Would you like some, sir?' McGurk volunteered.

His boss frowned at him. 'I'm not bloody helpless, son. If I did I'd get it.'

'Sorry, sir.'

'Yes, well . . .' Suddenly Skinner stopped; his frown deepened. 'No, Sergeant, I'm the guy who should apologise. That was plain rudeness. I'll tell you what, maybe you could fetch some bottles of water from the fridge beside my desk, and some glasses from the table.' He looked back at his visitors. 'Or would you guys like a beer?'

Archbishop Gainer put his hands together in supplication and glanced upwards for a moment. 'You see,' he said, with a grin, 'prayer does work sometimes. I thought you were never going to ask.'

49

McGurk fetched two bottles of Becks and two of Highland Spring and handed them round, then took his seat. 'So,' Skinner began at last, 'let me do some guessing. My outburst this morning has got a result. Number Ten's stopped pussying about and horned in on the visit.'

'Got it in one,' Gainer replied. 'I had a call from the man himself less than an hour ago, asking, very humbly, you understand, and appreciative of the great honour it would be, you understand, if the Holy Father would be prepared to allow him to attend the public events on the visit.'

Skinner smiled, not least at the accuracy of the Archbishop's mimicry. 'What did you tell him?'

'I told him that he was a bit late in getting off the mark, and that technically it was an informal visit, but after that I said that His Holiness would welcome his presence. I told him that he'd even hear his confession if he wanted. That drew an uncertain laugh, I should tell you.'

'I'll bet it did. I'd like to hear that confession myself.'

'Sure, with two tape-recorders running.'

'I doubt if I'd hear much more than I usually do in those circumstances. I'd be better off bugging your box.'

'My dark side might let you,' Gainer muttered. He looked at Rossi, then winked. 'You didn't hear that, Gio.'

'I hear nothing, Your Grace,' the logistics man replied. 'And everything,' he added, with a grin.

'Have you broken the news to Tommy Murtagh, Jim?' Skinner asked.

'I didn't have to. He'd already been, ahem, consulted by the time I spoke to him.'

'How did he sound?'

'Enthusiastically and loyally underwhelmed would just about describe it.'

The DCC's smile was his broadest of the day. 'His loss is our fledgling nation's gain.' He sipped his mineral water. 'What do you need?' he asked Rossi.

'I'd like to meet with his people,' the Italian answered.

'You will,' Skinner promised. 'Someone will come up within a couple of days to do a recce; when that happens we'll do final visits to each venue.'

'Can we go firm on a date for that?'

'I guess so. This is Wednesday, so let's try for Friday.' He glanced at his assistant. 'Jack, will you set that up please? Contact the PM's protection officers and tell them what we want. They'll go along with it.'

'Even at such short notice?' Rossi sounded doubtful.

'Their boss is late to the table,' the Scot growled. 'They'll take what's put in front of them.' He looked at the Archbishop. 'Is anyone going to be chucked off the platform at any of the events because of this?'

'How many extra bodies are we talking about? I'm assuming it won't just be him and her who turn up.'

'You assume correctly,' said Skinner, 'but I can keep it to a minimum. There'll be his private secretary; she has to go everywhere. Then there'll be his official mouthpiece; they're joined at the hip. It'll be par for the course if the Cabinet Secretary tries to elbow his way in, but I'll tell him he's not on.'

'In that case I'll only have a problem at the main public

rally and mass at Murrayfield Stadium. The stage we're setting up there has as many seats on it as we can fit in. Much of the rest of the programme has His Holiness on the move.'

'I've noticed. Is he up to that? He's not a young man.'

'He thinks he is: he calls sixty-nine "middle-aged". Don't you worry about him, he had a medical a couple of months ago and they declared him good for another fifteen years.' Jim Gainer laughed. 'That would disappoint a few of the younger cardinals if they knew about it. He feels that not only could he kick off the Hibs–Celtic game on Saturday week, if he'd been able to stay for it, he could play in it.

'Nothing's all that strenuous anyway. He arrives next Thursday afternoon at Edinburgh airport; he'll be welcomed formally by the Lord Provost, who'll introduce the rest of the official party. Nobody sits down there so the PM and his wife can just get in line with the rest.'

'Before or after the First Mini-car?' the DCC asked.

'What do you think? What's the protocol?'

'I don't think there's any established. Personally, I think they go after, and sod 'em if they can't take a joke, but we'd best ask them.'

'Elegantly put, sir. I share your inclination, but I'll have di Matteo or Angelo Collins consult the First Minister's office about precedence at that and all the other events. I'm assuming that they'll want him to go everywhere.'

'That's a cert, Your Grace. This is the biggest photo opportunity of all time for these guys, and there's always an election around the corner. The only one they might duck out of is the council reception at the City Chambers, once he's driven into town from the airport. That's private, and the Lord Provost does not like Mr Tommy Murtagh. On the other hand, once he hears that the PM's coming he might invite him specially, just to annoy the wee man. If that happens he'll go there too. Are you still happy with the time they're spending there?'

'If we can get him out of there on time, it won't be a problem. If we can't . . . and he'll be meeting a lot of people he hasn't seen since his elevation . . . well, if the cathedral mass is a bit late in starting it won't be the end of the world. The congregation won't walk out on him. We don't have any political problems there, or at the Royal Infirmary visit on Friday. I know that he wants Lord Provost Maxwell and his wife there, though. He married them, you know, and he gave the Provost his first communion wafer, too, thirty-five years ago. No, the only problem I have is at Murrayfield.' He opened his briefcase and took out a copy of the document Skinner had prepared for that morning's meeting, and flicked through it until he found the page he sought. 'Looking at the platform party . . .' He paused. 'Too bad the deputy justice minister admitted to being an atheist,' he said. 'It's cost her and her partner their seats on the stage.' He took out a pen and scored through their names, then added two more at the top of the page.

'Can I ask a question, sir?'

The DCC glanced up at his assistant, involuntarily irritated. 'What do you want to know?'

'What exactly is planned for Murrayfield, sir?'

'A celebration, Sergeant,' replied the Archbishop. 'The city of Edinburgh is staging a rally to celebrate the election of Pope

John the Twenty-fifth. It's being held in Murrayfield Stadium because it's the biggest venue we have; we won't fill it, but forty thousand tickets have been allocated. All of them will go to Scottish secondary-school students, but not to Roman Catholic kids alone. His Holiness is insistent that this should be an interdenominational event. The entertainment will be a selection of the Pope's favourites; the programme was announced six weeks ago. We'll have music by a school choir, Scottish dancing, pipes and drums, a marching band from Belgium . . . I'm not entirely sure why, but he asked for them specially . . . operatic arias performed by Donald O'Brien, the tenor, and a couple of songs by that lad who won a television competition a couple of years ago. It's all very homely and, if you like, parochial, but it's his style. It'll conclude with mass being said, and a sermon by His Holiness.'

'And afterwards he goes straight to the airport?'

'That's right,' said the Archbishop. 'He has to be back in Rome that evening. It's a pity for he'd have liked to stay on for the Hibs–Celtic game on Saturday. Father Gibb's had a seat in the stand at Easter Road for years, even if it's me who uses it now.'

'What did you call him?' asked Skinner.

'Father Gibb; it's a name his friends used, before his elevation. His name's Gilbert, but his family called him "Gibb" for short; those of us who were close to him got to call him Father Gibb. We all regarded it as an honour.'

'Maybe the Hibs will win for him on Saturday, then,' said McGurk.

Skinner snorted. 'You're into the realm of miracles there,

Sergeant.' He looked at his visitors. 'So, gentlemen, in addition to kicking Ms de Marco and her man off the stage and into the grandstand . . . I'll advise her of that . . . what other changes does this new presence impose on our operational plan?'

'It may raise the stakes a little,' said Rossi, 'but if nobody knows that he's coming until the day . . .'

Skinner shook his head. 'That's not the way it's played. Downing Street will brief the press well in advance; you can be sure of that. They won't be surprised either, any more than I was.'

'That's regrettable, but even then I feel that the level of protection we are giving His Holiness does not need to be increased.'

'In truth, I doubt if it could be,' said the Scot. 'All the same, I think I'll arrange for reinforcements to be handy.'

'More police?'

'No, military. I have a contact in the Ministry of Defence who can arrange for a special forces platoon to be in place. We'll distribute them round all the entrances.'

'What will they do?'

'Their job will be to look out for known terrorists. We've already agreed that we can't put forty thousand kids and their teachers through metal detectors, or we'd wind up frisking everyone with a belt buckle or a brooch. Only those people who will be close to the Pope will have to go through them. We'll have enough people inside the ground, watching the crowd constantly for any wrong moves, and we'll have close personal protection. We've also got our escape plan. But if I can stick guys in black suits at every entrance, each with a mental file of all the faces from the FBI and MI5 wanted lists, it'll give us a bit of added insurance.'

'Will they be armed?' asked Gainer. 'The Pope wouldn't like that.'

'They won't be obviously armed, Jim. It's best if we don't discuss who's armed and who isn't.'

'The Pope won't like anyone being armed in any way.'

'Except his potential attackers? Is that what you're saying? I'm sorry, but I'm not putting my officers at avoidable risk. Look, I really do think it would be best if we don't discuss this subject, Your Grace, and if you accept that such decisions are mine alone. You can trust my discretion.'

'Fair enough. If the Holy Father asks me, I'll tell him to talk to you.'

'Tell him to talk to Proud Jimmy. The chief's more of a diplomat than me.'

The Archbishop smiled. 'I'll bear that in mind.' He picked up the document. 'Do we need to amend this, then, before it's circulated to the need-to-knows?'

'Only to add in the new VIP names and to relegate Aileen de Marco. Jack'll take care of that, and we'll handle the distribution.'

'That's it, then,' exclaimed the Archbishop, briskly. He stood, and the rest followed his lead. Rossi and McGurk went ahead as Skinner showed them to the door. He held it open but Gainer took his elbow and whispered, 'A word in private, please, Bob.'

'Of course, Your Grace. Jack, please look after Signor Rossi till we're done.'

He closed the door once they were gone, and went back to his desk. 'What can I do for you, Jim?' he asked.

'Maybe it's more a case of what I can do for you, Bob.'

'What do you mean?'

The churchman flexed his big shoulders and settled into a chair facing the DCC's own. 'Is anything troubling you?' he asked.

Skinner blinked. 'Why do you ask that, man?'

'I'm prompted by over twenty years' experience as a priest. I didn't actually need to ask: I can bloody well tell that something's bothering you. The way you spoke to your assistant shocked me, even though you had the grace to apologise. We were joking about confessions earlier. Would you like me to hear yours? Informally, as a friend, if nothing else.'

The big policeman leaned back in his chair, then swivelled round until he was looking out of the window into the fog. 'Is that stuff never going to clear?' he murmured.

'I'm sorry,' said Gainer. 'I was being presumptuous. Stop me, for my own sake, next time I start talking to you like a priest.'

Skinner swung back round at once to face him. 'No. Not at all, Jim; that's not the case at all. Even though I'm not an adherent of your church, I appreciate your concern as a friend.' He sighed. 'Ah shit, do you fancy another beer?'

The Archbishop smiled. 'This time I wasn't praying for it, but okay. I'll tell Giovanni to get a taxi back to the residence on his own.' He stood and walked to the door, as Skinner bent in his seat for another Becks and more bottled water.

'Are you off the lager, then?' his guest asked, when he

returned. 'You've always liked a pint in all the time I've known you.'

'It doesn't improve my temper.'

His Grace laughed. 'Could it make it worse?'

'Jack McGurk would probably say "no" to that.'

'Would he now? And your family, what would they say?'

Without a word, Skinner replaced the water in the fridge, and took a beer instead. 'I hope they would say nothing,' he replied. 'My children's nursery is where I go to get away from everything else in the world. There is nothing in this life that I love as much as spending time with Seonaid, Mark and James Andrew.' He smiled. 'My younger daughter's a handful, I'll tell you. Now that she's fully mobile, she's developed a new hobby: hiding things. It's a game with her, but the trouble is that sometimes she forgets where she's hidden them. We spent an hour the other night looking for a silver bracelet. Eventually we found it in an old tea caddy of my mother's that she fancied as her jewel box. As for Mark, he's showing signs of real excellence in maths. It's always been his hobby, but now he's about five years ahead of his contemporaries, and picking up pace. We tried getting him special tuition, but he made his teacher feel inadequate.' He looked across at Gainer. 'You know, I was genuinely determined that all my kids would be educated at the local schools, like Alex, my daughter from my first marriage, was, but Mark's a specially gifted child. So he's starting at Fettes College prep school, just up the hill there . . .' He pointed out of the window. '. . . after Christmas; they have the flexibility to let him develop at his own pace in his area of excellence, and work alongside the other kids at the rest. And if he goes there, so will Jazz and Seonaid; they'll have to; it's only right.' He grinned, and suddenly he seemed twenty miles away, in a house by the seaside. 'You know, Jim,' he continued, 'one of the things I admire about you and about men like you, is the strength of your vocation, in that it denies you the pleasure and the fulfilment of family life.'

'Ah,' said the Archbishop, 'but I am a member of many families. They don't call priests "Father" for nothing. You and I are around the same age, give or take a few years, and we've been in our professions for around the same time. I'll bet you that I've married more people, baptised more kids, and seen more folk on their way at the end of the first part of the journey than you've locked up villains in your career. I'm welcome in the homes of all my flock. Can you say that?'

Skinner laughed. 'I'd need to go armed into the homes of many of my flock; that's all I can say with certainty.'

'Ah,' but I do too. I go armed with the word of the Lord Jesus Christ.'

'How big a magazine does He have? I've been using a compensated Glock Twenty-two pistol on the range, with a seventeen-shot capacity.'

'Jesus couldn't hit a barn door, I'm afraid. Nor, I doubt, would He approve of such weapons being used in His name.'

'We're allowed ethical choices,' Skinner pointed out. 'No police officer is compelled to do firearms training.'

'I know, and for that at least I'm thankful.' Gainer paused. 'You mentioned your mother back then, Bob. You may not be aware, but in the years I've known you, that's the first time I can recall hearing you speak of your parents.'

'That may well be so, Jim. I've always kept my private life very much to myself . . . as someone made me realise last night, in fact. I've never talked family around the office . . . or at least that part of my family . . . and I suppose that as the years have gone on, I've stopped talking about them anywhere.' He held up a hand, in a gesture that could have been unconscious self-defence. 'That doesn't mean that I'm not proud of them; of my parents, that is. My dad was a quiet, self-deprecating man. He was a war hero, but he never talked about it, nor did he encourage me to ask him. I didn't learn the whole story until after his death. If I'm a private man, as I've acknowledged I can be, I suspect it's a tendency I've inherited from him.'

'And your mother,' the Archbishop asked, 'what of her?'

'She was the life and soul of our house when I was a kid. My father was quiet, but she was always singing about the place; she was a great one for television-ad jingles . . . hands that do dishes being as soft as your face, that sort of stuff. She had a big circle of friends, too; they were bridge players and they used to take our front room over every six weeks or so. You could hardly see through the smoke when they were in there.'

'She's dead too?'

Skinner nodded. 'Has been for years. She passed away when Alex was a baby.'

'That must have been like a light going out of your life.'

'I suppose that losing your mother always is, but in truth that light started to fade a few years before.'

'Why was that? Was she ill for a long time?'

'No, she died suddenly. The fact was, she had a drink problem in her middle years, Jim. I don't mean she was scrabbling around in the garden shed for the last bottle of Red Biddy or anything like that, but she started in on the gin-and-tonics around lunchtime, and was quietly hazed for the rest of the day. With that, she stopped going around, and her friends, other than the one or two closest, stopped coming around. The singing stopped too; latterly, the house was like a mausoleum.'

'How did your father deal with that?'

'It broke his heart, but there was nothing he could do about it. I remember him once trying to persuade her to see the doctor about it: she bit his head off, and he never mentioned it again.'

'The mausoleum, Bob,' Gainer asked, quietly. 'Who was entombed there?'

'My brother.'

The Archbishop's eyebrows rose. 'You had another brother? When I read of Michael's death earlier this year, there was no mention of a third.'

'There was none, only Michael. She was mourning his memory.'

'Ah. There was a schism, then.'

'That's a fine Presbyterian way of putting it, Jim,' Skinner murmured. 'There was a fucking big bust-up, not to put too fine a point on it. My brother was no saint, but he was sinned against too, even though I didn't know it or appreciate it at the time. If you read of his death, you'll maybe recall that he spent the second half of his life in a Jesuit hostel in Greenock.'

Gainer smiled. 'In the care of Brother Aidan, the Irish leprechaun monk?'

'That's the guy. Michael went to live there after relations between the two of us broke down completely. Initially, it followed a period of treatment for alcoholism, but later, and for most of his time there, it was entirely voluntary.'

'There was more to it than that, surely.'

'Maybe, but that was at the heart of it. My father never came right out and told me, but I reckon now he was protecting both of us from ourselves when he arranged for him to take shelter there. Michael would have drunk himself to death, or into prison, eventually.'

'And you?'

The policeman frowned. 'And me? Let me put it this way, Jim. I've had to defend myself on many occasions in my life, but my brother Michael is the only person I've ever physically attacked in a blind, murderous rage.'

'Why?' The question was whispered.

'I was protecting my mother . . . or that's what I told myself. In truth, I could have called my dad. He was in the house at the time, and he'd have dealt with it in his own way. But I didn't, I just went berserk, and filled him in until the old man heard my mother screaming and hauled me off. Do you know the really shameful thing? Until recently, it didn't bother me. I felt no remorse, no guilt.'

'And what brought you to feel it?'

'Michael's death did; that and the discovery that he did feel remorse. He'd changed, as I learned from old Aidan, yet I never saw him again from that day on, nor did my mother.

The schism, as you put it, was the end of her happiness. One son was gone, and she could never look at the other in the same way. No wonder she went on the piss.' He looked at the ceiling. 'I drove her to it, Jim. I led her to break my dad's heart.'

'I see,' murmured the Archbishop. 'This is a hell of a guilt trip, isn't it?'

'Justified, the way I see it.'

'It's gone far enough, though. From what you're telling me of Michael, you had plenty of help in breaking your mother's heart. The other side of the coin is that you helped rescue him. I know the story, man; when I read about it in the press I called Aidan. He told me the truth, at least as much of it as he knew. Whatever his weaknesses of the flesh, your brother died in a state of grace, with his soul cleansed, and you were the catalyst that triggered the process. Like it or not, my unbelieving friend, you were God's agent.'

'I doubt if He'd think so.'

'I'm one of His vicars on earth and I'm telling you He does. He's forgiven me, so why not you?'

'What does He have to forgive you for?'

'All my little everyday sins, my son, and some big ones too. Back then, not long after you were having your confrontation with your brother, you know how I spent my free weekends?'

'Selling the *War Cry* round the pubs?'

'Would that I had. No, my hobby was beating the shite out of Rangers supporters, and getting across their women when I had the chance. I was a gang leader in Glasgow. The Dublin

Reds, we used to call ourselves, and we were feared. I was a tough boy, and nobody crossed me.'

'So what happened to save you?'

'Much the same as happened to your brother. In my case God's agent was a priest called Brendan McCarthy. He ran a youth club, and one night, there being no Proddies handy to bash, my crowd went in there for a ruck. Father McCarthy told us to behave ourselves; I, being an idiot at the time, squared up to him. Did he whop me? Did he ever. He'd been army light-heavyweight champion or some such; he kept on knocking me down, and I kept on getting up. The rest of the Dublin Reds were long gone, but I wasn't going to run. Finally, he really nailed me. I came to with him leaning over me, saying, "Do you realise, boy, that this is what's going to happen to you for the rest of your fucking life, unless you come over to the side of the righteous?" He was persuasive, that fellow: I left my gang and joined his. He taught me how to box properly, and he made me doorman at the club. But he also taught me the ways of the Lord, and left me wanting nothing but to be like him.'

Skinner looked at him. 'Do you still box?'

'Nah, these days I turn the other cheek. I'm not the boy I was then, any more than you are. Bob, if you want a penance from me, then here it is. Put flowers on your parents' grave and move on from there. You have no reason for shame, and no reason to be taking your remorse out on your colleagues.' He paused, taking a long breath. 'Always assuming, of course, that there's no other underlying cause for your ill-humour.'

The DCC took a long slug of his Becks. 'And why should there be?' he asked.

'I don't know. But I do know this. When you spoke earlier of the pleasure that you take in family life you spoke entirely of your children. Neither then nor at any other time since we've been speaking did you mention your wife. I remember a time, Bob, not so long ago, when her name peppered your conversation. Maybe I'm wrong, but I see this as a significant omission.'

Skinner shifted in his seat. 'With respect, Your Grace, it's entirely likely that you would be wrong. In this area at least, I might know more than you.'

'Ah, so I am right.'

'How do you figure that?'

'Hah!' Gainer laughed. 'You've just implied that, as a priest, I can't be expected to understand the nuances of what happens between man and woman. Leaving aside the raw experiences of my secular youth, throughout my priesthood I've been exposed to those very nuances, formally in the confessional, and informally in conversations such as this. You know this perfectly well, yet you try to sidetrack me. That tells me that you can't lie to me, yet you can't bring yourself to admit that I'm right. If this means that you simply don't want to get into this area, fair enough, but that's all you had to say.'

'What's your view on contraception?' Skinner asked suddenly.

'In line with that of the Holy Father,' Gainer replied instantly. 'But why do you ask me that?'

'I wanted to knock you off balance, that's all,' said the DCC amiably. 'But I see that I can't. Sarah and I have known better times, Jim. How can I put this?' he asked himself aloud. He thought for a few seconds then reached a decision. 'Try this. Since you're a marriage-guidance guru as well as everything else . . . you're a veritable hypermarket of counselling services, my friend . . . you'll probably appreciate that there, as in all areas of life, communication is everything. There have been occasions when Sarah and I have been unable to communicate properly with each other. Most of the time the fault has been mine, for not listening to her and considering her needs.'

'But not this time?'

'Sometimes communication backfires, Jim. Sometimes you learn things you'd be better off not knowing; when you do you have to work out for yourself whether you can live with them. Myra, my first wife, was a genius when it came to selective communication. As a result, we were blissfully happy until her car hit that tree. Yes, Sarah and I have problems. But what advice can you give me, as a minister of your Church? Only, I think, that we should work hard at it and see them through together, for the sake of the children.'

'True,' the Archbishop conceded.

'Then I thank you, for that's the advice I've given myself. But I thank you also for reminding me that I have to work hard at keeping it away from the office.'

Eight

Vernon Easterson, the general manager of the Scottish Farmers Bank, stared across his desk. Detective Sergeant George Regan knew the look of disbelief in his eyes well enough. He and his detective constable companion, Tarvil Singh, had seen it countless times, from their earliest days in the force, when they had been sent to break the news of bereavement to the unsuspecting bereaved.

'He's what?' the banker gasped, as he gazed at the photographic driving licence in his hand. It had been taken from Ivor Whetstone's wallet.

'He's been found dead, sir, hanged from a tree in the Meadows.'

'Suicide?'

'I can't say that, sir,' Regan replied. 'We're at an early stage in our investigation. What can you tell me about Mr Whetstone?'

'He was a most valued colleague,' said Easterson, firmly. 'He transferred to the business banking division a year ago from Kelso. He was our branch manager there, and I think he'd hoped that he would be able to see out his working life in the town. His main customers were landowners and farmers, and so many of his business meetings took place on the Roxburgh golf course . . . he was a very keen golfer.'

The man frowned. 'That wasn't to be, though. Thing is, personal banking as Ivor knew it is doomed. The days of the "financial GP" are over. Many of our high-street branches have been rationalised . . .'

'You mean closed, sir?' asked DC Singh.

'Correct. Private customers are being directed, wherever possible, towards our new telephone and Internet banking options. I could see Ivor didn't like it at first. It took him time to get used to the idea, but eventually he agreed to accept the job of associate director of Commercial Banking, here in Lothian Road, at our head office. I persuaded him that the primary business of the modern banker is lending money. While the personal-mortgage and hire-purchase sides are important, the main growth has to be achieved through expanding the base of business customers, financing new-start companies and helping those already established on to the next stage. Those were the marching orders handed down to me by the board, and it was up to me to find the brightest, the most experienced and the best to carry them out. Ivor was very definitely among them.'

'He was successful?' asked Regan.

'Very. There were several associate directors, all reporting to our senior director of Commercial Banking, Aurelia Middlemass. She's in her thirties; she came here from a career abroad. She's very highly rated and there are those who say she'll become the first female chief executive of a Scottish bank before she hits forty. A slight exaggeration, perhaps,'

Easterson murmured. 'Aurelia's a hard driver: she handed each of her people very steep lending targets to sort the wheat from the chaff. We had one resignation and one emotional breakdown within six months, but, within that same period, Ivor attained his lending target for the full year. Before his posting to Kelso he had done time in branches in London, Aberdeen, and Edinburgh, and he had maintained nearly all of the contacts he had made in each city. He had a ready-made network, and he put it to effective and profitable use. He was rewarded: he was made director of Commercial Banking, reporting directly to me, and he was given a raise and a better bonus scheme. He's never looked back since. He and Virginia had even bought a bungalow down in Kelso, for his retirement when it eventually came.'

'When did you see him last, sir?' asked DS Regan.

'Last night. He was still here when I left, but that wasn't unusual. Ivor was often first in last out.'

'Would you have known if anything was troubling him?'

'I'm sure I would. He and I were basically old school; we'd both adapted to the modern world, that's all.'

'Can you tell us anything about his family background?'

'Well, there's Virginia, his wife, and there's one son, Murphy. He graduated a couple of years ago; he works in the US; something with Jack Daniel's, Ivor said.'

Regan pulled himself out of his chair; his colleague followed. 'Thank you, sir,' he said. 'That's been helpful.'

'Are you going to see Virginia now?' the banker asked.

'Oh no, sir. That job's not for us: our bosses draw that short straw.'

'What should I do now?'

'That's up to you. But if you come across anything you think might help our investigation, please let us know.'

'You can count on that,' he called after them as they left.

'Would that be as the banker said to the actress?' Singh muttered to Regan.

Nine

'What do we say to this woman, Maggie?' asked Stevie Steele, as they sat in the inspector's car, outside the red sandstone semi-detached villa. Steele had an eye for the property market and he reckoned that in the Grange District, a house like that would fetch well over four hundred thousand pounds, and might even top the half-million mark.

They had been there for half an hour. They had been on edge when they had rung the doorbell: no police officer, however experienced, however senior, relishes the job of telling a married woman, or man, for that matter, that from that point on they will be using the word 'widowed' on official forms. But there had been no reply. Mrs Virginia Whetstone was not at home.

At first, they had assumed that given the wicked weather, she was away visiting friends, but Maggie Rose had noted that there were two cars in the drive.

'Maybe someone's heard about it, and beaten us to the punch in telling her,' Steele had suggested. 'Maybe she's with neighbours.'

'Maybe. But the name hasn't been released yet. Let's just wait here for a while and see if she shows.'

So they had gone back to their car, and waited in the fog as the minutes ticked by. It was still thick, but not as bad as it had been, and a few vehicles were beginning to venture out. 'How's Andrea?' Maggie asked casually.

'She's fine.'

'That's all? Fine?'

'Yup.'

'Are you still seeing as much of her?'

'Who says I ever was seeing that much? We're friends, and that's it.'

The detective superintendent smiled. 'No comment.'

'What does that mean?'

'No comment.'

'Are you saying I'm not capable of being just friends with a woman?'

'I'm saying nothing.'

'I manage to be just friends with you, don't I?' he challenged.

'I'm your boss: you have to be.'

'Not so. We could have a purely professional relationship; five o'clock, goodnight, that's it. But we don't. We've been out socially . . . as friends,' he added.

'And it's nice,' Maggie conceded. 'I enjoy going to a movie or for a meal with you. You're someone I can talk to; plus you don't see me as easy prey, and I appreciate that.'

He reached across and touched the back of her hand lightly. 'That doesn't mean that I don't find you attractive, ma'am. For the record, I do.'

'I've been aware of that too, don't you worry. And by the

72

way, it's mutual. It's just that I'm only interested in being attracted up to a certain point. Understand?'

Stevie nodded. He looked at her as she leaned back in the passenger seat. 'Of course I do,' he said. 'But . . . a purely hypothetical question, I stress . . . what might happen if you got attracted beyond that point?'

She smiled back at him, then squeezed his hand. 'If I did . . . of which, non-hypothetically, there's precious little chance . . . then before anything happened, you'd get transferred; or I would.'

He grunted. 'Just don't send me to your ex-husband's division.'

'You're not scared of Mario, are you? Did you see his New York photo in the *Evening News* on Monday, by the way, with that American cop, the guy who's coming over as the other half of the exchange trip?'

'Yes, I saw it, and no, I'm not scared of him. I just don't fancy the Borders, that's all.'

'That may not be an issue for much longer,' she said idly, to steer the conversation in another direction.

'What do you mean?' he asked, intrigued.

'Never mind.'

'Come on, what's up? Is Dan Pringle retiring?'

Her eyes narrowed slightly. 'Meaning that Mario'd get his job and I wouldn't?'

'No,' Steele protested, suddenly on the defensive. 'You're above him in the queue; and Greg Jay's ahead of you both.'

'You can forget Jay,' she said vehemently. 'But you're on

the wrong track anyway: Dan's not going yet, not that I know of anyway.'

'Someone is, though. You've let that much slip.'

'Rumour! It's rumour, that's all, and I should have known better than let anything slip to you. Change the subject. How much of what that man Easterson told George and Tarvil was news to you?'

'You don't get off that lightly, Superintendent. Let's go for a Chinese after work and I'll grill you further.' Steele grinned at her. 'Now, to answer your question, most of it was. I've been aware of the Scottish Farmers Bank since it was formed out of the demutualisation of the Agricultural and Rural Building Society a few years back. But I've always known it as a personal-service set-up, fiercely independent and very targeted in its approach to its clients. Its mortgage book as a building society was heavily weighted towards the top end of the market.' He pointed at the Whetstone villa. 'Houses like that one, for example, were very attractive to them; that sort in the towns, and in the country, properties with a bit of land attached. They've maintained offices in the four cities, London and key rural population centres in Scotland, servicing clients who are, in the main, minted. That's what I knew of them.'

'Comprehensive,' Rose acknowledged. 'So what didn't you know?'

'I didn't know that they now only have private banking halls in Edinburgh, Glasgow and London, for top-end clients. I didn't know about the Internet banking set-up, and I hadn't a clue that they'd sold their mortgage book to a Dutch bank.

And the fact that they've done a complete about-turn and were using the cash generated from the mortgage sell-off to attack the corporate banking and lending market came as the biggest surprise of all.'

'From what I'm told they've done it very successfully too,' the superintendent added, 'and according to Mr Easterson, a lot of the credit was due to the late Mr Whetstone. I find it hard to think of bank managers as debt salesmen, and yet it seems that's what they've become.'

'It's the way of the modern banking world, like he told the boys, and Whetstone was their top salesman. Knocks Manny English's suicide assumption even harder on the head, doesn't it?'

'I'm not so sure that's out of the question.'

'What do you mean?' asked the inspector. The detective superintendent pointed across the road at a taxi that had just drawn up in front of the Whetstone semi. A woman appeared on the pavement on the far side of the cab; as it drove off they saw that she was struggling with a number of cream-coloured Jenners carrier bags. Steele watched as the unknowing widow turned into her driveway. 'There's still the big "how" question, isn't there?' he finished.

'I'll tell you how he could have done it,' Rose replied. 'The call to the emergency services showed up on screen as coming from a mobile number, a phone that was nicked a couple of days ago. There were cycle tracks on the grass around the body. It could be that our anonymous tipster had also stolen the bike he was riding, that he stole the overcoat that Easterson said Mr Whetstone wore to work yesterday, and that he stole whatever makeshift stand he used to step off with the belt around his neck.'

'Who'd nick a milk crate?'

'Or a small stepladder?'

'Where would Whetstone get that?'

'He could have taken it from his office. No one saw him leave.'

'Well I'll tell you what; you ask the thief . . . only catching him might not be too easy.'

'I'm not so sure,' Rose argued. 'I could probably give you a dozen names, and he'd be among them. As it is, the emergency service has a tape of the call. I've told George Regan to get hold of it and have a listen. If nobody in our office twigs the voice, he'll take it around the CID offices to see if anyone else does.'

'But he won't have the gear any more, so he won't say a word . . .'

'Depends how I ask him.'

'You could get the DCC to ask him, and you still wouldn't get anywhere.'

'Time may tell, but for now, Mrs Whetstone's had time to get her coat off. Let's go and break the bad news.'

'Unless she's been out shopping for a new black suit already,' Steele muttered.

'Cynic,' Rose chided him. 'Come on.' She stepped out of the car, into the cold grey afternoon.

They crossed the street and opened the blue-painted iron gate, then walked once again up the paved pathway to the entrance porch. Steele rang the doorbell.

In fact, the woman was still wearing her heavy coat when she opened the door. She was naturally large and formidable, and it made her look all the more imposing. Although she was in her early fifties, she was fresh-faced and she wore no makeup, other than mascara and a very light lipstick. 'Not again,' she exclaimed.

'Excuse me?' said Rose.

'I said, not again,' she repeated. 'I had two of you people at the door on Monday afternoon. I thought I made my feelings perfectly clear then. If not, let me say it again. I am not sympathetic to fundamentalist religious views, I think that you are vain, silly, obsessive people and I would like you to go away.'

The detective superintendent took out her warrant card and held it up; Steele following suit. She smiled. 'Mrs Whetstone,' she explained, 'we're not Jehovah's Witnesses. We're police officers. I'm Detective Superintendent Rose and this is Detective Inspector Steele.'

The woman in the doorway blinked. 'You are?' She peered at their identification. 'Oh, I'm so sorry. They've been canvassing this area lately, you see, and I find that unless you are very firm with them you have trouble getting rid of them. How can I help you? Has there been a crime in the neighbourhood?'

'No,' said Rose, quietly. 'That's not what it's about. May we come in, please? It would be better if we did.'

The first sign of uncertainty showed on Virginia Whetstone's face. 'Of course.' She opened the door wider and stepped aside to allow them to enter, slipping off her coat as they passed her and turning to hang it on a hallstand. 'Go into the drawing room; first door on the left. Don't mind the dog; I've only just let him back inside, and it would be cruel to put him out again.'

Stevie Steele was a dog lover . . . he would have owned one, but for his single lifestyle . . . but he had never seen one quite like the animal that looked up at them as they entered the big, well-furnished room. It was lying on a rug in front of the fire, as big as a German shepherd, with a pure white coat. He might have taken it for an albino, but for the fact that it had vivid blue eyes. 'What is it?' he asked.

'He's a Siberian husky,' said his owner. 'The size of him scares some people, but Blue's as docile as they come, just a little down because I haven't been able to walk him in this damn fog. That should be my husband's job, of course, but he's never . . .' She faltered, as if she was no longer able to keep her anxiety at bay. 'This is about Ivor, isn't it? Has there been an accident?'

Maggie Rose found herself wondering how often she had been asked that question in her police career. 'No,' she replied. 'But what we have to tell you is still the worst possible news. The body of a man was found on the Meadows this morning. We believe it to be that of your husband.'

Virginia Whetstone blinked, then looked down at the dog. She reached out a hand and touched the back of a blue, cloth-covered armchair, then seemed to feel her way round it, until she sat down. 'I see,' she whispered. 'You believe that it's Ivor.'

'Yes.'

'You're certain?'

The superintendent glanced across the room at a large framed photograph that stood on a sideboard against the wall, beside the door. It showed Mr and Mrs Whetstone in evening dress; two tall, smiling, confident people. 'As certain as I can be without a formal identification. There was a driving licence in his wallet.'

'I see,' the widow said again. She looked quickly up at Rose, then back at the dog; she stayed motionless for several seconds, until suddenly she stood up. 'Would you excuse me for a few minutes?' she asked. 'I think I need to be alone for a bit.' Her cheeks, pink when she had opened the door, had a pale yellowish tinge to them.

'Of course,' Rose agreed. 'Would you like us to wait in our car for a while? We don't mind.'

'No, no. You stay here with Blue. I'll just go upstairs and,' she paused, 'compose myself.' She frowned. 'Or better still,' she said, with an attempt at briskness, 'I'll go through to the kitchen and make us all a cup of tea. They say it's called for at a time like this.'

Steele would have preferred coffee, but he decided not to ask for it. Instead he stood silently to one side as she left the room. 'Should we be doing this?' he asked. 'Leaving her alone, I mean. If this is a murder inquiry . . . and it bloody well is . . . she might be a suspect, for all we know at this stage.'

'She couldn't have got him up there,' the superintendent pointed out.

'Maybe she had help. I mean . . .'

'I know, I know. Stranger things have happened, but in the

absence of proof, let's just be kind, and assume that we've broken the worst news this lady's ever had in her life, and let's help her handle it the best we can.'

Steele smiled grimly. 'I suppose so. You're right, of course. Listen to me, for Christ's sake, quoting the book at you. It must have been exposure to Manny English this morning that did it.' He crouched down beside the dog and scratched it behind the ear; the animal rolled on to its side. He played with it for a while, and it was still licking his hand when Mrs Whetstone came back into the drawing room. She was carrying a tray with three mugs, a sugar bowl and a milk jug. Her face was still as pale, and the rattling of spoons on the tray told the detectives that she was trembling. Steele jumped quickly to his feet and relieved her of her burden.

She asked for no milk, one sugar; having been brought up to believe that hot sweet tea was a remedy for everything from shock to shingles, the inspector gave her two. She sipped the brew as she settled back into the armchair. The two detectives took their mugs and sat on the settee, part of a traditional suite.

'You understand that there are some questions we must ask you, Mrs Whetstone,' Rose began.

'Of course.' Her voice was strong and steady, but the officers could tell that it needed an effort to keep it that way.

'It doesn't have to be now, though. I can put that off for a bit, if you wish.'

The woman shook her head. Reflections of the room's central light sparkled in her hair. 'No, I'll deal with that now. I have some questions of my own first, if you don't mind.'

'What can we tell you?'

'You can tell me what happened to Ivor. Was he attacked? Was he mugged?'

Rose took a deep breath. 'He was found hanging from a tree,' she replied quietly.

Virginia Whetstone flinched; her hand shook violently for a moment, spilling some tea into her lap. 'Oh dear,' she whispered, pawing absently at the marks. 'Had he been there long when he was found?' she asked.

'All night; at least, that was the police doctor's preliminary view.'

She frowned, as if that would help her make sense of what she had been told. 'Are you telling me that Ivor killed himself?' There was incredulity in her tone. She looked from one detective to the other.

'No,' Steele replied. 'We're not telling you that.' He caught Rose's quick glance, and her message. 'The circumstances were such that we have to regard his death as suspicious,' he concluded cautiously.

'So he was attacked?'

'That's a strong possibility,' said the superintendent. 'When did you see your husband last, Mrs Whetstone?' she continued quickly, not wanting to be questioned any further herself.

'Yesterday morning, when he left for the office.'

'Did he use public transport? I notice that there are two cars in your drive.'

'Sometimes he used the bus, but quite often he walks.' The present tense registered with her at once; she bit her lip awkwardly. 'It's his main form of exercise, now he has less time for golf, although he hasn't been doing it as much lately.'

'So the MO was right, and he didn't come home last night.'

'He was right.'

'Didn't this alarm you?' The question was put softly.

'No.'

Rose was puzzled. 'It didn't? Weren't you expecting him?'

'No, because he called me in the afternoon, after the fog had closed in, when it was really very bad. He said that he could hear buses crawling along Lothian Road, and bumping into each other, and that the streets just weren't safe. He told me that if it hadn't lifted, or at least got a bit better by the evening, he might well take a room in the Caledonian Hotel. I assumed that he had.'

'So he didn't phone to confirm that?'

'No.'

'And you didn't phone the Caley?'

'No. I spent the evening with a neighbour, Connie Dallas. She'd just bought a DVD of the extended version of *The Two Towers* and she invited me to watch it with her. I didn't get back here until after eleven.'

'Did you think to check your answering service,' Steele asked, 'to see if your husband had called?'

'We don't have an answering machine, Inspector, and we don't use the BT service. Ivor has a mobile,' she flinched again at her mistaken tense, 'and that's all.'

'Did you try to call him at his office this morning?'

'No,' she said, stiffly. 'Why should I? I have never interrupted him at work, unless it was absolutely necessary.'

'Were you surprised that he didn't call you?'

'A little,' she confessed. She sniffed, and added, 'Enough for me to decide to get my own back. When the fog cleared a little I called a taxi and went to Jenners for some retail therapy. It's always been my way of letting Ivor know when I'm displeased.' As she spoke, her voice became a whisper, and her gaze dropped. 'Isn't that right, Blue?' she murmured to the dog. Finally, tears began to roll down her cheeks; she reached out to a side table and ripped a handful of tissues from a box, roughly, as if she was annoyed by her weakness.

Rose let the silence last for a few seconds, giving Virginia Whetstone time to gather herself, and to drink some of her tea. 'How was your husband's state of mind recently?' she murmured eventually.

'Robust!' The answer was fired back in an instant. 'Ivor has never been more successful in business, and we are both . . . have both enjoyed being back in Edinburgh.'

'He's never mentioned any worries?'

'None.' The widow knitted her brows. 'There were a few concerns at first, I suppose; he didn't care for the woman he had to report to, for instance.' There was something in Mrs Whetstone's tone which hinted that she had shared his dislike. 'The new approach to business came as a surprise to most of the managers, and as a terrible shock to some who couldn't adapt. Ivor could, though, as Vernon Easterson anticipated. After some self-doubt, his new post began to stimulate him far more than Kelso had in recent years. To be frank he'd become a bit of a boring old sod down there; he was just filling in the years to retirement. The change was a challenge and he embraced it very quickly. It made a new man of him.'

'Did he talk about his work at home?'

'When we were in Kelso, never; I knew many of his clients and so it would have been difficult. But here, since he took over the new job, he's spoken much more of what he's been doing. Why? Do you think this might have had something to do with . . .' As she looked across at Rose, it was clear that her emotional strength was all but spent.

'We don't think anything at this stage, Mrs Whetstone,' she answered. 'We're a few hours into our investigation, that's all. I think that we should end this conversation now. You've had terrible news, and we should help you to deal with it. You have a son, I believe.'

The woman seemed to be shrinking before her eyes. 'Yes,' she whispered, tearful again and no longer fighting against it. 'Poor Murphy. He's in the USA; he works there, in the drinks industry. I don't know how I'm going to tell him.'

'I'll tell him, if you like,' Maggie offered. 'If you give me a number for him, I'll break the news.'

Virginia Whetstone reached across and squeezed her arm. 'That's kind of you, my dear; I know it isn't part of the job. But it's something I have to do myself.'

'Do you have any other relatives nearby? Anyone who can come and be with you?'

'There's my mother, but she's very old, and anyway, I couldn't stand her fussing over me. Ivor has a sister in Kirkliston; yes, Aisling and her husband must be told.'

'Perhaps we could call her husband at work. Then he could go home, break the news to his wife and bring her to see you. I just don't feel right about leaving you here alone.'

'I appreciate that. Yes, maybe you could call Bert for me; he works for a finance house, Carpenter Dixon, in Edinburgh Park. His other name's Reynolds.'

Rose looked round at Steele. He nodded, stood up from the couch and stepped out into the hall, taking a cell phone from his pocket as he left. The dog stirred itself from its place on the hearthrug and padded after him.

As the door closed on them, Mrs Whetstone frowned and looked down, into her hands, now clasped together on her lap. 'You said something earlier about formal identification,' she murmured.

'Yes. It's necessary, I'm afraid.'

'When will I have to do it?'

'It will have to be done as soon as possible . . . but not necessarily by you. The fiscal will accept an identification by your brother-in-law.'

'Ohh!' Her hand went to her mouth. 'I couldn't ask Bert to do that.'

'No?'

'No, really I couldn't. I have to do it myself. It's my duty as a wife, isn't it?'

It was Maggie's turn to look at the floor, at the space the dog had vacated. 'When I'd just started going out with my husband,' she said slowly, carefully, weighing her words, 'there was an incident, and he was shot. He's a policeman, and I was taken to see him because everyone thought that's what I would want. The truth was, I'd rather have been anywhere else. I didn't want to see that big hunk of a man lying helpless with tubes coming out of him. I wasn't really given any choice. You have; you can ask Bert if you want, and nobody's going to think the worse of you. Not for one second.'

'Thank you, my dear,' Virginia Whetstone whispered. 'But Ivor might, and that I could not permit.'

Ten

Cold had come to New York City, down from the Arctic, banishing fall for the rest of the year. Mario McGuire had been completely unprepared for the change, but Colin Mawhinney had found him a heavyweight over-jacket from his precinct storeroom. The big Scots detective was quietly pleased by the experience of standing at the intersection of Seventh Avenue and Broadway with the letters 'NYPD' emblazoned across his back.

He looked around at the sea of neon, bright even in the morning light. 'Times Square, the centre of the universe,' said his escort. 'Tacky, isn't it?'

'It's Piccadilly Circus, mate,' McGuire retorted. 'Different shape, overall bigger, but the same idea.' He pointed along 42nd Street. 'You've even got theatre land going off it, just like in London they have Shaftesbury Avenue.'

'Do you have anything like this in Scotland?'

'We light up Edinburgh and Glasgow for Christmas. But we're too fucking mean to pay the electricity bill for a whole year.' He glanced up at the banner rolling around a building on the other side of the wide street, headlining the morning's news stories. 'Ach, that's not quite true. The castle's floodlit all year round, and damn nice it looks, but we don't have any of that stuff. Wouldn't be appropriate for my city. Wouldn't look right.'

'Edinburgh's that staid, then?'

'She's not as po-faced as she used to be, but compared to this she's still a tightly corseted old lady.'

'Sounds attractive,' said Mawhinney. 'I really am looking forward to seeing it. Will I enjoy it, do you think . . . as a cop, as well as a tourist?'

'As a cop you might well be bored. At your rank, in uniform, you'd spend a lot more time in the office than out on the street. The upside is that when you were out, your equipment belt would be a few pounds lighter.'

For a moment the American looked puzzled, until he caught McGuire's meaning. 'Ah yes, being unarmed. Do your guys have a problem with that?'

'We'd have a bigger problem if we were told that we had to be armed all the time. A lot of my friends would quit if that happened.'

'But how do you get by as an unarmed force in the twenty-first century?'

'We're not an unarmed force, Colin. We have more firearms at our disposal than ever before. They're just not routinely deployed, other than at sensitive sites; airports in the main. We're as lethal as you lot when we have to be, but we don't give guns to ordinary uniformed patrol officers.'

'Doesn't that put them at risk?'

'No more than they've ever been: not yet, at any rate. Gun

crime is a problem, I'll admit. We have a law in Britain banning the private ownership of handguns, but it was passed to keep them out of the hands of nutters, people who might suddenly go crackers and shoot up a street without warning. It was never thought that it would reduce the incidence of guns in street crime, for one obvious reason . . . criminals don't obey the law.'

'Mmm,' Mawhinney murmured. 'Interesting.' He motioned with his hand. 'Come on, let's walk up Seventh towards Central Park and watch how our officers handle street patrol. You'll see plenty of them: we believe in a strong visible presence. As a result, Manhattan is one of the safest tourist places in the world.'

'Oh, aye? And what about the rest of New York?'

The American grinned. 'Just don't get off the subway at the wrong station at night, that's all I'll say. Let's walk, Mario. If we're meeting Paula for lunch at noon on your last day in town, we've just got time to get there. If she's researching the deli business, she has to see the Carnegie.'

Eleven

Wee Moash Glazier stared defiantly up at the two faces as they towered over him in the Wee Black Dug, the pub he frequented whenever he stopped over with his Granton girl-friend. 'Ah dinna ken what yis are talking aboot,' he protested. 'Me go oot in that fog? Ye must think I'm fuckin' daft.'

'No, Moash,' Detective Sergeant George Regan growled. 'We actually think you're fuckin' clever. You looked at that fog and what did you see? Santa's lucky fuckin' dip, that's what! But you should have kept your sticky wee hand out, because this time it's pulled you into a murder investigation.'

The little thief's mouth fell open. 'It's you that's fuckin' daft,' he protested.

'Is that right?' the sergeant exclaimed heavily. 'In that case, you come with DC Singh and me, and we'll all go up to the Torphichen office for psychiatric evaluation.'

'Are you liftin' me?' Moash raised his voice so that the rest of the bar could hear him. He glanced around, in the hope, perhaps, that some of his fellow drinkers might dislike the police sufficiently to come to his aid. However, he saw nothing but backs turned towards him, and men lost in determined study of the bottom of their glass.

'By the balls if I have to,' Regan muttered, seizing him by an elbow and propelling him towards the door and out into the street, where their car was parked on a yellow line.

The little recidivist sat sullenly in the backseat as Tarvil Singh drove smoothly up through Muirhouse, and up towards Crewe Toll. As they navigated the busy roundabout, Regan heard him mutter, 'Yis have nae right. Ah've got nothing on me; yis have nae right.'

The detective sergeant turned in the front passenger seat and stared at him. 'You have the right to remain silent, and if you don't exercise it till we get where we're goin', you'll also have the right to a belt round the ear.'

His advice was followed for the rest of the journey. When they reached the Torphichen Place police office, Singh drove to the back, and parked close to the entrance; Glazier was hustled inside and deposited in an interview room. 'Keep an eye on him, Tarvil,' said Regan, 'while I go and fetch Stevie. This wee bastard would nick the table given half a chance.' He disappeared, ignoring the prisoner's muttered protests, returning a few minutes later with DI Steele.

'This is a fuckin' liberty,' wee Moash exclaimed as the inspector took a seat opposite him.

'Shut up,' Steele snapped. 'Speak when you're spoken to and give me straight answers to my questions, and you'll walk out of here. Piss me about and you will be off the streets for quite a long time.' He took a tape cassette from his pocket and inserted it in one of the decks of the recorder that sat between them on the table. 'Listen.' He pressed the 'play' button. There was a hiss, and then a female voice spoke. 'Emergency services. Which service do you require?'

Moash blinked, as the reply sounded around the room. 'Nane, but ye need the police in the Meadows. Fit o' the walkway, ahent the old Royal.'

Steele stopped the tape and rewound it. 'Again,' he said, and pressed 'play' once more. When it was finished, he stared across the table. 'This is the point, Mr Glazier, at which you tell me that you have no idea whose voice that is. Correct?'

The thief gave a tiny, cautious nod. 'Nae idea.'

'Okay. Predictable so far. Now here's the next step. DS Regan's already told you, I think, that we're investigating a suspicious death, a man found in the Meadows, the subject of that phone call. That means this is far more serious than anything that's ever brought you to our attention before. It means also that if I have to, I will bring in experts to listen to that recording, compare it with your speech pattern and determine whether or not it is you. Since DC Singh identified you at first hearing, I don't think they'll have any bother, but if I have to do that, you will be charged at the very least with withholding evidence in a murder inquiry. The fiscal might even go for accessory.'

He leaned forward. 'I'll ask you one more time, and I mean one more. Lie again and you're in the crapper. Is that your voice?'

Moash Glazier did not scare easily, but this young polis, a stranger to him, had his number. 'Aye,' he croaked, 'it's me. But I just found the guy, like.'

'I told you, straight answers only. This is one step at a time.

Did you steal the late Mr Whetstone's overcoat from off his body?'

The little man stared at the table silently.

'Fuck it, George,' said Steele. 'I'm fed up being nice to this wee snotter. I'm making this a formal interview and he's going down for everything we can nail on to him.' He looked over his shoulder at the bulky, grey-suited DC. 'Tarvil, go and get us a couple of fresh tapes.'

'Yes, sir.'

The junior detective had a hand on the doorknob when Glazier called out, stopping him in mid-stride. 'Aye, okay, okay. Ah get the picture; it's bash wee Moash day. A'right, Ah took the coat. It wisnae keeping him warm, that was for sure.'

'You didn't happen to nick a bike from Warrender Park Road as well, did you?' asked the inspector. The little man glared at him, trying to summon up some defiance. Steele answered his own question. 'Of course you did, but I'll deal with that later. Did you take anything else from the area around the body?'

Glazier peered at him as if trying to work something out, until finally his eyes lit up. 'Oh aye,' he said cunningly, 'Ah get it, one of you bastards lifted the guy's wallet and now you're going tae blame it on me. Well you just switch that tape on and I'll tell you loud and clear that I didnae take anything else aff him.'

'If I had time to take serious exception to that suggestion,' Steele told him icily, 'I would. But so far this is still your lucky day. I repeat,' he leaned over and stared into the thief's eyes, 'did you take anything else?'

Moash flinched. 'There was a wee stepladder; an aluminium thing. It was dead light, so I jammed it between the seat and the saddlebag. It fell aff though. Ah dinna ken where. That's the truth, honest.'

'You've never been honest in your fucking life, pal. Where's the coat?'

'Ah havnae got it.'

'Christ, I know that. You were in the pub, therefore you had drinking money, therefore you'd sold the coat and the bike straight off. I guess the stolen cell phone you called 999 on will be in the Water of Leith by now. Who bought the coat off you?'

'Fuck, Ah cannae tell you that. You'll do him for reset, and he'll do me for grassing him up.'

'I just want the coat, Moash. I won't do anyone if I get it back. But unless you tell me I will do you big-time. You were the first man to see Ivor Whetstone dead; it won't be all that difficult for me to prove to a jury that you were also the last man to see him alive.'

'You're as daft as Regan!' the thief protested.

'Nobody's as daft as Regan, but I'll let that one pass. You stole Whetstone's coat. Whether you tell us who bought it or not, we'll find him, and prove that. The rest's easy to work out; you mugged the man in the dark. You hit him over the head; but you hit him too hard. You thought you'd killed him, you panicked and to cover your crime you made it look like he topped himself. Tell me who you sold the coat to, or that's the way it's going to be.'

Wee Moash was convinced. Breaking with a tradition

handed down by the two generations of Glazier thieves before him, he muttered, 'Big Malky Gladsmuir, the bar manager in the Wee Black Dug.'

'Truth?' Steele fired out the question.

'On my kids' lives.'

'You don't have any kids, Moash,' Regan rumbled.

'In that case,' said Steele, 'we'll just keep you in custody till we actually have the coat. George, Tarvil, get back down to that pub fast and recover it, before Big Malky realises that it might be just a bit too warm for him to hang on to.'

Twelve

He had been in St Andrews House on many occasions, and for many reasons, since the creation of the Scottish Parliament and its Executive and before that, when Scotland had been ruled from afar and governed on a day-to-day basis by the Secretary of State.

From the start of his career, he had always kept his political leanings to himself, but those who assumed that he was naturally inclined to the right would have been surprised had they known the truth. He had voted for devolution and had welcomed it, on patriotic grounds, but also because he believed in social justice, and knew from experience that the remoteness of the Westminster Parliament and the constant battle for legislative time had been a heavy chain slowing down its delivery.

More than anyone else at the table that morning he had been angered by the interference of Miles Stringfellow, as he always was when he sensed that London was attempting to impose its will on Scotland. He had sometimes suspected that if he had lived his life two and a half centuries earlier it might have been ended on Culloden Moor.

As he rode up to the fifth floor, he was seized again by the feeling that the big stone building was a happier place under its new management.

Lena McElhone was waiting for him as the lift opened. 'Good evening, Mr Skinner,' she said as he stepped out into the ministerial office area. 'She's ready for you. If you'll follow me, I'll show you in.' She led him a short way along the corridor, stopped at a massive, varnished door, rapped on it with her knuckles and swung it open.

The deputy justice minister stood up behind her desk as he came in. The windows were uncurtained, he noticed, and the room was back-lit to an extent by the sodium globes outside in Waterloo Place. 'Hello,' exclaimed Aileen de Marco, moving round to meet him and extending her hand. He shook it, his smile seemingly automatically activated by hers. 'This is a surprise,' the minister continued. 'I didn't expect you to deliver the programme personally. I thought a biker would drop it off.'

He shrugged his shoulders. 'It's not a problem,' he told her. 'Besides, I wanted to update you on what's happened since our meeting this morning . . . and to break some bad news in person. I wasn't certain that I'd find you here, though. I thought you might have been off home to Glasgow by now.'

'I don't commute,' she said. 'Lena has a spare room in her flat. I rent it from her so that I have somewhere near the parliament and the office where I can crash. It's an unusual relationship between minister and private secretary but it suits us both. So what's this bad news you have to break?'

Skinner explained to her that there would indeed be two

more guests throughout the papal visit, and that as a result she no longer figured in the platform seating plan.

She laughed. It was a pleasant laugh, not a bray, but strong, musical and infectious. 'You think that's bad news, do you? It might be for my brother . . . he's coming with me . . . but it isn't for me. I don't mind giving up our places for the Prime Minister and his wife. In fact, making them happy is all I live for.'

Skinner looked at her and saw the mischief in her eyes. 'Not a fan, then?' he asked.

The young MSP smiled back at him. 'Come on,' she chided. 'That would be heresy, would it not?'

'If I was the investigating officer, I'd press for full-blown blasphemy on the charge-sheet.'

'Aah, but I'm an atheist, remember.'

'I don't think that would be a legitimate defence. It would be like saying that you didn't believe in traffic lights, so you have a right to drive through them. There are jails up and down Scotland that are jammed full of people who think like that. You should know. You're a justice minister; you're responsible for them.'

'Mmm,' she mused, 'I never thought of that. Maybe I had better guard my tongue in the future.'

'That depends.'

'On what?'

'On whether it's politically correct within your ruling group to be for the Prime Minister or agin him. From what I've observed the antis are probably in the majority.'

She looked at him in surprise, half sitting on the edge of

her desk, knee slightly raised, calf curving attractively. 'Is this Bob Skinner talking?' she challenged. 'The man who, or so the legend goes, once had a Secretary of State for Scotland by the throat? The man who's famous for his dislike of politicians? Is this the same man standing in my office talking like one of them?'

'Sure it is,' he replied easily, wondering when he had last felt so relaxed with someone who had been elected to office. 'You cannot conquer your enemies, Aileen, or even control them, unless you know how they think.'

'If you can't beat them, join them?'

'If necessary.'

She whistled softly. 'You are definitely not the product as advertised, Mr Skinner.'

'I've learned to adapt over the years. I've studied the beast in captivity.'

'And what have you learned?'

'I've observed that on occasion you come across one that you can let out of its cage to roam around freely, without worrying if it's going to bite you on the arse. They're the good ones: the ones who are there to make a difference for the people who gave them the job, not to preserve their own power base: the ones who'll steer the ship through heavy seas if they have to, not tie up and wait for the storm to pass. The trouble is, they're almost always found on the back benches or the cross benches, because their colleagues realise they're too dangerous to be trusted with the tiller.'

'And how do you spot them?'

'Small signs,' he replied. 'For example, they refer to politicians in the third person rather than the first, "they" instead of "we", as if they themselves realise they're not run-of-the-mill, not just another nose in the trough. You did it yourself, a couple of minutes ago.'

'Are you saying you'd open the door of my cage?'

He nodded. 'But don't tell anyone. Watch yourself. Guard your tongue. Go with the tide . . . until your chance comes. When it does, you grab the tiller and steer for the white water.'

Thirteen

Big Malky Gladsmuir was not particularly tall. His size was in his shoulders, which were as wide as a doorway, and in his chest, which resembled one of the barrels in the cellar of the Wee Black Dug: when that was allied to a disposition that was said to suck sunlight out of the brightest day, he inspired a reaction similar to that of sailors spotting a mine bobbing on the surface of the ocean.

Nonetheless, for all his outward ferocity, Big Malky appeared to be an exemplary citizen. As Tarvil Singh drove down Leith Walk, George Regan had taken the precaution of calling his CID colleagues in Queen Charlotte Street, headquarters of the division that took in Granton, and making enquiries about him. He found that he had never been accused of any offence, nor had he been detained by police for any reason.

'Man's a fucking bear, though,' he had been advised by his near namesake, DS George Grogan. 'He runs a quiet pub, mainly because he looks so ferocious that none of his regulars ever chance their arm; any strangers who look like bother don't get a second drink.'

'And he's really never been done for anything?'

'Malky's been a friend to us over the years: he understands the value of keeping on good terms with the CID. The one time we could have done him for something, we turned a blind eye; that was when he caught a smack dealer from Muirhouse trying to move stuff in his place. He broke the guy's jaw, nose and both his arms, then chucked him out in the street. When we asked about it, nobody had seen a thing, but there was still blood all over the bar. We could probably have matched it, but the drugs squad had been trying to nail the victim for about three years, so we didn't bother.'

'Is there stolen gear handled in his place?'

'No danger. The Wee Black Dug belongs to a chain, and it does tidy business; they wouldn't appreciate their licence being put at risk. If wee Moash says Malky bought something off him I'd take that with a pinch. Wee Moash is not the most reliable witness.'

'Most witnesses are reliable when Stevie Steele's squeezin' their balls, George. Thanks.'

The pub was busy when they arrived; they stood just inside the doorway for a while, eyeing up their surroundings. Regan did a quick head count and reckoned that there were over forty punters in there. A man and a woman . . . the only member of her sex in the place . . . were hard at work behind the bar; they refilled glasses on the nod, a sure sign that they knew their customers well, took the money and dispensed change with a minimum of conversation. Behind them a squat, heavy-browed figure stood by the till, ringing up the purchases; he was in his forties, with a greying crew-cut, and a dimple in the middle of his heavy chin. Regan moved close to the bar and caught his eye. As Singh followed him, one or two heads turned, glanced at him, read him for what he was and turned away again quickly.

Malky Gladsmuir called across to the female steward; she came across to take over the till, and he moved to the furthest corner of the bar, where there was a little space.

'You're the two guys were in earlier,' he said, in a voice that was quiet and not at all threatening. In Regan's long experience, that meant nothing at all. Tony Manson, Dougie Terry and Lenny Plenderleith had all been quietly spoken, and all quite lethal. Jackie Charles, on the other hand, had been loud, but had relied on people like Dougie the Comedian to back him up.

'Well remembered,' said the sergeant. 'I'm sorry we had to huckle one of your punters.'

Gladsmuir shrugged his massive shoulders. 'Wee Moash is not a big contributor to my profits,' he said. 'Guys like him are a fucking drain on the rest of us.'

'So why do you let him in?'

'He's useful to me. Moash hears things around and about; he'd never say a word tae you, other than "guilty", when he has to, but he talks to me.'

'And you in turn talk to us?' Regan murmured.

'Sometimes. When I think it's right, and when I know it's in absolute confidence . . . which is why,' suddenly his voice became colder, 'I don't appreciate you two swanning in here and waving me over.'

Regan understood. 'Worry not. We'll make enough noise

before we leave. In fact we might even wind up lifting you.'

That might not be so easy, said Malky Gladsmuir's eyes. 'What the fuck do you mean?' he exclaimed, loud enough to be heard by those nearest him.

The DS fell into character. 'I mean,' he bellowed back, 'that somebody in here's been buying knock-off gear.'

'You're fucking joking,' Gladsmuir protested. To their surprise, the two detectives found themselves believing that this was not part of the act for the punters; he seemed genuinely surprised, and angered.

'Wee Moash Glazier nicked a five-hundred-quid mountain bike, and a four-hundred-quid Crombie coat, this morning, in the fog, on our patch.' Tarvil Singh leaned across the bar; he was taller than Gladsmuir and almost as powerfully built. 'The owners of these items are not being reasonable about it. They want them back.'

The bar manager's heavy eyebrows rose. 'That wee bastard!' he exclaimed. 'He came in here wearing that coat. Miles too fuckin' big for him, but he told me he'd bought it in a charity shop. I says tae masel', "Aye, that'll be right," but I still had it off him straight away. Wee Moash owes me a quid or two, and I told him I was keepin' it until he squared me away. Haud on a minute.'

He turned on his heel and walked away through a door at the back of the bar. He had been gone for less than thirty seconds before he was back, holding a heavy dark blue overcoat in his right hand, raised up by the lapels, as though it contained an obstreperous customer whom he was seeing off the premises. 'Here.' He lifted it over the bar and handed it to Regan, who took it from him carefully. 'Take it away wi' yis. I know fuck all about a bike, though.' He turned and surveyed his customers; finally the scene in the corner was commanding their undivided attention. 'That said,' he continued, his voice raised, 'if I find that knock-off's been traded in this pub, then the guy that bought it had better get on it and pedal as far away from me as he fuckin' can.'

Suddenly, the bar was filled with outraged looks and shaking heads . . . and minus one drinker. The door at the far end opened with a creak and began to swing shut again on its closer. Without another word, Regan and Singh turned and headed for their exit, and business as usual was resumed.

'One more thing,' Malky Gladsmuir called after the two detectives. They turned in the doorway. 'You can tell wee Moash from me that the next time he comes in here he'd better have stolen a life-jacket: because he's goin' in the fuckin' river.'

Fourteen

James Andrew Skinner had been at Gullane Primary School for only a few weeks, but already, in that short time, he had made a name for himself . . . two names, in fact; one as a five-year-old with a reading age of eight, and the other as the best fighter in his class. His mother had been even more appalled by the second than she had been pleased by the first.

'He burst a kid's lip, Bob,' Sarah exclaimed indignantly. 'Then when the little boy's brother . . . his two years older brother . . . came in to stop the fight, he made his nose bleed.'

Bob made himself frown at the five-year-old, who was standing in the middle of the kitchen, trying to look remorseful, but not quite getting there. 'That's a bit excessive, Jazz,' he said severely. 'No Saturday television, my boy.'

'Aw, Dad!'

'Sorry, mate. That's the way it is.'

He looked at his wife. 'Why?'

'Pardon?'

'Did you ask him why?'

'No, I did not. Bob, I don't like being called to the head

teacher's office to receive an official complaint about my son's behaviour. The evidence was there. Mrs Rogers showed me the tissues they used to wipe the blood off those kids. She said that Jazz attacked the little one, then hit his brother as well.'

He picked his son up and sat him on the work surface. The boy's blond hair glinted in the light; he was sturdy, and big for his age. 'Right,' he said. 'Let's hear your plea in mitigation.'

'What?'

'Why did you hit him, son? The boy in your class, I mean. I doubt if it would be a fair fight; I don't remember seeing any kid your size in your group when we checked you in there.'

James Andrew shook his head, his jaw set.

'Hey,' said his father, 'not answering me isn't an option. Now out with it.'

'No,' the boy replied.

'Jazz,' Bob warned him. 'No telly for a month.'

He shook his head again.

'I'll tell you,' a voice exclaimed from the doorway.

James Andrew glared furiously at his brother. 'But not in front of Mum,' Mark added quickly. When he had been adopted, it had been his decision to christen Bob and Sarah as Mum and Dad, but they had always made sure that the memory of his natural parents burned strong in him.

'Wait a minute,' Sarah exclaimed.

'Ssh,' said her husband, soothing her. 'I want to get to the bottom of this. Mark's a sensitive kid; if that's the way he wants it, let's go with him. Remember, he's the reason this bruiser can read as well as he does; we owe him. Gimme a minute with the boys.'

Finally, reluctantly, Sarah nodded. She lifted Seonaid, who had been watching the exchange with obvious fascination, out of her high chair and tucked her under her arm. 'Us girls will rejoin you when we're good and ready,' she said stiffly, and hefted her daughter out of the room.

Bob knew that she would probably be listening outside, but he carried on. 'You might as well tell me yourself, Jazz.'

As he looked up at him, his younger son's eyes blazed with an anger he had never seen in them before. 'He called me a something stinking copper's brat,' he said, his voice high-pitched. 'And he said Mum was a something Yankee something.'

'That's true,' said Mark. 'He shouted it so the whole class could hear. I made one of them tell me afterwards.'

'So you pegged him one,' Bob sighed.

James Andrew nodded.

'Just the one?'

'It was a good one,' the boy whispered.

As he spoke his father noticed a slight bruise on his temple. 'The brother,' he went on. 'The head teacher said that he tried to stop the fight. Is that all he did?'

James Andrew shook his head. 'He punched me on the side of the face: from behind.'

'How often did you hit him back?'

'Three or four times. Till he started to cry,' a gleam of satisfaction came into his eye, 'in front of all the girls.'

'Why didn't you tell Mrs Rogers what happened?'

'Didn't want to say it. What he said about you and Mum.'

Bob felt an unfamiliar lump in his throat. 'Well, thank you, pal,' he murmured, and hugged him. 'In the circumstances, television privileges are restored.' He called over his shoulder, 'Sarah!'

She was grim-faced as she came back into the room, with Seonaid toddling along in front of her. 'Did you know that I'm a something stinking copper and you're a something Yankee something?' he asked her.

He turned back to his son. 'Jazz, I'm not going to ask for these kids' names. If this happens again, I want you to tell a teacher. But do no more than that; don't go thumping any more kids. There's a reason for this. The wrong sort of people might use it to try to hurt Mum and me; they might tell stories to the papers, stuff like that. Understand?'

'I think so.'

Bob ruffled his hair and lifted him down from the work surface. 'Good lad,' he said. 'On you go now, you can play a game with Mark till it's time for bed.'

As the boys trotted off together Sarah looked after them. 'God,' she whispered, 'he's so like you. But he's still so little; he's only five. What if this is only the start? What's going to happen once Mark goes to Fettes? What if he's going to be bullied?'

'In that case,' said Bob, with a faint grin, 'I'd better start teaching him some restraint holds, so that he isn't just slugging kids all the time . . . or to hit them where it doesn't show, so that it's deniable. But I don't think that's going to happen. Jazz is not the bullyable type, as he's just shown with some effect. There's more than that, though: I've lived in this village for a long time. I know the people here, I know the kids and I know that school. This incident's as far from typical as you can get. It never happened to Alex when she was there, and it's never happened to Mark. I'm pretty sure it won't be repeated. Just to be on the safe side, though, I think you should go back to see the head teacher, and tell her the other side of the story. I don't want things taken any further, but I'd like the staff to keep their eyes and their ears open, just in case.'

'Don't you want to come with me?' She was frowning slightly.

'I will if you insist, but I don't think that would be a great idea. I am what I am; there's no getting away from that. I don't know Mrs Rogers all that well, and I wouldn't want her thinking that the deputy chief constable's come to lean on her. A quiet word from you would be better.'

'I suppose you're right,' Sarah conceded. She watched him as he took an onion, some mushrooms and a large red pepper from the fridge, and put them in the drainer section of the sink. As cold water ran on them from the column tap, he put a frying-pan on the hob, poured in a coating of olive oil and a little balsamic vinegar, added a little salt, then turned up the temperature wheel. As the pan heated, he took the vegetables from the drainer, dried them, then began to chop them, carefully, on a thick teak board. 'What's this?' she asked, intrigued.

He grinned, keeping his eyes fixed on what he was doing. 'What's it look like? I'm cooking. It's Trish's night off, and the bears were fed by the time I got home, so I thought you and I would have a quiet dinner together. If you go and put the lady Seonaid to bed, I'll be done when you are.'

Fifteen

'How was the identification?' asked Stevie Steele. 'Was he reasonably presentable?'

Maggie Rose grimaced. 'Yes,' she replied, 'he looked dead, but otherwise okay, if you get my drift. But I really do hate those things, all the more so when it's a wife or husband who's doing it. I wish to God Mrs Whetstone had asked her brother-in-law, as I suggested.'

'Bad, was she?'

'Not till the end. That was the worst of it in a way. She was so bloody stoic at first. She took a deep breath, and nodded for the attendant to turn back the sheet. Then she took another breath, and looked closely at the face. She must have gazed at it for about two minutes, quite impassively, until finally she nodded again and said, "Yes." She almost made it out of the room, but not quite. We were just short of the door when she collapsed; just sort of turned and leaned on me, as if she was giving in, and burst into tears. She'd me going as well, I don't mind telling you. Afterwards, when she'd got hold of herself again, she was embarrassed. I don't think I coped with that any better.' She looked away from him. 'I'm just not one of nature's comforters, I'm afraid, Stevie.'

'No, you're not,' he concurred. 'You're a police officer, not a social worker. You were there because it was your job . . . although you could just as well have sent me, or young Tarvil for that matter. So stop beating yourself up, for Christ's sake, and choose a starter.'

She looked at the menu. 'You choose. I've made enough decisions for the day.'

'Clispy duck, then?'

Maggie grinned. 'Fine.'

'Sweet and sour pork?'

'Fine.'

'Chicken and black bean sauce?'

'Fine.'

'House white?'

'Hell no! Chablis.'

'See, you can't get away from giving orders. That's why . . .'

'That's why my marriage broke up?' she shot at him, before he could finish, taking him by surprise.

'I didn't mean that at all. What I was going to say was it's no wonder you're a workaholic.'

'Who says I am?'

'I do. So does everyone else in the force. I'll bet that the next thing you were going to ask me was work-related.'

When her cheeks reddened slightly, he was taken aback for the second time inside a minute. 'Actually, you're right,' she confessed. 'I was going to ask you about Whetstone's coat.'

'We recovered it. I've sent it off to Arthur Dorward at the Howdenhall lab.'

'How about the stepladder? Have we recovered that yet?'

'No, and the chances are slim that we will.'

'It puts suicide back in the frame, though. It existed, that's for sure. There was no reason for Glazier to make that up.'

'It may be back in the frame,' said Steele, 'but I'm still not certain that I buy it.'

'Why not? He could have taken it from his office.'

'There's something else; I only heard about this late on, so this is the first chance I've had to tell you. He was hanged with a leather belt.'

'Yes.'

'When they got him back to the morgue, they undressed him and sent all his effects out to the lab. The man was wearing braces. Not just that. Ivor Whetstone had a thirty-six-inch waist. The belt that hanged him was a size forty-six; long enough to tie securely to the tree and still leave enough to put a noose through the buckle.'

'He could have bought the belt for the purpose.'

'I'm sure somebody did; it was expensive, very strong leather and it looked new. I'm nearly as sure . . . well, let's say I think there's a chance . . . that when we track down the purchase, whoever bought it won't fit Whetstone's description.'

'We'll see. That aside, and going back to the coat, someone from Howdenhall will need to see Mrs Whetstone.'

'For hair samples for elimination purposes? Yes. And the dog too. They'll need to clip some of its fur.'

'Maybe not elimination?'

'What do you mean?'

'I mean, as you reminded me at her place, if you're right, then for all her performance she still hasn't been ruled out as a suspect.'

'Oh, yes, she has,' Steele countered. 'While you went off with her to the morgue, and while George and Tarvil were at the Wee Black Dug, I went to see her neighbour . . . the one with the Tolkien video. She confirmed that they had supper together, then watched the movie, all three hours and whatever of it.'

She frowned across the table. 'I never told you to do that.'

'It's called initiative, ma'am. It had to be done, and quickly too. Don't worry, Maggie: I told Mrs Dallas it was purely routine and that there was no need to mention it to Mrs Whetstone, if she thought it would upset her.'

'Do you think she will?'

'No, I don't. She had a hell of a shock too when I told her what had happened, but she understood what I was saying. I told her that we were releasing the name after the identification anyway, and that it would be public by tonight.'

'Did you ask her anything else while you were there?'

'Of course I did. I asked her how well she knew Whetstone. She told me that he and her husband were pally, and that they played golf together. I asked her about his demeanour recently. She said that he'd been on top of the world, and really chuffed with himself over the way his job was going. She said that he was a workaholic as well, by the way, but that at least he found time for his golf.'

'But not for his wife?'

'She didn't say that, but now you mention it that may have been implied.'

'Mmm.'

'Don't tell me you've got a niggle yourself?' he asked.

'No, not really. It's just . . . I'll be happier when there's a clear line of inquiry. I'll be happier when we have Dorward's crime-scene report, and I'll be happier when we've got the post-mortem report. With those together we should be able to say whether we have a suicide, or something else.'

'If we do, I'm pretty clear where we go after that,' said Steele. 'Straight back to the bank. We should talk to his golf pals, just in case he had any worries that he mentioned to them, but I'm sure our best way forward lies in looking at his client relationships. Nobody loves their bank manager; maybe one of Mr Whetstone's customers was in trouble and had good reason to hate him.' He chuckled. 'We could always charge wee Moash, of course, but even the rawest advocate would get him acquitted if we did. He didn't nick the bike till this morning, and he didn't make the phone call till then, but the man died last night.'

'Agreed,' Rose murmured, 'but what if . . . We know Glazier didn't kill him, but what if it was just a random mugging that went wrong? What if the hanging was an attempt to cover it up?'

'The autopsy should tell us that. When's that happening, by the way? And who's doing it?'

'Sarah Grace is handling it, but she can't do it before tomorrow morning. It's longer than I'd have liked, but it's acceptable. Rigor mortis will have passed off by then. I want you to go along, incidentally: nine a.m. tomorrow, at the new Royal Infirmary.'

A corner of his mouth twisted in a smile. 'You've made my night,' he muttered.

'Don't think about it and it won't put you off your food,' she said, as the waiter approached.

Sixteen

'This is excellent,' Sarah pronounced, as she finished her first mouthful of fillet steak. 'Why don't I let you cook more often?'

'Why don't I volunteer more often might be a better question.'

'Okay, why don't you?'

'Because I like your cooking too much. How about that?'

She gave a gasp of surprise. 'What is this? Bob Skinner the diplomat? Am I hearing things?'

He reached across and poured her some more wine, a nice light Rioja called Marques de Griñon, that he bought by the case from a website with the well-chosen name of Simply Spanish Wines. 'Funny, you're the second person who's said something like that to me today.'

'Who was the other?'

'An MSP. A minister, in fact.'

'Does the thought that you might be mellowing worry you?' his wife asked, a tease in her voice. 'Does it make you feel like Samson with a short back and sides?'

'If it did, I'd be sure to remember who cut my hair,' he growled.

'Ouch. I see you haven't lost your bite.'

He cut off some more of his steak and forked up some of the *escalivada*, vegetables as he had learned to cook them in Spain. 'I hope I haven't lost anything,' he said, once they had been despatched. 'But it's good to learn things along the way.'

'Who's been teaching you?'

'Life's been teaching me, honey. But it's been a difficult process.'

'Is this to do with your heart trouble?'

'Don't call it heart trouble.' His sigh was full of exasperation. 'It's an inherited condition and it's been dealt with. I have a pacemaker, and that allows me to function exactly as I've always done. You're a doctor; you know that well enough.'

'I don't agree,' she countered. 'Physically you may be fine, but emotionally it's left a scar. You've never had to question your health before. As a result you're . . .'

'There are lots of things I've never had to question before,' he said, quietly, cutting her off.

A silence fell between them; they ate, not looking at each other. It was Sarah who broke it, pushing her plate to one side, leaving half of her meal untouched. 'Ironic, isn't it?' she exclaimed. 'I make a remark about your new-found diplomacy and you respond by tearing into me. I bet you didn't do that to the MSP.'

'No,' he admitted, looking a shade guilty. 'I didn't. I'm sorry, Sarah. I'm on a hair trigger just now, and I don't know why. I even had a small strip torn off me by Archbishop Gainer today for the way I spoke to Jack McGurk. He was right: the boy's like a coiled spring every time he comes into my room, and none of it, or very little of it, is his fault. Maybe you're right too, maybe it is the aftermath of the pacemaker thing but, honestly, I doubt it. I think it goes deeper than that. I reckon that more than my health has been called into question this year. And as I see it now many of the things I've believed to be true may have been way off the mark.'

'Things about me, I assume,' she murmured.

'No,' he retorted quickly. 'Don't assume that.'

'It's true, though. Let's face it, I'm not the gem you thought I was; I've got flaws just like everyone else. Most married women find another man attractive at some time or another; me, I did something about it.'

'Okay, you had an affair: but I'm no saint either. You've stuck by me before, and I'll stick with you now.'

'Is that what it's about? Sticking with each other?'

'For most people, I reckon that's exactly what it's about. It's easy to walk away from marriage these days, once the early glamour fades . . .'

'Like the McGuires, you mean?'

'No, not them: there's something deeper there.'

Sarah snorted. 'Yeah, she's got legs up to her armpits, silver hair and her name's . . .'

'Paula Viareggio didn't break them up,' Bob snapped. 'She came after. Anyway, Maggie and Mario aren't like us: they don't have kids.'

She frowned at him. 'You're saying our kids are the glue that binds us together?'

'Are you going to tell me they're not? If we didn't have them, wouldn't you have been tempted to stay in Buffalo after your parents' death?'

'Bob,' Sarah told him, 'I never want to see Buffalo again. I could have stayed, with or without the children, but I chose to come back here.' She paused. 'Now you answer me something. Who do you love the most, me or the children?'

He stared at her. 'What's that? The chicken-and-egg question? I love my family, Sarah, there are no degrees involved there. It's total.'

'Okay, I'll stop pussying around the real issue. If we had no children, like Maggie and Mario, would we still have a marriage?'

'For my part, yes, I think we would. What do you say?'

She reached across the table and took his hand. 'You "think" we would; hardly a straight answer, is it? You've changed, Bob, you've grown more remote, and I can't help wondering whether it's because, for all you say, you can't really handle what happened with me.'

Bob looked down at his plate; the remnants of his meal, and hers, lay cold before them. 'That was a fucking waste of two fillet steaks,' he said heavily.

'Maybe not,' she countered, 'if it's what it takes to make us sit down and talk to each other.' She picked up the bottle and refilled both their glasses, draining it in the process. He picked his up and drank deeply.

'Why don't we just go to bed,' he suggested, 'and fuck each other's brains out? That usually sorts us out.'

She smiled weakly. 'That's a palliative. This time we're attacking the root cause of the problem.'

'Well, it's not you,' he told her firmly. 'We haven't been talking to each other enough, that's for sure, and maybe we have been sweeping some marriage problems under the carpet, but that's not what's been eating me.' He got up from the dining table, walked through to the kitchen and returned a minute later with another bottle of Marques de Griñon, from which he topped up his glass.

'I've always laughed at the thought of mid-life crises,' he continued. 'I've seen them as post-yuppie status symbols. But not any more, not now I'm having one myself. I've suddenly started to look at myself objectively, and that can be a terrible thing. I realise now that for much of my adult life I've been intolerant, unforgiving, arrogant. I've made decisions about the lives of people close to me, as if I was God Almighty.'

'Are you talking about your brother?'

'Yes, I mean Michael. His death has been the trigger for all of this. My pacemaker incident, you losing your parents, our personal difficulties, I admit they may all have been contributory factors, but that lies at the very heart of it all. It's made me look at myself, and at the way I behaved towards him, and I do not like what I see.' He picked up his glass in both hands and took a sip, leaning forward, elbows on the table, shoulders hunched, peering into the dark wine as if the truth was written there.

'I hated him when he was alive,' he said hoarsely. 'I really did. For all his faults, his weaknesses, and his cruelty towards me when I was a kid, still he was my only brother, and yet I could find no forgiveness towards him in my heart. As it turned out he was a victim himself, but I was never interested in that. I was his jury, his judge, and I might even have been his executioner, but for my father. I told Jim Gainer all about it this afternoon. He patted me on the head, sort of; he told me that as it worked out I'd done right by him, but I can't buy that. I left him living as an outcast for years, when I could have brought him back into the family. You know, Big Lenny Plenderleith might get out quite soon, on a form of early parole, training for freedom. There was no parole for Michael, though; not in my heart. I left him to rot.'

He frowned savagely, knitting his eyebrows together. 'What sort of a man does that make me? What sort of a policeman does that make me? I've made some momentous decisions, Sarah, when I've had to. I'm looking back on them now, and I'm looking for compassion within me when those things happened. I don't see any. Don't get me wrong. I've always known that I'm a hard guy when I have to be and that there's a merciless streak in me; it's kept me alive a few times. But I thought that I was fully aware of it, and that I could control it. I never appreciated until now just how much a part of me it is.'

'You're exaggerating, Bob. There's compassion in you: look at how you handled Jazz tonight.'

'Jazz is a five-year-old in his first playground fight. I'm talking about judgement at a whole different level, and honestly I'm not certain any more that mine is up to the job that I have. Sarah, I made a promise to Alex a while back that the moment

I feel that I'm burned out in the police, then I'll pack it in and do something else. I wonder if that moment's here.'

'Wow!' She whistled. 'That's something I never expected to hear from you.'

'How would you feel if I retired?' he asked.

'Not so long ago I'd have said, "Roll on the day," but now I think I'd dread it. You're right about your mid-life crisis. You're racked with self-doubt and for the first time ever you're questioning yourself. For the moment you're unsure and indecisive, and yet here you are, talking about making a career decision. You cannot do that in your present state of mind. If you quit now, there's a fifty per cent chance you'd spend the rest of your life hanging about the house regretting it, and I do not think I could stand that. Tell me something. On a day-to-day basis do you still feel functional in your job?'

'I suppose I do,' he conceded.

'You don't feel insecure about the preparations for next week's visit, for example?'

'Not at all. That's routine; top-end stuff, but still routine.'

'Any other command decisions you're having to take just now?'

'There's a personnel thing; a senior CID post.'

'Any doubts about that?'

'No. I've known the people involved for years.'

'So?'

'That's all peripheral stuff, decisions based on training and experience. It's what's at the heart of me that concerns me.'

'Bob, you're on a guilt trip: don't take it out on the rest of us.'

'I'm trying not to, but it's no trip. As far as Michael's concerned, I am fucking guilty.'

'Man,' Sarah exclaimed, 'get it through your head. You are no closer to infallibility than the rest of us. You are no angel. I'm no angel. There are no angels. Let me ask you one last thing. Are you proud of James Andrew?'

'More than I can say,' he answered.

'Me too. Now let me tell you one last thing. As I said earlier, he is you, everything you are, in miniature; if you could stand back and see the two of you together you'd understand exactly what I mean. My rough-and-tumble son is a lovely guy; you can see his soul through his eyes, and every time I look at him I thank you from the bottom of my heart for making him, and the others, the way they are. They're the most important achievements of your life, and in their light you can make allowances for everything else.'

He closed his eyes for several long seconds, as if he was trying to find words. When he opened them and looked across at her, they were filled with tears. 'That's another thing,' he said, as a smile broke through. 'I never used to get emotional either.'

'That's nothing to be ashamed of,' she told him, although, in truth, she found that more disturbing than anything else.

'I'll keep it under control, don't worry.' He grinned. 'Let's get back to firmer ground. What have you got in your professional diary?'

'I'm working for you tomorrow,' she told him.

'Uh?' He stared at her, surprised.

'Well, for Maggie Rose, really. I'm doing a post-mortem

examination on a man who was found hanging from a tree in the Meadows this morning. The early CID view is that he may possibly have had some help, from person or persons unknown.'

Bob's expressive eyebrows knitted together once more, and the fragile link they had woven between them was snapped. 'It's the first I've heard of it,' he growled. 'I tell you, Chief Superintendent Pringle's in for a kicking tomorrow!'

Seventeen

There was one thing about England that the drummer loved, and it was the same thing he loved about Belgium.

Once he had revelled in the universal dream of youth, of seeing the world, of following a martial life in glamorous, interesting and preferably sunny surroundings. It had been his ambition to go into private security work, not the kind that involved wearing drab uniforms and crash helmets but the upmarket type that would take him to Hollywood riding in the front seat of limos with movie stars in the back. He had made some early enquiries about possibilities, and had even registered with an agency that had promised him the sort of life he was after within a couple of years, once he had acquired the sort of experience they required.

But somewhere along the line . . . not very far along either . . . it had all gone wrong. It had been nothing of his making. He had simply been the wrong man in the wrong place at the wrong time. A finger had been pointed at him, an order had been given, and he had obeyed. He would not have volunteered, and while he had been unsure of the consequences of refusal he had been smart enough not to invite them.

That was all it had taken: a couple of minutes out of a hot day long ago, and his life had been changed irrevocably, his dream snuffed out, his imaginary CV of ten years on crumpled metaphorically and thrown in the waste bucket. He had called himself 'Idiot!' many times since, but unfairly, he knew. He had been given no choice.

Since then, his life had known no more dramas. He had been looked after and he had nothing really to complain about. His existence had been comfortable, almost pampered, and the envy of many of his friends. But it had been essentially ordinary, and worse than that, it had been spent in Belgium, a pleasant country, he conceded, but one that he had always found desperately dull.

True, the band had livened things up for a while. It was not the most orthodox of hobbies, but it was one for which he was trained and it was also one that kept him in touch with old friends. There were the trips too, the annual jaunts to Spain and Germany, with hospitality laid on, as much free booze as they could drink, and the occasional fumbling congress with a friendly lady, although, as the years had passed, those pleasant encounters had become fewer and fewer.

Nothing had been said, but he sensed that for some of them this would be the last outing. He and his contemporaries were all past sixty, and the colonel himself was closer to seventy. They didn't have the stamina for these road trips any longer. Let's face it, he had told himself, too often, they were all fucked. He could count on at least three nocturnal pisses, uncomfortable ones at that. It was a grievous curse for a man of his passions and he suspected that a few of his friends were afflicted in the same way.

He felt the pressure again as he walked away from the bus, two fresh packs of cigarettes tucked away in his pocket. His first port of call back in the club had better be the lavatory rather than the bar. It had been a good night though. They had been welcomed by their hosts in Hull as comrades in arms, as he supposed they were in a way, ex-servicemen all, linked by a martial bond that was international.

They had marched and played their way through the town centre that afternoon, and he could say with some pride they hadn't been too damned bad at all. If it was to be a swansong, then it would be sweet and no mistake. It had taken him a while to summon up enthusiasm for the trip, but now that it was under way he was looking forward to every moment of it.

Of course, it was the beer that had lifted up his heart, the true love of his bachelor life, and the common passion that united the ordinary Belgian and his English counterpart. It was a symbol of their nationalism, a thread in each country's flag, even if it was expressed in very different ways.

The bandsman believed in embracing the culture of others wherever he went, and so he took readily to the strange, warm, hoppy English ale, even though it was as different as one could imagine from the golden Stella or from the strange fruit-based brews of which Belgium was so proud. Beer was the champagne of the common man and much more interesting in its variety and in the range of experiences it offered. For him, England meant the *premier cru*, the pinnacle of the craft.

That night he was in heaven. The Humberside Ex-servicemen's Association had taken the Bastogne Drummers to their club, and there they had seen, bright fonts gleaming along the bar, the legend of legends, the range of champion ales made by Timothy Taylor of Keighley, Yorkshire.

He smiled as he thought of his evening. He had heard of Taylor's ales, of course . . . who hadn't? . . . but they were as rare as hen's teeth, other than the bottled Landlord which he had found once in Antwerp. He had never seen the full range of draught before, and he had set about them with the relish and enthusiasm of a youth.

He had sampled the best bitter, then the draught Landlord and the dark mild, followed by the Golden Best, an extraordinary creation that looked like Stella but tasted like holy nectar. And there was more to come. He had still to reach the mighty Ram Tam and the Porter, which, he had been promised by the comrade with whom he was billeted for the night, made Guinness taste like French tap-water.

But first, it was necessary to make room. The lights of the club shone bright on the other side of the silent roadway as he stepped out of the coach park. He looked at the Taylor's sign above the entrance, trying to imprint it strongly enough on his memory for it to survive the evening, no matter how many more times he went to the well.

The noise of the vehicle did not register in his brain until it was far too late. When it did, he was in the middle of the road. Finally the roaring of the engine broke through his reverie and drew his eyes to his left. All that he saw was a dark shape, unlit, a big, high, thick-wheeled monster.

He had no time to run, no time even to freeze; it took him in mid-stride. Bull-bars shattered his legs, and the hard edge of the hood smashed through to his backbone, powdering vertebrae and severing his spinal column.

The veteran drummer was hurled high in the air and over the vehicle as it sped on. As he crashed head first on to the hard road, his last thoughts were of Timothy Taylor, of Keighley, Yorkshire.

In his rear-view mirror, the driver saw him hit the ground, and knew that there was no need to look for reverse gear. Two hundred yards further along the road, he turned left, flicked on his lights and drove away quietly, into the night.

Eighteen

Detective Chief Superintendent Dan Pringle knew that something unspoken was hanging in the air; his problems were that he was not entirely sure what it was, and that he did not know when Bob Skinner would give it voice.

It was in the DCC's manner, and in his eyes. He had seen it before in recent weeks when something had been irritating the Big Man, and on each occasion it had been an advance warning of trouble.

And trouble was something that Pringle did not need; not any more, not at his time of professional life. He had come late to the job of head of CID, towards the end of a career which he thought had culminated in his appointment as a divisional head in Edinburgh, and after he had thought he was being parked in a siding when he was transferred to the Borders post.

He was honest enough to recognise that when he had been recalled from that out-station and named as Andy Martin's successor, most of his colleagues had been surprised. In truth he had been astonished himself. But Bob Skinner had told him that what he wanted most in the job was a pair of safe hands, and that his were the most experienced and reliable around.

In his first months, he had fancied that there had been resentment at his appointment. Ultimately, though, he had put it down to over-sensitivity on his part, and had become more relaxed. He knew that the only person who had really coveted the job had been Greg Jay, whose command took in the Leith area. The rest were either nearer the door than him, or young in post, like Rose and McGuire, and if he was a stop-gap, well, that did not worry him one bit.

Bob Skinner's demeanour did, though, as they worked their way through the agenda of targets achieved and investigations in progress. The goals that had been set for the year were stiff. Both men knew that and the head of CID had gone into the meeting pleased with his success rate. The war against illegal drugs was, in fact, a series of battles being fought across Scotland, under the general oversight of the Scottish Drug Enforcement Agency but with the local forces as the shock troops. No chief constable wanted to sit at the foot of the enforcement league table, and significant year-on-year increases in detection were always being sought. Pringle had been told to achieve an increase of twenty per cent on the previous year's enforcement figure, in terms of dealer convictions. With almost half of the operational year left, he was already at sixteen per cent.

'That's good, Dan; very good,' Skinner conceded. 'Bringing Mary Chambers across from Strathclyde was a nice bit of poaching on Willie Haggerty's part, and it's paying off.'

'Aye, but now I'm losing her to Division,' Pringle felt

compelled to point out, 'and you still haven't agreed to her replacement.'

The DCC nodded. 'I'm aware of that, but I've been keeping it up my sleeve until I had it confirmed. We're going back to Strathclyde to fill Mary's job in the Drugs Squad. I'm bringing in DI David Mackenzie from North Lanarkshire CID, on promotion to chief inspector; "Bandit", they call him over there. He is too, a cocky bastard, but he's a bloody good copper.'

'Why are they letting him go, then?'

Skinner looked at him severely. 'Because I asked for him, Daniel.' Then a half-smile crossed his face. 'I did a bit of trading though. You know Ian Pitkeathley, the DI from Mary's team? He's marrying a girl who's in a promoted teaching position in Glasgow. It's easier for him to move job than her, so that's what'll happen. He goes to Cumbernauld as a straight replacement. I want you to keep an eye on the Bandit when he gets here. Take him round the divisions, make sure that everyone knows who he is, and that they know whose appointment he is too. His job's too important for him to be hampered by any petty jealousy.'

Pringle nodded, then picked up the last biscuit from the plate on Skinner's coffee table. 'I'll do that,' he said, just before he crunched it.

'That's about it then,' said the DCC, 'now that they're finished.' He pushed himself up from the low leather couch.

A small wave of relief swept through the head of CID; his suspicions must have been wrong after all. Someone else must be for the high jump.

He was almost at the door when a big hand squeezed his shoulder. 'By the way,' Skinner drawled casually, 'Sarah was telling me last night that she's got one of ours on the slab this morning: a guy found topped in the Meadows yesterday morning. Imagine my surprise and delight, Dan, when the wife tells me across the fucking supper table that we've got a potential homicide investigation on our hands, and I haven't heard about it from anyone else.'

An ice-ball dropped in Pringle's stomach. 'Ah, well,' he began slowly, 'the division felt that it would be a bit premature to go calling it a murder inquiry before the SOCOs and the autopsy confirmed it. There were some anomalies at the scene that made suicide look unlikely, but I heard from Maggie Rose last night that they've all been sorted out and that suicide's now seen as a possibility.'

'I see.' The big man scratched his chin. 'It'll be an unusual one if it is, him stringing himself up from a tree in the middle of the city. Usually they go into the garage, lock the door and turn on the car, or they swallow a bottle of single malt and a bottle of Valium, or they get out the twelve bore and blow their fucking heads off.'

Pringle sighed. 'Sorry, boss, I should have got word to you. But I didn't hear about it myself until Maggie called me at half four, once the ID was complete.'

He looked up at Skinner and saw that he was smiling. 'It's all right, Dan. If I hadn't heard about it from Sarah, there was always this morning's *Scotsman*. No harm done, and anyway, I had other things on my mind yesterday.'

He reached out and opened the door for his colleague. 'I

made some resolutions on the way in in the car this morning. One of them is to stop giving the people around me such a hard time. If I made you run and tell me right away about every serious incident that goes down on our patch, then neither of us would be doing his job properly. But in this case, I gather that the victim's a corporate banker. Just to be on the safe side, I want you to keep a close eye on the investigation, and keep me in the loop as well.'

The chief superintendent nodded. 'I'll do that, don't worry. I won't lean too hard on Maggie Rose, though. Stevie Steele gets upset when I try it, and there's worse than that. She doesn't like it herself, and sometimes her eyebrows can be as bloody heavy as yours!'

'Mmm,' said Skinner. 'Mags can be frosty from time to time, I'll grant you, but you won't have to handle her for much longer. Put your kid gloves on for now, but keep me in touch.' He patted Pringle on the shoulder. 'I'll talk to you later. As you leave, ask young Jack to come and see me. There's some air I have to clear with him too.'

Nineteen

'Is this new place an improvement, or what?' asked Stevie Steele, his blue tunic rustling as he looked around. 'There was something about the old Royal Infirmary that always gave me the creeps. Every time I went to an autopsy there I found myself thinking about Dr Knox, and Burke and Hare.'

'The resurrectionists, you mean? The body-snatchers?'

'They're the boys. Every time I saw one in the old Royal I imagined the ghost of Knox the anatomist standing there instead of you or Prof Hutchinson.'

Sarah Grace Skinner, who was dressed identically, smiled at him. 'You're a romantic at heart, Stevie, aren't you? It would have had to be Knox's ghost. I doubt that he ever set foot in any part of the old Royal. He pre-dated that; his school was somewhere up near Surgeons' Hall, I believe. Mind you, Burke's still around.'

'Uh?'

'Well, his skeleton is, at least. After they'd hanged him, his body was given to the medical school for dissection; I guess it seemed appropriate at the time. His bones are still there. Plus there's a pocket book made from his skin on show at the police museum.'

Steele shuddered. 'We're a ghoulish lot, us Scots, aren't we?'

'Not just you. I believe that Ned Kelly's skull became a desk ornament in an Australian jail.'

The inspector looked round the autopsy room once more. 'This is a different era, though. This place is purpose-built, everything's stainless, there's proper drainage, a high-pressure water supply and most of all,' he pointed at the big fans set in the ceiling, 'there's a proper air-extraction system.'

Sarah gave a grim laugh. 'They're still looking for the ultimate air-freshening system,' she said, 'as you will discover when I open up the late Mr Whetstone.' Steele winced, and moved a few feet away from the table.

She switched on the microphone above the examination table. 'Let's get started. The subject is a white male, mid-fifties, found hanging by the neck from a tree.' She lifted the body's right arm. 'Rigor mortis appears to have worn off, this is consistent with the initial medical examiner's estimate of time of death as approximately . . .' she checked her watch '. . . thirty-six hours ago.'

She turned the head to one side. 'The imprint of the belt is clearly visible.' She felt the neck carefully, for over a minute. 'However,' she continued, 'there is no apparent dislocation of the cervical vertebrae. Subject to more detailed examination, this would indicate that death was due to strangulation.' She took a pace back, and looked at the corpse carefully, from head to toe then back again, walking around the table as she did so.

'There are no visible marks on the torso or limbs,' she paused, 'except . . .'

She moved forward again, close to the body, and took the right shoulder in both of her white-gloved hands, probing with her fingers, manoeuvring it slightly. 'Inspector,' she said, 'can you confirm for the record that when the body was taken down rigor mortis was complete?'

'Yes, I can,' Steele replied, speaking loudly to make certain that the microphone picked him up. 'Mr Whetstone was absolutely stiff when my officers took him down.'

'And they handled him carefully?'

'Certainly.'

'In that case, this shoulder dislocation could only have happened *pre mortem*. It would have been very painful, and the shoulder would have been immobilised. Therefore it would have been very difficult for the victim to have made all the necessary preparations before hanging himself. That suggests he may have had help, or may have been attacked. Either way, since there's no such thing as assisted suicide in Scots criminal law, it looks to me as if you could possibly have a murder investigation on your hands after all.'

'Can I make a call to let Maggie know?' Steele asked.

'I'd rather you waited till I'm finished; unless you'd like to go outside to make it, then change into fresh blues.'

'No, I'll wait.'

'In that case . . .' she said, picking up a scalpel.

The inspector watched in a kind of haze, doing his best to keep his heaving stomach under control. The only policeman he knew who did not mind witnessing a post mortem was

George Regan, but his grandfather had been a village joiner, one of the last to combine funeral undertaking with the carpentry business. George liked to regale young coppers with a story from his childhood, which he swore was true, of watching Grandpa Regan lay out a late customer. In life the man had worn a wig, without mishap. In death as he lay in his coffin, it kept slipping sideways. After several attempts to fix it in place, the old tradesman had turned to his grandson. 'Lad, wid ye pass me ma claw hammer, and a big nail.'

He was no George Regan and he knew it, but he managed to master his revulsion. Sarah worked methodically, in the knowledge that she might well be cross-examined in the High Court, and thus taking care to leave no questions that she might not be able to answer, to the detriment of the prosecution case. Fortunately, she was assisted by a pathology student, and that saved considerable time.

After just over an hour and a half, as her helper began to reassemble the remains of Ivor Whetstone and sew him up, she turned back to Steele. 'Death by strangulation, as the result of hanging,' she announced. 'Apart from the dislocated shoulder, the other things I found that were significantly out of the ordinary were in the lungs: there is a significant tumour in the left and a slightly smaller one in the right. I've taken sections for biopsy, and I reckon that'll show malignancy, a small-cell carcinoma. There are clear signs that it's spread into the chest wall; if it's there it's probably in other organs too.'

The detective started to speak, but she held up a hand to cut him off. 'All that said, I can't tell you for certain that he would have been aware of its presence, not even at this stage of its growth. He may have thought, or hoped, that he had bronchitis; too many people play down symptoms that need investigating until it's too late. Therefore it does not necessarily offer a reason for suicide, even if he could have managed to do it with that damaged shoulder.'

'Any other marks on the body?'

Sarah nodded. 'There was a cut on his right wrist, on the inside. It was fresh, and had been bleeding at the time of death. You saw the body. Can you remember whether there was any jewellery on it?'

Steele's eyes narrowed as he replayed the scene in his mind. 'Wristwatch,' he said. 'Worn as normal on the left wrist; it had a leather strap. And yes, there was a bracelet on the right wrist. It was a chunky gold thing.'

'That's what I thought. If the forensic technicians examine it, they'll probably find traces of skin and blood. That raises the possibility that if the man was helped, or more likely attacked, he was grabbed by the wrists and the gold cut into him.'

'So if we're lucky we might get prints as well?'

'Exactly.'

'Good. I'll tell Maggie when I call her. I'm clear to do that now, yes?'

'Yes, but next door, please.'

She led the way from the autopsy room, and through to an office area, unfastening her tunic as she went, and ripping off her blue surgical cap. Steele did the same, and threw his protective garments into a wastebin on top of hers.

'What do you do now?' he said.

Sarah grinned. 'Right now, I'll have a shower, and after that

I'll grab a bite, then get round to working on a report for you and the fiscal. What about you? Off to catch a potential killer?'

'Eventually, but first I'm either going to have a late breakfast or an early lunch, depending on how you look at it. Knowing what I was going to be looking at, I decided not to chance it.'

'You and me both. I never do when I've a morning autopsy to perform. You never know what might crawl out when you open one of these up. So my brunch agenda's the same as yours. Why don't we team up? Where were you thinking of going?'

'Actually, I was going home. My place is between here and the office, more or less.'

'Sounds okay,' she said. 'Got enough for two?'

Steele felt a strange cold tingle in his stomach. Later, hard as he tried, he was never able to work out why he answered, 'Yes, of course.'

Twenty

Colin Mawhinney stepped away from the reception desk, key in hand. 'Thanks, Mario,' he said. 'This is a nice hotel. Normally I don't like them; I find that in the States they treat you like a number not a person, but that guy there couldn't have been more friendly.'

His host, until recently his guest, smiled. 'Yes, it has a comfortable feel about it, doesn't it? I have to confess I've never slept here, but Paula and I use the dining room quite a bit: it's excellent. We checked out the suites before we booked you in here, and they're up to the same standard. It's as well after that flight. It's a long haul to Edinburgh when you come through Heathrow.' McGuire had been concerned about flying with Mawhinney, given his terrible experience on September Eleven, but he had handled the journey calmly, even if he had been even more than usually serious throughout.

'I hate airports, period,' said the American, 'but they are a necessary evil of our time.' He grinned. 'The taxis in this city are pretty good, though. They're even more colourful than our yellow cabs and, better still, the drivers seem to know where they're going. Dunno if you noticed, but New York taxis have a customer charter on display inside. It says you're entitled at all times to a courteous driver who speaks English and knows his way about the city. Two out of three is pretty good, but you'll never get all three in the one cab. No-hits are not uncommon.'

McGuire glanced out of the window at the police patrol car, bright Day-glo flashes on its side and hood, that was waiting outside. 'Trust me,' he said, 'we got lucky today. The traffic inspector had the good sense to send a sergeant to collect us. If we'd had a rookie, he'd have taken the normal route, and we might still be stuck in Corstorphine.'

'We may have come here by a back way, Mario, but I really like what I've seen of your city so far. And the waterfront out there is just great. The air's so fresh I can hardly believe it; it's warmer than what we left in New York, too.'

'From what I hear we're lucky we didn't arrive twenty-four hours ago. My pal Neil told me that we've just had the worst fog in forty years; he said it was worse than anything he's ever seen. The airport was even closed, so it must have been bad; they're supposed to be able to land blind there. It's cleared up now, though. You will be able to see the city, thank Christ.'

'Good. So what's on the agenda?'

'Today, nothing. I guessed you'd want some time to settle in, and maybe grab a couple of hours' sleep, so I thought we'd leave you here, then come back for you around half five. We'll go to my place for a drink and then maybe go uptown for something to eat.'

'You live close by?'

'If you step outside and look across the water you can see it. I have a penthouse in a block over there.'

'Where do you live, Paula?'

Their companion smiled wearily. 'In Leith,' she replied, 'just off Great Junction Street. That's not far either, but I'll crash at Mario's. If I go back to my place I'll get into opening mail, and I'll be at it all afternoon.'

'So,' said McGuire, 'does that sound all right to you?'

'It sounds perfect. Where will we eat?'

'We'll find somewhere with a bit of class; the Secret Garden, maybe. It won't be a deli, I promise you that. Nice meal, nice glass of wine, and a decent night's sleep, that's the idea. Get you ready for the official stuff. That starts tomorrow. You'll meet the chief, the DCC, and ACC Haggerty, and we'll give you a presentation on how our force works. After that we'll show you it working. For now, you head on up to your room, and we'll see you later.'

They shook hands, then Mario and Paula headed for the door and their waiting car. Less than five minutes later they were in his living room looking back across the water at the Malmaison Hotel.

'Nice guy, that,' Paula murmured as she stepped out of her shoes.

'Yeah, he is. There's something infinitely sad about him, though. I can't imagine what it must have been like for him, being there and seeing that second plane hit, then knowing after the event that he had watched his wife die.' The big detective shuddered. 'God save us from that, eh?'

'Too true,' she agreed. 'Mario, I'm knackered. I was going

to run a bath but I think I'd fall asleep in it, so I'm going straight to bed. You coming?'

'In a minute. I'll check my messages then I'll be through. Set the alarm for about four o'clock, okay?'

'Sure.'

He grinned after her as she shuffled sleepily off towards the bedroom. Not long before, Neil McIlhenney had asked him to put into words what it was that he and Paula had in their relationship that made it gel. 'Softness.' He had said it without even thinking. 'When we're together everything in the world seems peaceful. We blend together; each of us knows instinctively what the other's thinking, or wants, or needs. They say that you have to work at a partnership. We don't. We make each other content, and it's effortless. I don't think I've ever smiled as much in my life.'

'No,' his friend had conceded. 'I don't think you have.'

He thought of that conversation as he listened to his first phone message. It was from McIlhenney, inviting him, Paula and Colin Mawhinney to lunch with him, Louise and the children on the following Sunday. He made a mental note to consult the American before accepting, in case such a family event might be a strain for him.

The second message was from a caller who identified himself as Ainsley, breaking the wonderful news that he had won a voucher for two thousand pounds towards the cost of a luxury fitted kitchen, and inviting him to call and confirm his prize. He pushed a button and deleted it.

The third voice was that of Jack McGurk. 'I'd be grateful, Superintendent McGuire, if you could call me as soon as you get this message. The DCC wants to see you in his office at Fettes at the first opportunity.'

Mario sighed. He could always creep quietly off to bed and pretend that he had not checked his answering system until later, but that was not the way things worked with Bob Skinner. He called McGurk's direct line number.

'Jack,' he growled, 'I'm warning you, you're speaking to a jet-lagged bear.'

'It won't take long, sir, honest. The boss wouldn't ask without a good reason. He's in all morning or he can see you at four thirty, if you'd rather.'

'Let's get it over with. We've just been dropped off by a Traffic car. Turn it around if you can and have it pick me up; I'll be waiting at my front door. But warn him, he's getting me unshaved and honking, and not at my most attentive.'

'You will be, sir,' said McGurk, quizzically.

Intrigued, he hung up, and went through to break the bad news to Paula. She was asleep and looked as if she would be so for a while. Still, to be on the safe side, he wrote her a note, left it on her bedside table, and headed downstairs, feeling a growing interest in whatever it was the Big Man might be wanting.

Twenty-one

She followed Steele's car from the new Royal Infirmary complex, which had been built in an outlying part of Edinburgh known as Little France since the sixteenth century, when the servants and courtiers who accompanied Mary, Queen of Scots, on her return from Versailles had set up residence there.

It was a short trip, down to Cameron Toll, then negotiating three roundabouts to turn into Gordon Terrace, where she parked behind him in front of a solid red sandstone house.

'I have a piece of that,' he told her, nodding towards it.

'Very impressive,' she exclaimed, meaning it.

'I bought it when I made sergeant, when interest rates were higher than they are now, but before Edinburgh property prices went crazy. No way could I afford it now, even on a DI's pay.' He led the way up a narrow path to a door in the side of the building; he unlocked it and they climbed a curving flight of stairs into a spacious hall.

'It's a sort of duplex, really, not a flat. I have a couple of bedrooms upstairs, and here there's a living room, small bedroom, bathroom, and this.' He opened a door and showed her

148

into a vast dining-kitchen, with a five-burner gas hob and double oven, a big oak table in one corner and a seating area in another. 'I live here, basically,' he told her. 'The living room's my playroom, more or less, with my music and my main television. Take a look round if you like while I whip up the grub. Scrambled eggs, toast and coffee, okay?'

'Perfect.'

She took him at his word and left him to cook. She went from room to room, admiring the old house more and more as she did so. The ceilings were high, with cornices and plaster centrepieces that were undoubtedly original. The bathroom fittings looked original too, including a high chain-pull cistern above the toilet, but they had all been replumbed. Steele's playroom was exactly as he had described it, with a Bose home-entertainment system, a big Toshiba television set, a computer on a table in the corner and a soft, three-seater settee in the centre. She climbed the stairs, feeling the mahogany banister smooth under her hand.

The attic ceilings were lower than below, but the bedrooms were as immaculate as the rest of the house. The larger of the two had an *en suite* shower room.

'This is beautiful, Steven,' she said, as she stepped back into the kitchen, 'and so well decorated. It must cost a bit to maintain.'

'I do my own,' he replied. 'I'm not saying I'm a DIY freak, though. I have an older brother who's a painter to trade, and he gives me a hand with some of the more difficult parts, the plasterwork and such. Come on, it's ready.'

He showed her to the dining table, which was set out with

two plates piled high with scrambled eggs, a basket of toast and two mugs of black coffee. *Thank God he's got a weakness*, she thought. *No napkins.*

'Sugar and milk?' he asked, as she took her place.

'No thanks. I'll take it as it comes.'

The coffee was hot and strong; it was percolated and had a Colombian flavour. The taste stayed with her as she spread butter on a slice of toast.

'You're a strange guy for a cop, Steven,' she said quietly, as she picked up her fork.

He looked back at her, just a little warily. 'In what way?' he asked her, as they ate.

'You're atypical. Most of the policemen I've met, and come to think of it, most of the policewomen too, have an air about them. It's as if they have something to prove. I don't get that feeling from you. You seem . . .'

'Too sure of myself by half?' he suggested, with a smile.

'No, I didn't mean that at all. I was going to say that I sense confidence within you, in your own ability, a sort of self-awareness. I can only think of two other people I know who give me the same feeling.'

'Who's the other one?'

'What do you mean? Aah, you're assuming that Bob's one of them. God, you couldn't be more wrong. I was thinking about Neil McIlhenney and Andy Martin. My husband is one of the most driven men I know. He's trying to prove something to someone every day of his life, but mostly to himself.'

She ate the rest of her eggs quickly. At first Steele thought she was ravenous, but soon he saw that there was an anxiety behind it. When she was finished, she stood up, abruptly, her mug in her hands. 'Let's move over there,' she said, stepping towards the corner seating.

He followed her, lowering himself on to the cushions beside her. 'Are you still not any happier?' he asked her quietly.

'What do you mean?' she retorted. Her voice was bold, but as she looked at him she saw that her eyes were defensive.

'You know damn well what I mean. I'm talking about the last time I had to attend one of your autopsies, a few months ago. We went for a drink afterwards, and we sort of got too close together, and lips brushed. I apologised and you apologised. We both said we'd pretend it never happened, and I'm still sticking to that, even though I still feel slightly mad for bringing you back here now.'

She looked into her mug, and nodded. 'I remember.'

'That really would never have happened if there hadn't been something wrong then, would it?'

'Maybe not,' she whispered.

'The same thing that's maybe wrong now?'

'Maybe so.'

'So what is it? Or should I mind my own business?'

'It is your business in a way.' She made a half-turn to face him. 'That night, I don't know where it all came from, but you were attentive and kind and you spoke to me softly, as if you sensed then that something was troubling me, and I realised quite suddenly it was. I hadn't articulated it until then, but part of me felt very lonely and alienated from my husband, and from my marriage. I'm the model mother, Steven, don't get me wrong, and I'm an attentive wife too, in every respect. And yet . . .' She grasped the mug as if she was trying to break it. 'You've never been married, have you?'

'No.'

'Ever been close?'

'No. I've always backed off before that. There's someone I've been seeing lately, but that's a friendship thing.'

'Maggie Rose?'

His eyes widened in astonishment, and he gasped. They both laughed.

'Are people talking about Maggie and me?' he asked.

'There are those who hope quietly that you'll get it together,' she told him, 'people who like you both.'

'Well, Maggie doesn't share their hopes, I promise you, and I'm happy with the way things are between us. I wasn't talking about her just now, but she falls into the same category as that girl. Sure she's attractive, but friendship . . . and work . . . are more important to us both.'

'That's almost a pity. For there's someone else who's attracted to you, and she's a lot more hazardous to your all-round health than Maggie. In a way it would be better if you and she were an item.'

'I'm intrigued. Who is this mystery woman?'

'Steven, you are neither dumb nor blind. You know who she is.'

He shook his head. 'That's crazy.'

'I know. But craziness happens. What I was saying before . . . I work hard at my marriage, and so, to be fair, does Bob: most of the time, until something comes up that he sees as so important that he doesn't have room for anyone else in his life until it's dealt with. In the main, though, he tries to be a good husband, and I try to be a good wife.'

'But?'

'But . . . somehow we're both failing. The excitement that used to be there just isn't any more. I'm sure that's a lament that you might hear from wives all over the world, but it's true, and it's the reason why I can be Mrs Bob Skinner, mother of three, and love my husband, and yet still be attracted to you.'

She reached out, took hold of his tie, pulled him down towards her and kissed him, long and tenderly, much more than a brushing of lips. 'Go on,' she whispered, as they broke off. 'Pretend that didn't happen, Steven Steele.'

Twenty-two

When the intercom phone on his desk buzzed, Bob Skinner was lost in thought. He was replaying his dinner-table conversation with his wife, and reflecting on the things she had said, admiring the way that, with a few words, she had helped, even more than Jim Gainer, to cut his personal demons down to size and restore his sense of balance.

'You should have specialised in psychology, not pathology, my darling,' he murmured aloud. But at the same time he recognised that her attention to his problems had diverted both of them from facing their joint crisis. He had hoped that it would stay behind them in America, but it had boarded the plane like an extra piece of baggage. It was an issue, all right, and one that would have to be faced, sooner or later, not least because of some other disturbing and very private thoughts he had been having over the past twenty-four hours.

He started, in spite of himself, when the buzzer sounded, feeling a twitch in his chest, just below his left collarbone; it happened sometimes when the muscles tensed and disturbed his pacemaker. Bringing himself back to the present, he reached out and picked up the handset.

'Superintendent McGuire, sir,' Jack McGurk announced. 'He's arrived.'

The DCC smiled, glad of the distraction. 'Send him in,' he said. 'Will we be needing coffee, do you think? My filter machine's empty.'

'Looking at him, I'd say so, sir. I'll get you some from the kitchen.'

Skinner stood up, went to the door and opened it, to find Mario McGuire outside, almost in the act of knocking. The big detective was dressed in jeans and a creased jacket, his shirt was open at the neck, he looked several hours overdue for a shave, and there were dark shadows under his eyes. 'Jesus,' the DCC laughed, 'you look at your best. Come in and sit down before you fall down. Anybody'd think you just came off a transatlantic flight.'

'You wanted me here right away, boss; what you see is what you get. However,' he added, 'out of deference to the command corridor, I did give myself a squirt with the deodorant before I came out.'

'That's big of you. No, don't sit at the desk: grab a comfy seat by the coffee table.' He followed and lowered himself on to one of the two couches, which formed an L in the corner of his office.

'So how was New York? What was the weather like, for a start?'

'Hot when we arrived; cold when we left.'

'And the city?'

'I love that place,' McGuire admitted. 'I'd have taken some holiday there, had I not been bringing Colin Mawhinney back with me. Maybe we'll go back next spring. I might even persuade my mother to meet us there. She'd love the art galleries. That Frick collection's something else.'

'It is, if you can stand the thought of one person having all that wealth. What did you think of NYPD?'

'It's an excellent force, no doubt about it. But it's the sheer size of the thing. I don't know how it's manageable.'

'Me neither,' Skinner admitted, 'especially with so much power in the hands of the mayor. I tell you this: if Jimmy and I had to report directly to the Lord Provost of Edinburgh, I'd be off. The joint board can be bad enough.'

He paused at the sound of a knock at the door. 'Come in,' he called out, and Maisie, the dining-room waitress, appeared with coffee and biscuits on a tray. 'Thanks,' he said, as she laid them on the table. 'I'll sign for them at lunch time. Our visitor,' Skinner continued, 'what sort of guy is he?'

'Let me put it this way,' McGuire replied. 'If there was an ACC post going, I'd suggest you offered it to him. Colin Mawhinney's a potential police chief. I only spent a few days with him and I could see that. I learned a lot in New York, but to be honest, I can't think of a bloody thing we can teach him.'

'Neither can I. That's why I'm going to show him how Greater Edinburgh works while he's here, rather than stick him in a patrol car and send him round Muirhouse. Jack's put together a programme for him that'll give him a flavour of how our city works. He'll meet the senior officers tomorrow, and I'll give him a presentation on the type of work we do.'

'You'll do that yourself?'

'It's either me or Haggerty; he'd need an interpreter for

some of Willie's Glaswegian, so it's down to me. After that Brian Mackie will talk him through the planning for next week's papal visit; when that takes place I'm going to slot him in beside Mackie as a close observer. He might even get to meet the Pope.'

'He'll love that,' McGuire exclaimed. 'He's a Catholic. He was going to take Paula and me to mass at St Patrick's on Sunday, but she bottled out.'

Skinner raised an eyebrow. 'I'm not surprised. The roof might have fallen in on you.'

'That's what I thought too, between you and me.'

'Aye, best be on the safe side. That apart,' the DCC continued, 'the rest of his visit's going to be spent meeting people.'

'Movers and shakers, and the like?'

'That's them, and that's how he'll spend the early part of next week. He meets the Justice Minister on Monday morning, then in the afternoon he's got a session with the Chamber of Commerce. Neil will pick him up and take him to those meetings. In the evening, the chief's having a reception for him here, with a guest list that's made up of professionals . . . accountants, lawyers, bankers and the like. Tuesday and Wednesday, ACC Haggerty will tour him round the various divisional commanders, showing him the scenic variety of our patch, in contrast to his. Before that, of course, there's the weekend; that'll be informal, but since he's a single guy I'm not just going to leave him on his own. I'm going to invite him to dine with Sarah and me at the golf club on Saturday evening, but unless you've had enough of each other, I was going to ask you to take care of him for the rest of that free time. I've got you tickets for Tynecastle . . . Hearts are playing Aberdeen . . . on Saturday afternoon, and for the rugby international on Sunday. Of course I'd like you and Paula to join us for dinner at the club.'

McGuire was taken aback. 'Do you mean that, boss? Paula as well?'

'Of course I fucking mean it. She's your regular partner, isn't she?'

'Yes.'

'Well, enough said.'

McGuire was touched by Skinner's rough and ready blessing on his new relationship. He was about to say so, when the DCC moved on. 'Since we've started talking about you, that brings me to the real reason I wanted to see you today. Tell me, do you love the Borders? Has your territory carved out an indelible place in your heart?'

'Are you taking the piss, sir?'

'That's what I thought you'd say. You've done a good job down there, Mario, carrying on what Dan Pringle started in bringing that division into this century, after all those years under dear old John McGrigor. But you're a city copper; I know that. So to cut to the chase, there's some stuff happening at a senior level, movement.'

'Dan Pringle?'

Skinner smiled and shook his head. 'I know there's been speculation about him retiring, but it's not that. He's going to soldier on till sixty. No, it's Manny English, the uniformed commander of western division, who's taking early retirement.

And that's led to some healthy debate between Willie Haggerty and me. He's been looking round for a while for Manny's successor. He's identified half a dozen candidates, but I've pulled rank and made the final choice . . .' He saw the superintendent's sudden frown. '. . . and it's not you, so you can get that worried look off your face. You'd be no more comfortable in a uniform than I am.'

He shook his head. 'No, the new commander in Torphichen Place will be Chief Superintendent . . . Margaret Rose.'

McGuire smiled, then suddenly his frown returned, deeper still. 'You're not . . .'

Skinner laughed out loud. 'Of course I'm bloody not! I couldn't possibly move you into her job. I don't care how amicable your separation is, I'm not going to test it. No, I'm transferring you to command CID in the coastal division, based in Leith. Your territory will stretch from South Queensferry all the way to Portobello. You fancy it?'

Mario could not hide his delight. 'Too right I do, boss. I'll even be able to walk to work.'

'Only if you keep the streets safe,' Skinner grunted.

'Can I take Sammy with me?'

'DS Pye? I reckon so. It'll do you no harm to have someone familiar around, and besides, my secretary, his wife, would kill me if I left him down there.'

'What about Greg Jay? Is he going to Western Division?'

'No, Greg needs a bigger shift than that. He's going to East and Midlothian, Alastair Grant's moving from there to Borders and Mary Chambers is moving from the Drugs Squad into Maggie's job, on promotion.'

'Two women commanders in the same station? That'll be a first.'

'Sure, and it'll be a good example to set.'

'As long as it works.'

'It will, don't you worry. They get on, and just as important they're two of the most professional senior officers I have.' The DCC paused. 'I won't kid you, Mario. Willie Haggerty wanted to move Brian Mackie in there, but I overruled him. The reason I gave was that Brian's too new in his present post, and ideally suited for it as well. I'm right on both counts, but it's not the whole truth. Strictly between the two of us, I wanted to position Maggie as a candidate to succeed Haggerty when he moves on . . . as he will, to be a chief constable somewhere . . . but also I wanted to avoid the prospect of having you two as rivals for Pringle's job when he does go. I'm thinking of myself, you see. It'll make that decision easier. Not that I'm saying you'll get that job, you understand: Grant's a strong runner, so is Lowe in Central Division, and Mary Chambers might well force her way into the picture too. I'm watching all of you from now on.' He hesitated again. 'That's always assuming, of course, that you're still committed to the force and that you're not going off to run the Viareggio family businesses with Paula.'

McGuire shook his head. 'Clearly, sir,' he said, 'your daughter does not discuss her business with you. Paula and I are in the process of restructuring the family trust. We're looking at incorporating: turning it into a limited company with shareholders instead of beneficiaries. That would let me back off. Your Alex is doing all the legal work for us.'

Pride showed through in Skinner's grin. 'You're right, she is tight-lipped. She's turned into a real lawyer, God help me. I'm glad to hear you're doing that, though. It might well make things easier for me in the future.'

'I thought it might. How about McIlhenney?' McGuire asked him suddenly.

'Neil's staying in Special Branch. He's too valuable to me in that job to move, and anyway he's got a promotion to chief inspector coming up, plus Lou's pregnancy to occupy his mind.'

'When do the changes take effect?'

'Manny retires tomorrow. I want you all in post on Monday, hence the need for this meeting.' He rose to his feet, smiling. 'With that in mind, Superintendent, I suggest that you bugger off home, and catch up on your sleep.'

McGuire's head was spinning as a panda car drove him away from the headquarters building. By moving him and promoting Maggie, Skinner had satisfied the top two items on his professional wish list. More than that, he had painted a picture of a future that, if it was not his for the taking, then at least was there to be won.

Fifteen minutes later, as he undressed, throwing his clothes into a corner of the bedroom, and slipped under the duvet beside the quietly snoring Paula . . . his note lay undisturbed on the table . . . he thought that he would never find sleep as he pondered the future. Less than two minutes later, he was proved completely wrong.

Twenty-three

Stevie Steele ran his fingers through his hair. 'Jeez,' he murmured, 'this is my day for surprises.' He was taken aback yet again, when he realised that his voice had been loud enough to carry across the desk.

'Oh, yes? What others have you had?'

He thought quickly: being kissed by the DCC's wife was not something he cared to discuss. It had gone no further than that, but at another time . . . Sarah had been right, there could be no more pretending, and he was like any other man in that his libido could overcome his common sense. George Regan would have put it another way, but he would have meant the same thing.

'Whetstone's dislocated shoulder. The homicide theory being put back on the table. I wasn't expecting that.'

'Maybe it hasn't been,' said Rose. 'It's not like Sarah to go headlong after one side of an argument, but . . . Since you called me, I've been thinking about it. Just suppose Whetstone had decided to top himself. Let's say he saw the fog and he decided that it was the perfect opportunity to go away and do himself in, undisturbed. Who knows why people choose the methods they do when they're in that state of mind? Let's just say he buys his belt, he nicks a wee ladder from the office and he heads off into the night. He's chosen his spot and everything. When he gets there, he gets up on the steps, makes the noose and ties the other end of the belt to the branch of the tree. And then he slips. Simple as that; he's nervous, probably shaking with cold and fear, the ground is frosty and he slips, comes off the stepladder and lands on his shoulder, dislocating it. Sarah's right, in that he couldn't have secured the belt one-handed, but suppose he'd done it before the dislocation happened. He could have climbed back up the steps, albeit in great pain, slipped the noose over his head with his one usable hand then kicked his support out from under him. Yes?'

'Yes, but what about the cut that Sarah found on his wrist?'

'That could have been caused in the same fall, couldn't it? Right shoulder, right wrist?'

'I'll grant you all of that,' the inspector conceded. 'What does the scene-of-crime report say? Is that consistent with your theory?'

'Dorward's report doesn't rule anything out. Even after its trip to the Wee Black Dug and back, there were traces of soil and grass on the shoulder of the coat. There were marks on the ground beneath the body that were consistent with a small stepladder having been placed there, and weight applied.'

'Footprints?'

'The only ones they could identify were those made by the trainers you took from Moash Glazier when he was lifted. Everything that might have been made the night before was obliterated by the fall and the freezing of the morning dew. In other words there's no evidence that anyone else was there other than the victim and Glazier. What have we done with that little bugger, by the way?'

'Let him go. We might need him as a witness at some point. It sticks in my throat, but we'll get him for something else, that's if Malky Gladsmuir doesn't do what he was threatening and chuck him in the Water of Leith.'

'Do you believe Gladsmuir's story about the coat? That he took it as security against a debt?'

'It suits me to believe it. Gladsmuir's on Mario's new patch, and by all accounts he's helpful. We got the coat back, so I'm not going to give him grief.'

'Yes, agreed. I take it we checked Glazier's whereabouts on Tuesday night, didn't we? Not that I think he's smart enough to cover his tracks by coming back to the scene of his own crime in the morning, but the fiscal will want to know.'

'He was in Jenny Ha's pub, with his Lochview girlfriend. The manager knows them both; she confirmed it. I wish we could find that bloody stepladder, but he's hardly going to have made that up. But even without it, "keep an open mind, Stevie" . . . that's what you're saying, is it?'

'Exactly. You'll have a new boss to impress next week. You won't do it by chasing false trails.'

'What's she like?' Steele asked. 'I've never worked with her.'

'Mary Chambers? She's a first-rate officer and she'll make a damn good commander. George Regan will have to watch

himself, not least because Mary's gay and he's an unrecon-
structed male chauvinist. But you'll get on well with her, not
least because you won't go out of your way to try to impress
her . . . just as you never have with me.'

'I thought I had.'

'Not you, Stevie, and you know it. You just do your job the
way you think it should be done, and you're usually right.'

'Not with Whetstone, though. I don't know which side of
the fence to land on there.'

'Just keep sat on it, then, till it all becomes clear. Maybe
our meeting at the Scottish Farmers Bank will give us a better
idea.'

'You're still coming to that?'

'I'm still in post till close of play tomorrow, and I made the
appointment personally. I think I should.'

'Suits me.' He looked at her across her desk. 'I'm going to
miss you, Mags,' he said.

'Why?' She chuckled. 'Won't you find me attractive in
uniform? I'll be in an office just down the corridor, remember.
Or are you going to cut me out of your social life? Is it getting
too crowded?'

There was a quick tension about his eyes, momentary, but
it registered with her. 'There'll always be room for you,' he
replied.

'Okay. In that case, celebrate my promotion with me.
Tomorrow evening will be a wash-out because of Manny's
farewell do . . . it'll be mine too, I suppose . . . but let's have
dinner on Saturday.'

'Sounds good. Where do you fancy?'

'My place. Just you and me, shoes off, no job talk; I'll cook, you bring the wine . . . and no rubbish, mind. Deal?'

'Deal.' He glanced at his watch. 'What time are we due at the bank?'

'Two thirty. We'd better be off. I'll drive; I've booked a space in their car park.'

They left the CID commander's small room, and walked out to her car, beside the back door of the West End police office. The fog had gone completely, chased by a cold east wind, but a persistent drizzle had replaced it. Rose took a circuitous but quick route, using the Western Approach Road to reach the financial centre, where a security guard admitted them to the bank's car park and directed them to their reserved space.

They took the lift to the fourth floor of the block and stepped out to find themselves facing a reception desk, in light beech, with a tartan-clad woman sitting behind it. She stood as they approached. 'Superintendent Rose,' she began, 'Security told me you were on your way up. Mr Easterson's ready for you, if you'll follow me.'

She led them out of the reception area, and along a corridor, stopping at a heavy wooden door, beech once more in common with the rest of the office's furnishing. A brass plate, at eye-level, bore the initials 'GMCB'. The receptionist knocked and opened it. 'They're here, sir,' she announced, then stepped aside.

The general manager, Commercial Banking, was on his feet behind his desk as the two officers entered his room. As Rose introduced them both, Steele glanced around. The office was tasteful, not ostentatious; ideal surroundings for meetings with clients one is out to impress but not intimidate. Its most impressive feature was a big, wide window which offered a view of the Usher Hall across Lothian Road and, behind it, of Edinburgh Castle.

'Welcome,' said Vernon Easterson, as he shook the super-intendent's hand. 'I only wish you weren't here on such grim business.' He turned to greet Steele also. 'Take a seat, please, at my meeting table. I'll let my colleague know that we're ready to begin.' He turned to a complicated-looking phone on his desk and pressed one of its many buttons.

'Would you like a refreshment?' he asked. Rose and Steele both declined. 'Are you sure?' he persisted. 'I can offer you tea or coffee, a soft drink or mineral water, perhaps. This is a dry office, I'm afraid. Unlike yours, I gather.' He laughed nervously, almost a giggle. 'My chief executive and I are invited to a cocktail reception by the chief constable. As it happens, neither of us can go, but Aurelia Middlemass, who's about to join us, will be representing . . .'

He broke off as his door opened again and a woman entered, perfectly on cue. She was tall, maybe five feet nine, halfway in height between Rose and Steele; her chestnut hair was close cropped and its highlights might just have been natural. Her eyes were her most distinctive feature, brown with a suggestion of a slant, set above high cheekbones. Even in her charcoal grey business suit, she was strikingly attractive, a complete contrast to the short, tubby, balding Easterson. The banker stood as she came in, and Steele followed him to his feet.

'Aurelia,' the GMCB exclaimed, 'so glad you could join

us. Superintendent, Inspector, may I introduce Aurelia Middlemass, our senior director of Commercial Banking, and at one point the late Mr Whetstone's line manager. Take a seat, my dear, take a seat.'

She followed his pointing finger to the chair beside his, directly opposite the two police officers. 'Good afternoon,' she said, unsmiling, laying a folder on the table before her. She had carried it in her left hand, on which a large diamond ring sparkled, alongside a gold wedding band. 'I gather from Vernon that you're trying to resolve some lingering doubts about Whetstone's death. Hopefully we can help you.' Her voice was deep and honeyed and, on first hearing, without any distinctive accent. 'I've read the statements that your press office has issued; they're guarded, to say the least.'

'Deliberately so,' said Rose. 'There was some confusion when the body was found, but that was caused by a petty thief, whose collar's been felt. The remaining doubt comes from a couple of injuries that were revealed during the autopsy.'

'Maybe I can help you resolve it,' said Middlemass. 'Vernon and I haven't had all the information you had. Maybe that's just as well, for when people in our position are faced with the apparent suicide of a popular and success-ful member of staff, some very specific concerns present themselves.'

Beside her, Easterson nodded gravely. 'Sad but true,' he intoned. The woman by his side flashed him a brief look of annoyance at the interruption.

'At Mr Easterson's request,' she continued, 'I've been carrying out a complete review of all of the late Mr Whetstone's business dealings and relationships.' She turned to the general manager. 'I'm sorry I haven't had a chance to run through this with you,' she tapped the folder, 'in advance of the meeting, Vernon.' Steele formed the instant impression that she was not at all sorry. 'To set this in context,' she continued, 'let me tell you a little bit about him. I have to admit at the outset that he was not someone I'd have gone out and recruited myself. He didn't fit my profile of the ideal corporate banker: he was twenty years too old, for openers . . .' The GMCB shifted uncomfortably beside her. '. . . and his background was restricted almost entirely to retail banking. However,' she said firmly, 'if I'd dug my heels in and flatly refused to have him, I'd have been wrong.'

A small smile of relieved satisfaction crossed Easterson's face. 'Ivor was the success of the team. I had a hunch about him and it turned out that my faith was well placed.'

'Yes,' Aurelia Middlemass agreed, 'it turned out that Whetstone had built up something of a network in his time with the SFB's predecessor, the Agricultural and Rural, and in the period after the demutualisation. He used it very shrewdly, and absolutely slaughtered his lending targets in his first year in post. As a result, he was given a promotion; he was also given a degree of extra autonomy on what he was doing.'

'I thought that Mr Easterson said you were his line manager,' Steele interrupted.

'I was at the outset; but when Whetstone had his review he asked if he might report directly to Vernon rather than through me.'

'Didn't you object to that?' asked Rose. 'In our set-up, that would be a bit like DI Steele asking if he could report directly to the head of CID.'

'Maybe it would, but maybe also we're a more flexible organisation. I didn't object because I reckoned it would be best for the bank. As I said, Whetstone wasn't of my generation, and our thinking was completely different, but I couldn't knock his performance. Frankly it seemed to me that having Vernon supervise him was an ideal arrangement all round.'

She paused and took a deep breath, drawing herself up in her chair. 'Of course, I assumed that there would be supervision.'

It was Easterson's turn to sit bolt upright. 'I beg your pardon?' he asked, his guests forgotten for that moment. 'What do you mean by that?'

'I mean, Vernon,' she replied evenly, 'that I understood that Whetstone really would be reporting to you, not doing his own thing.'

The little man's face turned a colour that if not pure beetroot, certainly looked hazardous to his health. 'I think we should continue this discussion in private, Aurelia,' he hissed.

Rose intervened. 'I'm sorry, Mr Easterson, if there's a disagreement between you but if Ms Middlemass has something to say that might have a bearing on Mr Whetstone's death, then we need to hear it.' She looked at the woman. 'Please, continue.'

The banker nodded. 'When I said that I've been carrying out a review of Mr Whetstone's business, I meant all of his business; not just the period when he was reporting to me, but the time since then. When I managed him, every lending transaction that he secured and every new business customer he brought to the bank was scrutinised by me and signed off by me, but only after I'd met the people involved and made my own risk assessment of each of them. It appears that hasn't been happening since he left my orbit.'

'Oh yes it has,' Easterson protested. 'Ivor brought every one of his deals to me for approval.'

Aurelia Middlemass turned towards him, her brown eyes seeming to drill into his head. 'I hope not,' she said icily. 'If you've heard of the Bonspiel Partnership, the situation is even more unfortunate than I thought.'

'What's the Bonspiel Partnership?' Steele asked. 'Something to do with curling?'

'Got it in one, Inspector,' she replied. 'Bonspiel's application for a credit facility says that the partnership is involved in the manufacture of curling stones made from traditional Ailsa Craig granite. The business plan proposes a distribution network throughout Europe and North America. The application is fine as far as it goes . . . only it doesn't go far enough. In a situation such as this, the bank would always ask for personal guarantees from the borrowers. That wasn't done in this case.'

'Okay,' said Rose, 'but there has to be more than that.'

'There is. The joint applicants are a couple called Alexander and Victoria Murray. Their business location is an industrial site in Stewarton, Ayrshire, and their home is listed as Galston. I've checked out both of those addresses; yes, they exist, but neither one has anything to do with the bank's alleged customers, or their alleged business. The industrial unit is vacant and unlet, and the house in question belongs to a couple whose surname just happens to be Murray. He's a teacher, she's a nurse.'

'Are the applications signed?'

'The signatures are a joke. They're just squiggles, that's all; one in black ink and the other in blue.'

'What's the borrowing facility?'

'One million pounds, all of which has been drawn down already.'

'And of course,' Steele anticipated, 'it's already been trans-ferred.'

'Correct. The money was moved last week to an account in the Isle of Man. As it happens, I have a contact in the receiving bank. The account holder is a Mrs Victoria Murray. Incident-ally, those two names bear a remarkable similarity to the forenames of Whetstone's wife and son.'

'That's true,' Rose conceded, 'but it's pretty tenuous as evidence. Is the money still there?'

'Are you kidding?' Aurelia Middlemass laughed. 'It was moved on the day after it was lodged, to a numbered account in a Swiss bank, and you may be sure it's been transferred out of that too.'

Vernon Easterson's face had gone from bright red to pale yellow. 'I knew nothing of this,' he whispered. 'How long have you been aware of it, Aurelia?'

'Since yesterday.'

'Have you told anyone else about it?' asked Rose.

'Absolutely not. Our chief executive, Proctor Fraser, has to be told, though. I've asked him to meet with Vernon and me once this meeting is over.'

'I don't believe it!' the GMCB gasped. 'How could Ivor ever have hoped to get away with it?'

'Without adequate supervision,' Aurelia Middlemass said slowly, 'he could have expected to, for a period at least. Sure, the auditors or someone would have discovered eventually that the application was fraudulent. Whetstone might even have worked a double bluff and blown the whistle himself; I've known that to happen. He could have claimed to have been shown the industrial unit, and that he had simply been duped. The worst that would have happened to him would have been an enforced early retirement. He'd have got away with it.'

'Not if the money was traced,' Steele suggested.

'The money's untraceable already. The Swiss are still holding on to their banking secrecy laws, in spite of pressure from the EU. They do co-operate in cases of money-laundering, but we'll need to go to court to prove it. But as I said earlier, the money won't be in Switzerland any more. There are still plenty of shelters around the world.'

Rose leaned back in her chair, and looked at her colleague. 'It could be, Stevie,' she said. 'Whetstone defrauds the bank, then panics and kills himself.'

'Or he really was conned, and once the money was transferred, he was killed by the fraudsters to cover their trail,' Steele suggested.

'No.' Vernon Easterson shook his head. 'He broke a strict banking rule in this transaction, by not obtaining personal guarantees.'

'Then maybe he was a partner in the fraud?'

'The problem I have with that, Inspector, is that Ivor has owned the Edinburgh house for years, since his first stint in the city, before he moved into the bank house in Kelso. His remaining mortgage on it is minimal. He and Virginia planned to sell it on retirement and move to Kelso; it's worth a good deal more than the third of a million you're suggesting he might have been in this for.'

'Point taken.' Steele turned to Rose. 'So what do we tell the fiscal?'

The superintendent shrugged her shoulders. 'On balance I think we suggest suicide and let him decide.'

'He might want to know whether Mrs Whetstone was involved.'

'There's no indication of that on the file,' Middlemass volunteered. 'My contact in the Isle of Man said that the application form was downloaded from the Internet, and that he never met the applicant. But he did fax me the signature on the form. It's a pretty good match for the scribbles on the loan application.'

'You have been thorough,' the superintendent murmured.

The woman shot a glance, full of meaning, at her colleague. 'It's as well someone was,' she murmured.

Rose looked at him. 'Did you have any luck with the equipment inventory I asked you about?'

Easterson shook his head dolefully. 'We don't possess an item like the one you describe. We use contract cleaners, and they might, but when I asked them they said they lose equipment all the time, and that they've more or less given up keeping track of it. So I'm afraid that I can't help you trace a pair of aluminium steps.'

The detective sighed. 'Don't worry about it. We know that they exist and that they were used. But frankly, finding them has become less important. What we've been told here shifts the perspective of this investigation . . . indeed it may open a new one altogether. If you're making a formal report of a theft, I'll need to open a formal investigation. In any event the information you've given me will need to be put in front of the procurator fiscal, since it may be material to the circumstances of Whetstone's death.' Rose turned to Middlemass. 'I'll need copies of all the papers in that folder for our report to the fiscal.'

'I anticipated that,' she replied. 'This file is for you.' She slid it across the table, and the superintendent picked it up.

'Come on, Inspector,' she said to Steele. 'That's us done here for now. Looks as if we have another unpleasant call to pay on Mrs Whetstone.'

Twenty-four

Skinner sat behind his desk, looking out of the window. He could have had another office, adjoining that of the chief, one that was slightly larger and which enjoyed year-round sunshine, but he had chosen to stay in his first room in the command corridor. It was cooler in the summer and, the clinching fact in its favour, it allowed him to look down the roadway that led up to the main entrance to the headquarters building, and to keep a watchful eye on the comings and goings.

He had been surprised a few hours earlier, just over an hour past midday, to see Sarah drive up the slope and park in one of the visitor spaces. He had been on the point of going along for lunch and had invited her to join him, but she had declined. So he had asked for a salad to be sent along from the dining room, and she had watched him eat.

At first he thought it might have been a business call, but she had assured him that it was purely social, following on from a food shop, before she went home to write her report on the morning's autopsy. She had been in a funny mood, but then, he had to admit to himself, so had he: he had felt a distraction, the reason for which he still found it hard to pin down.

He had kissed her goodbye as she left, but there had been a distance between them, one that he knew needed to be closed. On impulse he picked up the phone and dialled Sarah's private line in her office at home. 'What is it?' she asked him irritably. 'I'm busy.'

'Me too, but I've got time for this. I thought I'd take tomorrow afternoon off, and you and I could get in the car and go up to Gleneagles Hotel for the night: no kids, just us. We'll stay till about noon, then get back in time for dinner with the American at the club. How about it?'

She felt a shiver of crazy anxiety. Had she been spotted following Stevie to his place? Had someone told Bob? She discarded the notion in a second: she knew nobody brave enough to tell him. 'What's pricked your conscience?' she asked him.

'Nothing,' he told her truthfully. 'It's just something I think we need to do.'

'Maybe we do at that,' she conceded, after a few seconds' thought. 'Okay. Will you book it?'

'Sure. See you later. Maybe we can manage to finish dinner tonight.'

She laughed and hung up. Bob cradled the phone for a second, then buzzed through to Ruth Pye, his secretary. 'Do me a bit of extra-curricular, please?' he asked her. 'I'd like you to book me a suite for tomorrow night, dinner, bed and breakfast, at Gleneagles.'

'I take it Sarah's going too.' There was a laugh in her voice: he had told her earlier that her husband was being transferred back to Edinburgh from the Borders, and she was still basking in the news.

'What?' he grunted. 'Yes, of course. If I was taking anyone else I'd book it myself, Ruthie, don't you worry.'

'I hope you'd choose somewhere a bit more discreet than Gleneagles, in that case.'

'Discretion's never been my strongest card.'

'I'm saying nothing. By the way, you had a phone call just now, while you were engaged; a Ms McElhone, from the Scottish Executive Justice Department. She wouldn't leave a message, but she asked if you'd call her back as soon as you can. Will I do that first?'

'Yes, please. Get her for me, then call Gleneagles.'

He hung up, waited till the phone sounded again and picked it up on the first ring. 'Mr Skinner?' Like every ministerial private secretary he had ever heard, Lena McElhone sounded very young, very keen and very confident. 'Ms de Marco would like to speak to you. If you hold on I'll put you through to her.'

He felt himself smile as he waited, wondering whether the minister's brother had been so upset at being chucked off the Pope's platform that he had asked her to use some muscle. If that was the case, the ball would be passed to Jim Gainer, double quick.

'Bob?' Even in the way she said his name, there was something different about her voice; an excitement that he had not noticed before. 'I have some news for you. It's going to be breaking soon, within the next hour in fact, and you're one of the people I wanted to tell in advance. My boss, Crichton Griffiths, the Justice Minister, has resigned. He's been diagnosed with a form of leukaemia, and begins chemotherapy this week. The First Minister has asked me to take his place.'

Skinner took a second or two to let the news sink in. He knew Crichton Griffiths professionally, and had always found him polite and courteous. However, he had also regarded him as Tommy Murtagh's lackey, a bit too much his master's voice rather than his own man. 'Congratulations, Aileen,' he said. 'It's a big job you're taking on, but you're up to it. The Association of Chief Police Officers will welcome your appointment; I can assure you of that.'

'It's nice of you to say so. Crichton's always described them as a forbidding, argumentative lot, so I'm a bit apprehensive about facing them.'

'Hey, I'm one, remember, and I do my best not to be forbidding. I don't always succeed, I know, but I try . . .' he gave a soft laugh '. . . unless, of course, I come up against someone I really want to intimidate.'

'He said that too. You don't like the First Minister a lot, do you?'

'He talks too much. The first time I catch him listening I might start to respect him.'

'I'll have to bear that in mind.'

'You're different, don't worry. This phone call alone is evidence of that. You'll be a breath of fresh air at the cabinet table. I'm in no doubt about that.'

'Thanks for your confidence, Bob. I have to admit that, right now, I'm struggling to share it.'

'Trust me.'

'I do, as it happens, but I'm under no illusions. I'm wildly inexperienced for the job . . .'

'It's still a new legislature,' Skinner pointed out. 'You can say that about every one of your colleagues.'

'Fine, but this is me I'm talking about, my insecurity. I'm responsible for the administration of the courts, for the prison service, the probation service, the fire service and the police. I'm going to need help and advice.'

'You've got a small army of civil servants to help and advise you.'

There was a pause. 'Exactly.' They both laughed. 'It's okay,' she said. 'I told Lena not to listen in. It's part of the private secretary's routine, you know; hold the mute button and listen in on the minister's calls.'

'I know. But in the main, you can trust your civil service. Some of them might be a bit self-important, but they're conscientious . . . and they are experienced.'

'I appreciate that, but I'm not going to accept everything they say and recommend. I want to have other input available when I need it. I'd like to have a private group of advisers, in each of the areas I'm responsible for, and I was wondering . . . Can I count on you? Can I use you as a sounding board when I need one? You're your own man, the last person to tell me what you think I want to hear.'

'What makes you so sure of that?'

'You fell out with the Secretary of State, when you were his official adviser; everybody knows that. More recently, though, you told Crichton Griffiths to piss off when he offered you command of the Scottish Drug Enforcement Agency.'

Skinner chuckled. 'That wasn't quite what I said.'

'That's a fair summary of how he described your conversation to me.'

'It's true that we discussed the job. I told him that I had reservations about a national body that's focused on a single issue. If we're talking about fighting serious crime in general, that would be another matter, but Crichton didn't see it that way, or rather his boss didn't. As usual, he let the Scottish media set his agenda, so we got the SDEA. At that point your predecessor did try to lean on me to take the job; he suggested that it might be my only shot at chief constable rank. I didn't tell him to piss off, though; I told him to tell Tommy Murtagh to shove it up his arse, and not even to dream about threatening me again.'

'I doubt very much if he passed that on.'

'I doubt it too,' he laughed, 'but it might make you consider, Aileen, whether you really want me as an adviser, informal or not.'

'It makes me dead certain that I do. Consider it, please.'

'I don't need to. I'll do it. If you're going to be a listening minister, I'd be bloody stupid to pass up the chance to tell you what I think.'

She gave a small sound of pleasure. 'Thanks, Bob, thanks very much.'

'Don't mention it. So what do you want to pick my brains about first?'

'How about the SDEA? What should I do about that?'

'You don't have any choice. You have to give it your full backing. My view on that is irrelevant; your administration set it up and gave it a job to do. There are dozens of good officers out there now, working hard at it, and I will never do or say anything, in public or in private, to undermine them. My argument with Murtagh was strategic. I do not subscribe to the view that all serious crime in Scotland goes back to the drugs trade, simple as that.'

'We'll have a longer discussion about that,' said de Marco, 'and soon. Before I go though; you've got contacts, could you help me build up my advisory network?'

'I'll think about it, but I can give you a couple of names right now: Mitchell Laidlaw and Lenny Plenderleith.'

'I've heard of Laidlaw,' the minister murmured, 'but not Lenny Plenderleith. Should I?'

'As of today you should have. You've got him locked up for murder. Lenny was a gangster, and I put him away, but he's a very bright guy, and in a strange way he and I have become friends. His motivation has changed, and so has his outlook on life. He knows more about the prison service than most of the guys who run it. If you really want to understand what happens inside, he's the guy to put you right.'

'I'll read his file. Let's meet, Bob, privately; the evening would be best.'

Skinner hesitated. 'I can't do it before Monday,' he said cautiously.

'That suits me. We'll confirm arrangements later. I have to make some more calls now.'

He laughed. 'Not least to your brother. You can tell him he's back on the platform at Murrayfield.'

Twenty-five

'What did you think of that?' Rose and Steele had driven away in silence from Lothian Road; neither had spoken until they were through Tollcross, when the inspector could contain himself no longer.

'Just be thankful you don't have anyone like Aurelia in your team,' the superintendent replied. 'We get that type in the police from time to time, but they don't usually get rewarded for it. She will, though; maybe not right away, but in a few weeks, when Whetstone's death has faded into the background, poor wee Vernon will get the early retirement package and Ms Middlemass will move into his office. And if the chief executive of SFB has any bloody sense, he'll watch his back from that moment on.'

'I wonder what Mr Middlemass is like.'

'I don't think he is Mr Middlemass. I did some checking up on the key players at SFB in advance of the meeting. They're listed in the last *Insider* magazine banking survey. It said that she's married to a Spanish academic, who's on the staff of Heriot-Watt University. Maybe she's a pussycat at home, though, Stevie. A lot of people change personalities when they step through the office door.'

'As long as she, or anyone like her, never steps through mine.' He paused as a thought struck him. 'Mary Chambers isn't like her, is she?'

Rose laughed. 'A greater contrast you could not find.'

She drove on, in silence once more, until once again they reached the Whetstone house at the Grange. This time, Steele had phoned ahead to announce their visit, although he had not said what they wanted to discuss.

The door was opened by a woman they had never met; she was middle-aged, she wore black, and her puffy eyes showed signs of recent crying. 'You must be the police,' she decided, before Rose had a chance to speak. 'I'm Aisling Reynolds, Ivor's sister. Virginia told me she was expecting you. She's upstairs, resting; she's had precious little sleep, poor thing. If you'd like to wait in the drawing room, I'll tell her you're here.'

Blue, the Siberian husky, was in his usual place in front of the fire as they went into the bay-windowed room. Steele walked round the couch and knelt beside him, ruffling his thick fur. 'How're you doing, boy?'

'Missing his dad, I'm afraid,' said a voice from the door. Virginia Whetstone seemed to have shrunk in twenty-four hours, but as she moved into the room they saw that she was wearing sheepskin moccasins, with virtually no heel. She was dressed in black jeans and a crew-necked sweater, and her hair was tied back in a pony-tail. Like her sister-in-law, her grief showed around her eyes. 'I took him for a walk this morning, though; or rather, he took me. Did Aisling offer you tea?' she asked.

'No,' Rose answered, 'but we're fine, thanks.'

The widow nodded, and sat in the chair beside the dog. The superintendent took a seat close to her on the couch, and Steele joined her.

'How are your investigations proceeding?' Mrs Whetstone's voice seemed stronger as she turned to business.

'We have reached a conclusion,' Maggie Rose told her. 'We're going to report to the procurator fiscal that your husband probably took his own life. There was a slight doubt cast on that by the post mortem, but on balance that's how it looks.'

The woman drew in a breath and gazed directly into the detective's eyes. 'I see,' she said evenly. 'And if I choose to contest that?'

'I should tell you to consult your solicitor about that, but . . . You could ask the fiscal to hold an inquiry into your husband's death under the 1977 Act. He has the discretion to do that, and it would allow you to have all the circumstances examined in open court, before the Sheriff. You could have legal representation; you'd hear evidence in open court, and be able to cross-examine witnesses. Also you'd be able to give evidence about your husband's state of mind, and maybe even introduce other people who knew him.'

'Are you suggesting that I should do that?'

'It's not for me to make such a suggestion; I'm only telling you that it's a possibility. But before you go down that avenue, there are some things we have to discuss with you. Did you know that your husband was ill?'

Mrs Whetstone's look of blank astonishment answered for her.

'I'm afraid so,' Rose continued. 'He had lung cancer, sufficiently advanced for the pathologist to take the view that it would have proved fatal.'

'My God,' the woman whispered, 'poor Ivor.' She looked at the detectives. 'But even so, my husband was a man of some determination. I don't believe he would just have given up . . . if he knew about it.' She shook her head. 'He was never very good at keeping secrets from me, you know.'

'The pathologist did say that he might not have known about it.'

'Then what makes you so sure he killed himself?'

'That's the other thing we have to tell you; it relates to your husband's job.'

'Well? As they say . . . shoot.'

'Have you ever heard of the Bonspiel Partnership?' asked the superintendent.

'The what?'

'The Bonspiel Partnership; it's one of your husband's clients. Did he ever mention it to you?'

'Never. I'm quite certain of that. It's hardly a name one would forget. Why do you ask?'

'Because the Bonspiel Partnership does not exist: yet it appears that your husband approved lending facilities of up to a million pounds and that the full amount was transferred to an offshore bank account.'

'I don't believe it.'

'It's true, I'm afraid. It was revealed by an internal investigation at SFB. The offshore account was in the name of Victoria Murray. The money's moved on since then, and the bank's view is that it will probably be untraceable.'

Mrs Whetstone gasped. 'That's impossible.'

'No, it isn't.' She held up the document case she had brought from the car. 'All the papers are in here. I have to ask you again, Mrs Whetstone . . .'

'I won't listen to any more!' the woman shouted; her eyes were blazing.

Rose waited for her to subside. 'I have to, I'm afraid. To be honest, I'd be justified in making this a formal interview, given the information I've seen, but I'm bending over backwards not to do that. I just need you to answer this question. Did you know, or did you have any reason to believe, that your husband might have been defrauding his company?'

'No, I did not,' she replied stiffly. 'You can show me all the evidence you like, and I still won't believe it.'

'I'm not going to do that. I'll report to the fiscal, and he'll make the decision on how to dispose of the case. I'm sorry, but I cannot justify taking this investigation any further.'

'What would you expect him to do?'

'I can't say; it's his decision.'

'But based on your experience . . .'

'Each case is different, Mrs Whetstone; but informally, between you and me, I'd expect him to close the file. On the basis of the information that I'll put before him, I'd expect him to write it off as suicide under pressure of imminent incrimination.'

'Without an inquiry?'

'Your husband wasn't in his workplace, and he wasn't in custody; therefore an FAI is discretionary, not mandatory.'

'But if I pressed for one?'

'He might order it. Bear this in mind, though: at an inquiry before the Sheriff, your husband would effectively be in the dock. All the evidence against him would be led. On top of that, the Sheriff would probably ask you to give evidence about Ivor's demeanour in the days before his death; that would lay you open to aggressive cross-examination, should the bank instruct counsel. Before you do anything, think about the box you'd be opening.'

'Besmirching Ivor's memory, you mean? That's a box he'd throw open himself.'

'And your son? How would he feel about it?'

Virginia Whetstone pursed her lips. 'That is another matter. I have still to speak to Murphy, I'm afraid. When Bert called him at the distillery he was told that he and a couple of colleagues have time off, and that they've gone into the mountains. They're not due back until today. The company know what's happened; they'll make sure he calls me as soon as possible, but I don't expect to see him before Saturday. Monday won't be too late for me to speak to this fiscal man, will it?'

'Not at all. I won't be making my report until tomorrow.'

'I could consult my solicitor, couldn't I?'

Rose nodded. 'That would be a sensible thing to do. If he

wants to speak to us, and he probably will, tell him to ask for DI Steele.'

'Not for you?'

'I'm going to be busy tomorrow, I'm afraid. I have an in-tray to empty before five.'

Twenty-six

The DCC was tidying his desk, and thinking about the road home, when there was a knock at his door. The status light outside had been set to red, 'busy', but he pushed a button in his desk and turned it to green, 'come in'.

His visitor was the head of CID. 'Red lights mean nothing to you, do they, Dan?' said Skinner, amiably.

'Depends where they are. Traffic lights I generally take note of, but houses down in Leith I avoid like the plague.'

'I wish all our officers could say that.'

A smile seemed to ruffle Pringle's heavy moustache. 'Are you suggesting that some of our colleagues might not be above accepting sexual favours, Bob?'

'I know of at least one who has done in days gone by, but he knows I do, so it won't happen again.' He grunted. 'Anyway, he's probably fucking past it by now . . . or words to that effect. What have you got for me, Dan? Whatever it is, it had better not take long.'

'It won't. It's about the swinging banker; you asked me to keep you in touch, remember.'

'Aye, what about him?'

'I've just had Maggie on the phone. She and Stevie have wrapped it up; they're reporting it to the fiscal in the morning as a probable suicide.'

Skinner frowned. 'I'm not sure the pathologist will be too happy about that. Sarah came in to see me at lunchtime. She said she'd found injuries that offered another explanation.'

'I know,' said Pringle. 'Rose told me that. But she came up with a theory of her own, and I think it fits.' He explained the scenario that had been outlined to him by the outgoing divisional commander.

When he finished, Skinner sighed, and nodded. 'I can see that one,' he admitted. 'And I reckon the fiscal would buy it too. It's not like my wife to go out on a limb like that, and be wrong. In fact, I've never known it before. I'll need to be careful around the dinner table tonight.'

'There's merit in what she said, though, boss. It's just that when Maggie and Steele went to the bank this afternoon, they were given a folder that showed that the bloke had been at it. Almost certainly he'd have been rumbled. On the evidence it seems pretty clear-cut.'

'I suppose it does,' the DCC agreed. 'Weird, but clean-cut. Are you happy?'

'I have to be. We all have to be; that's what the evidence tells us.'

'Tell that to the ghost of Timothy Evans, my friend.'

'Who was he?'

'An accused of fifty years ago. The evidence said he was

guilty too, and they hanged him . . . a lot more neatly than this chap, by all accounts. But . . . cases like that are rarities. If you lot are prepared to report, I'm not going to rock the boat.'

Twenty-seven

'It gives me great pleasure to welcome you to Edinburgh, Inspector Mawhinney,' said Sir James Proud. He shook his guest's hand, holding it long enough for the five photographers to frame and take their photographs. Both men were in uniform; the chief's was heavy with silver braid, but the New Yorker's, bright with the ribbons of service medals, and with its badges of rank, was just as sharp and impressive.

Mawhinney's eyes were bright and sharp too, in spite of the fact that the time change had allowed him only three hours' sleep. He had eaten the night before with McGuire and Paula at a small restaurant close to the castle; he was still unsure whether it had been called the Secret Garden or the Witchery, but whatever, it had been very fine.

'It gives me great pleasure to visit your city, sir,' the American replied. 'I've been asked by my commissioner to thank you formally for your force's generous gift to our dependants' fund. It's greatly appreciated.'

'Before we go any further,' said Alan Royston, the force's media manager, to the three reporters he had ushered into the conference room, and the camera people, as they worked, 'a piece of housekeeping that I have to take care of. Press entry to all the events on the papal visit next week will be on a pass-only basis. If any one of you expects to attend any event but hasn't given me a formal application, please do so before you leave here today, with photographs. I've got forms you can complete. Now, we have time for a few questions.'

'Where are you staying while you are in Edinburgh, Inspector?' asked one of the photographers, a bearded, bespectacled freelance who was a newcomer to the press group.

'In a fine hotel down by the docks,' said Mawhinney.

'The Malmaison? They're really looking after you.'

John Hunter, the veteran reporter, threw his colleague an irritated glance. He was the senior man on the police beat and the rest usually deferred to him automatically. 'Your rank, Inspector Mawhinney,' he began. 'How does it equate to our own inspectors?'

'There are probably fewer of me than there are of them; that's the best way I can put it. Our forces are structured in a completely different way, so it's difficult to assess rank equivalents. In a way it's pointless too: we're all cops doing a job.'

'What do you hope to learn while you're here?'

'As much as I can. For example, I'm looking forward to seeing at first hand how your force handles the policing of the papal visit next week.'

'You'll be there?'

'I expect to be in the very midst of it. When my programme was put together, the chief constable was kind enough to suggest that I join Chief Superintendent Mackie's team, as a close observer. It's a great honour, and I appreciate it.'

'Are there any other specific areas you'll be looking at during your time in Edinburgh?'

Mawhinney nodded. 'Yes, I've been asked to study the way that your uniform and detective bureaux work together.'

'I've been studying that for twenty years,' said Bob Skinner from the side. 'I still find myself with more questions than answers.'

'Is Maggie Rose's promotion to uniformed chief super meant to improve that?' asked Hunter, switching his attention to the DCC.

'That wasn't the reason for it, and it's not what we're here to discuss, but I'm sure it'll be of benefit. Maggie's a fine officer, and I've got no doubt that her CID experience will help her take a broad view of her divisional responsibilities.'

'Is she the first woman to command a division?' The DCC looked across at his new questioner, Sally Gordon, the *Evening News* reporter. He knew that the photo-call was being hijacked, and that she was after a headline; he decided to throw her one.

'She is, but she won't be the last. If her appointment and that of Mary Chambers send out any signal, it's that this is an equal opportunity force. The days when the promotion ladder for female officers had snakes alongside it are well and truly over. The policy of this force, as established by Sir James, is quite clear: we appoint the best person for the job in question, regardless.'

'Does that mean that you're going to follow the example of

the NYPD and recruit more people from ethnic minorities?'

'I don't believe in tokenism, Sally; we're going to recruit the best, and that's it. No arbitrary restriction ever works in the public interest. When I was a very young man,' he told her, 'there was a legend about a village in the west of Scotland, where there was no crime.'

John Hunter smiled; he had heard the story before, over several beers. The old journalist had known Bob Skinner for a long time; their relationship was entirely professional, but it was close and based on respect. He had seen a change in the DCC over the last few months. He had never asked but his impression had been that for the first time in his career, and maybe even in his life, the absolute inner certainty that made him exceptional had been shaken. Skinner was approaching the final step in his journey through the ranks of the police force; every reporter in town knew that, and all but one of them assumed that it would take him into Jimmy Proud's office. The exception was John Hunter. He sensed Skinner's reluctance to step across the corridor, and to put on a uniform for the rest of his professional life. When the SDEA job had come up, he had expected the Big Man to move into it, but he had not; it was then that the change Hunter perceived had begun. Yet as he listened to him expound to Sally Gordon, he sensed a new, if suppressed, excitement in him, as if a new door, one that nobody else knew about, had somehow opened up.

'No crime at all?' asked the woman from the *News*, taking the bait.

'No reported crime,' said Skinner. 'If the police didn't see it, it never happened. The thing was that virtually the whole population of that village was Catholic, and all the coppers were masons to a man . . . and I mean to a man. Those were the bad old days, when a gifted woman like Maggie Rose would have had to leave the force for committing the career-ending offence of getting married. So in that village, the house-breakings, the petty thefts, the assaults went unreported, and were sorted out within the community.'

'Vigilantes?'

'No, just people. The legend continues though; finally the age of enlightenment dawned and the first Catholic officers were recruited. One of them was stationed in that village as its local bobby and, hey presto, people started to talk to him. It remains probably the only time in history that a chief constable has won universal praise for presiding over a quantum leap in recorded crime.' The laughter of the crowd made him pause for a few seconds. 'So to come back to your question, Sally,' he continued, when he could, 'we're not following anyone's lead in our recruitment policy, not even the NYPD, we're doing what we believe to be right. We're recruiting from the whole community because we serve the whole community, and because every senior police officer in Scotland is determined that an instance like that village . . . which could have been called Northern Ireland but wasn't . . . never arises again.'

'Does that mean that you think freemasons shouldn't be police officers?'

Skinner laughed out loud, and looked over at Hunter. 'I asked for that one, John, did I not?'

'Aye, you did,' the old man agreed. 'Now answer it.'

'Okay. If a mason wants to join this force, he won't be excluded, any more than will a Buddhist, a Rotarian, a train-spotter, or a collector of rare and exotic orchids. If a police officer wants to join the masons, that's fine by me, and I won't expect the fact to be reported. It's a hobby, an interest, and maybe even for some it's a way of life. But my rule's the same for it as for any other leisure pursuit. Don't bring it to work and, especially, don't get together with a bunch of like-minded people and try to use the police to impose your personal values on society. I'll be your enemy if you do, and my enemies tend not to last long.'

He turned to Mawhinney. 'Do you think that's a fair basis for running a police force, Inspector?'

'No sir,' said the New Yorker. 'I believe it's the only basis for running a police force.'

'A man after my own heart.' The DCC looked back at the media. 'And now, if you'll excuse us, lady and gentlemen, we have to explain to our guest how we put all that into practice.'

Twenty-eight

'What made you decide to pull the plug early, Manny?' asked McGuire, raising his voice above the noise in the crowded Torphichen Place briefing room.

For the first time in more years than anyone could remember, the retiring chief superintendent was in shirtsleeves in the office; half an hour earlier, he had been presented with a set of golf clubs, the result of a quick collection organised throughout the division, and he had made his farewell speech. At its conclusion he had surprised his colleagues by unfastening the silver buttons on his jacket, and taking it off for what he declared would be the last time.

'Your wife was running me ragged,' English replied, clutching a can of Tennents lager. 'That was a joke,' he added quickly, and wisely, for it had passed by Mario completely. 'I've never had a problem with Margaret. I'm a bit surprised that she's moving into my job, but she'll do very well there. She's a very capable officer, but I'm sure I don't have to tell you that.' The man was trying to shed his pomposity with his uniform, but it promised to be a tough task.

'No, the truth is,' he continued, 'that it was my own wife

who gave me a hard time. She's been pressing me to give up for a while, ever since it was made clear to me that my face didn't fit in the command corridor.'

McGuire considered telling him that it was his inflexibility that had held him back, but decided instead to stir the pot a little. 'Who made that clear to you?' he asked mischievously.

English killed his can, reached out to the table and took another. 'Since I'm on my way through that door, I'll tell you. The deputy chief constable did. He runs this fucking force now, and old Proud Jimmy lets him. You're all right; you're in his circle, you, and Margaret, and Brian Mackie, and that big pal of yours, Skinner's hatchet-man McIlhenney. But those of us who are not favoured, we're just filling in time.'

'Come on, Manny. We've all got an important job to do, even though only one of us, every ten years or so, is going to make chief constable. You know that.'

'I'll tell you what I know, son.' If there was one thing that usually triggered McGuire, it was being called 'son' by people like English, but he let it pass. He knew that the man had been summoned to the chief's office for a formal farewell and, even over the lager fumes, he could tell from his breath that whisky had been on the agenda. 'I know that I had seniority over every other superintendent in this force. I was in the rank before Skinner, or Dan Pringle, or Greg Jay or any of them. I know that there was no more meticulous officer than me on the strength, and that nobody ran a tighter division. Yet when Jim Elder decided to chuck it, and I applied for the vacancy, I was called in by the deputy and told point-blank that he could not have anyone hold command rank who didn't have the potential to be chief constable. And then he went ahead and appointed that roughneck from Glasgow, that man over there, that Willie Haggerty. And what a time I've had with him. Do you know, he actually questioned my judgement on occasion?'

The ex-commander's indignation was almost comic to watch, but McGuire kept his face straight. 'I'm sure that Margaret will get on better with him than I did; she'll be under the great man's protection, for a start. But you tell her to watch her back all the same.' He snorted. 'I notice the DCC hasn't deigned to join me this evening.' That fact had occurred to McGuire already. He knew that Skinner would not be intentionally ungracious, and wondered what had taken him elsewhere. 'I suppose I could call that the final snub.'

'Personally, I wouldn't,' said the younger man, 'but if you choose to, that's down to you. Do you know your problem, Manny?' he asked.

'What's that?'

'You didn't join the same police force as the rest of us. You joined one of your own. I wish you and your wife all the best in retirement. Enjoy the rest of your evening.'

He wandered across to where Maggie was standing, with Mary Chambers, Stevie Steele and Colin Mawhinney, who was holding a Budweiser, and biting uncertainly into the first Scots mutton pie of his life. 'What was that about?' she asked him quietly, turning her back on the other three. 'Were you winding him up?'

'I didn't have to; he's fully wound as it is. He thinks he should have got Haggerty's job. He says the Big Man shafted him.'

'Manny thinks he should have got the DCC's job,' Maggie retorted. 'But he's right about the second bit. The boss did shaft him, and thank God for it, too.'

'He says you should keep an eye on Haggerty.'

'If I keep a proper eye on what's happening in this division, I won't need to bother looking out for the ACC. If I don't, I'll hear about it.'

Mario grinned. 'And so will every bugger under your command, I'll bet. Don't fret, lass, you'll be a star. Your future's mapped out.'

'So's yours, from what I hear. Looking forward to Leith?'

'Too right. I think there might be a few people not looking forward to it, though.'

'I'm sure, knowing your style. If it helps, a couple of my guys were in a pub down there the other day; it's called the Wee Black Dug.'

'Malky Gladsmuir's place? I know it, not that I drink there. It's a fucking hotbed, but Malky keeps a lid on it. I plan to have a chat with him, soon.' He nodded towards Mawhinney, who was making the last of the pie disappear. 'What did you think of our friend Colin?'

'Fine. He's a very sharp guy; chief constable material if he was one of ours. Why do you ask? Are you trying to pair us off?'

'Don't joke about that. He lost his wife in the Twin Towers. And anyway, I wouldn't want to upset Stevie.'

'You'll upset me if you keep on like that,' Maggie said quietly. She looked up at him; for all that they were on course for divorce, Mario was the only person in the world who knew everything there was to know about her. Sometimes that thought frightened her, but she knew also that, whatever happened to them in the future, he would always be the man she could trust beyond anyone else.

'Sorry,' he murmured. 'For the record, I like the boy Steele; if he doesn't get on with Mary, I'll have him in a minute. Stevie and women, though, that's another matter, and it's got nothing to do with him and Paula, either.'

'Are you giving me a warning, McGuire?'

'I know better than to do that. But for all sorts of reasons you have to be careful, that's all I'm saying. Don't let anyone compromise you in the job, and don't let anyone hurt you. Mind you, if anyone does, they're in more trouble than they could imagine.'

'If you're planning on being my emotional security guard, why don't you just move back in?'

'Are you serious?'

'No.'

'Just as well.' He paused. 'I won't be looking over your shoulder, love. But if you need me, I'm there . . . That's all I'm saying.'

She smiled, amused by his awkwardness. 'Thanks. And however odd this may sound, the same goes for me too.'

Twenty-nine

The weather had been grey and wet all the way up the M90, but when they had turned at Perth, heading for Auchterarder, the skies had begun to lighten in the west, as if they were guiding them to their destination.

It had been dry when they had arrived, and mild enough for them to change into golf gear and play the best part of a round on the King's Course. Bob had given Sarah her customary shot per hole, two at the par fives and longer par fours, and had regretted it by the seventh tee, when he stood three down, a deficit that he had been unable to make up by the time the light and the growing cold had forced them to call a halt after the fourteenth, the closest green to the hotel, apart from the eighteenth itself.

As they sat in the bar, having a drink before dinner, he was still muttering about his game. 'All over the bloody place, I was,' he grumbled into his gin and tonic, 'and I putted like a gorilla as well. Honest to Christ, if you play a course like that, you should do it the honour of being in some reasonable form.'

Sarah was still basking in the afterglow of her rare success. 'If you practised more you'd play better,' she pointed out. 'When was the last time you played Gullane?'

'The October medal; shot a seventy-five . . . net.' He added the qualification.

'What's your handicap now?'

'Seven point three.'

'It's not that long ago you were playing off four. You're the detective, you work out why it's gone up.'

'You're the pathologist,' he countered. 'You tell me how my pacemaker's affected my swing shape.'

She laughed. 'Of all the excuses I've heard for a bad round of golf, that has to be among the lamest. Your pacemaker doesn't make you knock a four-foot putt six feet past the hole. Lack of concentration does that; plus lack of time on the course, of course.'

'Is that your roundabout way of saying I'm not spending enough time at home?' he asked.

'You're not at home when you're on the golf course,' she pointed out.

'Answer the question.'

'Maybe. The clubhouse is three hundred yards away from our house, and a round takes under four hours.'

'If it takes over three and a half, it's frowned upon.'

'I was allowing you a couple of pints in the bar afterwards. Anyway, once that's done you are home, and of course if I'm playing with you . . .'

'So if I take a morning off every week during the winter, as I could, and we hack round number two course, that would iron out the kinks in our marriage. Is that what you're going to suggest?'

'It wouldn't do us any harm. I wouldn't even mind losing once you got your game back.'

'Okay, suppose I've booked a morning off and a tee time, and big McGuire or someone phones while we're having breakfast and asks you to go and cut up a stiff, what are you going to do?'

'Tell him I'll do it in the afternoon.'

'But Mario needs it done in the morning, because they've got someone locked up, and they need the PM report double quick or they'll have to release him.'

Sarah gave a quick frown and sipped her sherry.

'Need I say more?' Bob asked. 'Listen, love, this is not about leisure time, or about my fucking golf handicap. I can only do my job one way, and that's flat out. You might have a different working environment, as a home-based consultant, but when your phone rings you're exactly the same as me. If either of us gets a 999 call we don't think, we act. And . . . it's . . . always . . . been . . . that . . . way.' He prodded the arm of his chair with a finger, to emphasise every word. 'It may have caused us a problem years ago, that time when you took Jazz back to the States, but we got over that and we lived happily with our respective lifestyles afterwards. What's wrong with our marriage now is not our work, and it's not my guilt over my brother . . . which I now accept was misplaced . . . it's us, you and me.'

'You can't tell me how I feel about you,' Sarah protested.

'I think I can. This year, when we were in America, and I

had my health thing and decided afterwards . . . wrongly, as you saw it . . . that I had to come back here to defend my job, you had a fling, an affair. It ended badly, and okay, I know we said we wouldn't speak of it again, but I have to. We started the other night, and we have to finish.' He looked into her eyes. 'I need to be honest about this, Sarah: I can't look at you in the same way I did before. I hoped I would, but I can't. That doesn't mean I don't love you, because I do; it means that my perception of you has changed.'

'If it has,' she said grimly, 'it's an ego thing. Go on, deny that.'

'I won't even try to. The idea that the great Bob Skinner's wife could ever be truly attracted by another man never entered my head. But you could, and you were, so that's me put in my place. Sure, I could try to dismiss it by telling myself you were angry with me at the time so it was really my fault, but I'd be kidding myself. You fancied him and he fancied you, and you had each other. So now when I'm feeling black . . . you know, the shade beyond blue, where we all go sometimes . . . I find myself asking myself, how many more times?'

'So why not ask me?'

'Okay, since we've been married, how many lovers have you had?'

'You know how many.'

'Accepted. Now, suppose you met someone who got you as hot as the guy in Buffalo did, and it was mutual . . .'

Dangerous ground. 'Bob . . . that's not going to happen,' she exclaimed. She felt her cheeks flush and feared for a second that he had noticed, but he was looking away from her, up towards the ceiling.

'You can't say that,' he murmured. 'It's happened once this year already. Look, I'm not going to ask you whether you would or you wouldn't, one, because I think I can guess the truth, and two, much more important, because I think what you're saying is that I don't affect you like that any more, I don't get you that hot. Be honest with me, I don't, do I?'

She sank back into her chair, as if she was trying to make herself smaller. 'Honestly? No,' she admitted finally. 'But whose fault is that?' she challenged him.

'Oh, that really is mine, and I admit it. But it's not because I'm not interested in you physically, or because when we do get it on we're just going through the motions. It's because where I've stood this year, you've stood before. We've matched each other in one respect, Sarah, and that's in the number of affairs we've had since we've been married. You told me once that you had your first so that you wouldn't be able to brandish my infidelity like a club to beat me with. I don't think I believe that any more, but I do recognise this. If I can't see you in the same way I did before, then you can't see me as your ideal, faultless, untouchable lover either. And don't try to tell me I'm wrong.'

Sarah finished her Bloody Mary, and signalled to the cocktail waiter to bring her another. She sat in silence until it arrived, then turned back to look at her husband. 'No,' she said gravely. 'I won't try to tell you that. So what sort of a marriage does it leave us?'

'One that's probably still better than many others,' he replied, 'and one that I want to continue. Do you?'

'Yes. I've never been in any real doubt about that. But is it possible?'

'As long as it's what we both want, and as long as our family unit is strong and our kids are happy, yes, it is.'

'Can we maintain that?'

'I believe we can, if we try. But if we decide that it would be impossible in the long run, should we chuck it now, take the hurt and get it over with?'

She looked at him. 'I don't think I could take the hurt,' she confessed.

'Then we settle for what we've got right now. Agreed?'

She nodded. 'Agreed.' She stirred her drink, rattling the ice cubes. 'Are you still hungry?' she asked him.

'Christ, yes!' Bob replied. 'We've played fourteen holes of golf, remember; I'm bloody starving.'

'Okay, let's go through to the dining room.' He made to rise, but she put a hand on his sleeve. 'Bob, you may have found out things about me that you didn't know, but maybe I've found them out too. I promise you, as long as we are married, I'll never again . . .'

He stopped her in mid-pledge. 'Don't say it. If you do then I'll have to make myself believe you.'

'Would that be so difficult?' she hissed at him.

'I'd rather leave it the way it is. I didn't ask you to promise anything, and I didn't expect it. In all my career,' he said, 'I have never solved a crime that nobody knew had been committed. Likewise in all the recorded history of the western world, I can't recall a case of a marriage that's ended purely because one partner slept with someone else on the side. Criminals and adulterers are no different; they're only ever caught because they let someone else find out what they've done.'

Thirty

Colonel Malou was impressed. The sight of the reception that had awaited the Bastogne Drummers in Haddington had taken him by surprise, and had made him think for the first time since Hull of something other than the death of Philippe Hanno. He had not been told of it in advance, and in other circumstances the sight of it would have gladdened his heart.

When their bus had pulled into the centre of the old county town, they had found an official welcoming party, headed by the chairman of East Lothian Council, and by the president of the area council of the Royal British Legion. There was another there too; a young priest, in a dark suit, looking sombre amongst the jovial councillors and their boisterous ex-service hosts. 'Colonel Malou,' he said, in French, when it was his turn to greet him, 'I am Father Angelo Collins, private secretary to His Holiness. He has asked me to give you his personal welcome to Scotland, and to tell you how pleased he is that you have been able to come to play for him.'

The old soldier was deeply moved. 'It's an honour beyond the dreams of any of us.'

'His Holiness has heard of the accident in Hull,' Father Collins continued, 'through the priest who attended. He sends his sympathy on your loss, and his prayers for the soul of Corporal Hanno.'

Malou simply nodded his thanks, for he could not speak them.

A civic buffet awaited the Belgians in the Corn Exchange and a marching route had been laid out for the afternoon. After Hanno's tragic death . . . the police in Hull had called Malou that morning in Newcastle, but only to tell him that they had had no success in tracing the drunken driver who had knocked him down . . . Malou had surprised many of the bandsmen by declaring that for the rest of the tour there would be no drinking before parades and that the Stella would be strictly rationed afterwards.

Some of the senior men had suggested that their fallen colleague would have wanted the opposite form of tribute, but the colonel had rebuffed them. 'This was always my intention,' he had told them, 'and Philippe knew it. We are on our way to play for His Holiness. When we do, every one of us will be at his sharpest.'

And so the crates of beer in the Corn Exchange had been untouched by the visitors . . . although not by the official representatives . . . and an extra supply of soft drinks had been fetched from the nearby supermarket. To the surprise of the Royal British Legionnaires, at least, Malou and his company had remained clear-eyed throughout the lunch.

At three o'clock sharp, they lined up outside the Sheriff Court building. The colonel was at the head of the parade, leading the twenty-three bandsmen in their blue uniforms, with the squad of twelve musketeers bringing up the rear.

Although they were known officially as the Bastogne Drummers, half of the instruments were brass, with six trombones, two tenor horns, two baritone horns and two tubas. Normally there would have been two bass drums flanking the ten side-drummers, but as Malou marched them out into Court Street, there was only one. They had left without reserves, and Hanno's place remained vacant.

The route was a short one; for traffic had to be held up for the march, and Haddington was always busy on a Saturday afternoon. Malou the bandmaster led them, playing as they went, from Court Street into Market Street; the pavements were not exactly lined, but many shoppers stopped to watch them pass through the wider area of the old marketplace, past Kesley's bookshop on the right, and the *East Lothian Courier* office on the left, before they moved into the bottleneck that led to Hardgate.

Malou had not been given an opportunity to rehearse the parade, but he found no difficulty as there was a strong police presence and officers were lined on either side of the marchers, showing them the way. He speeded the march as they took the right turn into the narrow section of Hardgate that led them towards, then past, the old George Hotel and into High Street. There the roadway widened out once more, and the colonel was able to slow the march again. The music was loud and martial, but tight and disciplined, as were his troops. A lump came to the old soldier's throat as he glanced to either side of him and saw genuine admiration in the eyes of many of the onlookers, where these days in Belgium he usually saw only amusement and ridicule.

If this was to be the Drummers' last tour, they would go out in style, he promised himself as he led his proud column past the Town House.

The march ended where it had begun, in front of the Sheriff Court and the old council buildings. As the colonel led the squad into the assembly area he turned them, so that the musket platoon was in front.

'Raise your weapons!' he called out; the command was in English, for the benefit of his audience. The ancient, heavy muskets, shouldered during the march, were pointed in the air.

'Prepare salute!' A dozen thumbs drew back hammers, and the side-drummers began a long roll.

Malou counted to ten. 'Fire!' he yelled, making himself heard above the bandsmen.

The noise was deafening. Several members of the official party were seen to jump backwards, and even across the street, the colonel saw that the crowds were startled. *Good*, he thought, as he always did at such a moment. *They should know, they should know.*

Thirty-one

B ob had always liked the smoking room in the Gullane golf clubhouse, the big front lounge with its oak panelling, and the gold-inscribed boards high on the wall, listing the club champions and past captains. Once he had entertained hopes of seeing his own name on the former, but his erratic putting stroke had thwarted him in each of the three or four years when he had come close.

He had told McGuire to be there for eight o'clock, but he and Sarah had arrived a good fifteen minutes early, to be on the safe side. He had chosen a bottle of Chablis from the list; it sat on their table in an ice bucket, as they waited, sipping the gentle white wine and making small-talk, sitting close together to make themselves heard above the conversation of the other dining parties.

The Gleneagles weekend had been a good move, Bob had told himself on the way back. The surroundings had encouraged them both to say things that had needed saying, and as a result there was a degree of restored warmth between them, where before the atmosphere had been chilly and unpredictable.

Their marriage was not out of the woods, but at least there was light shining through the trees.

If the clock above the fireplace had had a chimer, it would have struck eight at the precise moment that McGuire's bulky form appeared in the doorway. The big superintendent wore a navy blue blazer and slacks, but even in a white suit he would still have managed to cast a dark figure, Skinner thought. His hair, his complexion and his eyes worked together to create that impression, and also to radiate considerable menace to those who did not know him, although he was by nature the most amiable of men.

Skinner rose to greet his guests, making for Paula Viareggio first. They had met before at a few social events around Edinburgh; he had always found her as striking a figure as her cousin, although in a different way. She was as typically Italian as he could imagine, save for her silver hair, long and sleek and shining, which made her olive skin seem even richer. Heads at every table turned in her direction as she walked into the room.

'Hello,' he said warmly, leaning forward to kiss her cheek, bending only slightly, for she was tall. 'Good to see you.'

He turned to the American; the two shook hands. 'Inspector, welcome to Gullane. How's your day been so far?'

Both Mawhinney and McGuire smiled. 'Interesting,' the Scot replied, as they all took seats at Skinner's table. 'Colin's been learning some of the finer points of Scottish tribalism,' he continued, as their host poured each of them a glass of wine. 'We did the blue-rinse tour in the morning . . . Jenners, Harvey Nicks, Frasers . . . then we had a pint and a bridie at the Diggers' for lunch and finished up at Tynecastle. It was a draw, by the way, if you haven't heard.'

'That's good,' said the DCC happily. 'They've taken two points off each other; that suits me. What did you think of the game?' he asked the visitor. 'Are you a football man?'

'Neither ours nor yours, sir, I'm a baseball fan. But I enjoyed the match very much. A different atmosphere, I gotta say. Those songs! We hear nothing like that in Yankee Stadium, I promise you. And maybe just as well, because some of them would probably be in breach of our public-order laws.'

'Some of them might be against ours,' said Skinner, 'and we enforce them where we can, but how are you going to arrest a whole football crowd?'

'That's complacent!' Sarah protested. He turned, surprised by his wife's intervention. 'What if they all started chanting racial abuse?'

Bob frowned. 'You think that never happens? Maybe not in Edinburgh, but it does elsewhere. It's easy to say, "Arrest them," but sometimes it's impossible to do it. Not even NYPD would have enough officers to lift five thousand people.'

'So you'd let it go on?'

'No. If it was down to me, and it became intolerable, I'd change the law so that clubs could be fined for the behaviour of their crowds . . . and not just the home clubs either . . . and grounds closed if necessary. If there was serious racial abuse going on at a stadium on my patch, and the home support was clearly responsible, I'd like to give them one warning, and on a repeat offence, close the place for three months.'

'Sounds good to me,' Mawhinney concurred.

'Mmm,' said Paula, as the lady-steward handed out the dinner menu, in blue leather folders. 'You two guys, and Mario, you give the word "draconian" a whole new depth of meaning.'

'That's cops for you, the world over,' Skinner countered cheerfully. 'But you can relax. For a start the problem isn't that bad, and if it was, the politicians would take years to pluck up the courage to tackle it.'

'Speaking of politicians,' the American intervened, 'I read that you have a new Justice Minister.'

'Yes, we have. I have hopes for this one. Not many of them have what it takes to make a real difference; this lady might just be one of the exceptions.'

'If the men around her give her a chance.' Sarah snorted.

'They might not have the option.' He looked across the table to McGuire. 'By the way, how did Manny's do go last night?' he asked.

The superintendent laughed. 'He surprised everyone by getting rat-arsed. He wanted to take everyone on to Ryrie's for more, but we wound up sticking him in a patrol car and sending him home for the rest of his life.'

'I thought the chief was a bit liberal with the Laphroaig in the afternoon. I'm sorry I had to miss it, but we had other places to be.'

'Nice places?' Paula asked Sarah.

'Gleneagles.'

'Mmm. That qualifies. When did you get back?'

'Early afternoon. I can only escape the humdrum for so long. Saturday tends to be Tesco day, for the kids have to be fed.' She turned to Bob. 'Speaking of which, honey, I saw the strangest thing in Haddington this afternoon. It was a parade, by a marching band, in uniforms, with a squadron of guys following behind with muskets. They were very good, but at the end they lined up and they fired their old blunder-busses up in the air. What a hell of a noise they made. I had Seonaid with me, and she almost jumped out of her skin. For a moment I thought they'd really frightened her, until she started to laugh.'

Her husband grinned. 'Those must have been the Belgians,' he said.

'Who?' asked Paula.

'The Bastogne Drummers; they're a group from Belgium and they're over to play at the Pope's Murrayfield rally next week.'

'What a strange choice,' Sarah remarked. 'Whose idea was that?'

'Pope John the Twenty-fifth's idea; he asked for them. Monsignor de Matteo told me he'd heard them on a visit to Belgium.'

'He could have been on a trip to Holland and he'd still have heard them. They go off with quite a bang.' She glanced up at the waitress who had come to take their dinner orders. 'I'll start with the smoked fillet of beef, please.'

They placed their orders and talked quietly, the two women and the three men developing their own conversations, until they were called upstairs to the dining room. They were in the hallway when Sarah put a hand to her side, to the pocket of her cream-coloured jacket. 'Sorry,' she said, 'that's my phone, trembling away. I know it's anti-social, but I always like to be contactable for Trish. You all go up, I'll take it in the ladies' lounge.'

She walked through to another part of the building, while Bob led the way to their table, and seated the three guests. Sarah rejoined them in less than two minutes. He looked at her, a question in his eyes.

'The kids are fine,' she told him quickly. 'That was business. The police in Haddington want me to do an autopsy tomorrow in Roodlands Hospital.' McGuire's head turned towards her also. 'No, it's not suspicious. The doctor's certified it as a heart-attack, but it was unattended, so they need a post mortem. Ironically, it's one of those Belgians. I wouldn't be surprised if those muskets scared him to death!'

Thirty-two

'Are you pleased to be handing an empty pending tray to Mary Chambers?'

'I thought we said no job talk. Come on, bring your glass next door. We're finished here.' Maggie stood up from the table; it was past ten o'clock and the last of the coffee with which they had finished dinner was cold in the cups.

'Let me help you clear up first,' he offered, but she shook her head firmly.

'Later. You're a tidiness freak, DI Steele, that's your problem. Anyway, I never use anything I can't shove straight into the dishwasher.'

He followed her through to her living room. 'Is it too warm in here?' she asked. The coal-effect gas fire was lit and the curtains were drawn against the cold night outside.

Stevie plucked at his shirtsleeve. 'Not for me. I'm fine.'

'That's nice,' she said. 'What's that wee logo? Ralph Lauren?'

'Yeah. Polo. I'm a sucker for designer labels.'

'You and me both.' She looked down at the dark sheen of her blouse and skirt. 'DKNY, this is.' She sat on the sofa, which faced the silent television. Her companion headed towards the armchair, until she stopped him. 'No,' she said. 'Put some music on, and come and sit beside me.'

He moved over to the music centre on a shelving unit and looked at the CDs racked beside it. 'What do you like?'

'You choose.'

They were neatly filed, the artists listed in alphabetical order. He scanned through them almost to the end until he found *Fulfillingness First Finale* by Stevie Wonder, and put it on. 'Do you know,' he asked her, as he joined her on the settee, 'that album is thirty years old? It's been around for most of our lives and yet it still sounds better than most of the stuff that's churned out today.'

'The seventies was a pretty good decade,' Maggie replied. 'I mean, look at us; we're both its products . . . more or less.' She settled back into the lush upholstery, warming her short-stemmed wine glass between her breasts. She had drunk more with their meal than was her norm, but Stevie had reasoned that she was at home, and that it was, after all, a celebration of sorts. He had not stinted himself either; he had come by taxi and planned to go home the same way.

She smiled up at him. 'Thanks, Stevie,' she said quietly.

'What for?'

'For being a good copper, a good colleague, a good bloke, a good friend. Even today, it can be difficult for a woman at my rank in the police. Having you around always made me feel more comfortable. You may not have known it, but you were my shield against the George Regans of the world.'

He chuckled. 'Good old dependable Stevie, eh? Is that how people really see me?'

'Most of them. They trust you. They know that they can take a chance on telling you stuff, and that you'll keep it to yourself; but more than that, you'll know the right thing to say to them.' She drained her glass, then reached down for the bottle, the second of the Viña Hermina Riojas that he had brought with him, and that she had brought through from the table, and refilled it. 'Here,' she said, 'let me see to yours.' He did as she asked, and she topped him up.

'It's not just the women, either,' she told him. 'Nobody thinks you're a wuss, if that's bothering you. They know you're a hard bastard when you have to be. You've got old MCP Regan taped, and young Tarvil looks on you as a sort of role model.'

'You mean like I look on you?' he murmured.

'Are you serious?'

'Absolutely.'

'You're not taking the piss?'

'Mags, you are exactly the police officer I want to be. I think it's a fucking shame you have to leave CID, but I can see why you have to.'

'My ex, do you mean?'

'No I didn't, actually, but I can see where that could be a consideration.'

'Mmm. Me too. Do you know what he's doing tonight, by the way?'

He grinned. 'Surprise me.'

'He's having dinner at Gullane Golf Club, with the DCC

and Sarah, and our American visitor . . .' she paused '. . . and Paula.'

Stevie whistled. 'Now that is a surprise.'

Maggie shifted in her seat; as she did so, the top button of her DKNY blouse popped open, and he caught a glimpse of black bra beneath. 'Yup,' she murmured, 'Ms Viareggio's been accepted into polite society. Across the table from Dr Sarah, no less.'

'Does that upset you?'

'Not a bit, not any more at least. Shit, not that it ever did bother me much. Why? Does it upset you?'

Stevie blinked, then looked into his glass. 'What, Paula, you mean? She and I have been history for a while now. When we were seeing each other, I always knew I was filling in for someone; I just didn't know who it was, not then. After a while, I'd had enough of it.'

'Is she a good lay, then?'

He gasped. 'That's a hell of a thing to ask me; you don't expect an answer, do you?'

'Not if you're too much of a gentleman, which I suppose you are. Anyway, she's bound to be better than me.' He said nothing; he sipped his wine, and looked away. She reached out and touched his chin, to turn him back towards her. 'Sorry, Stevie, that was a stupid thing to say. I've embarrassed you.'

'No, you haven't. It's just . . .' He sighed, deeper than she had ever heard from him. 'Mags, you're not the first woman to pour her heart out to me this week. It should be great for my ego, but somehow it isn't.'

'I thought you'd love that. You a single bloke, and having it laid on a plate for you; what more could you want?'

'It wasn't like that.'

'Oh no?'

'Well, maybe it was, but the important thing is that I didn't eat any.'

'But it might be on the menu again?'

'It might, and that's what's worrying me.'

She nestled into him; if she was aware that her blouse had opened wider, she ignored it.

'Why? Are you afraid you'll be too hungry next time to pass it up?'

'Something like that. She's a very attractive woman.'

'So?'

'So everything would be wrong about it. But more than that, Mags; it would be bloody dangerous.'

She looked up at him. She blinked, then her eyes widened in surprise. 'When I asked you earlier about being upset,' she whispered, 'at first it wasn't Mario and Paula you thought I meant, was it?'

'I'm saying nothing.'

'You don't have to.'

'I feel as if I'm heading for trouble, Mags,' he said hoarsely.

She emptied her glass and let it roll on to the floor. 'That is something I cannot allow.' Her arm came up and round his neck, she drew him down to her and kissed him, holding nothing back. 'Come here, baby,' she murmured, 'where it's safe. My transfer's come through, remember.'

'Hey,' Stevie whispered. 'Are you taking pity on me?'

'No. I'm trying to make you a better offer. Or would you rather I didn't?'

'Are you crazy?' he asked, grinning.

In a single supple movement she was on her feet, pulling him up after her. He followed where she led, upstairs and into her bedroom. He glanced around; there was something austere about it, it bore the mark of her, and her alone. She began to unbutton his shirt, as he flipped open the remaining buttons of her blouse, and reached behind her for the catch of her skirt.

'I want you to know,' she told him, when they were naked, 'that although I've had a few drinks, I am very frightened, and I really wasn't kidding when I said that I'm no good at this.'

He reached down, flipped back the duvet, and slid into bed, pulling her after him. 'Show me,' he said, with a soft laugh in his voice.

'What do you mean?'

'I mean,' he answered, 'show me what it is you've been doing wrong.'

He lay back and she rolled alongside him, reaching down for him: he kissed her softly, on the lips and on each breast. They lay, fondling each other, until, to her surprise, she became moist; even then, though, he allowed her to control every step of what was happening. When, finally, she mustered all her courage and drew him into her, although she trembled, she felt no fear, no revulsion, none of the self-loathing that she had come to associate with sex. As she moved on top of him, and as he moved within her, what she felt most of all was peace, absolution and utter release.

No waves crashed on an imaginary beach, she had no shuddering, screaming orgasm, but as he spent himself, she experienced a brief, delightful climax, the very first of her life.

'Couldn't see a hell of a lot wrong with that,' he murmured into her ear, when it was over.

She lifted her head from his chest and smiled down at him. 'Thanks,' she whispered.

He laughed softly, contented. 'Shouldn't I be thanking you?'

'If you like, you can. But my thanks are different. They're great big thanks, as big as I can make them.'

'Why's that?'

She slid down from him, settling in the embrace of his left arm. 'Because of this,' she told him. 'When we waken tomorrow morning . . . both of us right here, I hope . . . you'll still be the same person you were before we climbed those stairs. But I won't. I'll be different; I'll feel like a proper woman, in a way I never thought I could.'

'What's your story, Maggie love?' he asked.

She laid a hand on his chest, tweaking its hair with her fingers. 'Some day, if this turns out to be anything more than a one-night stand, I might tell you. Or maybe I'll discover that I've forgotten it completely, and I won't.' She kissed him on the cheek, then nibbled his earlobe, gently. 'For now, though,' she whispered, 'let's concentrate on finding out if there's any more where that came from.'

Thirty-three

Sarah could have done the autopsy at Roodlands, the local hospital at Haddington, as the police had asked, but she preferred to use the new facilities at Little France, and so she asked for the body to be transferred there from the local undertaker's premises to which it had been taken.

As she drove there she was thankful that Mawhinney had declined Bob's invitation back to their house for a nightcap. Even on routine assignments she liked to work with a totally clear head.

The late Belgian, whose name had been Bartholemy Lebeau, was waiting for her on the table when she arrived. Joseph, the technician who would assist her, had him ready for examination, his head propped at an angle on a wedge.

She gave the cadaver a cursory examination, as she picked up the notes of the GP who had certified the death, and those of the police officers who had been called to the scene as a matter of routine. Like many victims of sudden death, he looked serene, as if he had simply gone to sleep. The lips were blue, but there were no other outward signs of distress. Clearly, Monsieur Lebeau had been overcome very quickly.

She glanced through the notes. The deceased was male, aged sixty-two; he was not grossly obese. In fact he had been weighed on his delivery to the mortuary and had been found to be around the average weight for a man of his height and age.

He, Colonel Malou and other members of the party had been billeted at the home of a British Legion member, a farmer with a large house near a hamlet called Bolton. They had been preparing to dine with their host and hostess, and Lebeau had decided that he would freshen up first. He had gone into the guest bathroom; when he had failed to emerge after fifteen minutes, the colonel had knocked on the door, to give him, he thought, the 'hurry up' sign. There had been no reply; when Malou had opened the door, he had found his friend lifeless on the floor.

Dr Lezinski, the emergency-service doctor who had responded to the call, had examined the body. Naturally she had looked for various options. She had eliminated cerebral haemorrhage as a likely cause, and had come to the conclusion that in view of the man's age, the drinking habits described by his companion, and the fact that he was a lifelong smoker, death had been due, subject to confirmation by post-mortem examination, to myocardial infarction.

'And you're almost certainly right,' Sarah murmured. She knew Jean Lezinski to be an experienced and very capable GP.

She put a tape into the recorder as usual, but before switching it on, she gave the body a quick external examination. There were no marks, no bruising from a fall that might have contributed to his death, nothing out of the ordinary, apart from an old scar on his upper right leg and another on his lower abdomen, almost certainly the result of an appendectomy. She pulled back his eyelids. The eyeballs were milky, and heavily bloodshot. She turned back his top lip. The remaining teeth, about half of the set God gave him, she estimated, were discoloured with age, coffee and tobacco, but they had been well looked after. On impulse she pulled the lip further back, and frowned. The gums showed signs of a furious irritation, a vivid rash. 'What the hell is this?' she murmured.

'Joseph,' she called out, 'would you pass me a torch, please, then hold the lips back for me.' The technician handed her a penlight and then did as she had instructed. She shone the light into the dead man's mouth. The rash was widespread.

'What do you see, Doctor?' the young man asked.

'I don't know,' she replied. She picked up Dr Lezinski's report and read through it again. 'I've got to speak to her,' she said aloud. She knew the medical emergency service number off by heart; she went over to the wall phone, found an outside line and dialled it. 'This is Dr Sarah Grace,' she told the operator. 'I'm in the mortuary at Little France, and I need to speak to Jean Lezinski, urgently. You've got her ex-directory there, I know. Either give it to me, or get hold of her and have her call me here at once. I'm on . . .' She looked for the extension number on the phone and read it out. 'Do it now, okay.'

She hung up and waited. 'What are you thinking?' Joseph asked.

'That rash on the gums, it's so bad that he must have been

taking some medication for it. I have to cover the possibility that there might have been a rare and fatal reaction with something he ingested that day. I'd rather talk to the certifying doctor before I look inside him, in case there's something she forgot to include in the report. It looks like an open and shut coronary case, and Jean would have had no reason to look in the man's mouth.'

She waited by the phone; after a couple of minutes, it rang.

'Jean,' Sarah began, 'thanks for calling. I'm looking at your Belgian. He exhibits what seems to have been a pretty severe mouth infection. Did you notice any medication lying around when you examined him?'

'No,' the GP replied. 'Nothing at all. As a matter of fact, when he had his fatal collapse, he was cleaning his teeth. I asked his friend if he was on any drug treatment. The poor chap was very upset, but he was coherent enough to tell me that he hadn't been. Why are you asking, Sarah?'

'I don't know for sure. It's just that this rash is very severe. In fact if he was brushing his teeth and he strayed on to his gums it might have been damn painful.'

'Not so painful as to shock him into a cardiac arrest, though.'

'Hardly. Jean, thanks. I won't keep you any longer.'

She hung up, frowning. 'Dr Lezinski says he was cleaning his teeth when he died,' she told the technician. 'There's no sign of any residual paste in the mouth.'

'The body's been prepared by the undertaker.'

'That was kind of him, he should know better than to do

anything to an autopsy subject. Let's get on with it, Joseph. Take a couple of photographs as he is, then I'll go straight into the heart.' She picked up her scalpel, as her assistant reached for his camera.

Thirty-four

'You got those morning-after blues, Stevie?' asked Maggie, as she looked at him across the kitchen table. 'You were miles away there.'

He grinned, then glanced at his watch. 'Just for starters, it's afternoon now, and no, I don't have any sort of blues. I was just thinking, that's all, about where we go from here.'

She smiled back at him. 'We don't have to think about that now, do we?' They had wakened together at around nine, after the best night's sleep that Maggie could recall in her recent past. After they had proved to each other that what had happened the night before had been no fluke, they had half dozed again, listening to Steve Wright on the radio and enjoying the peace of the Sunday morning. Eventually they had risen, showered together, then dressed, and Stevie had gone to the nearest Scotmid store to buy rolls, bacon, eggs, milk and a selection of newspapers. He had brought back the *Sunday Post* and *Scotland on Sunday*, Maggie had noticed, classic signs of a conventional Scottish upbringing.

'Nah,' he replied, 'you're right, we don't. It's just that I'm a compulsive thinker.'

'Well, since you can't help yourself, where do you want to go from here?'

'Back to my place.'

'Have you had enough of me?'

'Not nearly. I was hoping that you'd come with me in fact, and that we'd spend the day together.'

'I'd love to . . . except that you're forgetting one thing, typical CID guy that you are. There's a rugby international today; Murrayfield's in my area. Brian Mackie's team is providing operational support, and since I'm in a transitional role, so to speak, he's in command. Still, as the new divisional commander I've got to put in an appearance.'

'What, uniform, cap and everything?'

'The full bloody regalia; it's in my wardrobe, with the new badges sewn on already.'

'I'll come with you, in that case. You watch the crowd, I'll watch the game.'

She laughed. 'And nobody would notice?'

'Am I going to embarrass you?' he asked her. 'Is that how it's going to be? Because if I am, I'll ask for a transfer.'

'Don't be daft. It's just that it's my first day in the new job. But does that answer our original question? Where do we go?'

'I want to go forward,' he said, 'with you. I don't go in for one-night stands, Maggie; it's not my style, any more than I think it's yours.'

'What about the competition?'

'You don't have any.'

'Are you sure? What if that offer's repeated?'

'It'll be turned down, politely; but I plan never to get into a situation where it could be. That's me, though. What do you want?'

She rose from her seat, walked round the table, and stood in front of him, taking both of his hands in hers. 'Listen, Stevie,' she said, 'last night I began to put behind me things that have been troubling me for, oh, so many years. This morning, I can look forward to a nice, happy relationship, and that, for me, is wonderful. I don't need to look too far ahead; for now I just want you to keep on making me happy.'

He drew her down to sit on his knee, and kissed her. 'Snap!' he whispered.

'Good. So this is what I propose we do today. I take you home, and I go to work. You watch New Zealand cuff Scotland on telly, then after the game I'll come back to your place, and we'll get cosy. Does that sound okay?'

Stevie grinned. 'Sure, as long as you bring your uniform for tomorrow, your toothbrush and your girlie stuff.'

She jumped to her feet. 'All of that shall be done,' she promised. 'Now you catch up with "Oor Wullie" in the *Sunday Post*, and I'll get myself ready for action.'

She headed for the stairs. He was still smiling as he cleared the brunch table and stowed away the crockery and cutlery in the dishwasher. He almost laughed out loud at the cartoon section of the famous Dundee Sunday tabloid that had been a part of his life since boyhood. When his mobile sounded on the work-top, at first it was no more to him than background noise.

He reached out, picked it up and pressed the green button. 'Sir,' said an earnest voice. 'It's DC Singh here.'

'Hi, Tarvil, what's hit the fan this time?'

'Nothing, sir, nothing major at any rate; I've had a call from Mrs Whetstone, the widow of that bloke that topped himself. She was looking for you. She said that her son's just arrived home from the States, and that she'd like you to talk to him.'

Steele sighed. 'Today?'

'No, sir, it's okay,' the young detective constable exclaimed hastily. 'She said that the lad's knackered after the flight and that she's made him go off to his bed. She's asking if you could see him tomorrow morning.'

'That's not so bad,' said the DI, with relief. 'I've got to see Superintendent Chambers at nine tomorrow morning, but ten thirty should be fine. Call her back, Tarvil, and tell her that. I don't know what I'm expected to say to the boy, though. His dad strung himself up and that's it. Even I believe that now.'

Thirty-five

James Andrew Skinner had few favourites in his simple, uncomplicated young life. He loved his parents to equal degrees, if infinity can encompass the concept of equality. He looked up to his older brother, admiring rather than envying his skill on his computer, and taking no advantage of Mark's lack of co-ordination in the ball games they played. He worshipped the ground his younger sister crawled on, diverting attention whenever he could when her mischief seemed to be heading her towards trouble, and always sharing the blame when she found it.

Yet whenever Alex came to visit, his heart always seemed just a shade bigger in his chest. He kept a special place there for her; she wasn't like anyone else. He knew that she was his sister, like Seonaid, yet she seemed to be almost as old as his mum. He had asked her about this constantly in his nursery years, and she had told him that she had had a different mother, who had gone away, although Dad was her father too, as he was his.

She had arrived that morning, in her funny little car with the round roof that folded back in the summer, just after Mum had gone to work . . . he knew that his mother was a sort of scientist . . . and after Dad had gone off to the golf club for what he called a 'bounce game', with his three pals, Ken, Bobby and Eric. Jazz assumed that they would be using softer golf balls than usual.

To him, Alex shone with her own special light; if he had only known it, their father saw her in exactly the same way. She seemed to smile all the time, and she talked almost as much. She was important, like his mum and dad, a solicitor . . . Jazz never called her a lawyer . . . and had a big job in Edinburgh. She always brought presents too, whenever she came to see her brothers and sister. That morning she had arrived with a doll for Seonaid, a brand new WWE computer game for Mark and a football DVD for Jazz, with all the goals from that summer's European championship, which they watched together. Alex liked football just as much as he did; that was another reason for him to love her, had he needed one.

'What do you do, Alex?' he asked her, after the winning goal in the final had been slammed into the net, the champions had celebrated, and the losers had cried . . . James Andrew thought they had looked really silly.

She gazed down at him, amused, as they sat cross-legged, facing each other on the living-room floor. 'What do you mean, wee brother, what do I do?'

'In your office, where you solicit.'

She gave a really loud laugh at that, and he joined in, pleased that he had amused her. 'We don't use that verb, Jazz,' she told him. 'We practise.'

'You mean so you'll get even better at it?'

'If you like.'

'So what do you practise at?'

'There's all sorts of law. There are solicitors who do nothing but family law, that's buying and selling houses for people, and personal stuff like that. Then there are others who do nothing but criminal law, that's appearing in court to defend the bad guys that Dad and Uncle Andy and Uncle Neil catch.'

'What do you mean, to defend them?'

'When they're put on trial, they don't always admit that they did it. If that happens there are people who have to decide whether they did it or not; they're called a jury, and lawyers have to try to show them what really happened.'

'Like that woman in Judge John Deed, in the funny wig?'

'Exactly. As well as all of those, there are corporate solicitors . . .'

'Copperate? Something like Dad, d'you mean?'

She shook her head, stifling a smile. 'No,' she replied. 'I said "cor-por-ate"; that's what I am. We work with businesses, making sure that the things they do are in accordance with the law, helping them with takeover bids, and big stuff like that.'

'Do you work with famous people?'

'Sometimes.'

'Like who?'

'I'm not allowed to say; our clients are confidential.'

'What does that mean?'

'Private.'

'Secret?'

'Sort of.'

'I think I'll be a solicitor.'

'Not a policeman?'

James Andrew shook his head. 'Dad doesn't want me to be a policeman.'

'He didn't want me to be one either when I was growing up. Dads never want their kids to be what they are . . . unless they're lawyers. You know, both your granddads were lawyers, and they were both disappointed when Dad and your mum decided to do other things. Come on, tell me. Do you really want to be a policeman?'

He nodded, with a smile that was just between them. 'Yes,' he said. 'Unless I'm a sort of a scientist like Mum.'

She laughed. 'You've got plenty of time to decide, don't worry too much about it yet.'

Jazz smiled up at her; sometimes his facial expressions were so much like those of their father that she could hardly believe it. 'I'm not worried,' he told her. 'Alex,' he continued quickly, 'you know when your mum went away?'

She felt herself frown, wondering what was coming. 'Yes,' she answered hesitantly.

'Did she go away like Granddad and Grandma Grace went away?'

Alex nodded. 'Yes. She died. I was just a wee girl at the time; even younger then than you are now.'

James Andrew had no concept of the mechanics of death; all he knew was that it made the people who weren't dead very sad, and as he looked at his sister, he realised that sometimes that sadness never went away. 'I'm sorry,' he whispered, and reached his hand out to her.

She was saved by the bell, saved from making a sap of herself by having her kid brother move her to tears. Across the room, the phone on the sideboard rang out its loud trembling tune. She jumped to her feet, but she was beaten to it. The boy picked up the handset; 'James Andrew Skinner,' he answered, as he had been taught.

'Jazz.' He smiled when he heard his mother's voice. 'Is Dad back yet?'

'No, not yet. Alex is here, though.'

'Good, put her on, please.'

He handed the phone up to his sister, who had guessed by his tone who was on the line. 'Sarah? Hi. Wassup?'

'I need to speak to Bob, and it's kind of urgent. I'm at the new Royal, doing what was supposed to be a routine autopsy, only it's not. Normally I'd call the divisional CID office, but there's a restructuring going on, and I don't know who to ask for.'

'Leave it with me. I'll phone the club. If he's in the bar, I'll have him call your mobile. If he's not in yet, I'll ask the steward . . .' As she spoke, she heard a door open. 'Hold on, that might be him now.' She put a hand over the mouthpiece. 'Pops!' she called out, and in seconds he was there, his hair ruffled and his face still red from the November chill.

She held out the phone. 'Sarah.'

'Hi, love. What is it? You want me to hold lunch for you after all?'

'If only. Bob, this dead Belgian. This is no simple coronary; apart from a rather abused liver there was nothing wrong with this guy until the moment he died. His heart, his lungs,

241

everything else was in fine working order. Tissue tests will have to be run but I don't need them. This man was poisoned and I'm damn certain I know how it was administered. I need to know which officer in your great organisation I should inform about this.'

'At this moment, love, you're talking to him. You wait there; I'll be with you directly.'

Thirty-six

Brian Mackie's chief superintendent's uniform was still new; he looked as awkward in it as Maggie Rose felt in hers. The strangest part of it was the peaked, braided cap, which looked uncomfortable and out of place on his domed head.

'Hello there,' she called out as she closed the door of the police command room behind her.

Mackie's head and those of the two inspectors who were with him turned towards her. 'Maggie,' he exclaimed, 'I didn't expect to see you today.'

'Sure you did, Brian.' She laughed.

'Yes, well,' he admitted, 'maybe I'd have been surprised if you hadn't put in an appearance.'

'How's everything going?'

'No problems to speak of, although they've just had a small incident near the east turnstiles. One of the civilian security guys took it upon himself to try to body-search a member of the public for concealed alcohol, and actually laid hands on him. The man took exception to it, shoved him away and called a constable; rightly so, for the security fellow was absolutely reeking of drink himself.'

'What did you do with him?'

'I told the officer on the scene to arrest him, and to note the address of the complainer, so that we can take a statement later. I'm of a mind to charge him with assault; I won't have these people behaving like that.' He smiled. 'Apart from that it's just another day at the office. These events are not quite like the Hearts–Hibs derby games. They attract just as many prats, but a different sort, if you know what I mean, plus there's never any aggro between the rival supporters. The main problem we have is with pickpockets. They've been known to work in organised groups on days like this; I think they see all these half-cut Watsonians and Academicals as easy game.'

'Can that not be a bit risky?'

'It certainly can,' Mackie agreed. 'At the last match, a couple of weeks ago, one of them picked the wrong pocket and got his jaw broken.'

'What did you do about that?'

'I'd have charged them both, but the pickpocket wouldn't make a complaint, so only he got done. A pity in a way; the lad involved was a judge's son. That would have been fun had it come to court.'

Rose frowned. 'The judge wasn't Lord Mendelton, was he?'

'As a matter of fact he was. Why do you ask?'

'Because his son's car was torched outside his house last week. George Regan's still looking for the guy that did it. I'll pass that on to Mary when I see her on Monday.'

'Be my guest,' said Mackie. He led her over to the window of the command room, and together they looked out across the great bowl of the Scottish Rugby Union's national stadium. With thirty minutes remaining until the scheduled kick-off time, it was less than half full; on the field a pipe band was playing and the New Zealand squad, massive in black tracksuits, was warming up.

'It won't look like this in a few days,' Rose murmured, 'when the Pope comes here. I am more than happy that you'll be in charge of that one.'

'Cheers, pal,' her colleague grunted. 'As you say, the stadium will look a bit different then,' he told her, pointing out on to the field. 'The main platform will be on the pitch, just beyond the centre spot.'

'What's the programme?'

'Let's go outside and I'll take you through it.'

The two chief superintendents left the room and walked down the long staggered stairway that led, eventually, into the tunnel that would be used by the players in twenty minutes or so. As they stepped out of the huge west stand, on to the green, white-laned synthetic running track, the purpose of which was one of the great unsolved mysteries of Scottish sport, Mackie pointed towards the vehicle entrance to their left.

'It's relatively simple,' he said. 'The papal convoy, the glass bubble thing in front, and limos behind, will enter through there, and drive up to the platform. The youngsters will be in the west, north and south stands; the east won't be used. His Holiness will get out and will be received at the foot of the steps by the Prime Minister, the First Minister and Lord Provost . . . if they don't fall out over the order of precedence. Then they'll all mount the steps where some other people will be presented, the three wives of course, then the deputy First Minister and his wife, then the Justice Minister and her partner, then the Moderator of the Church of Scotland and his wife, and finally the chief and Lady Proud.'

Maggie was surprised by the last-named dignitary. 'It's not like him to put himself forward.'

'The Pope insisted,' Mackie told her. 'They're old friends. After all the introductions,' he went on, 'there'll be the entertainment; the bands, the dancers and the singers. Once that part of the programme's complete, they'll all line up, and the Pope, the Prime Minister and the First Minister will come down from the platform and review them.'

'All of them?'

'Every last one. His Holiness wants to bless them all, personally. Once that's done, he goes back up on stage and says mass, preaches a sermon, and closes the rally.'

'At which point,' said a voice behind them, 'you all breathe hearty sighs of relief and head for the Roseburn Bar.'

They turned to see Mario McGuire behind them, looking even more solid than usual in a sheepskin-lined bomber jacket, flanked by Neil McIlhenney and Colin Mawhinney.

'We should be so lucky,' said Mackie.

'It'll be a cakewalk, Brian, don't you worry.' He smiled at Maggie in her uniform. 'Suits you, ma'am,' he chuckled.

She beamed back at him. 'So does yours. I can just see you smoothing around the pubs in Leith in that, making your ominous presence felt.'

They turned and headed back towards the tunnel. 'I wasn't

kidding,' he said. 'You really do have a spring in your step in your nice blue suit . . . or is it just you?'

'Maybe it is me. Maybe I've got what I want at last.'

'In that case, love, I'm happy for you. Just don't put all your cash on one horse.'

'Sometimes we have to, Mario. Your trouble is that you're scared to bet at all.'

Thirty-seven

If there was one place in the world that Bob Skinner preferred not to be it was an autopsy room. While in the main he missed the day-to-day contact with criminal investigation that his rank denied him, attendance as a witness at post-mortem examinations was a duty that he was happy to leave to others.

When he arrived in the suite in which his wife had been working, still in the sweater, shirt and slacks that he had worn for golf, the late Bartholemy Lebeau was still on the table . . . at least, those parts of him were that had not been consigned to slides and jars for transfer to the police laboratory at Howdenhall, and examination by a toxicologist. He tried not to look at him.

Sarah was sitting on a workbench, waiting for him, as he swept into the room. 'What have you got?' he asked her, before the door had even closed behind him.

'At first examination,' she began, 'I had some of the signs that I'm used to seeing in massive and instantaneous heart-attack victims, a little vein suffusion, mainly. It was only when I looked in the mouth that I saw something unusual, a violent irritation of the gums. After I opened him up and found no signs of cardiac malformation or malfunction, I went looking for something else, poisoning.'

'Any specific poison?'

'In a case like this, it's usually cyanide, because it's easy to administer and because it's lethal in very small doses. The man who first isolated hydrogen cyanide in the eighteenth century died when he broke a jar of the stuff and inhaled it. It kills by inhibiting the ability of tissues to metabolise oxygen, and in sufficient quantity it will shut down the brain in seconds. Its most famous application was in the suicide capsules that were given to secret operatives in wartime, and used by some of the Nazi high command, like Goering and Himmler, to beat the executioner to the punch, but there are many examples of its criminal use, most notoriously, the Tylenol case in the US, twenty years ago.'

'Can it happen accidentally?'

'In theory it can, but this man did not have a large quantity of apricot or peach stones in his stomach, and he hadn't eaten half a ton of chickpeas either. Forget accidental, Bob. Every case of cyanide poisoning I've heard of has involved the spiking of food . . . apart, that is, from the people who were executed in gas chambers . . . and apart from this one. I've sent the stomach contents for analysis, but there hardly were any. This man hadn't eaten for several hours before he died.'

'So how was it administered, if he didn't swallow the stuff?'

'Cyanide can be absorbed through the skin; the more tender the surface the quicker the absorption. That takes me back to the irritation of the subject's gums. When he died, he was brushing his teeth. You're looking for toothpaste, Bob. Take, say, three grams of hydrocyanic acid, about an ounce, and inject it into a tube; you have just laced it with sixty times the lethal dose. From the extent of the rash, and the rate of ingestion it implies, he'd have been dead before he'd even had time to wash his mouth out. Your friendly local undertaker did that for him but, fortunately, he left a trace between two of the back teeth. That's one of the samples that's going to Howdenhall.'

Sarah raised herself up and jumped down from her perch. 'I may have been a little over-confident about that banker suicide the other day, Bob, but if this guy wasn't murdered, I will quit and take up landscape gardening.'

Her husband threw back his head and let out a great sigh. 'Just what I fucking needed,' he exclaimed.

'It's not for you, is it? You delegate it to Division like everything else. I suppose that in this case it's East Lothian, since the death occurred in Haddington.'

'No way,' said Bob, emphatically. 'Greg Jay's getting nowhere near this one. This man was due to play before the Pope in a few days' time. That alone moves it on to a different level altogether, and makes it one I will definitely be keeping my hands on. But there's another consideration too, one that makes my blood run cold.'

He took his phone from the pocket of his slacks, and scrolled through his phone book until he found the number he was looking for, under P. He called it and waited, until a gruff voice answered. 'Dan? It's the DCC here. How's your Sunday been?'

'Okay,' said Pringle, cautiously, 'but I've a hell of a feeling . . .'

'You're right. It's going to get worse. If there's a saving grace, it's going to make you feel like a real detective again.' He smiled, wickedly. 'Do you know that my wife's a sort of old-fashioned fortune-teller? That's right; she can look at your entrails and tell how bad your luck's been. In this case she's been looking inside a deceased Belgian, Monsieur Lebeau, who was signed off as a coronary case. Sarah says that's wrong, though; she says he's a cyanide case, and that it couldn't have been accidental.'

'Jesus. Where did it happen?'

'Haddington, last night.'

'East Lothian? Greg Jay, then.'

'He's not even in post yet, Dan. I want you to head this investigation personally. This isn't your ordinary famous Belgian. This one's a bandsman, and he was due to be playing for the Pope this week, at his personal invitation. That makes it a wee bit sensitive. Pick your own team, but run it hands on and keep me in touch all the way.'

'Okay boss. I'll use my own guy, Ray Wilding, for a start. I don't suppose you'd lend me Jack McGurk, would you?'

'You're welcome. I was going to offer him anyway, as my eyes and ears.'

'Good. Where do we begin?'

'With the undertaker who moved the body from the house where he died. You need to talk to him and confirm that he washed residual toothpaste from the dead man's mouth. We reckon that's how the poison was administered. If he still has the wipes that he used, we'll need to get hold of them, as evidence and on safety grounds. You come to Little France to meet up with me, then we'll head for the house where the man died. I've got all the relevant notes here.'

He looked at the brief report of the attending constable, and read the address at which Lebeau had died. 'While we're doing that, get McGurk and Wilding out to the undertaker's to interview him and take possession of anything that might be relevant. We'll try to find the man's toothbrush and toothpaste, although we'll need to handle them with great care. The things are probably still lethal.'

'I'll bring evidence bags, then. I always keep some around.'

'You do that, and . . .' His voice tailed off.

'What are you thinking, Bob?' asked Pringle.

'I'm thinking what I've always been trained to think . . . the worst. This man was killed by poison administered through toothpaste. What if the tube that he bought wasn't the only one that was spiked? What if someone went into a chemist's or a supermarket and planted a whole shelf of the bloody things? As well as your evidence bags, Dan, maybe you should bring a panic button . . . just in case we need to press it.'

Thirty-eight

'So what did you think of your first rugby international, Colin?' Mario asked as they walked from the ground to his car, in the police park.

'Impressive,' the American admitted. 'Some of those guys make our gridiron players look like pussies. It's fast, it's continuous . . . we have time-outs in our game . . . and it is certainly rough. Did you ever play the game?'

'I played at school, and for a while after I left. I was a prop forward, but I was a bit light for the top class.'

'You were? Man, you're a brick shit-house.'

'Maybe, but in those days my top weight was a hundred kilos. You try shoving against a hundred and twenty kilos for eighty minutes; it does your back in. I did think for a while about switching to the back row, but I was too slow for that.'

As they approached his car, a silver Alfa Romeo sports hatchback, he pressed a remote control to unlock it. They climbed inside and headed for the exit, McGuire flashing his warrant card at the young constable on traffic control to pull rank shamelessly on the civilian vehicles coming from their area.

Soon they were at the Western Corner traffic lights, where he turned left, heading westwards until he came to Clermiston Road. 'It might seem like we're going to Glasgow,' he said, 'but this'll get us back quicker, I promise you.'

The journey back to the Malmaison took less than fifteen minutes. 'If we'd gone the straight way we'd never have got back,' said McGuire, 'and that would have been bad news. Paula's cooking tonight and we do not want to keep her waiting.'

'Man,' the American exclaimed, 'we had lunch at Neil's already. I can't let you feed me again.'

'Do you want to tell her that? 'Cause I sure as hell don't. Besides, what else are you going to do?'

'That really is too kind of you both,' said Mawhinney.

'Mince,' McGuire replied amiably, as he pulled up outside the waterfront hotel. 'You get yourself round to my place for six. We'll walk up to Paula's and maybe call in at the Wee Black Dug on the way. I want to check that place over.'

Thirty-nine

*O*ld *soldiers are the same the world over,* Skinner thought, as he looked at the Belgian veteran. Colonel Auguste Malou cut an imposing figure in his civilian clothes; he was a little overweight, but he had a crispness about him, a neatness that the Scot recognized as the mark of the military man.

Nonetheless, he was also extremely distressed; his moustache quivered as he spoke. 'It was terrible, gentlemen, most terrible,' he said, in accented English that was as precise as his dress. The shock of his friend's death was still written all over his face.

The two detectives had not told him the reason for their visit, but his host, Major Alfred Tubbs, another old soldier, turned farmer rather than bandsman, was worldly enough to know that a deputy chief constable and a detective chief superintendent did not turn out in the aftermath of an ordinary sudden death. He hovered in the background as Skinner spoke to Malou.

'I'm sure it was,' the DCC replied. 'As I understand it you found him, that was all.'

'That's right. Bart went to the bathroom to shave and freshen up for dinner . . . he had a very heavy beard and often shaved twice a day. He didn't come back quick and I wanted in there, so I went to give him a hurry-up call. He did not answer my call, so I went in and found him on the floor.'

'He had been brushing his teeth, I understand.'

Malou nodded. 'Yes. There was paste all around. At first I thought he was having a fit and was foaming at the mouth, but then I took a closer look. I've seen dead men before, sir. You can believe that. I've seen them blown up, seen them with their throats cut, seen them with bullets through their brains, but their eyes were all the same. When I saw Bart's eyes, I didn't need any lady doctor to tell me he was dead.'

Major Tubbs tapped Skinner on the shoulder. 'What's this about?' he asked quietly.

The deputy chief constable saw no need for further delay. Quietly he told both men about the outcome of the autopsy on Lebeau. Malou stared up at him, his ruddy face suddenly devoid of colour. Tubbs gasped. 'In my house? This happened in my house?'

'I'm afraid so. Technically it's subject to confirmation, and I've got our toxicologist working on tissue samples right now, but I can't afford to wait for that. There are all sorts of considerations, and the most pressing is that of public safety.' He looked at the Belgian. 'Colonel Malou, do you still have the toothpaste that Monsieur Lebeau used?'

'Yes,' he replied. 'It's still in the bathroom, and so is his toothbrush.'

'Thank your lucky stars you didn't use it yourself,' Dan Pringle exclaimed.

'I thank those stars that I have false teeth, sir,' the bandleader retorted.

'Do you know, by any chance,' asked Skinner, 'where your friend bought the toothpaste he used?'

Malou shook his grey head. 'I have no idea.'

'Then we'll have to look through his effects, to see if we can find a receipt. It's vital that we identify the source.' He turned back to Tubbs. 'Major, we have a forensic team on the way here. I'm afraid there's going to be a degree of disturbance to your household. You might like to explain to your wife what's happening. But please, ask her not to talk to anyone about it in the meantime. This has to be kept quiet until we have some answers; I cannot afford to start a public panic.'

Forty

When he opened the door, he was wearing an apron emblazoned with a naked, voluptuous female form, its breasts cupped in two large hands that appeared to come from behind.

Maggie laughed. 'Who the hell gave you that?' she exclaimed.

'Technically, my three-year-old nephew, last Christmas, but actually it was my sister-in-law.'

'And you wear it?'

'Of course I do ... but never outdoors,' he added, taking her overnight bag from her and following her up the short stairway into his hall. She had been there once before, briefly, when she had called in on him after shopping at the nearby Cameron Toll shopping centre.

'Nice day at the office?' he asked her, as she hung her hat on the stand in the corner.

'Entertaining. I didn't have anything to do really; Brian was in charge, and it all went fine. But please, let me get out of this uniform.'

Stevie showed the way upstairs, carrying her bag and depositing it on his bed. He leaned over her and kissed her softly. 'Make yourself at home.'

She grinned, and began to unbutton her jacket. 'I can do that,' she murmured. She nodded towards the open door of the *en suite*. 'Can I have a shower as well?'

'You do that too; there's plenty of towels. I have to get back to the sauce.'

'Oh, Stevie,' Maggie called after him as he turned to leave, 'there is just one thing, I sort of forgot to mention before. I'm not on the pill or anything. I don't think it's a high-risk time, but . . .'

His smile dazzled her. 'I thought about that,' he replied. 'Worry not.'

She undressed, arranging her uniform on a hanger she found in his wardrobe, then stepped into the bathroom. As the warm jets of the power shower pulsed over her, she found herself wondering whether she had ever felt so relaxed before.

He was stirring a large pot when she came into the big kitchen, concentrating so hard that he did not hear her as she came up behind him, her hair still damp, dressed in a sweatshirt, jeans and moccasins. She slipped her arms round his waist, pressing her unfettered breasts against his back. 'Can I do anything?' she asked.

'You're doing it,' he told her. 'I'm just about finished here; I'll give it an hour to cook gently then I'll do some rice. Go on through to the living room and put on some music; I'll be there in a minute or two.'

When he joined her, there was a CD on the player that,

although it was his, he failed to recognise. 'What's that?' he asked, trying to pin down the guitar riff.

'Blue City: Ry Cooder. He's one of my heroes, but I've never heard of that one.'

He located it in his mental filing cabinet. 'Ah, yes, that one. It's an obscure movie soundtrack album from the eighties, very good, only nobody went to the movie.' He slid down beside her on the couch and handed her a glass of white wine. 'What did you think of the game, then?' he asked her.

'I didn't watch it; I was being professional, and watching the crowd. I gather the result was as predicted, though.'

'Yeah,' he sighed, 'we'll never beat those guys.'

'That's what Mario always says. I saw him at Murrayfield, by the way; he gave me a blessing and a warning at the same time.'

Stevie's mouth fell open. 'You mean you told him?'

'Of course not. D'you think I walked up to him in my chief super's uniform and said, "Guess what? Stevie made me come and you never could"? Mind you,' she mused, 'I might as well have done. Mario can read me like a book. I'm sure he knew just from looking at me that something of that nature had happened.'

'What was the warning?'

'I think he told me not to trust you too much. I sort of told him that he didn't trust people enough.'

Stevie nudged her with his shoulder. 'You can, you know. Trust me, I mean.'

She kissed him. 'I wouldn't be here if I had any doubt about that, love.'

'Say that again?'

'What?'

'That word you just said.'

'Love?'

'That's the one. Did you mean it or was it just a casual familiarity, like?'

She put her head on his shoulder. He looked down at her, feeling the dampness of her russet-coloured hair through his T-shirt. 'I think I did. But what I feel most of all is comfort in a way I never have till now. It's taken me completely by surprise, and I can't tell you how good it feels, how good you make me feel.'

'You ready to tell me your story yet?'

'No,' she whispered, 'the time's not right. Let me enjoy this.'

'Whatever it is,' he told her, 'you needn't be afraid. There is nothing you could tell me about you that would make the slightest difference to the way I feel about you.'

'What? Not even my sex change?'

'They've made a bloody good job of it,' he murmured into her hair, 'that's all I can say, sir.'

She exploded into a laughter that was more natural and spontaneous than he had ever heard from her. He felt her shaking against him and he joined her in it, hugging her to him as Ry Cooder played a tender tune.

'I love your house, Stevie,' said Maggie, when they were both still once more. 'It's got real character.'

'Yeah, hasn't it? It's just a house, though: it's what happens within its walls that's really important.'

'I agree.' She kissed him again. 'I wish we could take tomorrow off work.'

'Me too; of all the bloody days, though. You making your debut as the big boss of Torphichen Place, and me being sized up by Mary Chambers.'

'Mary's already sized you up; she asked me about you on Friday.'

'What did you tell her?'

She shrugged. 'Aw, you know, that you were a solid, dependable plodder; a real *Sunday Post* reader who thinks that there truly is a Francis Gay.'

'But there is,' he protested. 'He rides shotgun on Santa's sleigh.'

'That's good. Mary'll be pleased to hear that, her being gay as well. If you really want to know what I told her, I said that she should let you run things for as long as it takes for her to get to know all the troops and to familiarise herself with the territory. That's what she plans to do.'

'Nice to know. I've had a word with Regan, by the way. I've told him that the first time I hear a gay joke in the office he'll be singing soprano. Actually,' he continued, 'I've got an outing planned for her tomorrow. I forgot to tell you, but I had a call earlier from Mrs Whetstone. She wants me to go and talk to her son tomorrow; explain to him personally what's happened. I thought I should take the new boss along, just in case there's any follow-up from the fiscal's office.'

Maggie patted his chest. 'Good thinking, Stevie boy,' she said. 'If there are any more waves to be made in that investigation, I wouldn't want them to splash on my new uniform.' She slid a hand under his shirt. 'And talking about making waves,' she murmured, 'how long have we got till that curry's ready?'

He grinned and slid an arm round her. 'As long as we need, love. As long as we need.'

Forty-one

'Sarah, this is excellent,' Dan Pringle mumbled, as he finished the last of his steak pie in the Skinners' dining room. 'It's good of you.'

'It's good of Alex,' she replied. 'She made it while her father and I were out creating mayhem.'

An hour earlier, the DCC and the head of CID had left DI Arthur Dorward's meticulous crime-scene officers poring over Major Tubbs's guest bathroom, and headed for Skinner's home.

They had briefed Sarah as soon as they had arrived. A toothbrush and a tube of combined tartar control and whitening-formula toothpaste had already been bagged and were on their way by car to the Howdenhall lab. No trace of a receipt had been found among Bartholemy Lebeau's effects, but the manufacturer had established from an examination of the tube's bar-code that it was part of a batch dispatched a week earlier to a pharmacist outlet in Newcastle.

'But that's terrible,' she had exclaimed. 'There could be little time-bombs ticking all over that area, just waiting to explode.'

'Seven of them to be exact. That consignment was opened and put on the shelves on Friday; they've made eight sales since then. But that's just the tip of it. Potentially, your bombs could be all over Britain. The rest of the batch has been pulled, and the shop's checking its till records to see if any of the customers used cards and can be traced. The manufacturer's implemented recall procedures for all shipments made up to seven days before the Tyneside lot and since. When they get them back they'll start to test for contamination, but if it's been done at random that'll be a massive job. As that begins, we're making public announcements on all television and radio news bulletins nationally. It'll scare people, but it can't be avoided. By the way, when did we last buy toothpaste?'

'Six weeks ago. I bought two big pump dispensers, one for us and one for the kids.' She shuddered. 'Brings it close to home, doesn't it?'

'No, love. It brings it right inside the house.'

Sarah was still grim-faced as they finished their meal. 'It doesn't bear thinking about, guys. Right now all over the country there could be people doing what we've just done, then going to brush their teeth and . . . Poof! It's horrible.'

'I know,' Bob agreed. 'But maybe if it was going to happen it would have happened already. If there had been a mass con-tamination, I'd have expected more than one incident by now.'

'Maybe there have been,' his wife pointed out. 'Lebeau's death was taken for a heart-attack at first, remember.'

'True, but you spotted the real cause within twenty-four hours. The worst case is that this is part of a national emergency;

the best . . . although not for Lebeau, I'll grant you . . . is that it's a one-off.'

'So, while the manufacturer and the retailers are doing their things, where do you go?'

'Tomorrow I go back to the office to bring the chief fully up to date, and to field calls from Tyneside and any other forces with information. Dan and his team go back to Haddington. We need to talk to more of those marching Belgians.'

Forty-two

It was solitary, in comparison to that of most of his fellow officers, and it was of necessity secretive; in addition to that Neil McIlhenney's job was one of the most stressful in the modern force. Heads of Special Branch at regional level were not especially high-ranking; his soon-to-be-formalised step up to detective chief inspector was as high as he would go in the post. However, the responsibilities they carried were awesome.

The quirks of history had conspired to make it so. The first great SB target had been the insidious spread of Communism, even if it was more imaginary than real across Britain. As it faded, it was replaced as top priority by the Irish threat, much more significant and, in England at least, much more deadly. Even if the bombers had never targeted Scotland there were historic undercurrents that required continuous vigilance from the country's secret policemen.

Ireland had not gone away . . . privately, McIlhenney and Skinner doubted that it ever would . . . but it had been overtaken by another danger. Outside the corridors of the CIA and MI6 headquarters, the threat posed by the fundamentalists of al Qaeda had been underrated, even after several incidents and a punitive strike against them by the Americans. But September Eleven had changed all that.

No single event, McIlhenney mused, as he drew his car to a halt outside the Malmaison Hotel, not even the assassinations of the Kennedys, or those of Sadat, King, three Gandhis, or Lennon had reached out and touched personally so many people. It was a particularly bitter truth for him that morning, as he was going to collect one of those on whom it had inflicted the greatest loss.

When he walked into the hotel's small reception area, the duty manager recognised him at once: he was not a man easily forgotten. 'Good morning, Mr McIlhenney,' he greeted him. 'Are you here for Mr Mawhinney?'

'Got it in one, Saeed. Will you call him for me, please?'

'I will, but I'm not sure that he's in. He hasn't been for breakfast yet, I know that; but the last couple of mornings he's got up early and gone for a walk first. Could be he's been and gone and I've just missed him. I'll call him.'

He picked up a phone, dialled Mawhinney's room and waited for a full minute before hanging up and shaking his head.

'Is his key there?' the detective asked.

'No, but that doesn't signify. It's a card thing and guests never leave them behind.'

'I'll go up anyway and knock on his door. Maybe he was in the shower when you called. What's his number?'

'One oh six.'

McIlhenney walked up a single flight of stairs and found

the room quickly. He knocked on the door, loudly, and called out, 'Morning call, Colin. You've got a nine-thirty appointment, remember.' He waited, with growing impatience, until finally he gave up and went back downstairs.

He sat in Reception for ten more minutes, grumbling to himself and checking his watch. 'This is a bit of a damn nuisance,' he muttered to himself, then took a decision. 'Saeed,' he called out, 'have you got a pass key?'

'Of course. You want to look in the room?'

'Just to be on the safe side, we'd better.' The two men climbed the stairs once more, and the manager unlocked the door to room 106. It was beautifully furnished, and immaculately serviced; its double bed in the centre of the room was made and, apart from a suitcase in a stand behind the door, there was nothing to indicate that it was even occupied.

McIlhenney frowned and took out his cell phone; he found McGuire's mobile number and called him. 'Yes,' his friend replied, unusually impatient, as if he had been disturbed.

'Mario, if I'm interrupting anything I'm sorry, but did Colin Mawhinney stop at your place last night?'

'No,' McGuire grunted. 'But neither did I. We were at Paula's for a meal. I stayed there, Colin left about ten to walk back to the Malmaison. Why? Is he not there?'

'No, the bugger's out. You sure he knew I was supposed to pick him up to take him to meet the minister?'

'Absolutely certain; I remember mentioning it to him.'

'Any chance he misunderstood?'

'None at all. I was speaking English at the time. I suppose

he might have forgotten, though. Best thing you can do is phone the minister's private secretary and ask her to call you if and when he turns up there. After that all you can do is wait there for a while and see if he comes back.'

'Maybe you could get some of your boys to check the saunas,' McIlhenney suggested. 'He's a single guy, after all; maybe he's gone for an early-morning massage.'

'No, Neil,' Mario replied. 'Not this man. Early-morning mass, maybe; massage, certainly not.'

Forty-three

It made Stevie Steele feel strange to see someone else sitting behind Maggie's desk, yet, given their life-changing weekend, it gave him less difficulty than might have been the case otherwise. They had wakened together for the second morning in succession, the difference being that this was a working day.

There had been no awkwardness, though. He had left the *en suite* bathroom to Maggie and had used the one downstairs to prepare himself for the day. He was not sure what Mary Chambers's style would be so he had selected one of his better suits, a white shirt and a plain, sober tie.

'Mmm, smart,' Maggie had said, eyeing him up as he came into the kitchen.

'You can talk, ma'am. Are you going to wear that uniform every day from now on?'

'Why? Does it make me look like an old frump?'

'Not in the slightest, honey. Does this make me look like a civil servant?'

She had grinned at that. 'It makes you look like an ambitious young DI who's out to make an impression on the new boss.'

'Am I overdoing it?'

'Not at all. She'll take that as a compliment.'

She had too. In fact, Detective Superintendent Mary Chambers had dressed much as he had for her first morning in the new rank, in a dark, almost formal trouser suit. Her plain, square early-forties face was adorned by a minimum of makeup, and her dark grey-flecked hair was cut short, but not severely so.

He had made for her office as soon as he had arrived at the station; he had given Maggie a five-minute head start before leaving Gordon Terrace, yet the unpredictability of the traffic flow had resulted in them driving into the car park as if they had travelled in convoy. Twenty minutes short of nine, but his new boss had been there, and for some time too, as the papers piled around her indicated.

'Let's sort out the ground rules, Inspector,' she said, as he settled into the chair opposite, the one from which he had looked at her predecessor so many times. 'I'm an informal operator, like Maggie, so between us it's Mary and Stevie, unless you've any problem with that.'

'Fine by me, boss.'

'Boss!' she grunted. 'I like that. It makes me sound like Fergie.'

'Which one?' he asked, and they both laughed, breaking any ice between them for good.

'Maggie's marked my card about the team. What's your take on them?'

Steele went through the divisional CID staff one by one, appraising each. He began with Tarvil Singh, but left George

Regan till last. It did not escape her. 'Will I have any bother with him?' she asked. 'I've heard that Dan Pringle's his role model.'

'George is all right; his views of women officers may sound non-PC, but in the main they're bullshit, for show. He likes to think of himself as a dinosaur, but actually he's reasonably warm-blooded. That makes him vulnerable to the image of him walking round the track at Tynecastle in a sergeant's uniform, and aware of the need to do everything he can to avoid that ever happening.'

'He can cope with having a female boss?'

'Sure.'

'One who lives with another woman?'

'Regan is many things, but he's not prejudiced. For example, he's coping fine with having a Sikh for a partner. He's also coping without having my size eleven up his arse, and he wants to keep it that way.'

'You've got a way with words, young Stevie. Now tell me, how am I going to get on with Dan Pringle? I've heard it said that Maggie's promotion wasn't his idea.'

Steele frowned. 'I doubt if Dan was even consulted. He's only got a couple of years left, at most; moving Mags, and you for that matter, was a strategic decision, and its effects will be felt after he's gone. Sometimes DCS Pringle feels as if he's been parked on a siding . . . and maybe he has. From time to time that makes him throw his weight about. The only advice I can give you on that is, when he's right listen to him, and when he's wrong bloody well tell him.'

'Thanks, Stevie, I'll bear that in mind. I won't have to worry about him for a day or two, though. He called me just before you came in to apologise for not being here to welcome me, but he's hands-on with this toothpaste crisis.'

The DI looked puzzled. 'What toothpaste crisis?'

'Where have you been for the last twelve hours?' Chambers exclaimed. 'A guy out in East Lothian was poisoned by toothpaste laced with cyanide. He bought it in Newcastle on Friday. The whole thing's gone national; there have been emergency announcements on the box and everything. The DCC's put Dan in charge of the investigation.'

'Mary, I haven't seen a news report or read a paper since yesterday lunchtime. Are we involved?'

'Not yet, and hopefully we won't be. They're hauling back all the toothpaste they can and testing it. As of this morning they haven't found any more spiked tubes, and there haven't been any other deaths. I imagine there are a lot of yellow teeth in Newcastle this morning, though.'

Steele grimaced. 'I'd rather not think about that.'

'Me neither. Let's just hope it's a one-off and they catch the nutter soon, well off our patch. And speaking of our patch, I've been reading the files on active and recent investigations. Anything you want to add to any of them?'

'As a matter of fact . . . Have you read the Whetstone file?' The new superintendent nodded. 'What's your take?'

'Same as everyone else's. The man topped himself in the light of potential exposure, and possibly also in the knowledge of fatal disease.'

'Yes. So now his son's arrived back from the States and his mother wants us to talk to him, to explain it to him, I suppose.'

'Is it our job to do that?'

Steele found himself wondering if her question was a test. 'Technically no, but I've always found that in this job I can make myself feel a bit better as a person by doing what's right, not just what's required. I'll go alone if you'd rather, but I thought you'd like to come.'

Mary Chambers smiled and rose from her chair. 'You thought right. I think you and I are going to get on, young Stevie; I can see now what the new chief super sees in you.'

He blinked, hard.

Forty-four

'Having a guest go AWOL in the middle of a carefully prepared programme is something that I did not need,' Bob Skinner growled to Sir James Proud, 'and certainly not this morning, of all bloody mornings.'

'There's no accounting for it, is there?' the silver-haired chief constable mused.

'What?'

'The unpredictability of the individual. I'd marked down Inspector Mawhinney as a remarkable young man; I got a feeling from him of absolute self-discipline, of someone who wasn't given to indulgence of any form.'

'McGuire says he isn't. He reckons we should be checking the churches to see if he's there. He says that there's an undercurrent of grief in the guy that goes straight to the death of his wife. He saw it happen, you know, Jimmy. He was looking up at the towers when the second plane hit the very floor that she was on.'

'Poor fellow; poor lass. It doesn't bear thinking about, does it, my friend? At least it would have been quick for her, though.'

'But not for Mawhinney. After all this time, and the lad's still suffering inside, so says McGuire. He's spent over a week with him now, and he's got to know him pretty well.'

'What do you propose to do about his absence?'

'I've put the word out already to all the Traffic cars to keep an eye out for him. That's all for now; he could still turn up on foot for his meeting with Aileen de Marco. He's not due there for another couple of minutes. If he hasn't shown up anywhere by this midday, though, I'll have to consider starting a wider search and informing NYPD that he's missing.'

'Could he simply have headed for home?'

'His plane ticket was still in a drawer in his room, under the Gideon Bible. His passport wasn't there, so in theory he might have, but without his clothes, his personal effects . . .'

'Maybe he had some bad news.'

'If he did, it was after he left Paula Viareggio's place. But it didn't reach him through the hotel, and he didn't have a cell phone.'

Sir James sighed. 'It's a mystery, right enough; but like most mysteries, we'll get to the bottom of it sooner or later, when he turns up. What about the real crisis, though? This toothpaste thing?'

Skinner looked at him, grim-faced. 'I was up most of the bloody night, you know, Jimmy. I couldn't sleep for thinking about what might be happening, or what might happen in the morning when the nation woke up and started brushing its teeth. But,' he reached out and patted the top of the chief's rosewood desk, 'touch wood, there have been no reported incidents, and every minute that passes without one takes us nearer safety. The other piece of good news is that the manufacturer has been testing recalled stock all night at regional labs, and so far they haven't come up with any more contaminated tubes.'

'What about our own tests?'

'Oh, they're conclusive enough,' the DCC muttered. 'The toxicologist confirmed Sarah's finding straight away, and as far as the toothpaste was concerned, testing showed that there was enough hydrogen cyanide in that tube to have killed the whole fucking band, never mind Monsieur Lebeau.'

'How was it spiked? Do we know?'

'It was probably injected with a hypodermic. That brand has a foil security tag under the cap that you have to remove before use. Put a fine needle through it and the victim would never notice . . . anything, ever again.'

The old chief constable blew out a breath. 'As you know, Bob, I've always been against capital punishment. But someone who could do that sort of thing indiscriminately . . . I tell you, it's a test of my principles.'

'Mine too, Jimmy, but let's hold on to them. Neither of us ever wants to see the black cap put on in our courts again.' He turned to leave. 'I'd better go and call Pringle, to see if he and the boys have made a start to interviewing those Belgians.'

He left by the side door and walked across the corridor to his own room, where he settled into his swivel chair and picked up the phone. However, instead of calling Pringle, he flicked through his index and punched in another number. As always, Lena McElhone answered on the third ring. 'Aileen de Marco's office,' she announced.

'Bob Skinner's office,' the DCC replied. 'Is the minister free?'

'She shouldn't be, but she is. Just a minute.'

In fact, he had to wait for only a few seconds before she put him through.

'Good morning, Bob,' said the new Justice Minister; there was a hint of annoyance in her voice.

'Lena dropped a subtle hint that I should apologise for standing you up,' he began, 'so I will. I'm sorry. My guy turned up to collect the American at his hotel as arranged, but there was no sign of him. I don't know where the hell he is. When he turns up he's going to wish he was back in Manhattan, I promise you. As a matter of fact, he's going to be on the first bloody plane back there. I really hope it hasn't inconvenienced you, Aileen.'

'It has, but I can hardly blame you for your guest's rudeness.'

'Thanks for taking it that way. Did you cancel other arrangements for him?'

'I'm supposed to have a formal meeting with the Lord President of the Court of Session. He wanted to do it at nine thirty, but I put him off because I was seeing your man.'

'He won't mind. Lord Murray isn't one of the more precious judges.'

'That's good, because it's important that he and I get on.' She paused. 'By the way, the department has arranged a visit to Shotts Prison for me a week on Friday. While I'm there I plan to have a chat with your friend Mr Plenderleith. I'm also having lunch with Mitchell Laidlaw today, at his office.'

Skinner grinned. 'You don't waste much time, do you?'

'No, I do not; which brings me to our meeting. How about dinner, tomorrow?'

'Fine by me. Where do you want to go?'

'Somewhere very discreet.'

'This is Edinburgh; discretion and this city are strangers to each other.'

'How about the Scottish Arts Club?'

'The place in Rutland Square? Are you a member?'

'No, I'm a part-time nude model. There's a studio on the top floor.' There was a silence, which she broke by laughing. 'Gotcha! Ministerial joke; of course I'm a member. I can arrange for dinner there; I've already checked. There are no other parties booked for tomorrow evening.'

'Sounds fine. What time?'

'Seven thirty. Could you pick me up from the office?'

'Sure; see you around quarter past.'

'Good. I'll have Lena confirm the booking. But Bob,' she added, with a light chuckle, 'you won't stand me up too, will you?'

Forty-five

'There are bits of Glasgow that look just like this,' said Detective Superintendent Chambers as she surveyed the big stone villas and semis, 'but they're damn hard to find.'

'Where do you live, Mary?' Steele asked.

'Ratcliffe Terrace; not far from you, actually.'

'You know where my place is?'

'Maggie mentioned it when she was briefing me. Funny thing; I drove past Gordon Terrace last night on my way back from the M and S food store at Fort Kinnaird and I could have sworn I saw her turning in there in her car.'

Steele took a deep breath. 'Listen . . .' he began.

She laughed. 'I wasn't spying on you, Stevie, honest. That's exactly how it happened, and if I can't add two and two, I apologise. But if you're sleeping with the chief super, it's as well I know. You needn't worry; nobody else will hear a word about it from me.'

'We're friends, Mary,' he offered, knowing as he spoke how lame he sounded.

'Sure you are. Listen, I don't mind . . . Christ, I'm the last person to concern myself about other people's relationships. But if you want some advice, and I mean the pair of you, don't be shy about it. It's not as if you're working together any more. You report to me and Pringle. She reports to Haggerty. Don't try to keep it quiet; I did that once myself, when Serena and I got together, and it was a big mistake.'

'I'll bear that in mind. I'll talk to Mags about it tonight.'

'Fine. It's off my agenda as of now.' She looked along the street. 'Which of these houses is theirs?'

'That one,' said Steele, drawing to a halt outside the Whetstone semi. He glanced at the car clock; it showed ten thirty-three, but he always kept it a couple of minutes fast.

As they stepped into the front garden, Virginia Whetstone was in the bay window; looking out for them, Steele guessed. She opened the front door as they approached it; she was dressed casually, her hair was swept back and she wore no makeup. She looked several years older than the woman the DI had first met only a few days before. 'Mr Steele,' she exclaimed. 'It's good of you to come.'

'Not at all,' he replied. 'This is my new boss, Detective Superintendent Chambers. Ms Rose has been promoted, with effect from today.'

'I'm not surprised,' Mrs Whetstone muttered. 'A very capable woman. Come in and meet Murphy.'

They followed her into the drawing room. For once the dog was not there; where he had lain, there stood a towering young man; at least six feet six, Steele guessed, even taller than Jack McGurk. His mother introduced the two detectives and he reached out and downwards to shake their hands. Glancing up at him, they saw dark circles under his eyes, odd in such a youthful face.

'I'm sorry I wasn't up for this yesterday,' he said, in a soft voice, which hinted at the faintest of American accents. 'But it was a hell of a flight, coming on top of a few days up in the mountains with my pals, with no sleep involved.'

'I'll make some coffee,' his mother announced. 'I don't think I want to hear the details again,' she added as she headed for the door.

Murphy Whetstone lowered himself into what had been his father's chair, and looked at the two officers as they sat on the sofa. 'Tell me,' he murmured. 'All of it, please. My mother couldn't bring herself to; she said I should hear it from you if I'm to believe it.'

'If you're ready,' Steele began. 'Your father was found in the Meadows, last Wednesday morning. He was hanging from a tree and he had been there all night. The weather was extremely foggy; that explains why nobody came upon him sooner. My first thought was that he had been attacked, since there was no obvious means by which he could have done it himself. As it transpired, there was an explanation for that.' He told the young man of the unhelpful intervention of Moash Glazier, and watched his face darken.

'The bastard actually stole my dad's coat off his body?' he exclaimed.

'I'm afraid so, and the steps that were lying underneath him. The guy's a professional thief. His saving grace was that he phoned in an anonymous tip-off to tell us about it.'

'It won't save him if I ever get my hands on him. I don't suppose you'd give me his name.'

'Not a chance.'

'Worth a try. I've got friends in the police, though; I'll be asking around.'

'Please don't do that,' Mary Chambers asked. 'Anyone who gave you information about him would be fired. Go on, Stevie.'

'Yes. Finding that ladder made suicide a possibility, Mr Whetstone; indeed, it made it the likeliest explanation. There are two things you should know. The first is that a post-mortem examination showed that your father was suffering from a type of lung tumour which almost invariably proves fatal. The second came to light when we visited the Scottish Farmers Bank. We were given a copy of a file that shows that your father set up a dummy account and diverted loan funds to an offshore bank account.'

The young man's face flushed as he shook his head. 'I don't believe that, and I never will. That is not my dad you're talking about; he was the most honourable man you'd ever meet.'

'I expected you to say that, and I understand. But these are the facts.' The DI recited, virtually word for word, the contents of the Bonspiel folder. When he had finished, he looked across at Murphy Whetstone, and saw that he was smiling.

'Do you actually believe that crap?' the young man asked.

'The procurator fiscal believes it; he's accepted our report. I'm sorry; I know that it's very difficult for you to take in, but those are the facts.'

'No, not facts; a load of nonsense actually. I'm sure that

there's been a fraud, and I'm sure that the bank's lost money, but it wasn't my father who did it. I am absolutely certain of that.'

'Why?' asked Mary Chambers, quietly.

'Are you a curler?'

'Pardon?'

'Do you curl? Do you play the roaring game?'

'No.'

'How about you, Inspector?'

'No, me neither.'

'Well, my father did, and so do I. And I can tell you one thing. If he was going to set up a dummy company to defraud the bank, he'd have set one up that wasn't an obvious con from the word go. In particular, he wouldn't have involved it in making stones out of Ailsa Craig granite. Any curler would tell you how bloody stupid that is.'

'So tell us,' said Steele, intrigued.

'Ailsa Craig curling stones are made by one firm and one firm alone. They're called Kay's, they're from Mauchline, in Ayrshire, and they have exclusive rights to Ailsa Craig granite. My dad knew all that. I'm telling you; even if he was bent he wouldn't have done that.'

The two detectives exchanged glances. 'But he signed the application off himself,' said Steele.

'Or someone else did and made it look like him. I know it, he wouldn't have done something as obviously phoney as that.'

'But would it matter?' asked Steele. 'If your father knew that he was terminally ill and intended to kill himself, he'd only care that the money was beyond the bank's recovery. He'd know the set-up was bound to be discovered after his death.'

'And did he know that? Had he consulted his GP?'

'No,' the inspector admitted, 'he hadn't.'

'There you are then,' the young man challenged.

'Very well,' said Mary Chambers. 'We'll look into it, Mr Whetstone. We'll go back to the bank and we'll insist on carrying out our own investigation of the alleged fraud. But from what I've read of the files in this matter, it'll take quite a bit to make us alter our view that your father committed suicide.'

Forty-six

Moash Glazier had deemed it wise to lie low for a few days. In particular, he had deemed it wise to stay out of Leith, in case someone spotted him and reported his presence in the area to Malky Gladsmuir.

He knew how unpopular he would be with the bar manager and had decided to give him time to recover from his visit from the CID and from his embarrassment over the coat that he had taken from him. The longer he delayed their inevitable meeting the more likely he was to escape a kicking. One thing was certain, though; never again would he be allowed a slate in the Wee Black Dug. In future it would have to be cash on the bar.

If anyone understood the meaning of the phrase 'cash economy', it was Moash Glazier. He kept his contact with the official world to a minimum; he had been given a National Insurance number once but he had no idea what it was, or what obligations it imposed on him. Moash wanted nothing to do with formal society. Somewhere he fitted into a chain of supply and demand, but he would have scoffed at the idea. He lived on what he stole and on the money realised by its sale, and that was that.

His lifestyle carried the hazard of imprisonment, but paradoxically it offered the priceless benefit of freedom from the drudgery that made him pity those ordinary straight people who went to work eight hours a day, five days a week. He was glad of their efforts, though. After all, who else filled the great lucky dip in which he delved for his living?

If he had been able to recognise it, though, he was trapped in a work cycle of his own. He had no bank account, no nest egg; he fed and watered himself on a day-to-day basis, and holidays were a luxury he could not afford. His close call in the Meadows had rattled him, and he had hidden away with his Granton woman over the weekend, but the cash he had raised from the mountain bike, the boots and the wee stepladder . . . which had not fallen off during his flight from the Meadows, contrary to the story he had told the police . . . was running low, and it was time to go on the prowl.

He decided that the city centre was off limits for a few more days. That young inspector, Steele, had scared the crap out of him, and he had no wish to run into George Regan for a while either. So when he left his bolt-hole, he headed east for Leith and the docks, where there was always stuff lying about.

He passed by Newhaven harbour but paid a quick visit to the flour mill, where someone had been kind enough to leave a very fancy vacuum flask, a CD Walkman and a heavy-duty torch in the saddlebag of a bike that was chained outside. The saddlebag was secured only by two small buckles, so he stole that also.

He was so pleased with his take that he almost decided to go home at that point, but he thought that the day was too full of promise to cut so short, especially since the weather was grey and drab, the kind that he knew from experience kept folks' heads down, rather than looking out of their office windows.

There were too many windows in the Scottish Executive building, though, too many to take a chance on a quick trip through the car park, so he kept on walking down Commercial Street, until he crossed the bridge and reached the shore.

Moash was sometimes tempted by the Malmaison Hotel; it attracted a lot of moneyed folk, and in theory healthy pickings. But he had the sense to know that the rich were increasingly cashless, and that to make anything from them he would need access to their unguarded valuables. That would not be easily gained, though, as posh hotels usually had security systems, with concealed video cameras and other stuff that could get you banged up in no time.

So he sniffed at the Malmaison and passed it by; there were other places behind it, industrial units where people were sometimes careless, and the goods yard which on the right day was Aladdin's bloody cave. He wandered along casually, with the practised slouch of someone who was inherently skilled at drawing no attention to himself. When he nipped into an open office doorway and won himself a fat wallet from the pocket of a so-called security guard who had left his jacket hanging over his seat while he went for a slash, his day was complete.

Moash never retraced his steps. That was the second stupidest thing that a professional thief could do, a sure way of landing yourself in the treacle. The stupidest was to run once you had made a score. If the loss was discovered quickly, there was no better way of identifying yourself. So he kept on walking, until he was almost past the Albert Dock, where the road took a turn that would ultimately lead him out on to Salamander Street.

He stopped at the corner of the dock and glanced around, not to see if he was being pursued, but to see if anyone was looking in his direction. Happy that he was unobserved, he unzipped the fly of his jeans and urinated contentedly into the dull green water.

As he followed his yellow arc, his eye was caught by a strange movement. As is the case with all commercial harbours, it was impossible to see anything clearly that was more than a few inches below the surface, but he could just make out a shape down there. Moash knew that curiosity killed cats, but he also knew that they had nine lives. Beside him on the ground there was a long docker's pole; when he had zipped his fly, he picked it up and thrust it into the water.

Something moved at its touch, something solid. Moash frowned. And then the object turned and rose, until it was just below the surface, close enough for him to see the dead face of a man staring up at him.

Had there not been a helicopter close overhead, drifting in to land on the nearby pad, someone would have heard his scream.

As well as being totally amoral, and a parasite sucking sustenance from the community in which he lived, Moash Glazier had a third great weakness. He believed in omens and in the signs that they drew for him. And so when he saw the thing beneath him, tethered somehow to the wall of the dockside, its heavy jacket ballooning out around it, he read its meaning loud and clear. Finding one stiff was a major misfortune, but coming upon another less than a week later, that was an unmistakable message. All things came in threes, and if he hung around this place, he knew all too well who the next would be.

He dropped the pole into the water, and he broke his number-one rule. He turned and ran, taking the shortest route out of the docks, not caring who saw him, and not stopping until he was halfway up Constitution Street, when he saw a taxi and hailed it.

Gasping, he instructed the driver to take him to Waverley Station, where he used the stolen credit card of G. Gebbie, offering an acceptable facsimile of the smudged scrawl on the back, to buy a one-way ticket to London King's Cross. His train was past Dunbar before his heartbeat returned to something approaching its normal rate.

Moash realised that a whole new chapter of his life was unfolding, but that was infinitely preferable to the closure of the whole bloody book. As the train sped south, he counted the cash in Mr Gebbie's wallet . . . three hundred and thirty-five pounds, the remains, if he had known it, of a very successful Saturday in the bookie's . . . then took the fancy vacuum from the expensive-looking saddlebag.

He unscrewed the cup on top, then the inner plug, and sniffed. 'Bastard,' he growled. 'Fuckin' oxtail. Ah hate fuckin' oxtail.'

Forty-seven

Bob Skinner's day was looking up. His worst waking nightmares about a wave of cyanide deaths across the country had not come true, and negative test results were being reported from all over the country by the toothpaste manufacturers.

More and more the investigation was being focused on Newcastle; the DCC had spent some of the morning in telephone conference with his opposite number on the Northumbria force. He had been told that the sale of Bartholemy Lebeau's fatal toothpaste had been identified, thanks to bar coding and a computerised till system. It had been a cash transaction, at four thirty-five in the afternoon; one item only, five-pound note tendered, three pounds thirty-seven pence change.

Further enquiries were being pursued and when Ruth Pye called to tell him that DCC Les Cairns was on the line once more, he had been expecting him.

'Have your people spoken to the assistant?' he asked at once.

'Yes, but she's a kid,' Cairns replied, 'a sixteen-year-old part-timer; there's no way she remembers the sale, let alone anything about the buyer. We've taken her prints, though; I guess you'll need them for elimination.'

'Yes, thanks. Have they got video surveillance in this store?'

'I'm afraid not. I wish to hell they had, because in the absence of any other contaminated product, there's a growing possibility that the victim's tube was stolen, spiked, then put back on the shelf. It would have been nice to catch the perpetrator on tape.'

'Sure it would, but since when did real life get that nice? You're right, though, Les. We've got an integrated investigation here; I've got a murder on my patch and you've got product sabotage on yours. It needs high-level handling; I've put my head of CID in charge up here.'

'And mine is in Newcastle,' Cairns interjected, 'so do we exchange information through them?'

'For efficiency yes, but let's you and I talk on a daily basis. Meanwhile, I'd be grateful if you'd e-mail that girl's prints to DI Arthur Dorward, at our forensic lab.'

'Will do. Cheers.'

Skinner hung up and walked across the corridor to brief the chief on developments, catching him just before he left for an ACPOS meeting in Glasgow. He was smiling as he came back to his room, having put the poisoning investigation to one side for the moment as he contemplated his meeting with Aileen de Marco. He wondered what they would have to talk about, and how much insight she would give him into her own thinking on policy.

'She's still a politician, though, Bob,' he whispered to

himself. 'She'll be out to pick your brains and that'll be it.'

The phone on his desk cut into his thoughts. It was his direct line, and that meant urgent. He snatched it up. 'Yes.'

'Boss, it's Neil. I'm on my mobile, and there are people here, so I can't talk, but I need you down here straight away. Albert Dock, Leith.'

Forty-eight

Interviewing Belgians was not the way that Jack McGurk would normally have chosen to kick off the working week, but the opportunities to escape the office were few and far between. He felt that he had turned an invisible corner with Bob Skinner over the previous few days, but he still welcomed the trip to Haddington with Ray Wilding.

Their interviewees had been waiting for them in the Town House, a public building at the fork of Market Street and High Street. There had been thirty-five of them listed, twenty-two bandsmen, twelve musketeers and the bus driver who had driven them from Brussels. Dan Pringle had also recruited two interpreters, secretaries from the staff of the French Institute in Edinburgh, thanking his stars that he had not needed to find a Flemish translator.

The one name missing from the list was that of Colonel Malou. The head of CID had told the two sergeants that if he needed to be re-interviewed, he would do it himself.

McGurk and Wilding both felt that the interviews were a formality, but neither of them was about to argue with the

DCC or the chief super, so they began, splitting the group into two and taking a desk and an interpreter each.

There's something about them, McGurk thought, as he surveyed the group of men before him. They were all dressed casually, but some wore expensive leisure clothes while others were clad in shirts and jeans that could have come from any Sunday stallholders' market in Europe. They sat three or four to a row on the stacking chairs, waiting for their turn to be called to the interview table. But it was the look in their eyes that caught the sergeant's attention. He had never seen anything quite like it before; he guessed it was the expression he had seen, descriptive of men in warfare, and how they looked after their closest comrade had been blown away at their side, shocked, but with an undisguised element of relief.

He called the first one forward. '*Parlez-vous anglais?*' the interpreter asked. The man shook his head.

'Did you know Monsieur Lebeau well?' McGurk asked him, then waited for the translation. The Belgian shrugged, then muttered a reply.

'Not much,' his aide translated. 'He's been in the band for fifteen years and he was there when he arrived, but they never got close.'

'Did you all go shopping in Newcastle last Friday?'

'No. He certainly didn't. There was little time, he says.'

'Did you speak to Monsieur Lebeau that day at all?'

'Only once when he missed a beat . . . he was a . . .' The interpreter blushed, then paused. 'He was not a very good drummer,' she concluded.

McGurk noted the man's name and moved on to the next.

The result was the same, as was the next, and the next. 'A waste of bloody time,' he murmured to his helper, as the fifth man approached. This one spoke English, and gave his name as Bernard Simenon. 'Same as the writer,' he grunted.

'Can you tell me anything about Monsieur Lebeau?' the sergeant asked him.

'Barty? There is little to tell. He had his own group within the band, his own friends, but I was not one. He and his lot were ex-military, old bandsmen; I'm an engineer who likes to play the trombone.'

'That's funny. Someone said that he wasn't a very good drummer.'

'I never noticed, not behind the noise I make. He couldn't have been that bad, though, or Auguste would have kicked him out.'

'You don't call him "Colonel", then.'

'I told you, I'm not a soldier.'

'I don't suppose you went shopping with Monsieur Lebeau, did you?'

'When?'

'On Friday, in Newcastle. We know that's where he bought the toothpaste that killed him.'

'I don't know when he managed to do that. We played at a school in Sunderland in the morning, and then in a big shopping mall in the afternoon . . . the Metro Centre, damn big place. What time's Barty supposed to have bought this stuff?'

'Just after four thirty.'

'Impossible, he was still banging his drum at quarter past.

We didn't get to the city till almost five, and then we went to the British Legion club, because Auguste had said it was okay to have just a couple of beers. How sure are you of the time?'

'It came from the till in the shop; every transaction's recorded.'

'Then its clock must be wrong.'

McGurk frowned, and made a note on his pad. 'It's possible,' he conceded. 'I'll have it checked.' He glanced up at the trombonist. 'Your beer's on the ration, is it, Monsieur Simenon?'

'It is for this trip. Our little colonel wants us marching in straight lines before the Holy Father: but he's not alone, for we all want that. I cannot tell you how great an honour this is for us, or how great a surprise it was when we were invited. It's a mystery almost worthy of my namesake. I asked Auguste if he knew the reason, but all he did was shrug his shoulders and tell me I should take it as a gift from God.' The Belgian frowned. 'But if it is, then since He gave it to us He's clearly had second thoughts.'

'I wouldn't blame Monsieur Lebeau's death on God,' said McGurk, quietly.

'You say that,' Simenon exclaimed, 'but coming on top of poor Philippe . . .'

'Who's Philippe?'

The man stared at him across the table. 'Philippe Hanno. Who else?'

'I'm sorry, that name means nothing to me.'

The Belgian's face took on an agitated expression. 'It means everything to us,' he shouted. 'I cannot believe you can say that.'

'But why?'

'Because Philippe Hanno was knocked down and killed in England, in Hull, by a drunk driver. They still haven't found him.'

It was Jack McGurk's turn to stare. 'You're not kidding me, are you?'

'Why would I do that?' Simenon protested.

The sergeant shoved his chair violently back from the heavy table. 'Ray!' he bellowed across the hall.

Forty-nine

A security guard tried to stop Skinner's BMW as it swept through the entrance to the Leith docks complex. He flashed his warrant card at the man and drove on, barely slowing his road speed. He had no idea where the Albert Dock was, but he followed signs until, on taking a left turn, he saw a temporary screen by the waterside, and knew that he had reached his destination.

He swung off the roadway and pulled up alongside Neil McIlhenney's car, which was parked between a patrol vehicle and an ambulance. Its rear doors were open and its paramedic crew sat inside, their life-saving skills clearly not needed.

The DCC stepped out on to the dock, glad of his heavy jacket in the November cold, and walked behind the big green screen, past the two uniformed constables who stood guard, bracing himself for what he would see. He hated moments like these, but did his best to keep that to himself.

The first person he saw was not McIlhenney, but Mario McGuire. The big superintendent's back was turned to the thing on the ground, beneath the tarpaulin, but the look on his face told Skinner everything he needed to know and confirmed the conclusion to which he had leaped following the guarded call that had brought him there.

'Fuck,' he whispered to himself, as he approached.

McIlhenney heard his footstep and turned. 'Boss,' he began.

'It's the American, yes?' the DCC asked brusquely.

His colleague nodded. 'I'm afraid so.'

'What happened?'

It was Mario McGuire who answered. 'He's drowned himself,' he told him, in an anguished voice.

'Easy, big fella,' Skinner murmured, stepping up and taking the superintendent by the elbow. 'You've been close to Inspector Mawhinney for the last couple of weeks, maybe too close to be here.'

'This is my patch, sir. I belong here.'

'Okay, but keep it under control.' He turned to Detective Sergeant Sammy Pye, McGuire's assistant, who had transferred with him that morning from the Borders division. 'Sam,' he ordered, 'send those two PCs up to the main entrance. I just drove past one of the security guys on the gate like he wasn't there, and I don't want the press doing the same thing. Get another couple of uniforms from the Queen Charlotte Street office to take their place here. A lot of people work in these docks; we could need some crowd control.'

He moved over to McIlhenney. 'Has the ME seen him?'

'Not yet. We're still waiting for him. Do you want to look?'

'I'd better, I suppose. Will Mario be okay?'

'He's had a shock, but he can handle it. He and Sammy

were on the scene first; he called me while they were on the way.' He leaned over and turned back the tarpaulin.

Skinner looked down at the body of Inspector Colin Mawhinney. His hair, slacks and his heavy navy-style pea-jacket were slicked with green slime from the dock, and in death, his face had a similar, if very faint, tint in its colouring. He looked as if he could simply have fallen into the dock and drowned, had it not been for one thing; a long, thick and very heavy chain lay on the ground beside him, its links leading under the jacket. Skinner crouched beside the dead man, turned back the garment, and saw that it was twisted and lodged in his belt.

He turned and glanced up at McGuire. 'Again, Mario, what happened?'

The detective superintendent pointed towards two men who were standing a few yards away at the water's edge, watching the scene; one wore worker's overalls, and the other a suit, beneath a raincoat. 'They found him, sir,' he replied. 'You'd best hear it first hand.' Skinner straightened himself and followed him across to the pair. 'This is Benny McCaffrey,' he said, introducing the labourer first, 'and this is Stanley Guinness, from the port office. Tell the DCC what you told me, Benny.'

The man nodded; he looked to be in his mid-fifties, with a grimy face; strands of grey stringy hair protruded from a dirty woollen cap. 'Ah saw a fella,' he began. 'Ah was working over there and Ah saw this wee bloke. Ah thought he was maybe frae the pipe works or somewhere. He nivir saw me, mind.'

'What was he doing?'

'Just walkin', like, mindin' his ain business, ken. He was carrying a bag thing, that wis a'. He stopped, and he took a quick shooftie round, then he had a pish in the dock.' McCaffrey chuckled. 'Probably improved the watter quality. But when he wis finished I saw him looking doon, doon the dockside. Then he picked up a pole somebody hid left lyin' and poked it in the watter, like that.' He made a prodding movement as if he was gripping a pole himself, one hand above the other. 'Next think I kent he wis runnin' like fuck.'

'And what did you do after that?'

'Ah came doon here, tae see what had scared him, ken. Ah saw all right. That poor bloke there. Ah went straight tae the port office and got Mr Guinness.'

'Who took the body out of the water?'

'My men did,' the port official replied. 'I always have a couple of people handy who are trained divers and who can go into the dock in . . . emergencies like this. They freed him and brought him to the surface.'

'When you say they freed him,' Skinner interrupted, 'what exactly do you mean?'

'That chain you can see there,' said Guinness. 'He'd secured it in his belt as you see, and wound it round his waist, several times, for ballast I assume, to make sure he'd go down. There were stones in the pockets as well.' He paused. 'But when he went in, the end of the chain seems to have caught in the dock wall and held him there. The basin's tidal as well, so when the water level dropped a few feet, he became visible.'

'What about this man? The guy Mr McCaffrey saw pissing in the dock?'

'I can't help you there, I'm afraid.'

'Sammy had a word with Site Security, boss. One of them saw a bloke legging it through the gate and up Constitution Street, but he couldn't get near giving a description.'

The DCC scowled. 'That's a poor show,' he muttered. 'I don't suppose it makes any difference, though. Mawhinney was in the water for longer than a couple of minutes. Whoever that guy was he can't tell us anything we haven't found out already. Come on, Mario,' he said, turning and leading him away from the other two men. 'Let's you and Neil and I go up to your new office; there's some things I need to ask you, away from here.'

'I want to stay, boss, till the ME's been, and they've taken him off to the morgue.'

'No. Sammy Pye can do that, and organise formal statements from McCaffrey, Guinness and the divers. Then he can fix up a pathologist to do the post mortem.'

'But, boss . . .'

'It's not for discussion, Mario.'

The superintendent sighed. 'If you say so, sir. But there's something else I've got to do, and that's break it to Paula. She'll be gutted.'

'So will Sarah. She liked the man too.' Skinner looked at him. 'Tell you what, where will Paula be right now?'

'In her office, round in Commercial Street.'

'Okay. Let's go there. We should probably talk to both of you.'

'Why?'

The DCC looked at him patiently. 'Mario,' he said, quietly,

'I know you've had a hell of a shock, but get your heid in gear, will you? As far as we know right now, you two were the last people to see that man alive.'

Fifty

Dan Pringle glared at Auguste Malou across the table in the Dalkeith police office. When Ray Wilding had called to explode the bombshell in his lap he had gone incandescent, and ordered that he be picked up and taken to the East Lothian divisional headquarters, rather than to the Haddington office.

'I've been dancing to those buggers' tune since yesterday. I'll be fucked if I'll do it any longer.'

He had calmed down a little on the drive from Fettes, but not so much that he was about to defer to the Belgian. Equally, the peppery colonel was irate at the sudden and unexplained summons, which, he protested, had been presented with all the indignity of an arrest.

'Father Collins shall hear of this,' he bellowed at the chief superintendent. 'Monsignor di Matteo shall hear of it. Before I am finished, His Holiness himself will hear of it. When he does, sir,' he gave a grim little laugh, 'yours will be a heavy penance.'

'This may seem like sacrilege to you, Colonel,' Pringle drawled, 'but I answer to Sir James Proud and Bob Skinner. If you've got a problem with me, you tell them about it. In fact,' he picked up the interview-room telephone, 'if you like I'll call DCC Skinner right now and you can speak to him. I don't advise it though. If you think I'm a bear when I'm angry, you don't want to rattle his cage.'

Malou gave him one last icicle stare. In spite of himself, Pringle found it strangely disconcerting: it was as if the old eyes were made of frosted glass. 'I will accept your apology,' he said, in a grudging tone, as if one had been offered. 'Now get on with it. Tell me the reason for this outrageous behaviour of yours.'

'My reason, Colonel,' the head of CID replied, 'can be expressed in one name: Philippe Hanno.' The eyes seemed to mist over. 'I want to know why the first time I heard it was this morning, when one of my officers phoned from the place where they're interviewing your bandsmen. Why the hell didn't you tell me about Hanno yesterday?'

'Because you didn't ask,' the older man spat back at him. 'And what difference would it have made anyway? Philippe was killed by a drunken English driver, and poor Barty was made victim by some English lunatic who gets his kicks by poisoning toothpaste tubes.'

'What difference would it have made? Jesus Christ, I don't believe I'm hearing this. Two of your group die within three days of each other and that doesn't strike you as even a wee bit odd?'

The first sign of conciliation appeared on Malou's face. 'Look, I was there when Barty died, actually in the next room, through the wall. It was a terrible shock to me.'

'What happened to Monsieur Hanno?'

'It was in Hull,' the Belgian replied. 'We were in a club, and I had let the boys make it a party night. Philippe ran out of cigarettes, so he went across to our bus to get more . . . you can never buy Gauloises in England. When he didn't come back, they found him on the road outside. He'd been hit by a car; they took him to hospital, but he was dead. The driver who killed him didn't hang around afterwards. The police who came said that he was probably drunk, or that he panicked, or both.' He spread his hands wide before him in a classic gesture. 'Now Barty, Monsieur, that was completely different. When he collapsed, I thought it was a heart-attack, so did Major Tubbs, my kind host, and so, I remind you, did the lady doctor who answered the emergency call. It was only when your very clever pathologist did his tests that anybody knew differently.'

'Her tests,' said Pringle.

'Pardon?'

'Her tests: the pathologist was a lady too.'

'Indeed?' Malou replied, as if it was of some consequence. 'But, Monsieur Pringle,' he continued, 'suppose I had been alert in my sorrow, and had told you this yesterday, what difference would it have made?'

'It would have changed the whole focus of our inquiries. It opens a new possibility, that Monsieur Lebeau's death and that of Monsieur Hanno are linked. I'm not saying that it would have stopped us from ordering a nationwide recall of thousands of toothpaste tubes, but as it is, we've lost twenty-four hours when we'd have been doing things differently.'

'In what way?'

'For openers we'd have been interviewing your bandsmen

in a different way. Now we'll have to go back to the start with them and ask them a couple of new questions, the ones I'm going to put to you now.'

'Go ahead.'

'I will. Does your band have any enemies in Belgium that you know of?'

The colonel frowned. 'No, but why should we? We harm nobody and we entertain many. I'm honest enough to admit that there may be some who think we are a bit of a joke, and that we're, how do you say it, an anana . . . anach . . .'

'Anachronism?'

'That's the word. But no, on the whole the Bastogne Drummers are popular. I won't say we're an institution, but people like us. I suppose, though, we can never be certain.' His sharp eyes seemed to lose focus for a moment. 'There are crazy people in the world.'

'I'm glad you accept that, at least. So can I ask you to think back and try to recall whether you've seen anything odd around the band in the last few weeks? For example, have you been aware of the same face, or faces, showing up in different places? Have you ever had the feeling that someone might have been watching you?'

'People watch us all the time, sir. Believe it or not we have some fans in Belgium, people who like us and follow us when we play. So as leader, I see a lot of faces, and I am aware of them. However, I cannot say that I have seen anyone odd as you describe, or had the feeling that anyone who was watching us might wish us harm.'

'That's good,' Pringle conceded, 'but keep thinking about

it, please, and if anything or anyone does occur to you, tell me at once.'

'I'll do that, but don't put the rest of your life on hold waiting for me to remember something. When you get to my age you tend only to remember those things you'd rather forget.'

'I'm getting to your age, Colonel,' Pringle growled. 'I know. Still, let me ask you something else. Was there a connection between Philippe Hanno and Bartholemy Lebeau outside the band? Were they close?'

'Close?'

'Were they good friends?'

'I only know my bandsmen as bandsmen,' Malou replied. 'I don't concern myself with their lives outside the Bastogne Drummers. I care that they turn up for practice, that they keep their instruments in tune and polished, and their uniforms clean and with creases, and that they march sharply and play well. That's all I care about. As for Philippe and Barty being good friends, they were okay, they knew each other a long time, but I wouldn't say they were brothers.'

'What sort of men were they?'

'Good men, never been in any trouble I know of.'

'But could they, do you think? I'm trying to establish whether they might have been involved in something outside the Drummers that might have got them killed.'

'Then you will have to try somewhere else, for I wouldn't know any of that.'

'How long have you known these men?'

'They were in the band for fifteen years.'

'What did they do outside?'

'Barty had a small job as a concierge; Philippe did nothing. They were pensioners from the army, like me.' He paused. 'Actually we go back longer than fifteen years. When I was with the band of the First Guides Regiment . . . it's very famous in Belgium, you know . . . they were with me, on my staff.'

'So,' said Pringle, 'there is a connection beyond the band.'

'But historic, Monsieur, and ancient history now.'

'Maybe so, but it exists; and what's more it ties into you as well.'

Malou gave something that was half snarl, half snort. 'Hah,' he exclaimed. 'Are you suggesting that I might be next?'

'I'm not suggesting anything, Colonel. However, I am telling you this: from now on, I want your men lodged at a single location, where we can offer you proper protection.'

'*Mais ce n'est pas possible,*' the old soldier protested. 'That means a hotel; the band cannot afford that.'

'That's not a consideration you need worry about. But it is necessary, and it is going to happen.'

Fifty-one

Paula Viareggio looked old; that was the only way that Skinner could describe her. He had allowed Mario to break the news of Mawhinney's death in private, and had only gone into her office with McIlhenney when he had called to them.

Her eyes were red with tears, as unexpected and incongruous on her as on a man, and her olive complexion had gone white; somehow the effect robbed her silver hair of its striking quality and made it look that of a woman in her fifties, not one twenty years younger. As he looked at her he saw the image of her redoubtable grandmother, Nana Viareggio: he saw her future.

'I can't believe this,' she murmured hoarsely, sitting on the edge of her desk, and leaning on her cousin for support. 'He was in my house last night. He ate with us, and he left to go home and then . . .' She looked away and gripped Mario's arm, hard.

'We all ate with him the night before that,' Skinner reminded her. 'It's as big a stunner to me, and to Sarah; I've just called to tell her.'

'In that case, guys,' said McIlhenney, the calmest person in the room, 'since you were all involved with the deceased on a personal basis, it's best that I put the questions that need asking. Strictly speaking Sammy Pye should do it, since you've put him in charge, boss, but he might just be a bit nervous interviewing you two.'

'What do you think happened, Neil?' Paula asked.

'I don't think anything,' he replied. 'It looks as if Inspector Mawhinney went down to the docks after he left you, found a length of heavy chain, tied it round his waist as a sinker, stuffed his pockets with stones to make sure, and jumped in. That's what it looks like; but we have to establish his state of mind. So, how did he strike each of you? You first, sir.'

'I only met the man twice, Neil, as you know,' Skinner said. 'The first time it was in official surroundings, so I hardly had a chance to consider him as a private individual. Even on Saturday, although I tried to make it a social night, I felt that he was a bit shy, a bit reserved. I won't say he was humourless, just quiet. But on neither occasion did he make me think that he was considering walking the plank. That's all I can tell you.'

'Thanks. How about you, Paula? What did you think of him?'

She sniffed, then blew her nose on Mario's handkerchief. 'I thought he was just a lovely man, a very nice guy. He couldn't have looked after us better in New York; he knew everything about the city and he went out of his way to make my visit interesting in the time he spent with both of us. He was a friend.'

'Did he talk about his wife a lot?'

313

'He never talked about her to me, and I didn't like to ask him about her. Mario told me, of course, but I thought it was best left undisturbed.'

'Last night,' McIlhenney asked, 'how much did he have to drink?'

'He didn't get pissed, Neil, if that's what you think!'

'I'm not suggesting that. I just want to know.'

'Nothing excessive. We kept off the Amarone, stuck to Valpolicella. I got the Strega out later on, but Colin didn't like that too much, so I gave him some Remy Martin. If he had been showing it, I'd have made him take a taxi back to the Malmaison.'

'But he didn't?'

'No. He insisted on walking.'

'What time did he leave?'

'Just after ten. We turned on the news on telly just after he left, so I remember.'

'Fine. Thanks.' McIlhenney turned to McGuire. 'Now you, Mario. You knew him better than any of us. What do you think?'

'I'll tell you what I think,' his friend told him bitterly. 'I think that if I'd walked back with him last night, if I'd gone back to my place, and seen him into the Malmaison, we wouldn't be here now, having this bloody awful discussion. That's what I think, and I'll always fucking think it.'

There was a whiteboard on the wall of Paula's office, with a ridged platform below it holding some magic markers and a long pointer. McIlhenney picked it up and handed it to McGuire. 'What's that?' the superintendent asked.

'It's a big stick; you can beat yourself with that as well if you like. This was a grown man, Mario, a senior New York police officer. He didn't need a chum home, and anyway, if he was planning to top himself, you seeing him to his front door wouldn't have stopped him. So let me ask you again, but more specifically this time. What was your opinion of Colin's mental state? Do you find it beyond belief that he should kill himself?'

McGuire walked over to the window; he looked out and along Commercial Street, back towards the dock where Mawhinney had been found. Finally he turned back to face McIlhenney and shook his head. 'To be honest, I don't. There was a great well of grief in the man, not far below the surface, and if finally he's decided to jump into it, it wouldn't, it doesn't, astonish me. When I stood beside him the week before last in Ground Zero, and when he told me that as far as he was concerned we were standing on his wife's grave, I had a strong feeling that he wouldn't be bothered if he had to join her there.'

He went back to Paula and took her hand. 'Maggie told me last week that she had a probable suicide on her patch but that there were a couple of unresolved doubts about it. If that's how the fiscal wants to dispose of this one, he won't have a problem with me.'

He handed the pointer back to his friend. 'And by the way, you know what you can do with that.'

Fifty-two

'Why have I never heard of this bank, Stevie?' asked Mary Chambers as they stepped from the lift into the beech-clad reception area. 'My grandpa was a potato farmer in Lanarkshire.'

'That's not for me to say, Superintendent,' Steele chuckled, 'but I think this lot were after barley growers and big beef and dairy producers.'

'Spuds weren't good enough for them? Is that what you mean?'

'I think that the founders of the Scottish Farmers Bank, and before that the Agricultural and Rural Building Society, regarded all root vegetables as beneath them. They were the posh people's lender, until they found the competition in that sector too hot, and reinvented themselves as a business bank.'

The inspector walked up to the tartan-clad receptionist. 'Hello again,' he said. 'I called earlier and spoke to Mr Easterson's secretary. We're expected.'

She smiled at him, brightly, professionally, and superficially, with the twinkle that reminded him of an ad for dishwasher tablets. 'Yes, Mr Steele, I know. If you'll give me just a second.'

She picked up a phone and dialled, then spoke briefly and in a whisper that he could not decipher. Hanging up, she pointed to the waiting area. 'If you'll just take a seat over there, we won't keep you long.'

'You're bloody right you won't,' Mary Chambers muttered under her breath, as they walked towards the leather chairs and the table strewn with that day's newspapers. 'We're the polis, hen.'

After only half a day with his new boss, Steele knew that they would work well together. Mary Chambers was a straight talker, and he welcomed that. He had seen that she felt awkward about raising the subject of his relationship with Maggie, but she had gone ahead anyway because she had felt it necessary; that was okay with him, since he had never beaten about too many bushes himself. There was a surprising humour about her too, bubbling beneath her plain exterior, looking for opportunities to show itself.

In fact they were kept waiting for five minutes. Steele was on the edge of annoyance, when a stocky, middle-aged man swept into the foyer and came straight towards them. 'I'm sorry to have taken so long,' he exclaimed, 'but I had my chairman on the line. Unfortunately he's not given to short conversations.' He extended a hand to the inspector as the two detectives rose to their feet. 'Superintendent Chambers, I take it.'

'Does he look like a Mary?' the new divisional CID commander asked cheerfully, managing somehow to intercept the handshake.

'Terribly sorry,' the man exclaimed, without convincing

either of them that he actually was. 'I'm Proc Fraser, the chief executive.'

'I was under the impression we'd be seeing Mr Easterson,' said Steele. 'I made the appointment with his secretary.'

'Yes. Indeed,' Fraser muttered. 'Come along to my office and I'll explain.'

You don't bloody have to, thought the inspector. *It took her even less time than I thought.*

He stayed silent, though, as they were led along the narrow corridor, and shown into an office, larger than that of the absent GMCB and more expensively furnished, although still stopping short of opulence. There was a jug of coffee on the meeting table, and three china cups; Mary Chambers wondered if he would ask her to pour, but he did that himself.

'You called Vernon?' he began. 'Why was that?'

'We've been speaking to Ivor Whetstone's son,' Steele told him. 'He's raised some concerns about our view of his father's death, and he's pointed to a possible anomaly about the fraud of which he's been accused. We've decided that it warrants a few more questions, and maybe even a full-scale investigation by us. Where is Mr Easterson, sir?'

'He's not here,' Fraser replied superfluously. 'He's on leave, in fact. He was really rather overwrought in the wake of Whetstone's death. Ivor was very much his man, if you know what I mean, and he's taken it very badly, so I've suggested to him that he has some time at home to let him come to terms with things.'

'Would that be what they call gardening leave, sir?' Mary Chambers caught his eye as she spoke.

The chief executive attempted a wry smile. 'There's no fooling you, Superintendent, is there?'

'It doesn't happen often.'

'Well, as it happens, you're right again. A million-pound embezzlement is a serious business in any bank, especially for the line manager who lets it happen.'

'What is your management structure here, sir?'

'We have a five-person board, of which I'm the only executive member. I manage the organisation, which has two divisions, Commercial Banking and Personal Banking. Each of those is run by a general manager, and they report to me.'

'So Mr Easterson is your deputy?'

'One of two, Superintendent; he and the general manager, Personal Banking have equal status in the organisation. We run the two divisions entirely separately. Several of our private clients . . . in fact I think I'm correct in saying the majority . . . are directors or senior executives of companies to which the commercial-banking division is the principal lender. Therefore it's only right that we should have very effective Chinese walls between the two sides of the operation, and we do.'

'It's a pretty short line of command,' said Chambers, 'and it begs a pretty obvious question.'

'I know.' Fraser sighed. 'Who investigates me in circumstances like these? That's what my conversation with the chairman was about. He wants to put the matter in the hands of our auditors. He feels, and he's right, that we have a duty to our shareholders to have an external investigation.'

'I feel that you have a duty to the law as well,' the superintendent countered. 'This is a criminal matter. Last week we were satisfied by your senior executive's, and by my pre-decessor's, study of the papers you provided, that Whetstone was guilty, and we reported that to the fiscal. He looked at the file in his turn and agreed with us. However, what Murphy Whetstone told us this morning has persuaded us that we should take a second look. You can forget your auditors, sir. This is our investigation.'

As she finished, Stevie Steele frowned. From the moment of Fraser's unexpected appearance he had sensed that there was something wrong with the picture, something else behind the chief executive's patently obvious anxiety. All at once, he realised what it was.

'Where does Aurelia Middlemass fit into your structure?' he asked. 'I thought she was Mr Easterson's number two in Commercial Banking. If that's right, why isn't she here?'

The banker's face reddened noticeably. 'You have the advantage of me, Inspector,' he replied. 'That's a question I've been asking myself, all morning. Aurelia didn't come into the office this morning. She doesn't have any holidays booked, and even if she had, I'd have asked her to cancel them in the current circumstances. Her secretary's called her, I've called her myself. Neither of us has had any reply on her home phone or her mobile. I don't know where the hell she is.'

'That's another complication,' said Chambers. 'All the more reason for us to be involved here. I'd like the official request to come from you, Mr Fraser.'

'You have it. What else do you need?'

'Two things. Actually the first is only a suggestion, but it's one you might find appropriate. Since there are only you and

Mr Easterson in the line above Mr Whetstone and Ms Middlemass, it might be in the bank's best interest if you relinquished executive duties during this investigation to your other deputy.'

'I tend to agree,' Fraser admitted. 'What's the other thing?'

'I need all the papers relating to the Bonspiel Partnership. The folder Ms Middlemass gave us last week was only a copy. We need the originals to see, if we can, whose sticky fingers are all over this thing.'

'I only hope they are Whetstone's. Frankly it would suit me best if it was him all along.'

'I'm sure it would, although finding his prints on the documents won't be conclusive by itself. If anyone was setting him up, they could have done it with blank paper that he had handled. We'll need more than that.'

'Where will you get it?'

Mary Chambers smiled. 'Let us find Ms Middlemass first. Maybe she'll be able to tell us.'

Fifty-three

'My love, I hear what you're saying to me,' Bob Skinner told his wife. 'I appreciate that as soon as your thing loses the protection of total impersonality, it becomes very, very difficult. And I promise you that if old Joe Hutchinson was available, we would not be having this conversation.' He paused. 'I don't like being seen, personally, to give you police work. I'm scrupulous about leaving that to the judgement of others. Yet here I am: that, and the fact that I've driven out here to talk to you about it, when I should be back at Fettes helping young Crossley and Ruth cancel Proud Jimmy's cocktail party, must tell you how serious I am.'

She stood in the big glass-walled room gazing out to sea. 'I don't know if I can, Bob. What about that woman in Glasgow? Couldn't she handle it?'

'She was my second choice after the Prof, Sarah. I called her, but she's out of town at a conference; ironically, it's in New York. I can't, I wouldn't, I won't entrust this autopsy to anyone who isn't top-drawer. I know that it appears to be routine, but I have to report to the commissioner of the NYPD on this, and I need to be one thousand per cent sure of every piece of information I give him.'

'Bob,' she protested still, 'I knew this man. He'd be more than an empty vessel lying there on the slab. He's someone I've talked with, eaten with, laughed with, and all less than forty-eight hours ago. All the time I was working I'd be hearing his voice. Have you any idea how difficult that would be?'

'Yes, I have. Now will you call on every scrap of skill, strength and professionalism you have and do it for me? Today?'

She turned. 'Are you giving me a choice?'

'Yes. You can let me down.' He saw her flinch. He started to form an apology, but knew that it would be an empty gesture, for he had spoken what he saw as the truth.

'I couldn't do that again, could I?' she said. 'Very well. Where have they taken the body?'

'The Western General.'

'That'll do. You'll need to give me time to line up an assistant, a student if I can get one. Plus I'll want one of Arthur Dorward's photographers, and I'll want a police witness.'

'I'll ask Neil to do it.'

'The hell you will!' she snapped at him. 'You'll be there. If you're laying this on me, then I'm laying it right back on you, honey. I know you hate these things, but you will not delegate this one.'

'If that's what you want,' he said lamely. 'You fix up the student and I'll call Dorward.'

Skinner left her to use the phone on the sideboard and went upstairs to use the unlisted line that was reserved in the main for Internet access. He made the call to Arthur Dorward at Howdenhall, then phoned his own office. 'Do you have that phone number for me?' he asked Ruth Pye.

'Yes sir,' said his secretary. She read out a New York City number. 'That's the direct line of the chief of Department. I told his assistant that you need to speak to him as a matter of urgency. He's in his office now, waiting for you to ring him. There's one other thing, sir, that's come up since we spoke last. The head of CID's been on; he asks if you'd get in touch with him as soon as you have a moment, on his cell phone, since he could well be travelling back to the office when you do.'

'Did he say what it's about? The Belgian investigation, I suppose.'

'Yes. He said there's been a development.'

'Bugger it! That's all I need. Okay, Ruthie, I'll get to him later.'

He hung up, then made the New York call. The chief of Department was the most senior sworn officer in the NYPD, reporting only to the appointed commissioner. His secretary picked it up, but put him through at once when he identified himself. 'Good morning, Chief Skinner. This is Ralph Lovencrantz speaking.' The voice was smooth and cultured, with just a hint of Massachusetts twang; it was also cautious.

'Good morning, Chief,' said the DCC. 'This call should really have been made by my chief constable, but he's out of town, and it can't wait for his return. I have some bad news for you, concerning one of your officers.'

'That can only be Colin Mawhinney; I can't think of

another who's in Scotland at the moment. What's happened?'

'He was found this morning in a dock near his hotel; drowned.'

The chief of Department's sigh carried three thousand miles. 'I knew you weren't going to tell me anything good; I just hoped it wouldn't be the worst. Were you at the scene yourself?'

'Yes.'

'So how did it look to you? Did he fall, was he pushed, or did he jump?'

'If I said it looks as if he jumped, would you be surprised?'

'Is that an official question?'

'Was yours?'

Lovencrantz's laugh was humourless. '*Touché*, Chief, *touché*. No, let's keep this between cops. I won't quote you, you don't quote me. To be frank, if that was the case I wouldn't be astonished. Many of our police officers and fire-fighters suffered from post-traumatic stress after Nine Eleven. As you can imagine, losing his wife in the tragedy, Inspector Mawhinney was more deeply affected than most. I told the South Manhattan borough patrol commander to send him on compassionate furlough, but Colin just refused point-blank. He insisted on staying at his post. I ordered him, personally, to have counselling but that was as far as I was prepared to push it. To be honest, Chief Skinner, at that time, I needed all the heroes I could get.'

'Has he had any time off since?'

'Oh yes, but not voluntarily. Just before Christmas of that year, he finally had a breakdown; his counsellor reported that he was in a very fragile emotional state. At that point, I intervened, and ordered him to take some time off.'

'Did he have family other than his wife?'

'His father's been dead for around ten years. His mother remarried and moved to Maryland but Colin didn't like his stepfather; he didn't regard him as a particularly upright citizen. When he did take a break, he went to the Florida Keys to do some fishing. It was supposed to be for a month, but he came back after a couple of weeks and begged me to let him go back to work. He told me, and right now I can hear him say it as if he was standing beside my desk, "Chief, if I'd stared at that water any longer, I'd have been in it." I guess finally he couldn't stop himself.'

'That's the way it looks,' Skinner admitted. 'He was weighted down with a chain, so falling in isn't an option.'

'And he couldn't have been mugged?'

'It's unlikely in that area, and even more so where he was found. If he'd gone in a bit up-river, maybe, but he wouldn't have drifted with that chain round him. He went in where he was pulled out, and that was in a commercial dock that he could have seen from his hotel-room window.'

'Sounds open and shut, then. You'll autopsy, I take it.'

'It's mandatory.'

'You'll use your top pathologist?'

'Be sure of it. I'll copy the report to you.'

'Thank you for that. What about your media? Has this hit the press yet?'

'They know a body was recovered from the dock. That of itself isn't big news, but when they find out who it is, it will be.

As of now we're hiding behind the standard line of not revealing the identity until next of kin have been informed. In this case, that means you; now that we've spoken I'll authorise a formal statement through our communications manager.'

'Could you see your way to doing something for Colin? In that statement could you call it accidental?'

'I can do that. How it's filed eventually isn't my decision, but I've got some influence with the guy who'll make it.'

'Thanks. NYPD appreciates that.' Chief Lovencrantz was silent for a moment. 'I'm going to send someone over to Scotland, Chief Skinner, as an honour guard, to bring the body back home. It'll probably be Inspector Nolan Donegan, the commander of Sixth Precinct; he was Colin's best friend on the force, so I guess that's appropriate.'

'Fine. Once he's booked his flight, let my office know his itinerary and I'll have him received. Meantime, I'll ask Mario McGuire, our man on the exchange between our forces, to take charge of his personal effects.'

'Thanks,' said Lovencrantz. 'I'll be in touch. Now I'd better go downtown for what will surely be my worst duty of the year, and break the bad news, personally, to the officers of the First Precinct.'

Skinner replaced the phone and sat for a while at his son's desk, staring out of the window. 'It's a shit job,' he murmured, 'that can do that to a man. So why do I love it?'

He picked up the handset once more, found the head of CID's cell-phone number in his notebook, and dialled it. 'Dan. DCC here. What's up?'

He listened as Pringle described the hand grenade that had

been thrown into the midst of his investigation. 'Bloody hell!' he exclaimed, when he was finished. 'Did you ever have one of those days, my friend, when all you wanted to do was go home, pack a suitcase and fuck off somewhere nobody could find you? Well, I'm at home right now, as it happens, and the temptation's hard to resist. I will, though. Have you found a hotel?'

'It wasn't easy, but I'm putting them in the Alpha. I just hope my budget can stand it.'

'You leave that with me. I'll have a word with Jim Gainer; I'm sure the archdiocese can stand that tab. What's your next move?'

'I'll be back at Fettes in ten minutes,' said the chief superintendent. 'Once I get there, I'll call my opposite number on the Humberside force, and see what he can tell me about this drunk-driver hit-and-run.'

'You're making a big assumption there, Daniel,' Skinner murmured into the phone.

'What's that?'

'That the guy was drunk.'

'You don't think so?'

'Call me a world-weary cynic if you will, but when I see two fatalities in two days, involving members of the same small group, "accidental" is not the adjective that jumps into my mind.'

Fifty-four

'How was she, then?'

'Very professional, very sharp, very good; Mary's going to do fine.'

Maggie smiled as she hung her uniform on one of the handles of his wardrobe. 'So it's "Mary" already, is it?' she said.

'We got off on the right foot; plus, as a person she's not given to excessive formality. A bit like yourself, Chief Superintendent Rose.' Stevie hugged her to him, grinning back at her.

'It's a bit hard to be formal when you're standing in your bra and knickers.' She wriggled free of his embrace and reached for her jeans. 'If Sauce and Charlie Johnson could see us now, eh.'

He sat on the edge of the bed, looking up at her as she dressed. 'That's something we're going to have to think about.'

'I know,' she agreed, 'but in our own time, yes?'

'Not necessarily. Mary's an even better detective than you gave her credit for, and she's got a knack of recognising people by their cars. She spotted yours turning in here yesterday evening.'

'And she asked you about it?' Maggie gasped.

'Straight out.'

'What did you tell her?'

'I didn't have to tell her anything. Like I said, she's a very good detective; she wouldn't have asked the question unless she'd been damn sure of the answer. It's nothing to worry about, though. Mary Chambers of all people knows how to be discreet, and she's not going to fall out with you.'

'Let's hope not, but what does it mean? For us, that is.'

'Mary says,' he began, 'that is, her advice is, based on her personal experience, that we shouldn't try to cover anything up.'

'We could always walk away from it, of course.'

'What do you mean?'

'We could say to each other, "Thanks, that was nice, but let's just stay friends," and back off before it goes any further.'

'Is that what you want?' he asked her quietly.

She looked down at her hands, then up at him, into his eyes, and shook her head. 'No,' she whispered. 'What about you?'

'No more than you do. I want the opposite.'

'What do you mean?'

'I mean that I'd like you to move in with me.'

She raised her eyebrows, then sat beside him on the bed. 'Do you mean that?'

'Am I a serious guy or am I not?'

'You're a serious guy.'

'So?'

'I'm a handful, you know.'

'I can handle you.'

'I reckon you can at that.'

'So?'

'This is happening awful fast, Stevie.'

'No, it isn't, we've been working up to it for months, and you know it.'

'You were that sure of yourself all that time, were you?' She chuckled.

'Yup. Weren't you?'

'Scared shitless at the prospect, but yes, I do admit now to having fancied you something rotten for a while. I should be thankful to She Who Cannot Be Named for making me pluck up the courage to do something about it.'

'So?'

'So what?'

'Oh Christ, Maggie, do you want me on one knee? Will you please come and live with me and be my partner, and let me love you and look after you?'

She looked at him, soberly, as they sat side by side. 'What have you got planned for the next hour of your life?' she asked him.

'Nothing.'

'Good.' She jumped to her feet and took his hand, pulling him after her. 'In that case you can come back to my house and help me start to pack.' His heart leaped in his chest as he followed her downstairs, and out to her car.

'You happy now?' she asked, as she drove out of Gordon Terrace.

'Happier than I can ever remember,' he told her honestly.

'Shop or no shop?'

'What do you mean?'

'We have to have a house rule; either we talk shop or we don't. Which is it to be?'

'I've never lived with another cop before. You tell me.'

She smiled, so brightly that it seemed to light up the car. 'Thank you, darling, for reminding me that I'm still a married woman. But you're right, experience counts and you have to learn from it. We talk shop. Mario and I had a no-shop rule, and at the end we'd bugger all to talk about. So what else have you been up to with Mary today?'

'Quite a lot actually. We went to see young Mr Whetstone, and told him what his old man had been up to. He told us we were idiots for not knowing all about the manufacture of curling stones, that his father did and wouldn't have set up a dummy company to do that.'

'Would a detail like that matter, if he was planning to top himself as soon as the money was unreachable by the bank?'

'Maybe not, but we went back to the bank anyway.'

'What did Vernon say to that?'

'Vernon wasn't there; the boss had sent him home to prune his roses.'

'No real surprise in that.'

'No, but the absence of Ms Middlemass, that was.'

'Really?'

'Really. She's done a runner. We went to her address, a nice townhouse out in Cramond, but there was no sign of her;

the company car was there, but she wasn't. The neighbours were little help. Those that we found said she and her husband never mixed socially; they were strangers to them. One of them thought that there had been coming and going at their house last night but he couldn't be sure.'

'What about the husband? The Spanish academic?'

'Señor Jose-Maria Alsina, you mean? We went out to the Heriot-Watt campus to look for him. He wasn't there either. Nobody there was bothered about that, though; technically he might be on the staff, but he's actually doing a Ph.D. in chemistry. He takes some tutorials, and a wee bit of teaching, but that's all. Otherwise he makes his own hours.'

'So what's the conclusion?'

'It's all pointing to them being off to parts unknown with the bank's million. Tomorrow we start taking a serious look into her background.'

'Hold on, though. Maybe they've just gone off for a long weekend without telling anyone,' Maggie suggested.

'Hah,' Stevie exclaimed. 'One day in the new job and you're thinking like a plod already.'

'Hey! That's Chief Superintendent Plod, if you don't mind.' She grinned as she drove. 'But you're right; that's where it points. So why did Ivor top himself, in that case?'

'The cancer, I suppose. If he did top himself, that is. What if he found out about the fake company and was about to expose her?'

'Indeed.' She paused. 'By the way, speaking of topping oneself, while you were out on the chase with Mary, I had a call from my ex, very upset. Remember his American visitor?'

'The New Yorker? Yes.'

'Well, last night he had supper at Paula's, walked back to the Malmaison and into the docks, wrapped a heavy chain around his middle and jumped in.'

Stevie whistled in the darkened car. 'Jesus,' he whispered. 'I don't remember Paula's cooking being *that* bad.'

Fifty-five

The Archbishop's residence was an anonymous villa in an anonymous Edinburgh suburb. Bob Skinner had never been there before, and so as he parked in the street outside and turned into the driveway, he expected to find a sober place with white-curtained windows and a monastic look.

What he saw was a light, airy garden strewn with plaster sculptures and with fountains playing musically on either side of the pathway. There was a garage to the left with a Chrysler PT Cruiser parked in front and a Suzuki SV1000 . . . a very serious motorcycle, the DCC knew . . . alongside it.

Father Angelo Collins opened the door in answer to his ring of the bell. 'Whose is the bike?' Skinner asked the young priest. 'Yours?'

'You have to be kidding.' Archbishop Gainer's voice came from within the hallway. 'This boy thinks a Ford Fiesta's a bit racy. No, that's my toy out there. I saw *Easy Rider* when I was a kid and I was hooked. Come in, Bob. Actually, I've been meaning to get in touch with you. Come on through to my study.'

He led the way to a room at the back of the big, airy house, furnished with a desk, swivel chair and two armchairs. There was a flat-screen computer monitor on the desk, and a television in the corner. 'Sit down, Bob,' he said, collapsing into one of the armchairs. He was wearing black cords and a grey sweatshirt with one word, 'GOD', in large letters on the front. He saw it catch Skinner's eye as he sat opposite him and grinned. 'If you support a team, you have to wear the colours,' he said. 'What about that poor Belgian? What's the story?' he asked, then paused. 'Sorry, how inhospitable can I get? Would you like a beer?'

'I'd like several . . . I have to go to witness a post mortem . . . but I daren't have even one. About the Belgian, that should be plural, not singular.' He told Gainer about Jack McGurk's discovery halfway through his so-called routine interviews. 'Dan Pringle called me when I was on my way here. He's been in touch with the Humberside police. They've got no witnesses, they've got no vehicle, but they do still have the body, pending shipment back to Belgium. Pringle's contact told him some very interesting stuff. The man Hanno was hit by a heavy vehicle going fast. They reckon it was an off-roader or a pick-up; whatever it was it had bull-bars, because the marks of them could be seen clearly on the victim's shattered legs. The most significant thing was what they didn't find.'

'What was that?'

'Skidmarks. There were none on the road where the body was found. None at all. That means . . .'

'I know what it means,' the Archbishop intervened. 'It means that the driver didn't even try to stop, but just steamed straight through the poor bloke.'

'Correct; and that in turn says to me this was a deliberate hit-and-run. I've never seen a fatal involving a drunk where the driver didn't brake hard and leave some sort of trace on the road.'

'What about the other one, Lebeau, the one who was poisoned?'

'It changes our thinking altogether. We're no longer inclined to believe that he was a random victim of a contaminated product. We know the tube that killed him was bought in Newcastle on Friday while the band was there.'

'By one of them, do you think?'

'Not possible, they were playing at the time. I guess it was bought there to make it look as if Lebeau had bought it himself, and to make us react in exactly the way we did, by blowing the whistle and starting a national product recall.'

'Do you think these two men were picked out, or were they random victims within the band?'

'We don't know for sure, but on the evidence we have at the moment, they're random. Hanno ran out of fags and went to get more from their bus; that's why he was outside. How could the driver of the car have known that was going to happen? It suggests that he was just waiting for any one of them. In that case,' he continued, 'we'll have to give the whole bloody lot protection from now on. I've booked them into a hotel . . .'

'The Church will pay for that,' Gainer told him at once.

Skinner smiled. 'Thanks for that. I'm glad I didn't have to ask you.' His expression grew serious once more. 'There is something, though. What is it with these people? Why are they here at all?'

'I wish I could tell you,' the Archbishop murmured, 'but I can't, for I've been asking that myself. Without bragging, Bob, I'm probably closer to the Holy Father than anyone except his brother, but not even I know why he's invited the Bastogne Drummers to play at his rally. If you want answers, you'll have to ask him yourself.'

The DCC's gaze went to the ceiling. 'Not me, Your Grace,' he said. 'There are very few occasions when I hide behind my chief constable, but this will be one of them. If anyone's going to question the Pope as a potential witness in a murder inquiry it's going to be him!'

He turned to leave, and the Archbishop moved to show him to the door. As they went along the hall, he asked, 'What's happened to you, Bob?'

'What do you mean?'

'I mean that, compared to last week, you're a different man.'

Skinner glanced sideways at him. 'You sure, Jim? Are you sure it isn't the old one coming back?'

Fifty-six

As was the case with many pubs, Monday was the quietest evening of the week in the Wee Black Dug. There were fewer than a dozen customers in the saloon when McGuire walked in and Malky Gladsmuir was behind the bar with only one assistant.

'What can I get you, sir?' he asked, eyeing the detective up and down.

'A pint of seventy and your undivided attention.'

'Oh, aye?' said Gladsmuir, giving a slight smirk as he started to draw the beer.

The detective looked him dead in the eye. 'I want you to think hard about this,' he said, under his breath. 'Do you want to cross me? I mean it, do you reckon you want to get on my bad side?'

'Fancy yourself, do you?' Gladsmuir growled, but there was a tiny flicker of hesitation in his voice.

'All the fucking way, Malky, and any time you like. Now you listen, and take note; the name is Detective Superintendent McGuire, and I'm not here to bring you good news. My predecessor probably came across to you as a guy you could

339

keep stringing along. A wee bit of info here, another wee bit there, and you were left alone to get on with whatever fucking scams you run in this place.'

'Ah run a straight pub. You ask your guys.'

'Like hell you do. You hammered that drug-dealer because he moved gear in your bar . . .'

'That's right. See what I mean?'

'. . . without giving you a cut,' McGuire concluded. 'Greg Jay might have placed too much trust in human goodness to have figured that one out, but I'm not like him. So if you want any sort of slack . . . and that will not include drugs being dealt in here, by the way, not ever again . . . you will do what I tell you.' He took a deep swallow of the beer. 'Not bad,' he conceded. 'The first thing I'm going to tell you is this. We pulled a friend of mine out of the Albert Dock this morning.'

'Another copper, I hope,' the bar manager mumbled.

'In your office, now.' McGuire pointed to the door behind him and stepped through the hatch. He followed Gladsmuir into the private room, closed the door behind them, and in one continuous movement swung his right fist up and buried it in his belly. The breath left him in a groan and he sat down hard on the floor.

The detective stood over him, glaring down with angry, dangerous eyes; Malky Gladsmuir had the good sense to be scared. 'You might be a hard man in your own league,' McGuire said quietly, 'but you're not in mine, so don't you ever show disrespect to a police officer in front of me. As I was saying, we recovered the body of a friend of mine from the water this morning. There are a few questions in my mind that still need answers, and I want you to help me. My pal left my partner's place at about ten last night . . . she lives in the warehouse conversion just off Great Junction Street; you know the one I mean. He walked from there, back to the Malmaison Hotel, only he never went in there. They're trying to say he jumped, and maybe he did, but I need to be certain. We called in here for a pint earlier; you were off duty, but there were a few people in. On his way back, he'd have gone past this place, more or less. I want you to ask around, and I want you to find out if any of your regulars remembers seeing him. He was about six feet tall, slim built, but he was wearing a big heavy jacket so he'd have looked quite bulky. If that does ring any bells, I need to know also whether there was anyone else around, anyone, or maybe more than one person, who might have been following him.'

Gladsmuir looked up at him from the floor. 'I'll see what I can do.' He winced.

'No, you'll fucking do it. I'll bet Greg Jay gave you his direct line number, didn't he?'

'Aye.'

'Well, that's my number now. Call me on it as soon as you've got anything for me. And don't get cute and make up any stories to get me off your back. So far you've only seen my friendly side.'

Fifty-seven

'Hey,' said Skinner, quietly, as he helped Sarah fasten her sterilised blue gown, 'before we go in, there's something I want to tell you. I'm sorry I leaned on you to do this; moral blackmail isn't very nice and I wish I hadn't said what I did, about you letting me down. It wasn't right, and it wasn't even true.'

'Sure it was true,' she replied. 'That was how you saw it at the time, and if you were being honest with yourself rather than simply trying to be nice to me, you'd see that it still is. I've got no ethical problem with doing this; my reluctance was personal. So can we please stop saying sorry to each other? It's all right for us to disagree, Bob, and it doesn't even matter who's right and who's wrong.' She pulled on her cap. 'Now let's do this thing.'

She led the way from the dressing room into the autopsy theatre, where a postgraduate pathology student and a police photographer were waiting, standing over the body of Colin Mawhinney as it lay on the stainless table, naked, washed clean, white, still and cold.

She went straight to work, running through the preliminaries, giving the corpse a thorough external examination, speaking into the microphone above her head as she did so, dictating the notes that she would type up later. 'I can find no marks on the body,' she said, 'no signs of injury, not even any old scars.' She turned and nodded to the photographer, who snapped off a couple of shots. 'I'm now going to look inside the mouth,' she continued, picking up a spatula, and pulling the jaws apart. 'Inside, I can see traces of weed, and general debris that's come from immersion. That's what I would expect. We'll take samples later. Let's have a look at the hands now.'

When the first phase was complete, she turned to the student. 'Mike, I want you to do a couple of strong compressions on the chest wall. Not too strong, though; mustn't break any ribs.' As the young man did as she had asked, she turned to her witness husband. 'Do you know what this is for?'

'No.'

'It's . . . Wait a minute. Yes. Come here.' Reluctantly, he followed her beckoning finger. 'Do you see that foam, around the nostrils and mouth?' He leaned over and saw as she had described, a light froth, white, with a very faint pink tinge. 'That's a vital sign,' she told him. 'It's a mix of water, air, mucus and a little blood, whisked up by respiratory efforts. Basically it tells us before we do anything else that he was alive when he went into the water.'

'We never doubted that,' said Skinner.

'Well, you know for sure now. Okay, I'm ready to begin the internal examination. In the circumstances,' she said to her assistant, 'I'm going straight for the lungs.' Skinner backed off, quickly; when she picked up her scalpel, he cheated, as he always had done at that moment in every autopsy he had witnessed, by staring into the lights, blinding himself to what was going on before him. He could not shut out the sounds, though, as she opened the abdominal cavity then spread the ribs.

As she worked, her assistant came to join her on the opposite side of the table, mercifully blocking Skinner's view. He knew what they were doing, and he tried not to imagine it, but as always he failed. She removed the lungs, and placed them in a wide dry basin, which the assistant hooked on to a scale. 'Seventeen hundred and ninety grams,' he announced.

'That indicates that they're still full of water,' said Sarah, as the student laid the organs on a steel bench. Leaving the opened corpse, she walked round the dissection table and began to examine them. 'They're voluminous and ballooned,' she called out, speaking up for the microphone. 'The pleural surface appears marbled; they feel doughy and are pitting on pressure. I'm going to start to section now.' The assistant came over to her with several dishes ready to receive tissue samples. 'But first, I'm going to be a little unconventional and aspirate some of the water content.' She reached out and selected a syringe with a long needle, inserted it carefully into the lower lobe of the right lung and began to draw off liquid.

'Bob,' she called out, when she was finished, 'I think you should see this.'

Her husband tore his eyes away from the bright, near-blinding light. 'Must I?' he replied.

'Oh yes, you must.'

He blinked hard as he walked round to her, trying to restore some focus to his vision. 'Don't worry,' she said, 'I'm not going to make you look at any squidgy bits, but tell me,' she held up the syringe, 'what you make of that.'

He peered at the fluid in the chamber. 'It's slightly pink,' he murmured.

'Blood traces; to be expected. Anything else?'

'Nothing I can see.'

'Exactly. And that's what's giving me a problem.'

She laid down the syringe, and turned to him. 'Go on,' she said, 'get your large ass out of here.'

'Eh?'

'You heard. I don't need you here any longer; Mike's a witness, the photographer's a witness. This autopsy has just become anything but routine. I am going to have to work super-carefully from here on. I'm going to have to take several sections of the lungs from different lobe locations, central and peripheral. I'm going to have to take samples of the stomach contents, and do a lot of other testing. I do not need the distraction of having you in the room and wondering all the time when you're going to puke.'

She patted his chest. 'Thanks, you've got me this far, after I was reluctant to do this; now the best way you can support me is by digging out a technician, regardless of the time of day it is, to take water samples from the part of the dock where the body was found. We'll need to analyse them. After that, you can go home . . . but don't wait up for me: I could be some time.'

Fifty-eight

The top hinge of the front door squeaked. It had done for the last year, and every two months Bob had promised that he would buy a new tin of Three-in-One and fix it. On the odd occasion, though, it served him well.

He checked his watch: the time was ten past one. Killing the insomniac's movie on BBC2 with his remote, he walked into the hall with a glass in each hand. One contained red wine; the other, which he handed to Sarah, was a brandy goblet. 'That's been getting warm for the last hour and a half,' he told her.

Dropping her briefcase where she stood, she accepted it, gratefully, and took a sip. 'I told you not to wait up,' she said, 'but I'm glad you did.'

He led her through into the darkened garden room, and dropped into a couch, looking out of the window at the lights of the Fife towns, across the river. 'Sleep wasn't an option, not knowing what you've been doing.'

'Did you do your part?' she asked, as she joined him.

'Not personally, but it's taken care of.' He glanced at her as she sat beside him. 'So what's your story?'

'You're not going to like it. It's all subject to confirmation by test, but I don't believe that Inspector Mawhinney drowned in the Albert Dock. When I checked the stomach, there was dirty, oily water present, and other detritus that almost certainly did come from there, but that need not have been swallowed. It was also present in the large airways, but it need not have been inhaled. It wasn't in large quantities in the stomach, and it wasn't present in the further reaches of the bronchus. You saw the water I aspirated with that syringe; it was clear, and it was abundant in the lower areas of the lungs. It may also have diluted the dock water in the stomach. Bob, I think that he was drowned in fresh water and was put in the dock afterwards, weighted down with that chain to make him sink.'

He leaned back and let out a huge sigh. 'You're right about one thing, without any lab confirmation. You haven't exactly made my night. Was there anything else?'

'Yes. There were signs of bruising to the shoulder girdle and the neck. That can happen occasionally in drowning fatalities, but usually it's caused by the victim struggling in the water prior to death. Muscles can even rupture in those circumstances and you can find haemorrhaging, but not in this case. Here, the bruising could have been caused by his being restrained and held under water.'

'Christ on a bike,' Skinner muttered. 'You're saying that someone snatched the guy off the street and drowned him in a bath or something similar.'

'That is my hypothesis.'

'Not your everyday mugging, is it?'

347

'Not even close.'

'What are you thinking?'

'Mafia?' she murmured. 'Has he upset someone in New York?'

'And been taken care of over here, you mean, in the hope that it would raise less heat?'

'The trip was publicised.'

'The Mafia don't rely on the papers,' he told her, 'they bribe informants; but essentially you're right. I tell you, love, the sooner the Pope gets here the better. I'm going to need divine assistance to sort out all the mess that's landed in my lap in the last twenty-four hours.'

Fifty-nine

'Neither Aurelia Middlemass nor Señor Alsina showed up for work this morning,' said Stevie Steele. 'I've just confirmed that with the bank and with the professor of chemistry at Heriot-Watt.'

'Did you think either of them would?' asked Mary Chambers.

The inspector shrugged his shoulders. 'Not really, but you never know; I had to check.'

'Of course you did; now where does that leave us? What more do we have to go on than we had yesterday?'

'First off, I've got a report from Arthur Dorward. He's examined the papers in the Bonspiel Partnership folder.'

'Does it take us forward?'

'Sideways. He's identified Easterson's prints on the documents from the samples he gave us yesterday, and Whetstone's, from matches taken from the body. There's a third set, though, as yet unidentified. Mr Fraser told me he never handled the documents, so I expect they'll prove to be Middlemass's, but we need something for comparison. Arthur's sending a couple of people to the bank this morning; they're going to look for a diary, or something else that she handled exclusively, and take what they can get from that. Once that's done, they're going to the house. I've got a warrant from the Sheriff to enter and search.'

'So all three handled the documents; what do we read into that?'

'Surely the presence of Whetstone's prints is important? If Aurelia, or even Easterson, had set him up they wouldn't be there.'

Chambers smiled. 'Oh, no? Let's say I'm one of those two, planning this thing. I'd have discovered that I was out of loan-application forms, then I'd have stuck my head in Whetstone's office and asked him if he had a spare.'

'The document runs to several pages. His prints were on every one.'

'I'd have asked him to flick through it to make sure that all the pages were there.'

'You're too good at that, Mary. You're not bent, are you?' He gulped as the words left his mouth.

'Hell of a question to ask me,' the superintendent replied cheerfully. 'Actually, I've made a point of studying the method-ology in every fraud case I've ever worked on. That's quite a common one; I've nicked a car salesman and a building-society clerk for setting up phoney deals, and both of them tried to set up their mates that way. So just having handled the document doesn't prove he done it.'

'There is something else about him,' Steele said. 'We know that Whetstone didn't consult his Edinburgh GP about his illness, but I had a thought that I asked George Regan to follow up for me. It paid off yesterday. His doctor down in Kelso was a pal, and a member of the same golf club as him. Whetstone visited him just over three weeks ago, at his home, not his surgery. He listened to his chest and sent him for an X-ray on the spot. It came back with a big shadow on one lung and a smaller one on the other. He referred him straight away to an oncologist, a man called Nigel Goodyear, who has a private practice in Glasgow. George phoned the man, and when he heard that Whetstone was dead he was happy to talk to him. He saw him at Ross Hall Hospital within a couple of days. He put him through a CT scanner, then did needle biopsies that confirmed malignancy.'

'And the prognosis?'

'Goodyear said surgery was out of the question; it was way too late for that. He said he could only offer him chemotherapy and radiotherapy, and then purely as a delaying tactic. He had to tell Mr Whetstone that the best practical help he could give him was by arranging for him to go into a hospice when the time came.'

'And when did he reckon that would be?'

'Two or three months.'

'Poor bugger. I guess he didn't fancy the hospice idea, then.'

'Apparently not; that dislocated shoulder still worries me a bit, though, just as it worried Sarah at the time. Her first thought was that he'd have needed help. What do you think, Mary? I've been involved in this from the start. You can stand a bit further back from it than me. How do you read it?'

The superintendent swivelled in her chair, round and back again, round and back again, as she thought. 'Show me the money, Stevie,' she murmured. 'That's where we normally find the answer in a situation like this. But it's gone, hasn't it? And so have Aurelia Middlemass and her husband.'

She gave a grim smile, a hunter's smile. 'Their disappearance changes everything; young Murphy must have been right. It wasn't his dad who set up the Bonspiel Partnership, it was her, but to guard against discovery before she was ready she did it in a way that pointed at Ivor Whetstone. Maybe he found out about it, or just got suspicious . . . we know from the widow that he never liked her . . . and she and her husband killed him to shut him up. Or maybe he never knew about it, and just topped himself to save himself a lingering death. We'll ask her about all of it when we catch her.'

'That will be easier said than done,' Steele said gloomily. 'If we don't know where the money is, we don't even know where to start looking for them. We've no idea where they're headed.'

'No, but . . .'

'Sure, I know,' he exclaimed briskly, 'we can try to pick up their trail. I'll start with the airports and railway stations, and get into her credit-card records, and her husband's, to see whether they've been used to buy travel tickets.'

'Yes, and another thing. Her car's still at their house, so check whether he had one, and if he did, get a description out.'

Steele nodded. 'I'll get the boys on it right away. Then I think I'll go and see Murphy and his mother. It won't bring Ivor back, but it'll be the nearest thing they've had to good news since he died.'

Sixty

The national rugby stadium was a far different place than it had been forty-eight hours earlier. A team of scaffolders were finishing the superstructure of the platform on which the Pope's official party would sit on the following Saturday, with carpenters beginning work beneath them on the steps and the flooring. They worked quickly and skilfully; they were used to erecting grandstands at golf events all over the country so the Murrayfield job was child's play for them all.

Skinner stood at the vehicle entrance to the great bowl-like stadium, watching them at work, although they were not the reason for his visit. Brian Mackie was by his side, in uniform and wearing a luminous yellow over-jacket with the word 'Police' spelled out on the back, superfluously, given his unmistakable cap. Beyond him stood Giovanni Rossi.

'This place is wide open,' said Skinner to the chief superintendent.

'That can't be avoided, not while they're putting up the infrastructure for the event, but we're running sniffer dogs through the place every day. The contractors will all be finished by tomorrow, and the performers will be allowed to rehearse on Thursday morning. After that, the stadium will be closed and sealed off; my people and Maggie's will be guarding it all night. There will be a further search on Friday morning, then we'll let the people in.'

'You happy with that, Gio?' the DCC asked the Italian.

'Entirely.'

'Have you got everything you need, Brian?'

It was said by colleagues that Mackie's smiles were rationed to one a day; he used up Tuesday's allocation. 'If you can fix up some decent weather for the event, sir,' he said, 'that would be good.'

'If anyone can do that it's John the Twenty-fifth.' Skinner looked at his colleague. 'Where are these bloody Belgians, then?'

'They're rehearsing out on the back pitches. They wanted to do it in the stadium, but there are too many workers about for that. I've got uniformed officers watching them, though. I'll show you where they are if you like.'

'It's okay, Brian,' the DCC laughed, 'I used to be a detective, remember. I'll find them; the noise of their drums might just give me a clue.'

He walked out of the stadium and round the west stand, past the Scottish Rugby Union offices and shop and out of the gate. A cold wind was blowing from the east, but even against it, he could still hear the martial sound of drumming and the blare of brass instruments. He looked across the big field and saw a group in military array, twenty-four blue-clad musicians in front and a dozen red-uniformed musketeers bringing up

354

the rear. He strolled towards them, but kept his distance until he saw the leader, Malou, give the 'fall out' signal.

The old colonel had seen him coming; as his men laid down their instruments, he walked to meet him. 'Good morning, sir,' he said. 'You come to watch us march?'

'That and some,' said Skinner. 'Do you practise every day?'

'No, but today we must. On Sunday I sent for two replacements from Belgium, from the First Guides band; they arrived last night and they have very little time to get to know our repertoire, and our march routines.' He shivered. 'I wish it wasn't necessary. It's a cold country you live in. It is as well our uniforms are thick and made for the outdoors.'

'What do you do when it rains?'

'We have capes; transparent so you can see the uniforms.' Malou fumbled in his trouser pockets and produced a blue pack of cigarettes. He offered one to the DCC, who shook his head. 'You don't have the habit, then?'

'No. My brother forced me to smoke when I was about ten years old: made me sick as a dog. That put me off for life.'

'You might have wound up smoking Gauloises like me. You should have thanked your brother.'

'I didn't see it that way at the time,' the Scot mused, 'but you're right.' He watched as the old man lit up with a disposable Bic and inhaled deeply.

'Filthy habit, but it's one that's been with me since I was a young man. When I joined the army nearly everyone smoked, especially the officers. There were nights when we couldn't see across the mess, it was so thick.'

'Sounds like the fog we had here last week. Why do you smoke those things?' the DCC asked. 'They seem pretty strong.'

'I've smoked them for forty years and more. The main reason I got hooked on them was because they were good for keeping the mosquito at bay.'

'Would they work on midges? That's our big problem in Scotland.'

'I've heard that. A good friend told me so many years ago. As I understand the two creatures are essentially the same. Mosquito means "little fly", and so does your word "midge", doesn't it?'

'Yes,' Skinner grinned, 'but ours have sharper teeth.'

'So why are you here?' Malou asked. 'Do you have news of the deaths of Philippe and Barty, or did you simply want to see us march and hear us play?'

'There are some things I want to ask you. Well, one thing, really. Why are you here?'

The old colonel looked up at him sharply. 'What do you mean?'

'Why were you invited?'

'Because we are very good; we are an institution in Belgium and in Luxembourg, and Holland . . . or at least we once were, before age started to catch up with us.'

'I'm sure that's the case, Monsieur Malou, but there has to be more to it than that. You're here at the personal invitation of the Pope.'

'When he was a young priest, newly ordained, His Holiness spent some time in Belgium. The Bastogne Drummers have been around for many years; I didn't found them, I only gave them a lift when they needed it. I imagine that Father Gibb must have heard them then.'

'What did you call him?' Skinner asked quietly, as Malou dragged on his cigarette.

The colonel looked away; his face seemed to redden slightly. 'I'm sorry,' he mumbled, 'I forgot who I was talking about.'

'No, you didn't. That's a name that very few people use; the only ones who do are his closest personal friends. How long have you known the Pope?'

The old man finished his cigarette, inhaling the last of the smoke. 'We met during that time I spoke of, when we were both young men. And yes, we became good friends in those days. But it was a long time ago and it is not something I like to boast of; that would not be proper. I don't even like to talk about it.'

'Come on, it's more than a youthful meeting forty years ago for him to have invited you here. What brought you together?'

'That is something between Father Gibb and me,' Malou snapped, 'and I will not speak of it, to you or anyone else. And neither, I can promise you, will he.' He turned on his heel and walked away, leaving Skinner staring at his back.

Sixty-one

Murphy Whetstone was home alone when Steele called. As he led the detective through to the kitchen, to make coffee for them both, he explained that his mother had taken Blue off in her car for a walk around Holyrood Park. 'The poor dog's had barely any exercise since Dad died, and from what Mum said, his walks had been getting shorter before that.'

'Yet your father was in the habit of walking home from the office?'

'I know, but that had tailed off too, so Mum said.'

A night's sleep seemed to have done him some good. The circles had gone from beneath his eyes, and he looked more like a man of his age than he had on the inspector's first visit to him. He seemed also to have regained some spirit, as he handed Steele a mug. 'Are you here to ask or tell?' he said bluntly.

'Tell, in this case. There's been a development I thought you should know about.' As he explained about the disappearance of Aurelia Middlemass and her husband, Murphy's face seemed to light up. 'It all fits now,' he exclaimed, when the inspector had finished.

'What does?'

'Come into my dad's study and let me show you something,' he said. Carrying his coffee, Steele followed him into a room next to the kitchen that looked out on to a long, immaculately maintained back garden. 'My mother's pride and joy,' he said. 'Dad had his golf; she's got that.'

In one corner of the study, there was a desk on which a computer sat, up and running, showing moving stars as a screensaver. 'I've been looking through my father's files,' said the young man. 'To be completely honest, I thought that if he had left a suicide note, this is where it would be. The Old Man came late to computers, but when he did, he embraced them. His Filofax is gathering dust somewhere; all his personal records and notes were kept here. He had a web-cam, and he and I used to have video chats every couple of weeks or so. He didn't keep a daily diary . . . not the Samuel Pepys kind at least; he wasn't that sort of man . . . but I did find reminders and stuff, and notes, in a personal folder.' He looked at Steele. 'Before I show you this, I promise you, I didn't create it to try to prove anything. This is his own document.'

He touched the mouse and the screensaver vanished, to be replaced on the screen by a photograph of Blue, the Siberian husky. Murphy smiled. 'He used to create his own wallpaper,' he said. 'He had a video camera and downloaded pictures from it. He was always changing the image.' He moved the mouse and clicked on a series of folders, until a document opened. It was headed 'Countdown'.

It showed dates listed in sequence. Some were blank while others had entries against them. Steele scanned them and his eye was drawn to one in particular. It appeared on the day of his death, and it read 'Check AM/BP'.

'What do you think that is?' the young man asked.

'I think it's interesting. AM could be Aurelia Middlemass, and BP could be . . .'

'Bonspiel Partnership,' he finished. 'I reckon my dad was on to her, that she found out and that she killed him to shut him up, making it look like suicide so that when the fraud was discovered it would be blamed on him. What do you think?'

'I think it's a possibility, Murphy, that's all I'll say. I'll put it to her when we catch her, you can be sure of that, but without a confession there isn't enough to make a murder charge stick. Can I ask you, would the financial consequences for your mother be any different if the fiscal decides it wasn't suicide, and we can convict Middlemass of fraud?'

'No. After our solicitor showed them the pathologist's report, which said my father would have died within months, the insurance company paid out on his policy. His pension's ring-fenced as well, that passes to Mum and there's nothing the bank can do about it. All I care about is my dad's memory.'

'In that case, pal,' said Stevie Steele, 'I'll do all I can to help you protect it.'

Sixty-two

'That's definite, Chief Skinner?' asked the chief of Department. 'Your pathologist is totally certain?'

'A couple of hundred per cent certain, Mr Lovencrantz. Her findings have been confirmed by tests. I waited for the results before I called you. Colin Mawhinney was drowned in clean, fresh water . . . analysis shows that it was from the public supply, not from a pond or river . . . then weighted down and dropped into the dock.'

'That's no ordinary mugging, I agree.'

'No chance; he was targeted, and this was a professional hit. He was a strong, fit man, and there were no signs of a sedative in his bloodstream, so we're looking for two people, at least. Chief, we need all the information you can give us on Inspector Mawhinney. Who were his associates? Has he put away anyone in his career who might have held a long-term grudge against him? You know what I'm talking about. While your people are gathering that information, I'll be pulling out all the stops at this end. Our security service and Special Branch network has a significant database on organised crime. I have access to that, and I will use it. I'll be looking for intelligence about known figures from out of town heading for Edinburgh in the last few days.'

'Thank you for that, Mr Skinner. I'll call in the chief of our detective bureau, and the head of my Internal Affairs Bureau. They may have to go back a way, for Colin was a senior patrol officer for the latter part of his career, but he did have a detective's shield for a time. If he upset any Mafia guys, that's when he would have done it.'

Skinner frowned. 'Listen,' he said, 'I hope you won't be offended by this, but I have to ask. Is there any possibility that he might have been on the take, and that someone out there felt he wasn't getting value for money?'

'I do not believe that for one moment, sir,' Lovencrantz snapped. And then he sighed. 'But why do you think I'm going to brief Internal Affairs?'

'If it's any consolation,' the Scot told him, 'I ran that past Mario McGuire, and he went ballistic at the idea.'

'How's Superintendent McGuire handling it?' asked the chief. 'I gather that he and Colin bonded pretty well during their time together.'

'He's taking it very badly. The body was found in his division, and normally he'd be in charge of the investigation, but I couldn't allow that.' He glanced across the desk, at the two men opposite. 'It's being headed by Neil McIlhenney, who's in charge of my Special Branch unit. He's reporting directly to me.'

'McGuire must hate to be on the sidelines.'

Skinner chuckled. 'You don't know him; holding back the tide would be easier than keeping his hands completely off it.

When I gave him his orders I chose my words pretty carefully. He'll be causing trouble out there; be sure of it. He just won't tell me about it . . . not until he gets a result, at any rate.'

'We have officers just like him,' said the American. 'They tend to be our most successful detectives, so their chief tells me. Mr Skinner, I have Nolan Donegan booked on a flight today. He leaves Newark this evening and is scheduled to arrive in Glasgow tomorrow morning.'

'Tell him that he'll be met by Chief Inspector Mackenzie; he's just transferred to this force, and he still lives in the Glasgow area. But you appreciate, do you, that in the changed circumstances it may be a few days before our prosecutor's office authorises release of the body?'

'I understand that, but I'm going to send Donegan anyway. I will also send an officer from IAB. He'll be carrying with him Mawhinney's personal file, plus all the other information we can pull together between now and flight time. That will include anything we can get on known crime figures who might have been out of the country in the last few days.'

'That would be appreciated. We may wind up sending this investigation back to you for completion. Whatever happens, be sure of one thing: we want to catch the bastards who did this every bit as much as you do.'

He hung up and looked at McIlhenney, and at Dan Pringle, who was seated beside him. 'Apart from what you just heard me promise, have either of you any bright ideas for lines of inquiry?'

'Eyewitnesses, sir,' the inspector replied. 'Somewhere between Paula Viareggio's place and the Malmaison,

Mawhinney was abducted. As you said, he was a big guy, so there must have been some sort of a struggle. We could issue a public appeal for anyone who saw anything like that to come forward.'

'Tomorrow, if we have to.'

'Why wait?'

'Because most of the replies we get will be mistaken or time-wasters; yet they'll all have to be followed up. In a week when our resources are stretched by the papal visit, that's a last resort. Before we go there, we've a card up our sleeve. I think if you ask our friend McGuire, you might find he's been making his presence felt on his new patch. Anyone who was on the street at that time on a Sunday was probably going home from the pub, so that's the best place to start looking for assistance.'

'They're not very forthcoming in that part of town,' said Pringle gloomily.

'They will be, with an angry McGuire leaning on them.' The DCC looked at McIlhenney. 'Go to it, Neil. Dan, you stay for a minute longer, I want a word with you about something else.'

The big inspector nodded and left the room. 'About these Belgians,' Skinner continued. 'I had a talk with Malou this morning.'

'Did it get you very far?' The head of CID's tone said it all.

'It did, funnily enough, only I'm not sure of the direction I'm headed. And I need to be; these guys are here to play for the Pope, yet someone's bumped two of them off.'

'Couldn't we just send them home?'

'It's not that easy; they're our responsibility now. They're safe under our protection, and they'll be safe at Murrayfield. If there are others on somebody's hit list, we can hardly send them back into danger. We need to solve this, not pass the buck. Besides, they're not our guests, Dan. They're here at the personal invitation of His Holiness; if anyone sends them packing it'll be him. And he won't, because the wee colonel's an old friend of his.'

Pringle was astonished. 'How did they meet?' he asked.

'I don't bloody know; Malou wouldn't say. He wouldn't have told me about it at all, if I hadn't picked up on a reference he made to him. He used a name that only a few people know. Dan, I want you to pull all the information on this investigation together, in fact on both of them, ours on Lebeau and the Humberside police's on Hanno. I want to see all the interviews that you and the boys have done with the Belgians, and all the witness statements that the Hull people have taken; everything, post-mortem reports on both men, the lot. While you're doing that, I'll be trying to find some answers.'

Pringle nodded and left. As soon as the door closed, the DCC picked up the phone and called a cell-phone number. 'Yes?' a female voice answered.

'Aileen, it's Bob Skinner. Can you speak?'

'Yes, I'm alone, but how did you get this number?'

'I'll tell you when I see you. For now just call it a small demonstration of power. I'm sorry, but would it be a mighty inconvenience if we postponed our dinner this evening for, say, twenty-four hours? Something very important has come up.'

'If it's that important, sure. I'll call the club and tell them to move the arrangement back a day. Can you tell me what this thing is?'

The DCC chuckled. 'Not on this line. It's only slightly more secure than calling you through your office line.'

He put down one phone and picked up another, then dialled a scrambled Whitehall number that was lodged in his memory; the receiver at the other end rang once and was picked up. 'Hello, mate,' said a familiar voice, 'what fookin' crisis has befallen you today?'

'I'll say this about you, Major Arrow. You're nothing if not to the point.'

'And you, Deputy Chief Constable Skinner, always like a preamble. So how's the wife, how's the kids?'

'All in fine form, thanks. I won't ask about your home life; if I found out about it, you'd probably have to kill me.'

Adam Arrow laughed. 'We don't use that word these days, mate. "De-incentivise" is in fashion now, but it wouldn't come to that with you: a simple lobotomy would be enough. As it happens, I don't have a home life at the moment, so you're safe on all fronts.'

'Glad to hear it. To get to the point, Adam, you're my doorway into the murky world of defence intelligence, and I need your help again. I've got a double murder investigation under way here . . .'

'It doesn't involve soldiers, does it?' asked Arrow, sharply.

'Not ours, and certainly not on the active list any more. The victims are Belgian, and they're in their sixties. The only connection that I know of is that they were all in the army together, with the band of the First Guides Regiment. I need to ask some questions there, and I need a contact.'

'It won't be that easy, Bob,' Arrow warned. 'You'll need to go there.'

'I know that.'

'Even then . . . a foreign policeman, not even one of your rank, can't just walk in and talk to these guys.'

'I guessed that too.'

His friend sighed. 'So you want me to go with you.'

'You guessed it in three. Can you?'

'It's important?'

'We're got a major event in Edinburgh on Friday. There's a public rally in the rugby stadium, at which Pope John the Twenty-fifth will meet his people. The Prime Minister will be sat next to him. These dead Belgians were supposed to be playing for him. Their band still is.'

'It's important,' Arrow exclaimed. 'Right, the people we'll need to see are in the security division of the Belgian General Intelligence and Security Service. They can get access to everything without any questions being asked, so it'll be much quicker than going through their personnel section. The head of that division's a contact of mine; I see him regularly at NATO meetings. How soon can you get to Brussels?'

'There's a flight from Edinburgh this afternoon; there's a seat held on it for me. I can be there this evening.'

'I'll meet you at the British Airways desk in Brussels airport. Half six?'

'Make it six forty-five. See you there.'

Sixty-three

'Does it really mean anything, Stevie?' asked Detective Superintendent Chambers. 'This thing the boy found? It's only a few letters grouped together after all.'

'It could do, Mary. If Ivor was on to her, and she found out, it's possible she did away with him, or that she and her husband did. I'm assuming they're acting in concert.'

'Why should they run now, with Whetstone set up to take the blame?'

'Maybe they always intended to run, but maybe they couldn't just then, not until the money had hit its final destination.'

'That's plausible, I'll grant you. But as proof of anything, what does this all mean?'

'Next to bugger all, I admit, as I told Murphy.'

Chambers smiled grimly. 'Not next to it, Stevie,' she said. 'It means precisely bugger all. It doesn't tell us anything for sure and it doesn't lead us any closer to them either. If it makes the Whetstones feel better, that's good, but that's all it'll do.'

'I know, Mary,' Steele conceded. 'The lad was so pleased with himself, though.'

'And I hope he stays that way, but what are you planning to do next? I appreciate you keeping me involved, but this is your inquiry, remember; I'm still feeling my way into this job, so I don't plan on muscling in.'

'I'm going to dig into Aurelia's past,' he told her. 'I've requested her file, formally and in writing, from the SFB human-resources manager; she's consulting the data controller, just to stay on the right side of the Data Protection Act, but I don't anticipate problems. I want to see if it gives us any pointers to where she and her husband might have headed.'

'What about his file?'

'I've made the same request to Heriot-Watt University. They're more used to police requests for information. With a bit of luck I'll have both files by the end of the day. If I have to I'll take them home with me and look through them tonight.'

'They'll be well protected, then.'

Steele gave her a curious look. 'What do you mean by that?'

'Maggie had a quiet word with me while you were out. I don't know whether it was woman to woman, or senior officer to senior officer, but she told me about her . . . How do I put it? Relocation. I've never seen her look so happy; I'm very pleased for you both, and I really do hope it works out.'

'Thanks, Mary,' he said, 'that means a lot to us. I hope everyone takes it as well.'

'They will, don't you worry. Does Mario know yet?'

'I think he's guessed that we were seeing each other, but

not that Maggie's moving in. She wants to tell him herself, but face to face, first opportunity she gets. She's going to leave it for a couple of days, though. Apparently he's pretty broken up about the American guy.'

'He'll be steamed up now, after the outcome of the autopsy.'

'Why? What's up?'

'The DCC's wife found fresh tap-water in the lungs. She proved that he was drowned somewhere else then chucked in the dock. She's a sharp operator, that one; there's a few pathologists would have missed it. Dan Pringle called to tell me, as a courtesy, so I didn't hear about it first on the telly. There's a press conference this afternoon.'

'Is Mario taking it?'

'No, Mario isn't in charge. McIlhenney's running this one, and Alan Royston's handling the media himself.'

'Why big Neil?'

'Because Special Branch does organised crime, and that's where the investigation's focused.'

'Bloody hell!'

'That's more or less what I said, but when you think about it, who else would pick a New York copper off the street, and drown him in the bath?'

'There aren't many other candidates, I'll admit,' said Steele, just as the door opened behind him and DS George Regan's head appeared.

'Excuse me, ma'am,' he said to Chambers, then looked at Steele. 'Got a minute, Stevie?'

'If it's important, yes. What is it?'

'That car, the one you told us to trace?'

'Yup. Mitsubishi Pajero, number SQ02ZZL, registered to Jose-Maria Alsina.'

'We've found it.'

'Where?'

'In the long-stay car park at Edinburgh airport.'

'Outstanding. Any idea how long it had been there?'

'Can't give you that, sir, I'm afraid. You know how crowded that place is.'

'Anything from the airlines?' asked Chambers.

'We're working on that, ma'am.'

'No, you're not, George,' the superintendent replied amiably. 'You're standing in my doorway, waiting for someone to pat you on the head. Consider that done; now please go back and help Tarvil. We need to know which flight those two caught, and whether they had an ultimate destination beyond that.'

Sixty-four

If Bob Skinner had ever been asked to nominate, as a frequent flyer, his least favourite European airport, Brussels would have come a close second to Heathrow. For all its turn-of-the-century improvements, he still found it annoying, claustro-phobic and difficult to get around. Professionally he felt that its lay-out must make it a nightmare to police.

His flight from Edinburgh had been late, after an air-traffic-control departure delay had thrown it off schedule, so it was just past seven o'clock as he approached the British Airways information desk.

Adam Arrow was nowhere to be seen.

He walked up to the counter, where a richly dressed black woman was querying something on a flight ticket, then turned and looked around. Suddenly he felt something being pressed into the small of his back, something small and round.

'Turn around very slowly,' a voice growled.

Skinner began to do as he had been told, moving to his left. Then suddenly, he pivoted on his right foot, dropping his bag as he did so, knocking an arm aside and grabbing it by the wrist.

'Careful, Bob,' said Adam Arrow, 'or you'll break my fookin' banana.'

The Scot laughed out loud and released him. 'You daft wee bugger,' he exclaimed. 'How did I do anyway?'

'Not too bad,' Arrow answered, as he slipped the fruit back into his blazer pocket, 'but at best you'd have had a big flesh wound; at worst you'd have been minus your left kidney. Come on, let's get out of here, there's a couple of coppers over there giving us funny looks. I should have known better than to pull a stunt like that in an airport these days.'

Adam Arrow was a short man, with massive shoulders and a slim waist that gave him the overall appearance of a spinning top. His hair seemed to be cut shorter every time that Skinner saw him; the DCC suspected this was because there was less of it to cut. The two men had known each other for years . . . professionally at least, since Arrow only ever discussed business . . . and an absolute trust had developed between them.

They had met after Arrow had moved from undercover SAS work in Northern Ireland and other hotspots into a role in Ministry of Defence security that did not appear in any published documents and was defined only in vague terms to outsiders, even to those as close to him as Skinner. This was fine by the DCC; all he needed to know was that Arrow reported to very few people and that when something secret and serious needed doing, he was the man who could make it happen.

'Where are we going?' the Scot asked.

'There's a car waiting for us outside.'

Skinner picked up his bag, and the two men walked through the terminal building's arrivals exit. Less than twenty yards away, a black Citroën waited; its driver was in military uniform and stood beside it. He nodded briefly to Arrow and opened the back door.

'So now,' the Scot asked, 'where are we going?'

'We're booked into the Royal Windsor Hotel, on rue Duquesnoy. It's just about the best hotel in Brussels.'

'That's a bit extreme, isn't it?'

'Don't worry about it. They're looking after us, just as we look after them when they come to London. We don't piss about with two-star accommodation, mate: no fookin' security. The man we've come to see is meeting us there for dinner at eight thirty. One thing about your Belgian . . . he does like 'is food.'

Sixty-five

'Y ou're no feart, are ye?' said Malky Gladsmuir.

'Of you?' laughed Mario McGuire, amiably. 'There's a very small list of people and things that scare me, pal, and you're definitely not on it. I thought I'd convinced you of that. I don't like those big spiders you find in the bath sometimes, and my granny can still get to me, but not you, son, not you.'

'Maybe no', but meeting me here might not have been the smartest thing to do, if I'd brought a whole team wi' me.'

'I suggested this place, remember, when you asked for somewhere quiet. Anyway, give me credit, man. I watched you arrive from across the street. Only you and him came in here. If anyone else tries to join us, they'll find obstacles put in their way. It's you that's in bother, Malky, not me . . . if it turns out your man here's going to waste my time.'

The detective and the pub manager were in a half-built house on a site not far from Salamander Street, where investment by developers was turning acres of redundant warehousing into a residential district. There was a third person there too, a weedy man of medium height, in a woollen hat, a well-worn leather jacket and dark trousers.

'This is Spoons,' said Gladsmuir, 'the bloke I wanted you to meet. He's got something you might like to hear.'

The man looked at the superintendent with cunning eyes. 'Is it going tae be worth my while, like?'

McGuire glared at his escort. 'Is he serious?' he asked.

'It's no' like that, Spoons,' the publican barked at him. 'I told you. Now talk.'

The man shifted from one foot to the other. 'Aye, okay.' He looked down at the detective's feet, as he readied himself to tell his story. 'Malky said ye wis asking about Sunday night. Ah mibbe saw somethin'.'

'What time?'

'After ten.'

'Where?'

'Doon the shore. Ah'd come oot the Pheasant . . . Ah kent whit the time was 'cos the Spanish fitba' had finished on the telly, like . . . and Ah wis just comin' tae the bridge ower the watter, when Ah saw this on the ither side. There wis a man . . .'

'Describe him.'

'Quite a big bloke. No' as big as you, but quite big. He wis wearin' this donkey-jacket thing. That's a' Ah kin remember; it was dark, ken. Onyway, he's walking doon the shore, towards Commercial Street, when this motor pulls up alongside him; naw, a few yards in front of him. Jist as he got to it the passenger's door in the front opened, and the fella stopped.'

'How many people did you see get out?'

Spoons shook his head. 'Nane. There was naebody got out. The boy on the pavement just stood, as if he was starin' at it.'

'Could you hear anything?'

'Naw, Ah wis still only hauf-wey across the bridge; Ah wisnae near enough.'

'So what happened next?'

'The back door opened like, and the boy got in.'

'Of his own accord?'

'Whit?'

'Nobody forced him?'

'Naw. He jist got in, and the motor drove off.'

'Do you remember what sort of car it was?'

'Aye, it was a Land Rover.'

'Are you sure about that?'

'Course Ah'm sure. Ah ken whit a fuckin' Land Rover looks like.'

'Registration number?' McGuire asked in hope, not in expectation.

'Ah wisnae close enough. Ah think it wis wan o' the new sort.'

'Did you see anybody else around?'

'Naw, no' a soul. It's quiet doon there on a Sunday.'

McGuire looked at him, sizing him up, trying to gauge his honesty . . . questionable, going by his name . . . and what he would have to gain by making up a story . . . nothing, unless Gladsmuir had wanted CID off his back.

'Did you put him up to this, Malky?' he asked.

'No. I promise you I didn't. The manager of the Pheasant's a pal of mine. I asked him if he'd heard anything, and he remembered that Spoons had left his place around the time you were asking about.'

'Okay. I think I believe you both. I'll need a formal statement from you.'

'Aw, naw, come on,' the man pleaded. 'The word's oot that this was a hit; Ah don't want any o' that.'

'Have you ever heard of Bilbo Baggins?' Spoons stared at him as if he had been asked to recite Einstein's theory of relativity. 'No, maybe you haven't. What he said was true, though. Every time you step out your own front door you never know the trouble that might be waiting for you on the road. Come on, pal; you and I are going to Queen Charlotte Street, and you're going to tell all that to a tape-recorder.'

Sixty-six

For a hotel in the centre of Brussels, even a five-star, Royal Windsor was a very strange name, Bob Skinner told himself as he blew his grey hair dry with the device in his bathroom. However, there was nothing strange about the establishment itself; its facilities, its furnishings and its fittings were all of the highest quality.

His musing was interrupted when a sudden thought elbowed its way in and hit him. He picked up the phone, found an outside line and dialled home. He was pleased when Sarah answered, rather than Trish. 'Hi, honey,' he said. 'I'm going to be a bit late tonight.'

'How late?'

'Maybe twenty-four hours, maybe forty-eight; I don't know for sure. I'm in Brussels.'

'Brussels!'

'Yeah, the Royal Windsor Hotel. The Belgian thing's grown some wrinkles, and I'm trying to smooth them out.'

'Now you tell me!'

'Yes, I'm sorry. It's been a trying day.'

'Bob, this is not good.'

'Please, love, don't give me hassle. I have an important meeting very soon, and I need to focus on it.'

'Yes, and you have an important family, and you need to focus on it too.' He slammed the phone down, but she had beaten him to it.

When Adam Arrow knocked on his door, Skinner was ready, shaven for the second time that day, and wearing a fresh shirt. 'Smart,' said the major. 'It's as well, for this is posh.'

He led the way down to Les Quatre Saisons, the hotel's premier restaurant, and through its wide-open doors. The head waiter seemed to glide over to them. 'Yes, gentlemen?'

'We're dining with Lieutenant Colonel Winters,' Arrow told him, in the formal accent that he could don like a well-fitting jacket.

'Ah yes, he is here.'

They were led across to a booth in the furthest corner of the restaurant, set well apart from the nearest table. As they approached, a tall man rose to greet them. 'Adam,' he exclaimed, 'it's good to see you.'

'I'll bet it is,' the Englishman replied. 'You always like an excuse to entertain here.'

'It's the nearest thing we have to one of your London clubs.'

'This is a bit upmarket from the best of them. Pierre, this is my friend Bob Skinner.'

The two shook hands, as the waiter fussed around, anxious to help if any of them had difficulty pulling his chair into the table. Lieutenant Colonel Winters frowned at him and he withdrew, returning a moment later with three menus and a thick wine list, which he handed to the Belgian.

'We eat, then we talk business, agreed?' Skinner and Arrow nodded in unison.

The restaurant, the Scot had to admit as they finished, was pretty damn good, although he had a niggling worry about the garlic in the pâté. The older he grew, the less tolerant of it he was becoming. 'And so,' said Winters finally, as the wine waiter removed the Armagnac decanter, 'what brings you to Belgium?'

'Death,' Skinner told him.

'Hanno and Lebeau?' asked the Belgian.

'You know about them?'

'I read the newspapers. Two of the Bastogne Drummers die in unfortunate accidents and it makes the press here. The military notice too.'

'I thought the Drummers were a civilian group.'

'They are, but since Colonel Malou took them over, they have been operating under a degree of army patronage. We provide their uniforms and their equipment, and we give them a very small grant. We didn't before, but old Auguste pulled a couple of strings.'

'I see,' said Skinner. 'I notice that you described the deaths as accidents. Is that how they were reported here?'

'Yes, it was. The first one, Hanno, certainly. Lebeau's death was said to have been the work of some madman poisoning toothpaste.'

'We don't think he was that mad. My colleagues in England don't think Hanno was killed by accident either, and I tend to agree with them.'

'So how can I help you?'

'I've spoken to Colonel Malou; I understand that the two dead men served under him in the Belgian Army, that they were all members of the band of the First Guides Regiment.'

Winters laughed. 'That is something of an exaggeration. The band is very important, world famous we like to think; it is more of an orchestra, actually. If you have the idea that it is anything like the Bastogne Drummers, forget it. And as for Malou, Hanno and Lebeau being members, forget that also. I pulled their files when I knew you were coming. The band has an administration and a support team . . . I think the word in modern music is "roadies" . . . who are serving soldiers. That's where those three spent their careers.'

'All of their careers?'

'We all do basic training, even those who are non-combatants, but they all spent the best part of thirty years with the band. When Malou retired, he was its senior admin-istrator.'

'When they were serving, were there any suspicions about any of them; of improper behaviour in any way?'

'Absolutely not. The band is pristine; its reputation is above reproach and the same is true of anyone involved with it.'

'If there was anything in civilian life that might have got them into trouble, would you know about it?'

Winters smiled. 'Not necessarily, but I could find out. As Major Arrow is your friend, so I have contacts in our civil police. I will do so. If you come and see me tomorrow, at my office, I will tell you anything there is to tell. Eleven should be time enough, if Adam will bring you.'

'Thanks,' said Skinner. 'There's something else I need to pin down, about Malou. You know why the Drummers are in Edinburgh, I take it?'

'Yes, to play for the Pope. We Belgians regard it as a great honour, I don't mind telling you; it goes back to his time as a young curate in the Cathedral of St Michael, or Saint-Gudule, as we call it.'

'It may be more personal than that. Did you know that Auguste Malou and the young Gilbert White were close friends?'

Winters's eyes seemed to narrow, very slightly. 'You must not believe everything Malou tells you, Bob.'

'I believe this, though. It's true and I know it. But I don't know how that friendship began, and I need to. Two men have been killed; they form a line of acquaintance and personal history that leads to the colonel. Now I find that the line extends to connect with the Pope himself. Malou didn't boast of this; he wouldn't have told me of it at all, but for a slip of the tongue. Once he had, he refused to discuss it. You can see, can't you, that if he's keeping a secret and Hanno and Lebeau were a part of it, then I need to know about it?'

'I can see that,' the Belgian acknowledged. 'Again, I will see what I can do. When you visit me tomorrow, I may be able to tell you more.' He rose. 'I must go. There is an excellent piano bar in this hotel, gentlemen; you may care to end the evening there. It's called the Waterloo. The French hate it; I can't imagine why.'

Sixty-seven

Detective Chief Inspector David 'Bandit' Mackenzie was glad that he was one of nature's early birds. So was his wife; when the kids in their turn were very young and woke with the dawn, screaming to be changed or fed, in whatever order, David would always attend to them without complaint, leaving her to grab the extra hour or so of sleep that she needed to get her through the rest of the day.

The Bandit was proud of his nickname. He liked to claim that he had acquired it by locking up his own brother, but there was more to it than that. Throughout his CID career, his clear-up figures had spoken for themselves, but he had given the impression, through his relentlessly cocky demeanour, that they might have been achieved by cutting the odd corner, and sometimes the even one as well.

This was not true: in fact, he was guilty of nothing less orthodox than backing his own judgement and of relying on instinct first in pursuing a suspect, knowing that the necessary evidence would fall into place later. Almost invariably he had been right.

One of his few failures, however, had brought him briefly into conflict with Bob Skinner. He had been shown, forcefully, the error of his ways, but then, to his surprise, had found himself being taken under the wing of the Edinburgh DCC, whose legend as Scotland's hardest copper was well enshrined in the west, from which he had sprung.

Still, he had been surprised when his former boss, Mary Chambers, had whispered word in his ear that her job would be falling vacant and that it might be worth his while applying for it. He had been pleased too, because he had guessed that the hint had come indirectly from Skinner, who had actually cut far more corners in his time than Bandit would ever have dared.

He had been interviewed privately for the job by a panel that had included Skinner himself, Dan Pringle, and the formidable iron-drawered Maggie Rose, the most intimidating woman officer he had ever met. All his answers must have been right, for he had found himself transferred, on promotion, from the delights of Cumbernauld into a new office in Edinburgh.

He picked out the two Americans at once, watching through the one-way glass, as the queue from the Newark flight began to form at the non-EU passport checkpoint . . . big guys, hair cut too short and dressed too soberly to be anything but cops. So did the immigration officers, who had been briefed to speed them through.

'Inspector Nolan Donegan.' The older of the two, early forties as opposed to his companion's thirty-something, moved to shake his hand as they were ushered into the small room.

'This is my colleague, Lieutenant Eli Huggins, from our Internal Affairs Bureau.'

'Chief Inspector David Mackenzie. I'm going to drive you through to Edinburgh. We'll get moving as soon as your hold baggage is picked out from the rest.'

Donegan looked surprised. 'Chief Inspector?'

'Don't be over-impressed.' Bandit grinned. 'I live a few miles from here, that's all. It made more sense for me to collect you than for us to send a man and a car from Edinburgh.'

They were under way in a few minutes. Rather than join the Wednesday morning snarl-up on the Kingston Bridge, Mackenzie merged into the shorter queue through the Clyde Tunnel, the alternative crossing, and plotted a route through Broomhill and Hyndland that brought them on to the M8 at the point where the bottleneck began to thin out. 'Local knowledge,' he said to the Americans, as he picked up speed and headed for Edinburgh.

'What other knowledge have you guys been picking up?' asked Huggins. The Scot glanced at him in his rear-view mirror. The lieutenant was unsmiling; in fact, he looked as if, at some point in his career, he had forgotten how to smile.

Just the sort of cop you'd want to set on other cops, Bandit thought. He made eye contact, frowning back. 'Explain,' he said.

'Have you hit on anyone with a connection to Inspector Mawhinney?'

'I'm not involved in the investigation, but as far as I know, we haven't.'

'We hold you responsible, you know. Our man was in your country, now he's dead. We don't take that lightly, sir.'

The Bandit was riled. 'So what have you got?' he shot back. 'You're Internal Affairs; you're not here on escort duty. We need leads from you.'

'I'm not at liberty to say.'

'What makes you think you're at liberty to ask, then? I gave you an answer as best I could. Now it's your turn.'

'I'm not at liberty to say,' Huggins repeated.

'So that means you have got something relevant to this inquiry. Or are guys like you just so used to questioning other police officers that you've forgotten how to answer them?'

'Any information I have is exclusive to NYPD, only to be released at my discretion.'

'Gentlemen,' said Inspector Donegan. He turned in the front passenger seat and looked over his shoulder at his compatriot. 'Let's not get off on the wrong foot. Let's maintain some decorum here.'

'By all means,' said Mackenzie, 'but I'll tell you something, Lieutenant. If you try to hold that line when you meet my colleague who's in charge of this investigation, eventually you will be introduced to our boss. Then, I promise, you will come to believe that discretion is the better part of valour.'

Sixty-eight

Neil McIlhenney could have run the Mawhinney inquiry from his office at the Fettes building, but he had chosen to set up the murder room at the coastal-division headquarters in Queen Charlotte Street, to have immediate access to its manpower. He could also have excluded Mario McGuire from the investigation completely, but he had more sense than to try.

However, the superintendent knew that being seen to report to a junior officer only three days into his command would do nothing for his future authority, and so he had the sense in his turn to keep well clear. He was in his office when the door opened and McIlhenney came in.

'I wanted to thank you,' he said. 'That was bloody good work, bringing that guy Hughie Geller in last night. His statement's the only sniff of a lead we've got.'

'Has word got out that I was involved in it?'

'No. The statement's countersigned by the duty sergeant who took it, and that's all.'

'That's good. I told him I'd have his balls if my name was mentioned at all, or Malky Gladsmuir. That's a spin-off benefit. Gladsmuir's mine now, and I want to protect him.'

'I thought he was Jay's before.'

'He had Jay in his fucking pocket: life's changed for him.' He looked up at his friend. 'Where are we going with the Land Rover?'

'We've got the biggest magnet we can find, but it's still quite a task.'

'What do you mean?'

'Needle in a haystack, but I've got George Grogan working on it. He's been back to the witness and he's showed him Land Rover vehicle types. The best he could do was narrow it down to either a Range Rover or a Discovery, but that helps a bit. Total annual production's about a hundred thousand, and both models are big export sellers. We'll get accurate figures from the DVLA but I reckon we're looking at over fifty thousand new UK registrations every year. It's a new-style registration so we're going back three years maximum; that takes us up to a hundred and fifty thousand Range Rovers and Discos. We're trying to find one out of that lot.'

'You'll start with local, though.'

'Of course. That's George's priority.'

'Good. It means we . . . sorry, you'll have something to show the Americans when they get here.'

'Aye. And you never know; maybe they'll have something to show me.'

Sixty-nine

'Did you manage to do your homework last night?' asked Mary Chambers.

Stevie Steele looked up from his desk. 'No. I didn't get either report in until this morning. The SFB data controller was very nervous and waited for their solicitors to give her the go-ahead, and the Heriot-Watt office couldn't get a bike last night. They're both here now, though. The Middlemass folder arrived two minutes ago.'

The superintendent pulled up a chair and sat alongside him. 'What does it say, then? Let's have a look.'

Steele opened the yellow folder; it contained only three documents. 'Jesus, all that fuss over so little.'

'That's the Data Protection Act for you,' Chambers muttered. 'Another bloody barrier across the pathway to justice. What have you got there?'

The inspector picked up the top paper. 'A letter of application,' he announced, 'for the position of senior director of Commercial Banking, written on personalised stationery from an address in Dubai.' He laid it down. 'Next, a formal application on the bank's official form. Name, Aurelia

Middlemass, age thirty-five, place of birth Cape Town, South Africa, educated St Mary's School, Durban, and University of South Africa, graduated B.Comm. with honours in financial management, married earlier that year to Jose-Maria Alsina. For career see separate document.' He took it from the folder and read quickly. 'Vacation jobs in various law offices and banks, first full-time appointment as trainee in Federated National Bank of Zimbabwe, moved on to become a business account manager in the Commercial Bank of Namibia, then account manager with Friedman's, a merchant bank in Johannesburg, and finally director of High-Tech Investments, with the Jazeer Independent Bank of Dubai. Attached there's a letter of commendation from Nasser Alali, the bank's general manager, with a contact number.' He glanced at the superintendent. 'I think I'll call him.'

'You should. I'll let you get on with it. Give me a shout if you get a result.'

She walked back to her office, and set herself to working her way through her morning mail, and reading through the reports of officers on the lesser crime within her division, the day-to-day investigations that by their sheer volume were much more vital than the occasional high-profile incidents to the maintenance of an acceptable clear-up rate.

Mary Chambers possessed considerable powers of concentration, and a great ability to absorb information. The phone on her desk rang three times before she was aware of it, and again before she picked it up.

'Dan Pringle here, Mary,' said a gruff, familiar voice. 'I thought I should call at least, to see how you're doing. Normally

I'd have been down to see you long before now, but I've been up to my oxters in dead Belgians. On top of that there's the American. Think yourself lucky you're not involved.'

'I do, Dan, I do.' She laughed. 'How are those inquiries running?'

'The Belgians are running nowhere; they're just marching up and down, like always. So am I in terms of progress. The DCC's out of town; he hasn't told me where, but I think it's connected. As for the Mawhinney thing, McIlhenney's running that, and he wouldna' tell me if my shirt-tail was on fire. What about you? Have you had a quiet start?'

'If you call a million-pound bank fraud quiet, yes.'

'A million! Bloody hell. Have you got a suspect?'

'There is a suspect, but we don't have her. It was an inside job and it looks like she's got away with it. Stevie's on her trail, but it's pretty cold.'

'Keep me in touch, through Ray Wilding if you have to. Cheers.'

As he said his farewell, the superintendent's door opened. Stevie Steele wore the expression of a hunter; one who has just seen his quarry escape. 'What do you do with a bank,' he asked, 'that gives people access to millions without running proper checks on them?'

'Don't give them your money, or move it out if it's there. What's the story?'

'The contact number for Nasser Alali rang unobtainable. It was disconnected a year ago. Before that it wasn't in an office but in a private apartment, rented to a Spanish gentleman named Alsina.'

'And the Jazeer Independent Bank of Dubai? They've never heard of Aurelia Middlemass?'

'Oh, yes, they've heard of her. They flew her body back to South Africa, about eighteen months ago. She was out in the desert, off-roading big-time with her boyfriend, when their jeep exploded. They were both killed. The investigators decided that an electrical fault had ignited the fuel load.'

'Mammy!' Mary Chambers exclaimed. 'There's devious for you. So this woman, whoever she was, decided that it would be a good idea to steal her identity and use it to set up a scam in a bank well away from the Middle East. This was really well planned. She's out of here all right.'

'I know. George found the airline. They caught the first easyJet flight to Gatwick on Monday morning. One-way tickets, bought on the Internet the day before. Checked in four suitcases and paid the excess charge in cash. There's no record anywhere of any onward booking.'

'But there will be under another name.'

'Of course.'

'Shit.' She looked at Steele. 'You know, every so often in my career, I've run up against someone who's done something so clever and so audacious that part of me wants to take its hat off to them. This is one of those times.'

Seventy

The same black Citroën picked up Skinner and Arrow from the Royal Windsor Hotel at ten thirty. Both men had wakened with slightly thick heads, but an hour in the gym had set them up for breakfast.

Their driver took them through the city and towards the outskirts. The sky was cloudy and Skinner had no idea whether he was heading north, south, east or west, but eventually they broke out into clear, flat countryside. Not much more than ten minutes later, they turned off the dual carriageway on which they were travelling and into a two-way road, which led eventually to a gateway, barred by a hinged red and white pole. An armed guard appeared, spoke briefly to the driver, and the way was cleared for them.

Lieutenant Colonel Pierre Winters's office was on the ground floor of a grey concrete two-storey building. He came to greet them at the door, looking stiffer than ever in uniform, and even more solemn. He showed them to his sparsely furnished room, offering each of them a hard wooden chair.

'Monsieur Skinner,' he began, 'I am afraid that I will not

detain you long. I have examined the files of all three men in question, and I have made inquiries of the civilian authorities. I can tell you nothing that will help in your investigation. Your trip has been wasted.'

The Scot looked at him. 'Nothing? You've looked at their entire thirty-year army career and it doesn't offer a single potential line of inquiry?'

Winters sniffed. 'These were very boring men, sir. Exemplary soldiers.'

'Is that so?' Skinner exclaimed. 'If they were that bloody exemplary, how come they spent twenty-five bloody years as labourers to an orchestra?'

'We all have to do our part, sir, in whatever way. If you were a military man, perhaps you would understand that.'

Condescension always lit Skinner's fuse; his eyes caught Winters's and locked on, as if they were boring into his head. 'Listen, my friend.' He ground the words out. 'I am a member of a disciplined service, just as you are. To extend the point, I am a damned sight higher ranking in my force than you are in yours. I know how to handle the people under my command, and how to slot round pegs into round holes. When I see three men like Malou, Hanno and Lebeau doing the jobs that they did, I know that they're not there because they're exemplary. But if they were put there because they were no fucking good at anything else, they wouldn't have been kept on in the service till they were fifty. There was another reason; I know it, and it's written in your eyes . . .' Winters blinked, and his face reddened as if he had been slapped. '. . . that you do too. Will you let me see their service files?'

395

'Certainly not. They are private; available only to the Belgian military.'

'What? A colonel, a sergeant and a corporal who were, according to you, clerks and scene-shifters for the bulk of their careers? They're state secrets?' His expression as he looked at the Belgian was pure derision. 'I'll tell you, chum, you're another square peg in a round hole. For a spook you're not very good at it. You've had orders to pat me on the head and send me away with a smile on my face. You've failed, big-time. I came here with suspicions, and you've turned them into certainties.'

He turned to Arrow. 'Can we get out of here, or is he going to try to detain me until I promise to stop making waves?'

'Come, come,' said Winters, trying to recover some dignity and a degree of control. 'Of course you can leave. Your car is still at your disposal. It will take you to the airport.'

'For the first time in my life,' said Skinner bitterly, 'I find myself looking forward to seeing that place.'

Seventy-one

Normally, visits by the chief constable to the outposts of his empire were announced in advance. Sir James Proud did not believe in dropping in casually to divisional headquarters, or to any of the outstations. To some that would imply that he was trying to catch them off guard, and might damage their trust in him. Trust, given and received, was the foundation of his office, and it had seen him through a successful career that was now approaching its conclusion.

Thus, when he swept through the entrance of the Queen Charlotte Street police office, it came as no surprise to the young constable behind the public counter, or to Chief Superintendent Stockton Day waiting in front of it in his pristine uniform, or to Detective Superintendent Mario McGuire, standing beside him, jacketless, a pen clipped into the pocket of his white shirt. They had been alerted in a phone call from his secretary, as he had left Fettes.

Two men followed him into the building; one was in NYPD uniform, while the other, slightly younger, wore a grey tailored suit and a grim expression.

'Good morning, gentlemen,' the chief exclaimed. 'We

didn't need the welcoming committee but thank you anyway.'

As he spoke McGuire and Nolan Donegan nodded to each other, reached across and shook hands. 'You know each other?' Sir James asked.

The superintendent nodded. 'Yes, sir. Colin Mawhinney introduced us when he took me on a tour of some of the precinct offices. Sorry it's like this, Nolan.'

'Me too, Mario, me too.'

The chief constable introduced the two Americans to Chief Superintendent Day. 'I thought it right,' he said, 'that they should come straight to the heart of the investigation. Is DI McIlhenney in?'

'Yes, sir,' McGuire replied. 'He's in the office he's using. I told him I'd bring you through when you arrived.'

'Shall I organise refreshments, Chief?' asked Day.

'I'd appreciate that.' He turned to the Americans. 'How about you, gentlemen?'

Donegan nodded. 'To be truthful, I'm flagging after that flight. I'd welcome some coffee.' He turned to his colleague. 'Eli?'

The crew-cut lieutenant seemed to stand even more stiffly than before. 'No, thank you. I should check in on the investigation right away.'

As Donegan and the chief were led away by the divisional commander, McGuire showed Huggins through to the CID suite. 'Good trip?' he asked casually.

'No,' the American replied curtly.

McIlhenney saw them coming through the glass panel in

the door of the cubicle that McGuire had described as his office; he rose from behind his desk and opened it for them, then introduced himself to the visitor. 'Eli Huggins, Lieutenant, Internal Affairs Bureau, NYPD,' the man replied shortly.

Name, rank and serial number, thought McGuire. *He sees us as the fucking enemy.*

'Who's the senior investigating officer?' asked Huggins.

'I am.' McIlhenney was always amiable; but on occasion it was a little forced.

'You are? Maybe I misunderstand your ranking structure here, but isn't a superintendent superior to an inspector in your force?' He turned to McGuire. 'And are you, sir, not the divisional detective commander here?'

'Well done, you're right both times.'

'In that case, sir, I have to tell you that I do not believe that my chief of detectives would approve of command of this investigation being delegated to a junior officer.'

'Nor would he approve of me walking into his office and telling him how to do his job. You're not going to be a fucking seagull, are you, Eli?'

'What's a seagull?'

'It's a name the managers of American-owned companies in Scotland sometimes give to the guys from head office. It means that they fly in from far away, make a lot of noise, shit all over you and then fly away again. The story is that the man at the top of our chain of command has decided that it would not be appropriate for me to command this one. Colin and I became good friends in the time we knew each other . . .'

'You mean your objectivity is in doubt?'

'I mean I'm a potential witness to his state of mind.'

'There is another reason,' said McIlhenney quietly. 'When these people are apprehended, we do not want to have them carried into court by paramedics.'

'It's my Italian blood,' McGuire added. 'Makes me excitable; that and my Irish blood.'

Huggins showed his first sign of loosening up. 'Don't you have Scots blood to calm you down?'

'Nope. Fifty per cent Wop, fifty per cent Mick, that's me.'

'With breeding like that you'd be Commissioner of Police in New York.'

'I doubt that, very much. I'd probably be at war with myself over control of a labour union.' He reached out to open the door. 'I'm going to leave you guys alone, now. By the way, Lieutenant, Neil isn't on my staff, so I haven't delegated anything to him. He's Special Branch.'

'Is that something like me?'

'If you mean that you're both secret policemen, I suppose he is. But that's as far as it goes.' He left the room with a smile.

'Take the weight off your feet,' said McIlhenney, as the door closed, 'and tell me why you came in here like a man with a thistle up his arse.'

'I'm sorry,' said Huggins, as he accepted the first invitation. 'Before I left I had an interview with my boss and his boss. They both explained to me what the personal consequences would be if any of the information I'm carrying got into the public domain.'

'That's good man management.' The big inspector chuckled.

'Maybe, but I can understand why.'

'Are you telling me that your man Mawhinney was bent?'

'Absolutely not. There was no straighter officer on our force.'

'What's the story, then?'

'I'll get to that,' said the New Yorker, 'but maybe you could bring me up to speed on your investigation.'

'Sure.' McIlhenney ran him through everything they had, detailing all of Mawhinney's movements since he and McGuire had arrived for the second leg of the exchange visit, and ending with Spoons's statement, and the search for a single Land Rover among over a hundred thousand vehicles.

'He wasn't forced into the automobile?'

'Not according to the witness statement,' the inspector repeated. 'He stopped, there was a period of communication with the people inside, then Colin got in himself, and the vehicle drove off. Next morning he was found in the dock.'

'Do you think he was meant to be found?'

'It is only an opinion, you understand, but I don't. If he was, why bother taking him there? Why not just dump him in the river, or in one of the lochs in Holyrood Park? He was weighted down and dropped in deep water. It was a pure accident that the chain snagged and he didn't go to the bottom. He wouldn't have stayed there for ever, but I reckon the thinking was that he'd be down there long enough to fuck up the forensics.' He looked up. 'So what have you got?'

'Before I begin,' said Huggins, 'I need to know who will have access to this information.'

'If it's that sensitive, only two people: me and Bob Skinner, our deputy chief, my boss.'

'It will remain secure?'

'Bet on it.'

'I'm betting my career. That's why I was so awkward earlier. Okay, here goes. As you know, I am a member of our IAB. Before he was transferred to patrol division, Colin Mawhinney was also an IAB officer.' Huggins hesitated. 'You probably think of us in the way that most people do, that we're real bottom-feeders, cops who persecute other cops. But everything we do, and every investigation we undertake, is in response to a complaint from the public of corruption or serious misconduct, with the emphasis on serious. We don't go looking for work; we don't have to. It comes to us, by telephone, by letter and these days even by e-mail.'

'Understood,' said McIlhenney. 'It's a dirty job, but it has to be done properly in everyone's interests, cops included.'

'Right. In Mawhinney's time as a sergeant in IAB, he investigated a detective officer named Luigi Salvona. The complaint followed a killing in Brooklyn, a gangland execution in which the victim, one Al Tedesco, was lured to a restaurant in a quiet street and strangled as he ate. Salvona was at the table with him; he was the man who set up the meeting. He testified that the men who did the job wore masks, and that he was beaten unconscious. There were no witnesses; they were the only diners in the restaurant and both waiters were conveniently in the kitchen when the killing took place. Under questioning he said that Tedesco had been an informant of his, and that he assumed the execution had been a reprisal.' Huggins leaned across McIlhenney's desk, picked up his water carafe and a glass. 'May I?'

'Of course.'

He poured some water and took a sip. 'The complaint came from the victim's widow,' he continued. 'She said that her husband had been set up by Salvona, and that far from being a police informant, he was an organised-crime member himself, and that Salvona was on his payroll, not the other way around. When the FBI was consulted they confirmed that Tedesco had indeed been on their surveillance list, and that he had been under investigation, although not actively at that time. Such a complaint, a mobster's wife admitting his past and accusing a policeman of complicity in his assassination, remains unique in the annals of IAB. Sergeant Mawhinney was the investigating officer; he saw a problem from the outset with Salvona's story. He was a patrol officer, not a detective. How would he come to have an informant as connected as Tedesco?'

Huggins took another sip from the glass. 'Mawhinney did all the correct things. He interviewed Salvona's fellow officers, but learned nothing. He pulled his telephone records, but found nothing incriminating. He pulled his mother's telephone records: nothing. He gained access to his bank account: nothing. So he returned Officer Salvona to duty, and he put him under surveillance. Three weeks later it paid off. The officer was married; he also had a girlfriend, as the investigators discovered when they tailed him to her apartment one night, and watched him leave at three in the morning.'

He drained the glass. 'Bingo. Her name was Irene Falcone,

and she was the sister of a senior figure in a rival family to that of which Tedesco was a member. Mawhinney pulled her phone records; he found regular calls to her brother, but crucially, two days before the hit, he found one to Al Tedesco. Then he checked her bank accounts: the day after Tedesco's murder, the sum of one hundred thousand dollars was paid into a new joint account. It had two signatories, Irene Falcone and Luigi Salvona. That finished them both. They pleaded guilty to second-degree homicide and they were sentenced to ten to twenty years each. On the day he was sentenced, the judge asked Salvona if he had anything to say. He said, and I quote, "Yes, Your Honour, I would like to say the following. Sergeant Mawhinney, you are a fucking dead man." This is not an unusual remark from a convicted felon but . . .'

'But what?'

'Salvona and Irene Falcone were both released, on the same day, four weeks ago, and set up home together in an apartment in Queens. They had a scheduled meeting with their parole officer last Wednesday. They failed to appear: officers were sent to collect them but they were not at home. Then yesterday they walked into the parole office, apologised, and said that they had gone on vacation to Florida and had mixed up the date of their meeting.'

'Can you prove they left the country?'

'Not a chance. Irene's brother is still a very large fish; they'd have used fake passports.'

'But if we can match either of them to the hire of a Land Rover within the last week or so . . .'

'Yes, Inspector, only this is where it gets complicated. The day Salvona was arrested he was fired from the force. When he was arraigned, it was as a civilian, and his connection with NYPD was covered up. His presence at the Tedesco murder had never been revealed, nor was it announced in court, because of the guilty plea. However wrong it may have been, this was a decision taken to protect the image of the force. If it all becomes public now . . .'

'The shit flies ten-fold.' McIlhenney looked at the American. 'Are you asking me to fold my investigation?'

'A colleague of yours used the word "discretion" to me this morning, Inspector. I use it now to you.'

The big Scot leaned back in his chair and folded his arms. 'I don't have any,' he said. 'In these circumstances, discretion belongs with DCC Skinner. I think you'd better meet with him.'

Seventy-two

The policeman and the soldier faced each other across a table in a corner of the big restaurant in Brussels airport's departure area. They had barely spoken on the journey from Winters's office, not wanting to say anything that their driver might overhear.

Adam Arrow picked up his knife and fork to attack his gammon steak, saw Skinner staring absently at his salad, and put them down again. 'So?'

'Do you need to ask, mate?'

'Not really. The Belgians are throwing a fookin' blanket over something, that's for sure. What you said to my friend Pierre was dead right. He's not usually such a wanker, by the way. He was reading from someone else's script.'

'Can you get to its author?'

Arrow shook his head gloomily. 'I can do a lot of things, Bob, but this is the business of a sovereign state, one that happens, in addition, to be one of our European partners. I'd need a big wedge to get anywhere; first I'd have to persuade my own secretary of state, and he'd have to talk to his colleagues. Now if you were to tell me that, by withholding information,

406

the Belgians were compromising the safety of the Pope, they'd listen to that.'

'I can't tell you that for sure,' said Skinner, 'or I'd have told Colonel Winters, straight out. This started as a murder investigation, pure and simple, and it still is, only being denied information by the Belgian military means it isn't so simple any longer. There's something in these men's past that relates to all this. Maybe Malou's acquaintance with the young John the Twenty-fifth has nothing to do with it, but maybe it has.'

'Then why not go at it from the other side?' Arrow could hold himself back no longer from his lunch. He picked up his cutlery and set to work, with Skinner looking at him, frowning.

'You know,' said the DCC, 'you're bloody right.' He took out his cell phone and scrolled through his stored numbers until he found one under the name 'Rossi', and selected it.

The Italian answered in seconds. 'Sì.'

'English, please, Gio; it's Bob Skinner. I need you to get something for me. I know the Vatican maintains an official biography of the Pope, but is it exhaustive?'

'What do you mean?'

'Sorry; is it absolutely detailed? Does it cover every step of his career in the priesthood?'

'They have a long version, Bob, and a short version. I'll get you the long one. When do you need it?'

'First thing tomorrow, my office. Oh, and Gio, do you have a number for His Holiness's private secretary?'

'Father Collins? He's with me now. Hold on.' There was a silence as he handed his phone over.

'Mr Skinner,' said the young Scots voice, 'what can I do for you?'

'How often do you speak to the Pope?'

'Every day, even when I'm away on a mission like this: I have to call him this evening.'

'When you do, will you ask him a question for me?'

He heard Angelo Collins hesitate. 'I'm not sure. One does not interrogate the Holy Father.'

'I know, but it's a simple question. Does the name Auguste Malou mean anything to him? That's all. It's necessary, I assure you.'

'I think I can ask him that. Can you repeat it?'

Skinner did as he asked, then folded his phone and put it away. 'Let's hope I get more out of that than I did out of the bloody Belgians.'

Seventy-three

Something was disturbing the happiness that had enveloped Stevie Steele like a cloud since the previous weekend. It was nothing to do with his home life; he was convinced that getting together with Maggie was the best thing he had ever done. The night before, she had told him that he had liberated her; he had replied that all he had done was pull the stopper and let the genie out of its bottle.

He could still feel her warmth beside him, and hear her laugh in the darkness. 'In that case, you'd better put it back, so it's stuck out here for ever.'

No, the disturbance in his karma was purely professional. There was something about the Aurelia Middlemass business that was not yet complete, a question unanswered, because it had not yet formed within him, but one that was lurking there nonetheless.

Officers of his rank had perks; one of his was a computer, with an Internet link. He switched it on and waited while it went online, then entered two words into a search engine. A minute later he had a telephone number for the Dubai Police Department. He called it and identified himself; the operator spoke English, as he had assumed would be the case. He asked for the Traffic section, and found another English speaker on its switchboard.

'May I speak to your senior officer on duty, please?' he asked, then waited.

'Hello, this is Captain Sharif. How can I help you?'

'Good afternoon. I'm Inspector Steele, CID in Edinburgh, Scotland. I'm working on an investigation here and a name's come up. She was an employee in a Dubai bank and she was a victim in a fatal car accident at the beginning of last year. Aurelia Middlemass, South African.'

'Excuse me, that name again, please?'

'Aurelia Middlemass.'

'I cannot help you on that, Inspector Steele, I am afraid. This department did not investigate that incident. It was handled by someone else.'

'Can you transfer me to that section, please?'

For a few moments, only light static could be heard, the unmistakable sound of a man considering something very carefully. 'I do not think so. In the circumstances, I believe it would be better if they called you back.'

'Sure.' Steele understood that his identity was being checked; he gave the Torphichen Place switchboard number rather than his direct line. He hung up, and waited, and waited, and . . .

It was almost half an hour before the phone rang. When it did, he snatched it up. 'Yes?' he snapped.

'Ouch!' Maggie exclaimed. 'Who's been rattling your cage, Inspector?'

'I'm sorry, love,' he said. 'I've been waiting for a call and I'm beginning to think I've been pissed about.'

'Will it keep you late tonight?'

'I hope not. Why?'

'I just thought we might do something nice and domestic. Like a food shop.'

He could see her face in his mind's eye, and he smiled. 'My favourite hobby. How did you guess? As an alternative, why don't we go along to Fort Kinnaird, grab a pizza or something Mexican, then go to a movie?'

'I'll buy that. Then we can do the food shop afterwards. Asda's open twenty-four hours, remember.'

'Okay. By the way, did you have a chance to go down to see Mario today?'

'No,' Maggie replied. 'It wouldn't have been a good time. They were expecting Americans. I'll try to do it tomorrow. See you later.'

Suddenly, he was aware of George Regan approaching. 'Yes, ma'am,' he murmured, and hung up.

'Good,' said the sergeant. 'The switchboard's got a soldier on hold for you.'

Barely a second later, the phone rang again. He picked it up. 'Call for you, sir.'

'Inspector Steele?' The voice at the other end was deep, and precise. 'I am Brigadier General Hanif Aqtab. I am assistant chief of police in Dubai, in charge of the Criminal Investigation section. Your call to our Transport department has been referred to me.'

'May I ask why, sir?'

'Because of the name you mentioned, Miss Middlemass, the South African lady. She did indeed die here in a motor-car incident, but I am curious. Why do you ask about her?'

'I'm investigating a fraud, General, from a bank here in Scotland. The principal suspect is an employee of that bank, and she used the name Aurelia Middlemass. I've seen her file and her curriculum vitae, and all the details match the woman who was killed in your country. The suspect here appears to have assumed her identity and tricked the Scottish Farmers Bank into giving her a senior position. Unfortunately she has absconded.'

'She has what?'

'I'm sorry. She's disappeared. We're trying to trace her, but without success. In view of the identity she stole, I'm going on the assumption that she has a connection with Dubai.'

'Reasonable,' the General conceded. 'Do you have a photograph of this woman?'

'Yes, I do. She had a security pass at the bank; that vanished with her, but they have a duplicate of her mugshot. I'll have it scanned and sent to you as an e-mail attachment. I took your central address from your website.'

'Thorough, Inspector. Use the prefix "genaqtab": one word.' He spelled it out.

'Thanks. But may I ask, sir, if this was a vehicle accident, how did you become involved in its investigation?'

'Because of the other victim. The unfortunate Miss Middlemass's death was what our allies are fond of calling, these days, collateral damage. Tell me, Inspector, this suspect of yours, does she have an associate, a partner, someone close to her?'

'A husband, in fact. He's gone too.'

'What do you know of him?'

'He's an academic chemist, doing a doctorate.'

'And his nationality?'

'He claimed to be Spanish, but she claimed to be Aurelia Middlemass, so who knows?'

'I see.' He heard the general's breathing for a few moments; nothing else. 'Inspector, I can say no more over the telephone. I will arrange for people to come to see you.'

'How soon?'

'As soon as it can be done; it will not be long, I promise. When they do come, you may wish to have your most senior commander present.'

Seventy-four

Skinner called his office as soon as he stepped from the plane on to the air bridge at Edinburgh. As he expected, Jack McGurk was still there. 'What's happening?' he asked.

'Mr Rossi called,' the sergeant replied, 'to say the information you requested will be with you first thing tomorrow. DI McIlhenney phoned. He says he needs to see you tonight; he asked me to call him back to confirm as soon as your plane touched down. DCS Pringle rang as well. He said that Stevie Steele's got an investigation under way that might need your personal involvement, some time soon.'

'That's all I need, Jack.' He groaned. 'Did he say what he wanted?'

'No, sir; he said it was essential, that's all.'

'If he said that, it is. Is there a car waiting for me outside the airport?'

'There better be. I ordered it.'

'Okay. Tell Neil six o'clock.'

He ended the call then dialled Aileen de Marco's number. 'Hello,' she exclaimed breezily. 'You are calling to tell me you're going to make it this time, aren't you?'

'Yes, it's okay. I'll pick you up at seven fifteen as arranged, yes?'

'No, just go straight to the club. I'll be ready to leave in half an hour so I'll take a taxi, and wait for you there, away from the phones.'

'Fine. See you there.'

Two constables and a Traffic car were waiting outside as he walked through the main door into the cold November evening. They came to something approaching attention as they saw him. He waved them into the car and slid into the back seat, then checked the time: five thirty-five. 'Blue-light it if you have to,' he said. 'I must be in my office before six.'

He made it to Fettes with ten minutes to spare, and was in his chair, looking out of the window, as Neil McIlhenney's car rolled up the driveway. His eyebrows rose slightly when he saw that there was a man in the passenger seat.

He was waiting in the corridor when McIlhenney led the crew-cut stranger upstairs; as he ushered them into his room, he asked the inspector, quietly, 'Do we need anyone else?'

'Absolutely not,' his friend replied.

Leaving his visitors for a moment, Skinner went along to his assistant's office and told him that he could go home. When he returned to his office McIlhenney and the other man were standing in front of his desk.

'Boss,' the DI began, 'this is Lieutenant Eli Huggins, from NYPD Internal Affairs Bureau. He's got a story that nobody else needs to hear.'

The DCC looked at him; he seemed wound up tight. He smiled at him then reached out and shook his hand. 'You can tell it sitting down, then, Eli. How long have you been in Scotland?'

'Since eight thirty, sir.'

'And in all that time has anyone offered you a beer?'

'No, sir, they have not.'

'Bloody disgraceful,' Skinner muttered. He stepped round to his fridge and took out a bottle of Becks and two Cokes, all uncapped. 'I'm driving, so I won't. Neil used to be a fat bastard, so he won't. But you get outside that, and tell me all about it.'

Huggins's bottle was empty halfway through his story: the DCC stopped him and fetched him another, then listened until he was finished.

'Let me be clear on this,' he asked. 'Your police commissioner wants me to close down this inquiry to avoid opening a can of worms and having them crawl all over his office. Is that it?'

'I'm not allowed to ask you to do that, sir. My instruction is to explain the situation to you, to try to make you see how much damage might be done to the reputation of NYPD, and then to ask how far your discretion extends.'

Skinner looked at him. 'I can see the problem,' he said. 'If all our skeletons came out the cupboard we'd all be fucked. However, my problem is that a murder has been committed on my patch, and I am legally bound to pursue it to a conclusion. I'm also under media scrutiny, and that is something which, clearly, you understand.'

Huggins nodded, grim-faced; he looked ready to empty Skinner's fridge.

'So this is what I'll do. You've given me information that

tells me who Colin Mawhinney's murderers may have been. Do you have recent photographs of these people?'

'I have them with me, sir.'

'Then please let Neil have them. The game is easier if we're looking for a hired Land Rover; there are damn few of them around. We will show these photographs around the rental companies and the airports. If we can identify Salvona and Falcone, and show definitely that they were here, and had such a vehicle, then even if we never discover where Mawhinney was killed, we'll have a basis for prosecution.'

Skinner smiled. 'What we won't have are Salvona and Falcone locked up. Extradition of a non-US citizen from the States to this country is pretty easy. Extradition of a US citizen is not. So if we get to that point, to save our public purse the cost of long-drawn out hearings . . . which would be reported and which might prove prejudicial to an eventual Scottish trial . . . just to get them over here, I'd be prepared to recommend to our prosecutors that they turn the evidence over to you. In other words, Eli, if those circumstances arose, I'd be prepared to pass the buck. There would be one proviso: if your DA did pluck up the courage to put them on trial, there could be no death sentence. We couldn't have that. Does that sound like a deal?'

A smile of pure relief spread over the lieutenant's face. 'It does, sir.'

'That's good,' said Skinner. 'I want to help, but it's as far as I could go.' He laughed as he rose to his feet. 'Of course, if it turns out that Bonnie and fucking Clyde were in Florida after all, you will let us know, won't you?'

'That's a deal also, sir.'

The DCC walked them to the door and, as it closed behind them, glanced at his watch. It showed five minutes to seven. He ran his hand over his stubbled chin, then, decision made, went through to his bathroom. Twenty minutes later, showered, shaved, and dressed in the last of the supply of fresh clothes that he always kept in the office, he headed downstairs to his car.

The worst of the evening traffic was over; there were no hold-ups on his way to the West End, and when he had made the complicated turn past the Caledonian Hotel, he found a parking space without difficulty. He was standing in the hallway of the Scottish Arts Club, an unostentatious terraced house on the north side of the quiet, leafy Rutland Square, when he realised that he had not called Sarah since the night before. He was reaching into his pocket, when Aileen de Marco, blond hair immaculate, her white blouse looking as fresh as his shirt, came through a doorway to his left. He withdrew his hand and shook hers instead.

'Almost right on time, Bob,' she said, with a smile. 'Only twenty-four hours late.'

As she led him into the club's sitting room, he felt a strange flutter; he paused for a few moments, wondering if his pacemaker was kicking into action, but it passed and he followed her to a table near the window, with armchairs on either side, and a bottle of white wine in an ice bucket sitting on it. Two long-stemmed glasses stood beside it; one was half-full.

As he sat, she picked the bottle up and filled the second

glass. 'Chardonnay,' she said. 'Call me a prole if you want, but I like it.'

'Me too,' he confessed. 'But I'd better keep an eye on it. I have a car outside. So,' he asked, 'how are you finding your new job?'

'Much like my old one as deputy minister; but the salary's better, the car's a bit flashier and . . .' She flashed him a quick twinkling smile. '. . . I get access to all the secrets. Imagine!'

'That's good. It means you've passed your vetting.'

She looked surprised. 'I was never vetted for the job.'

Skinner laughed. 'You don't know all the secrets, then.'

The minister whistled quietly. 'Me too? I'm beginning to get an idea, though.'

'You've only just begun. How did your lunch with my friend Mitch go on Monday?'

'It was excellent. I learned more about the law in those two hours than in all my life up to then. Tell me, Bob, why isn't he a judge?'

'Because he's a solicitor, and always has been; he prepares cases and instructs counsel but he doesn't plead the case in court. Received wisdom is that to be a judge you have to have done that.'

'You don't go along with that?'

'Not all the way. Mitch has only ever lost one action in his life, and that would have been overturned had the pursuer not died before it got to the Appeal Court. I agree with you: he'd make a fine senator . . . if he wanted the job.'

'I must have a chat with the Lord Advocate, in that case.

Maybe we can put his name before the Judicial Appointments Board.' Skinner raised an eyebrow, and she caught its meaning. 'Do I take it that you're not a fan of the board?' she asked. 'We think it's one of our finest achievements.'

'I'm a great supporter of the Scottish Parliament, and the Executive,' he told her, 'except when it does something bloody stupid. The old system worked; it didn't need fixing.'

'What?' she exclaimed. 'Judges appointing judges?'

'That's not how it was, and you should know that. Politicians always made the appointments, on the basis of independent recommendations by people who were capable of assessing the fitness of the candidates for office.'

'Come on, it was Buggins's turn, and you know it.'

'I do not,' he countered. 'I could name you umpteen brilliant lawyers who did not make the Bench, because their appointments would have been dangerous, and maybe disastrous. Your system, a board that's made up of half lay members, who are not experts in the subject, and a minority of practising lawyers, who are, will let some of these people through. What's the next step? Telephone voting by the punters?'

'We won't go that far, I promise.' She threw him a mock frown. 'Here, this is my baby you're calling ugly.'

'Not yours.'

'I'm its guardian at least. Maybe I should appoint you to the next vacancy.'

'You'd have to wait a long time for that, till after I retire, and even then, if there was a remote possibility that I might be interested, I'd need to be chairman.'

'You're a passionate man, aren't you?' said the minister. 'I'd never have suspected that.'

'Why not?'

'Because you're iron-clad.'

'I'm passionate about justice,' said Skinner, 'and in particular about its impartiality. My father was a family solicitor, but he was a bit of a constitutional lawyer too. If he was alive, although he voted for your party all his life, he'd be dead against anything that eroded the essential distinction between the people who enact legislation . . . that's you lot . . . and the people who interpret it . . . that's the Bench.'

'Where do you fit in?'

'In the middle; we enforce it . . . the parts that relate to crime and public order.'

'And should you be independent of government too?'

'I think we should be removable by government, as ultimately we are, but I do not think you should have day-to-day supervision over us. Who investigates you?'

'Nobody, if we don't want it to happen. Isn't that the case?'

He smiled. 'So how come you didn't know you'd been vetted?'

She shivered. 'Spooky.'

'Listen,' he said, suddenly serious. 'However liberal a society may be, if it is to be safe, there have to be dark areas. All countries operate that way. Because of who I am and what I do, there are few doors if any that are locked to me in Britain. But this morning, in another European country, one was slammed right in my face.'

Aileen de Marco's eyes widened. 'Do tell!' she exclaimed.

'I might . . . since you've been vetted . . . but I thought you mentioned something about dinner. I had about a quarter of a fairly inedible salad eight hours ago; I am seriously hungry.'

She glanced at her watch. 'God, you're right; we should be upstairs.' She stood, smoothing her grey skirt, picked up its matching jacket, and led him once more, this time up a flight of stairs to the club's dining room. 'I've kept the menu plain and simple. Tomato soup, grilled sole, and ice cream.'

A waiter showed them to their table, left for a few moments, then reappeared with their ice bucket and glasses. Skinner glanced across the room; there was a party of two couples at a table in the furthest corner. He recognised both men: one was an actuary and the other was chief executive of an insurance company.

'When I changed the booking I was told we'd have company,' Aileen said. 'I hope you don't mind.'

'Not at all,' he replied, giving the group a nod of acknow-ledgement. 'If they were lawyers it would be all over town in twenty-four hours, but the only things actuaries ever tell people have numbers in them.'

They sat in silence as the waiter served their first course; home-made, he noted. 'So,' the minister whispered as soon as he had left, 'what was your sudden trip all about?'

'Dead Belgians. I wanted some information, and I thought their government would be helpful.'

'But they weren't?'

'They treated my colleague and me to dinner in the best

hotel in town. Then this morning they gave us the bum's rush.'

'I can't imagine anybody giving you the bum's rush.'

'It isn't over. I will find out what they're covering up.'

'Who's going to tell you?'

'That I can't say, not at this stage, anyway.' He picked up his spoon.

They did justice to dinner for the next half-hour, talking trivia about movies and music, discovering that they were both *Lord of the Rings* devotees, and Skinner admitting that his off-duty reading consisted mostly of crime fiction.

'Can't get away from it?' Aileen asked.

'What did you read last?' he asked her.

'*First Among Equals*,' she confessed. 'Okay, I know it's about politics, and I know it was written by a Tory, but it's still a first-class read.'

The coffee was poured and cooling before the minister steered the discussion back to business. 'The First Minister came by my office this morning,' she said. 'He asked me if I'd heard anything about that poor American policeman.'

Skinner frowned. 'Aileen,' he murmured, 'I'm happy to talk to you all night about policing, but I'm uncomfortable when you get into active investigations . . . especially when Tommy Murtagh's name's mentioned.'

'You really don't like the First Minister, do you?'

'Not a lot. I told you, when it comes to my view of politicians, you're one of the few exceptions to the rule. I don't trust them, and you should learn to do the same. Do you think Murtagh knew you were seeing me tonight?'

'It never occurred to me.'

'Well, it's the first bloody thing that occurred to me. As it happens we've got a strong lead in that investigation, but I don't want you telling him so. If he wants to know anything of that nature, he should be asking the Lord Advocate, not you, and he's well aware of that fact. He's testing you, just to see how compliant you are; watch him.'

She wrinkled her nose. 'I'd certainly never be compliant for him,' she murmured, with a smile. There was a movement in the doorway behind her. 'Bob,' she said, 'I think they want to close up.'

He looked round and saw that the other table was deserted. 'Sure,' he said. 'I didn't realise how the time had gone.' He glanced at her. 'Aileen, taxis can be hard to find at this hour. Can I run you home?'

She paused, for maybe half a second. 'Well, since it's on your way . . .' She stood up and slipped on her jacket. 'Wait for me downstairs, while I sign the bill and pay a visit.'

'Where are we going?' he asked her, as she eased herself into the passenger seat.

'We're heading towards Portobello. Lena's place is just off King's Road.'

'Fine.'

Skinner was not given to mixing conversation and driving: he found it too easy to concentrate on neither. As they drew away he switched on his CD player, and let Maria Callas fill the car. Aileen de Marco sighed. 'Ohhh! I just love her.'

'Unfortunately Onassis didn't. So she got fat and died. Silly woman.'

'Are you always such a cynic?' she asked.

'No, I just find it astonishing that someone who gave the world so much more than he ever did should have wound up pining away after he dumped her.'

'Thank God!' she exclaimed.

'What do you mean?'

'Thank God that you don't understand everything.'

He let the music take over and drove east. Lena McElhone's flat was in a modern block in a quiet side-street. He pulled up at the front door and turned down the volume on the great diva. 'Thanks for dinner,' he said.

'Thank you,' she replied, 'for making me realise how much I've got to learn, and for helping me shed my political blinkers.'

'Hah! That's what I'm doing, is it?'

'Absolutely. You're contributing to the better governance of Scotland.'

He shuddered. 'That's a horrible Harold Wilson word; you're from another era. I prefer "administration" myself. It implies more regard for the people.'

'Why, you're a closet socialist, Mr Skinner!'

'Aren't we all, if we care about people?'

She looked at him. 'Bob, the coffee was lousy back at the club. Would you like another?'

He glanced at the car clock. It showed ten thirty-six, and he always kept it fast. 'Yeah, okay. If Lena's not in her curlers, that is.'

'Lena's on a management course in Sunningdale.'

She jumped out of the car and opened the block's main entrance door with a key. The flat was on the ground floor, to the right; the heating had been on, for it was warm and comfortable. 'Living room's there,' said Aileen, pointing to a door off the hall. 'Make yourself at home, and I'll brew up.'

Skinner settled on to the larger of the two couches and leaned back, gazing up at the ceiling, feeling tired, and wondering vaguely what he was doing there. From nowhere, he thought of his children and felt a pang of longing, for peace, quiet and a life undisturbed.

'Hey,' her voice came quietly. He realised that he had been dozing.

'Sorry,' he said. 'I was meditating.'

'Do you always meditate with your mouth hanging very slightly open?' she asked as she laid a mug before him on the glass coffee table, and settled down beside him on the couch.

'That means I'm really getting into it.'

'You don't let much out, do you, Bob?'

'Not as a rule,' he admitted. 'Discussing my politics with a politician is a real first. Even my wife thinks I could go into the polling station, close my eyes, and my hand would still put the cross in the Tory box.'

'If we're into confessions, I'll give you one. I voted Tory once myself. It didn't count, mind you. It was in a mock election at school in 'eighty-three.'

'Everybody voted Tory in 'eighty-three. Would you like to confess something else now?'

She peered at him, over the top of her mug. 'What?'

'How did you know that this was on my way home?'

A faint pink flush came to her cheeks. 'I told you I had access to the secrets,' she murmured. 'My department has a file on you; I read it. I know that you live in Gullane, East Lothian, your middle name's Morgan, you've a two-one arts degree in philosophy and politics from Glasgow University, and you hold the Queen's Police Medal. You had a cardiac incident earlier this year in America. You had a pacemaker implanted as a precaution against a recurrence and you are now one hundred per cent fit. You've been married twice; your first wife was killed when you were twenty-eight, your second wife is American, a consultant pathologist. You have one daughter by your first marriage, one of each by your second, and an adopted son. Your adult daughter is an associate with Curle, Anthony and Jarvis, Mitchell Laidlaw's firm . . . but he told me that, it's not on your file.'

'Just as bloody well,' Bob growled.

'I could also take you through every step of your career, culminating in your rejection of the command of the Scottish Drugs Enforcement Agency, the reasons for this set out in your letter to the former justice minister.'

'Is there anything you don't know about me?' he asked her, when she had finished.

The pale blue eyes seemed to sparkle with her smile. 'I suspect there's still a hell of a lot that I don't know. In fact, I suspect that the really interesting things about you aren't on that file. Sure it told me where you come from, where you've been, how you've risen through the police and all that stuff. But it doesn't tell me why you have so many enemies.'

He frowned. 'Do I?'

'You know you do. There are people in my party . . . not in the controlling wing, I hasten to say . . . and in parties to the left of mine who are dead scared of you. They'd love to see you discredited, brought down, sent packing off to Gullane, or better still taken off the scene altogether.'

'That's not news to me,' he said. 'They've tried to get rid of me from my job already, a couple of times in fact.'

'You gave them the opportunity, as I understand it.'

'Maybe. And maybe they'd have succeeded in having me fired too, but they'd neither the brains nor the balls.'

'That's funny,' she said. 'I'd heard that Agnes Maley had both and you saw her off.'

Skinner laughed, softly. 'Ah, Black Agnes. She gave it a good try, but she's history.'

'Mmm. I heard she annoyed you so much you made a movie with her in the starring role.'

Skinner's grin vanished as quickly as it had appeared. 'Your boss,' he said. 'Mr Tommy Murtagh, the First Miniature. He's got a loose tongue; because he's one of only half a dozen people who know about that, and I can vouch for the silence of all the rest. I didn't make that movie, as it happens, but, luckily, I have more friends than I have enemies. Just in case you're harbouring any illusions about me, if I had known about it in advance I wouldn't have stopped it. The only regret I have about Agnes is that I couldn't do more to her.'

Aileen saw his eyes go harder as he looked towards her, saw the warmth in them turn to ice. 'You can be scary, you know,' she murmured.

'Only to people who need scaring; like Agnes Maley.'

'You may think that, but it's not true; you scared me.'

He frowned. 'When did I do that?' The moment was gone; she saw only concern in him.

'Just now, when you looked at me; it was as if you let me see right down inside you. Did you do that on purpose?'

'No, not knowingly at any rate. If I did, I apologise, but maybe, subconsciously, I wanted to warn you.'

'Warn me about what?'

'Never mind.'

She wrinkled her brow. 'Warn me not to exceed my ministerial brief, you mean? If you did, it didn't work. I like danger,' she said quietly, 'and you, Mr Skinner, are a very dangerous man. But the really scary thing about you is the way that it comes out of nowhere. Just there, when I mentioned Agnes, you went from sunshine to darkness in an instant. That's not in your file.'

'Of course it isn't. We all do things off the record.'

'We don't all kill people.'

'Who says I have?'

'That much is on your file; you must know that.'

He shrugged. 'They were terrorists. I was an armed officer.'

'They mean nothing to you?'

He held her gaze although, to his surprise, he found it difficult. Jim Gainer's phrase came back to him. 'I don't put flowers on their graves,' he said.

'Did you kill them in cold blood?'

'I don't like talking about it, Aileen.'

'Please, I want to know. I'm interested in what makes you tick. You're not frightening me any more.'

'If you're that keen it's like this: I'm a police officer. That means, literally, I'm an agent of the people. When I act I do so on their behalf, in the interests of the society which put me in that position. Emotion doesn't come into it. I didn't feel any then, and I don't now when I'm forced to look back on it, or persuaded to talk about it.'

'Why can't I believe that?'

'Because you've read too much crime fiction. You think that because I'm a copper I've got to have a tortured soul.'

'And don't you?'

'I did for a while, but I'm getting over it. I won't say that I'm entirely at peace with myself yet, but I've been persuaded that the bad's outweighed by the good. Most people can say the same about themselves . . . you included.'

'Yet you're still able to say to me that you could execute someone, just like that, and feel nothing.'

'Since I've told you I don't feel remorse, are you saying that I enjoyed it?'

'I hope not. I think I'm wondering whether you carry enough anger within you to make you able to do anything.'

He shook his head in denial. 'It's just a dirty job, that's all. When it's done I go home to my wife, and my children.'

'Could you kill me if it was necessary?'

'Don't be daft, woman.'

'Seriously. Could you kill me?

'If I found you threatening to use lethal force on me or

anyone else, I probably could. But that's academic, because you couldn't do that.'

'How can you say that so confidently? You hardly know me.'

An expression that she had not seen before spread across his face; there was mischief in it. She had not thought him capable of that.

'Sure I know you,' he told her, in a slow, easy drawl. 'You're thirty-six years old, the daughter of a chartered accountant and a nurse. You were educated at Hutcheson's Grammar School and Strathclyde University: you've got an honours degree in civil engineering.'

His smile vanished, and his voice grew serious. 'When you were twenty-three you went to South America to work on an irrigation project in Surinam. You were caught up in a revolution, and you set up a refugee camp for women and children running from the fighting. You fed, sheltered and saved the lives of hundreds of people. Then a platoon of rebel militia arrived; the government were winning, they were on the retreat, and they were out to scorch some earth. You faced them down, and they left your camp untouched. You weren't so lucky, though. You were raped by their commander. Luckily for you, he was one of the few men in that group who wasn't HIV positive, but you didn't know that until you were tested, after the revolt collapsed completely and the army arrived.'

He paused; Aileen de Marco's mouth was set in a tight line. 'After that,' Skinner continued, 'you came back to Scotland and you took a job with a firm of consultant engineers. You also became an active member of the Labour Party, where before you had only been a supporter. When you were twenty-six you were elected to Glasgow District Council. By that time you had established a charity which raises funds for the relief of refugees from civil wars, of which there is never any shortage. At the beginning of your second term on the council you were appointed chair of the planning committee. You were instrumental in uncovering a bribery scandal involving contractors, officials and a couple of your fellow councillors. They all got the slammer; as a result you've got some enemies yourself. They did their best to stop you getting a seat in the parliament, but they failed. That was their one chance. Now you've got power and you're going to get more in the future. You've become a career politician. You don't run a car, and you live alone in Glasgow, in a flat by the side of the Clyde. You've never married, although you had a relationship with another councillor that ended six years ago. Since then your male acquaintances have included a journalist and a musician. Currently unattached.'

He paused again. 'Oh, yes,' he added. 'And confirming your attraction to the oppressed and the underprivileged, you're a Partick Thistle supporter.' He looked at her. 'You couldn't kill anyone, and you couldn't even threaten it. If you saw someone threatened with death, you would say, "Kill me instead." And you know what? They probably would, because people who are capable of killing usually do it when they're challenged to.'

She sat in silence as he finished. 'That's me taught, isn't it?' she whispered eventually. 'Does it say on my file that I couldn't kill anyone?'

He smiled. 'No, Aileen, I said that. My wife made a forceful point to me a few days ago. There are no angels, she told me.' He flashed her a quick, wicked glance. 'But there are some who can call up the Devil when we need him.'

'And I should be grateful you're on our side?'

He nodded, and his grin widened. 'Very.'

She gave a snort of laughter. 'God!' she exclaimed. 'You're up front, aren't you?'

'Very rarely. You'd be surprised if you knew how few people I'd talk to like I've talked to you this evening.'

She shook her head. 'No, I wouldn't. You might be surprised too; the normal everyday Aileen de Marco's as private a person as you are. I guess that having read each other's files has given us a sort of intimacy.'

'I suppose.' He swung round in his chair, then suddenly looked her in the eye. 'Tell me something. That rebel, the one in Surinam: he didn't rape you, did he? Not forcibly, that is.'

He saw her cheeks redden. 'What do you mean?'

'I think that was the deal. It was the price you had to pay to save the people you were looking after. Am I right?'

She nodded, eyes downward. 'How did you know that?' she asked quietly.

'If he'd raped you, taken you by force, I mean, it would have been a violent act. He'd have killed you afterwards and his men would have slaughtered everyone in your camp. You took a chance that he would keep his word.'

'I couldn't do anything else.'

'Of course not. You were lucky that the guy had some sort of honour.'

433

'They killed him, you know,' she murmured. 'The government troops caught him and shot him, in front of his men. Then they shot the rest of them.'

Skinner shrugged his shoulders. 'Fair enough, in your man's case. You might pretend to yourself that there was a sort of treaty between you at the time, but in truth he did rape you, as sure as if he'd held a gun to your head.'

'I suppose you'd have shot him too,' she challenged.

He looked her in the eye, smiling cheerfully. 'Only if he was very lucky,' he replied.

'God,' she exclaimed, 'you mean that too, don't you? Stop it. Turn off that magnetism.'

'Hey!' He touched his chest, just below his left shoulder, where his pacemaker had been implanted. 'A magnet could do me some serious harm. I'm computer-driven, remember.'

She laughed. 'You mean that's your equivalent of a krypton necklace, Superman? That's a powerful hold you've given me over you.'

'I'll bear that in mind when they're putting you through the metal detector. "Look out for magnets!" I'll warn them.'

'Me too?'

'You too.'

'I don't think I'll bother going in that case.'

'Some chance. Atheist or not, you won't pass up the chance to meet Gilbert White. Oops, sorry,' he exclaimed, 'His Holiness. I haven't got used to giving him his title yet.'

'Are you an atheist, Bob?'

He grinned. 'Are you still trying to find my soul?'

'Maybe. Are you?'

'I thought I was, twenty years ago. Now I've seen some stuff, and I'd say I've slid into agnosticism. Talking with Jim Gainer, and with other clergymen, has given me a new slant on spiritual matters. It's made me realise that the older I get, I seem to be moving towards defining some sort of belief. Consider this. The New Testament portrays War, Famine, Pestilence and Death as anthropomorphic entities: the Four Horsemen of the Apocalypse. They're all too real in today's world, the whole fucking quartet, and you and I have no trouble accepting their existence. God's portrayed as an anthropomorphic entity, too, so why do we have trouble accepting its existence?'

'We're shown proof of the existence of the Horsemen every day. Where's the evidence for God?'

'By definition, that's where faith comes in: steadfast belief, in the absence of evidence. That's my problem, you see. I'm a copper and so I'm trained to require evidence. I'm still searching, though . . . and I *am* searching, believe me. I think I see a little every time I look at my daughters and my sons.'

'Mmm.' She mused. 'Maybe I should too. It can't do any harm, can it?'

'Not that I can see, as long as you don't become a zealot. Converts have a reputation as extremists.'

She smiled. 'Don't worry. I'm not that good.'

'Oh, no? Should I caution you, then?'

'Maybe you should.' She hesitated and then looked up at him. 'You haven't always gone home to your wife, have you?'

'Ahh. Back to my file, are we?'

'Sorry. I shouldn't have said that.'

'No, you shouldn't.'

'But since I did . . .' They met each other halfway, not pulling back. She opened her mouth and flicked his tongue with hers, pressing her body, her small, firm, hard-nippled breasts, against him. 'If you said, "Yes, Minister," ' she whispered as they broke off, 'I wouldn't laugh this time.'

He leaned back and looked at her. 'Aileen, when you said you liked danger, you weren't kidding.'

She bit her lip and looked down, suddenly chastened. 'I'm sorry. I don't know what made me do that.'

'I thought we both did it,' he said. 'And in my case, I know why. You are a very attractive woman, and I'm flawed and lustful, just like most on my side of the sexual divide. Listen to me! One minute I'm talking of searching for God, and the next I'm wondering whether I might find Him up your skirt.'

Aileen's chuckle was low and throaty. 'I'm not that complicated. I'm a single woman who's just realised it's been an absolute age since she's had any. I know, you're married, and I should be ashamed of myself. Crazy, isn't it? I now feel ashamed because I don't feel ashamed. I'm nuts, really.'

Bob shook his head. 'You're the most together woman a guy could encounter in a long day's march. But would you move you brain back up to your head for a minute, please, and consider this? If you and I got involved, and it leaked out . . . as you can bet it would . . . the tabloids would feed on us like maggots on a corpse. It would finish my rocky marriage, make me a louse in the eyes of my kids, and damage my career. But as bad as all that would be for me, so would the consequences you'd face. You have places to go: you will become First Minister, as everyone is forecasting. That would all be blown out of the water. You'd be lucky to keep your seat in the parliament.'

'I know.' She smiled: it was soft, sweet, with an odd mixture of shyness and seduction. 'But who said anything about getting involved? You've lived for years in a world that's populated by secrets, and now, so do I. So what's one more between us?'

Seventy-five

There were so many officers required for the briefing that it had to be held in the gymnasium at the police headquarters building. They were all there as ordered, at eight thirty sharp, when the chief constable, ACC Willie Haggerty and Chief Superintendent Brian Mackie strode in, followed by a silver-haired man in a sharp suit.

Heads turned and a few eyebrows rose at the sight of Sir James: usually he was content to let his deputy or assistants run such affairs. Even more rose when DCC Bob Skinner brought up the rear, with a slender, attractive blonde woman by his side. While the first four stepped on to the dais at the front of the gym and took seats, they slipped quietly into the far corner.

Sir James Proud stepped up to the microphone that the communications team had set up. 'I'd like to thank you all,' he began. 'Before we go any further I'd just like to do that. It's a privilege to command people like you; I don't have too many chances to tell you that, so I thought I'd take this one.' Skinner smiled; Proud Jimmy could lay it on when he wanted. 'I would like also to welcome,' he turned to his left and nodded to

Aileen de Marco, 'the newly appointed Justice Minister, who expressed her wish to come along this morning to lend you her support,' he turned to his right and nodded again, 'and Signor Rossi, of the Vatican logistics department.'

He paused, and looked around his force. 'In all my career,' he continued, 'this is, in my opinion, the most important event the city has ever seen. However, I want to get one thing out of the way at once. I recognise that Roman Catholicism is a minority faith in this country of ours. I appreciate also that there are sincerely held beliefs in Scotland that run contrary to its teachings. I'm not talking about bigotry, for I would like to think that I do not have a single bigot under my command. I'm talking about members of recognised churches, holding legitimate beliefs. I may also be talking to them. What I want to say is this, as diplomatically as I can. If there is any person in this room who feels, for whatever reason, that he or she might not be able to give one hundred per cent concentration to our task today, I'd like them to seek out their line commander after this briefing and ask to be excused duty. Similarly, if there's anyone out there who's not feeling up to snuff this morning, for whatever reason, I want them to do the same thing. Don't walk out now; I don't want anyone to feel self-conscious or stigmatised. If you've got a problem with this duty, do as I suggest, as quietly as you like.'

The chief's eyes scanned the assembly once more. 'Now that's off my chest,' he concluded, 'I'm going to hand over to ACC Haggerty, the commander of uniformed operations within the Edinburgh divisions.' He stepped back, and yielded the mike.

'Good news, bad news,' the pugnacious Glaswegian barked. 'First, the weather forecast for the next two days says it's going to be fine and sunny. Second, by the time this is over you're all going to be bloody tired. We've got six events to cover, three today and two tomorrow, culminating in the rally at Murrayfield.'

The ACC ran through the detail of the timetable from the arrival of the Prime Minister at Edinburgh airport, half an hour before that of the Pope, to their departure from the same point twenty-four hours later, then handed over to Brian Mackie.

The tall, slim chief superintendent removed his ill-fitting cap, laid it on his chair and moved over to three boards on easels at the side of the platform. They showed a route map, a ground plan of the airport and a plan of Murrayfield stadium, as it would be set up for the centrepiece event.

'I want to begin,' he glanced across at Skinner in the corner, 'by emphasising that this briefing is confidential and that if certain things that I am going to tell you appear in the media, I will personally hunt down the person who leaked them and subject them to cruel and unusual punishment, something far worse than duty at Tynecastle. If the phrase "nuts for breakfast" means anything to you, bear it in mind.'

The assembly laughed. A young constable in the third row raised his hand. 'Does that apply to the minister too, sir?' he called out.

Mackie froze him with a glare. 'If you think I'm joking, son, ask my senior colleagues how often I do that.' He looked round the hall. 'Any other comedians here?' There was dead silence.

'That's as well for, as the chief said, this is as responsible a task as we've ever faced. Okay, this is where I start to get confidential. I can tell you that there are no specific intelligence reports of a threat against the person of the Pope. However, the man who's greeting him at the airport and accompanying him throughout the visit is one of the world's top half-dozen terrorist targets. At this point, if he wasn't struck dumb, our funny friend in row three might ask why he's coming. The answer to that is that he's the head of the government of this country and he feels that it's his duty. He feels that if he doesn't show here, the terrorists will have won. So whether individually we agree with that or not, as a force we have a responsibility to protect him . . .' he paused and looked around once more '. . . with our lives if necessary, just like young Barry Macgregor.'

Seventy-six

There had been no word of the 'people' who the soldier policeman had promised would visit. As he had undertaken to do Steele had sent a JPEG image of Aurelia Middlemass's security image to Dubai. He had also given Mary Chambers a detailed account of his conversation with the general.

'That all sounds a shade heavy,' she had pronounced, putting his own view into words. 'I'll talk to Dan Pringle about it, and I know for sure what he'll do. This one will be passed straight up the line, so when your contact's friends do get in touch, you'd better be ready to bring the DCC in on the act, and have all your loose ends tied off.'

'There are no loose ends. Don't worry, I'll have a full report ready for him.'

He had spent the rest of the day preparing it, waiting all the time for the phone to ring. When it had not, he had told the night staff when he left that he was to be advised of any call, whatever the hour. Of course, he had told Maggie of the development; she had been as keen as him to learn who the visitors might be.

The mystery remained unsolved. Steele sat at his desk,

reviewing Arthur Dorward's report of the search of Aurelia Middlemass's home, under warrant from the Sheriff. The team had found clothes, male and female, in the wardrobes, bank statements, utility bills in Aurelia's name, and fingerprints in abundance. There were no clues to where they might have gone, but there was a clear indication of how they had been living. The young inspector found it intriguing.

The house had three bedrooms, but one was completely unfurnished. The largest of the three was *en suite* and in its bathroom the searchers found Aurelia's fingerprints on the taps, toilet handle and mirror, and hair in the bath and basin that matched strands found on her clothes and on the pillows of the room's double bed. But there was no sign of Alsina: his prints, hair and other traces were found in the main bathroom and in the second bedroom. His clothing was hanging in its wardrobe and his shoes were on a stand.

As always, Dorward's team had been thorough. They had checked the sheets on both beds for any traces of bodily fluids, but had found only a trace of menstrual blood on those taken from the main bedroom. There was no indication anywhere that Alsina and Aurelia had been living as man and wife.

He was pondering this when his phone rang. He snapped to attention and snatched it up.

'Front desk here, sir,' said a woman officer. 'There's a gentleman to see you.'

'Is there a free interview room?' he asked at once, imagining that the general's envoy might not like being paraded through the CID suite.

'Number two.'

'Okay, Briony, show him in there and I'll be down. Did he give a name, by the way?'

'Yes, sir. He said his name was Whetstone, Murphy Whetstone; he's a great big lad.'

'Shit,' Steele exclaimed involuntarily. 'That's not who I was expecting. Scrub the interview room; bring him up here instead.'

A few heads turned, as the exceptionally tall young man was led through the CID room. 'Hello, Murphy,' the inspector greeted him, curiosity overcoming his earlier frustration. 'What brings you here?'

'I don't know,' he replied. 'I guess it's the way I was brought up.'

'What do you mean?'

'I mean I think I had a chance to get away with something that would have left me in blondes and Porsches till I got tired of them, but I just couldn't do it.' He reached into a pocket of his jacket and produced an envelope, a big one that had been folded over to make it fit. He laid it on the detective's desk.

'The company's looking after me very well while I'm over here,' he began. 'Among other things, all my mail's being couriered over to me, express delivery. I had a consignment first thing this morning. Take a look; you might think I'm crazy when you do.'

Steele picked up the envelope and shook out its contents: two smaller envelopes, one white, with UK stamps and an air-mail flash, the other brown, with US stamps. Each was addressed to Murphy, at what the inspector assumed was his home in Tennessee. He picked up the British envelope first, and shook out a letter. He unfolded it and saw that it was printed, on A4 paper.

Dear Murph [it began],

By the time you read this, you'll know that I have gone to the great clubhouse in the sky. To cut a painful story short, a few days ago I was told by the sort of doctor who doesn't make mistakes that there was a room in St Columba's Hospice with my name on the door, and that it was ready for immediate occupancy.

I've never enjoyed sleeping in a strange bed, and although I've never had the experience, I'm sure I wouldn't enjoy being ministered to by strange women either. So, since I'm a firm believer in one's right to choose the time and manner of one's passing, I've decided to exercise it. You may find my choice of method a bit melodramatic, but it seems the easiest way to do it, and a strange opportunity has arisen of doing the deed away from well-meaning interferers and most of all away from home. Your mother has always loved that house and I would not want to have her associate any gruesome memories with it.

This sudden turn of events has made a bit of a hash of my intentions for you, old son. Your mother is well provided for, worry not, but it was my plan to use the last years of my career, and the wholly unexpected earning power I have been given, to do something to help provide for your long-term future as well as my own. However, when the chips are down I have always been a resourceful type, as many of my golf companions will testify. I'm going to let you into a secret. I have always been an old-fashioned banker, always been the sort who likes looking ordinary people in the eye, giving them good news when I can, and helping them through crises when I can't. It's one of my proudest boasts that I've never foreclosed on any client in my life.

Even though I have proved to be remarkably good at the job I'm doing now, so good that in a few months I was able to rid myself of the strange ice-maiden whom they tried to make my boss and out-perform her in every way, I have to tell you that I hate, loathe and detest everything that the Scottish Farmers Bank has become under the people who are now shaping its policies, and generally making a balls of implementing them. So it is without any conscience whatsoever that I have made certain arrangements for your benefit. I have done this in a way that will even now be causing ructions in Lothian Road, and which will I hope result in a culling of the incompetents, whose names I need not list here. I have also done it through a route which is completely untraceable, based on a knowledge of international banking law and practice which my so-called superiors never suspected I possessed.

Today I confirmed to my complete satisfaction that all my arrangements are complete. Very soon, you'll receive items in the US that will put all of this into context. You need have no fear about putting them to use in making what I hope and expect will be a bloody good life for yourself. The other letter I enclose with this is for your mother. I want you to give it to her yourself, when next you see her. I don't want her getting it through the mail, and didn't want to leave it for her in the office. It tells her why I've done this, how much I love her, what a privilege it has been to spend my adult life with her, and all that sort of stuff. I'll say the same to you now, son. I wish we could have had a few more years to enjoy each other's company, but none of us has the privilege, or rather the curse, of knowing the hour of our departure too long before the train is ready to leave the station.

Enjoy your legacy, and yourself. Drive straight and putt even straighter. Goodbye and God speed.

All my love,

Dad.

PS. I trust you'll have the bloody sense to burn this letter.

To his considerable surprise, Stevie Steele felt a lump in his throat. He blinked, to keep his eyes clear. He folded the letter, replaced it in its envelope and picked up the other. He reached inside and withdrew its contents, an American Express card, holder M. Whetstone, and a green bank book. He opened it and saw that it was the key to an account in a Delaware bank. The amount on deposit was very slightly over one million eight hundred thousand US dollars.

'You see the name?' Murphy asked. 'Bank of Piercetown;

that's "BP", the initials on Dad's note to himself. "AM" probably just meant morning.'

The detective looked across the desk at the young man. 'He was right, you know,' he told him as he held up the book. 'We'd never have found this.'

He smiled back at him. 'You mean I am crazy?'

'That's for you to work out. What did bring you here? You could have burned that letter as he says.'

'I know. I've been trying to make sense of it since that lot arrived, Mr Steele. The best conclusion I can come to is that my father did this as one last gesture, just to show that he could, then he left the deciding to me. He wasn't a flamboyant man, but he was a gamester inside. He taught me most of what I know, but one thing the course didn't include was how to live my life on the basis of something like this.' He shrugged the shoulders of his enormous jacket. 'On top of that, it's not my money.'

'That's the best answer.'

'What should I do now?'

'Nothing. Leave all this with me; I'll give you a receipt.' He looked through the glass wall of his cubicle, caught DC Singh's eye and waved him inside. 'Tarvil,' he said, 'I want you to find a typist . . . use the chief super's if you have to; ask her nicely and it'll be okay. Get me a formal receipt for one letter, an Amex card and a bank book . . .' He read out the bank's name and the account number. '. . . handed over by Mr Murphy Whetstone. It's to be signed by Mr Whetstone and by me with you as a witness signatory.'

The young constable nodded; he returned a few minutes

later, bearing two copies of the receipt. All three of them signed beside their printed names.

'Have you given your mother her letter?' Steele asked, as he walked Murphy to the top of the stairs.

'Not yet. Will I have to tell her about the other one?'

'I hope not. I'll go and see the acting chief executive at the bank. If he has any sense he'll just accept the return of the money. You may have to sign some form of legal document, but I hope that'll be all there is to it. With that done, the fiscal's file on your father's death will be closed as a suicide, and your mother need never know the whole story.'

'If you can do that, I'd appreciate it. Thanks.'

'No, it's for me to thank you. Thanks a million, in fact.'

Steele was smiling as he settled back into his chair . . . until the phone rang once more.

Seventy-seven

'Who was Barry Macgregor?' Aileen de Marco asked.

'He was a young detective constable, one of my boys. He was killed on duty, a few years back.'

'I knew it had to be something like that. Was Chief Superintendent Mackie there when it happened? He seemed a bit emotional for a second, when he mentioned him.'

'We were both there,' said Bob quietly. 'I was holding him when he died; I had his blood all over me. Brian took down the man who did it; picked him right off the back of a motorbike. Best damn shot I've ever seen. He wasn't emotional then.'

'That quiet man in a uniform? He did that?'

'Absolutely: didn't bat an eyelid. Brian's the finest shot on this force, with any weapon.' He looked at her across the low coffee table in his office. 'That stuff we talked about last night, about killing and everything; no fantasy, it really does happen. The boys and girls that people like your man Godfrey Rennie regard as statistics, they really do put their lives on the line.'

'I suppose I knew that,' Aileen admitted. 'But being there this morning, listening to Mr Mackie explain that although the Pope had asked for no show of weapons, there would be snipers hidden all over the place, and men with wee gold badges in their lapels to signify that they were armed . . .' She shivered. 'It brings it right on to my doorstep, the whole global-terrorism thing. As a deputy minister, I wasn't involved with heavy stuff like that.'

He reached across the corner of his table and squeezed her hand. 'Get used to it, love,' he told her, 'because it's the reality of my job and, from now on, of yours too.' He looked into her eyes. 'I have this vision of you, one day, as First Minister of an independent Scotland, as a national head of government. You should start to prepare yourself for that, right now.'

She let out a quiet laugh. 'God, you're not a Nat as well, are you?'

'Nah. I just think it's inevitable, like night follows day; it has been since they passed the Scotland Act.'

'That's not what the people who wrote it intended.'

'Since when could politicians see beyond the next election?' he asked her.

'Is that what you're trying to do? Make me take the long view?'

'Exactly. And it's why I won't do anything to compromise you. I haven't known you long, but already I believe in you as much as I believe in myself. You've got a destiny, same as I have, only I can see yours more clearly. I won't let anything or anyone get in the way of it . . . especially not me. That's why the . . . encounter . . . we had last night has to remain just that.'

Aileen gave the smallest of nods. 'I know,' she said. 'I'm ambitious enough to realise that too. Plus, I wouldn't want to hurt you.'

'Or my wife?' Words once spoken can never be recalled. 'Sorry, that was a crass thing to come out with.'

'No, it was honest. Bob, I know enough about married men to tell when they're only after a leg over on the side . . . they've got no chance with me, by the way, no chance at all . . . and when things are bad at home and they need somewhere to go, even if it's only to talk. You didn't have to tell me your marriage was rocky; I'd worked that out for myself. I promise you this, though; I won't make anything worse.'

'You don't need to tell me that,' he told her. 'You're not the *Fatal Attraction* type. But you're right. Sarah and I have been in trouble for a few months now, and nothing we try seems to make it any better.'

'Are you going to keep trying, though?'

'Right now, I really don't know. If we don't, can I tell you?'

Aileen smiled. 'You'd better.' She eased herself to her feet. 'My car should be downstairs by now. I have to get to the office. Will you be around tomorrow at Murrayfield?'

'I don't know,' he said. 'I'm not a player in the operation, although I helped put it together. If I turn up, Willie and Brian might think I don't trust them. If I'm there, I won't be high profile, that's for sure. It'll be a private visit.'

'Part of your search for God? Now I've told you He's not up my skirt after all?'

He stood, quickly and supply. 'Don't sell yourself short.' He chuckled, as he walked her to the door. 'Should we shake hands?' he asked.

'Don't be silly,' she whispered. Rising up on her toes, she kissed him. He was still gazing at the dark door well after it had closed on her, still aware of her perfume lingering behind her, the ghost of her presence in the room. He gave himself a shake back to reality and returned to his desk, ready to start his morning's work in earnest.

He buzzed McGurk. 'Jack, the minister's gone. Give me a couple of minutes then come along please, and bring the mail with you.' He switched on his computer, let it boot up, and checked his e-mail. There was nothing in his official mailbox . . . there rarely was, since his executive assistant routinely printed out all the incoming messages, other than those from certain listed contacts . . . but when he signed on to his personal address, he found one from 'dmacphail' asking if he would make that evening's gathering of his five-a-side football group, the Thursday Legends . . . 'Not a chance tonight, mate,' he muttered . . . two with headlines guaranteeing to increase his penis size, another offering him Viagra online . . . 'So I can cope with the new cock, I suppose,' he chuckled . . . and a fifth, from 'dr_sarah'. He moved the cursor to open it then changed his mind and deleted all five.

There was a rap on the door; it swung open and McGurk came in with a bundle of documents. 'Thanks,' said the DCC. 'Do you want to talk me through any of that stuff?'

'Just two items, sir.' He laid a brown envelope on the desk. 'That's from Signor Rossi.' He placed a bulky package beside it. 'And that's from the head of CID; all the paperwork on the

Belgian investigation.' He dropped the rest into the DCC's in-tray. 'That's just the usual stuff, I'd say.'

'So much for the paperless office,' Skinner grumbled. He reached out and tapped the pile of material that Pringle had set him. 'When I get round to this,' he said, 'I might ask you to come and help me. I'll be trying to find something that's out of shape, something that doesn't square with the facts as we know them. If you're helping me, we'll be twice as likely to spot it; four eyes are always better than two, especially when you don't know what the hell you're looking for.'

'I'll be there, boss,' said McGurk. 'Is that all for now?'

'Yes, Jack, thanks; and thanks in general too. You've settled in very well, in spite of me sometimes. I feel that my back's being well watched, and that's what I value most of all in an exec.' He slapped the fat folder again. 'I'll give you a shout when I need you.'

Alone, Skinner picked up the big brown envelope, slid out its contents and examined them. It was a three-page fax with a cover sheet, which showed that it had been sent to Giovanni Rossi from an Italian number. As he had been promised, it was a detailed biography of Gilbert White, Bishop of Rome, latest in a line of succession that stretched back to St Peter. As he read it, Skinner could see in his mind's eye the last occasion on which he had met him, just over three years earlier at a reception hosted by the former first minister in Bute House, his official residence. In his red robes and cardinal's hat, he had seemed to fill the room. If his election to the papacy had surprised the rest of the world, it had been seen in Scotland as no more than his due.

The DCC began to read. He found that the paper was written almost in reverse order; the first part dealt with the Pope's life since his elevation, his pronouncements, his views on major issues facing the Church and the world, and the two formal visits he had made, the first to his old college in Spain, relocated since his time to Salamanca, and the second a dramatic mission to the Democratic Republic of the Congo, in a successful bid to snuff out the last traces of the long-running civil war. It was only when he reached the last page that he found the information he had been after. The young Gilbert White had been educated at St Patrick's High, Coatbridge, and had studied for the priesthood at the Royal Scots College in Valladolid, Spain, established in the days when Catholicism had been an outlawed religion in Scotland. He had been ordained in Glasgow at the age of twenty-six. In the first year of his priesthood, he had chosen to broaden his education and experience and, through the influence of one of his former tutors, had been granted a two-year attachment as a curate to the great cathedral in Brussels. When that was complete he had returned to Scotland and, apart from a period on the staff of the Pontifical Scots College in Rome, had spent his entire pastoral career there.

Skinner finished the document, then read it through for a second time. He leaned back in his chair and scratched his head. He must have met Malou in Brussels, over forty years ago; there could be no more to it than that.

He laid the biography aside and turned to Pringle's folder. He was about to open it when his phone rang. 'I have Father Collins on the line, sir, from the Pope's secretariat.'

'Put him through.'

'Good morning, Mr Skinner.' The young priest's accent betrayed his Western Isles origins. 'I spoke to the Holy Father last night and asked him your question. He asked me to tell you that the name Auguste Malou does mean something to him. He met him during the period of his attachment to the Cathedral of St Michael in Brussels, and they've remained in touch ever since. Their friendship is the reason for his invitation to the Bastogne Drummers to play at Murrayfield.'

'That's all he said about him?'

'That is all, sir.'

'I see. Thank you for your trouble, Father.'

'Don't mention it, sir. His Holiness also asked me to tell you that he's looking forward very much to seeing you and Sir James Proud again. After this evening's mass, he'll be having supper with the Archbishop, at his residence: he's staying there, as you know. He wonders whether you and the chief constable would care to join them; around nine thirty. He promises that the conversation will be almost entirely about football.'

The DCC was taken aback. 'I think I can speak for Jimmy on that,' he said. 'We'd both be honoured. I'll let him know. Mind you,' he added, 'being a Hibs fan, the Pope may have little to talk about.'

'Don't you believe it,' said Angelo Collins, laughing as he hung up.

Skinner did not have time even to reach for Pringle's folder before his phone, barely in its cradle, sounded again. 'Yes, Jack,' he said.

'Boss,' began his assistant, 'remember that thing I mentioned last night: the investigation that DI Steele might need to involve you in? Well, it's come up. DCS Pringle's just been on the phone; and he'd like to bring Stevie to see you. He said it was urgent, so I said okay. They should be with you in ten minutes, tops.'

'Okay. I guess Dan's folder will get done some time. There have been no more reports of incidents involving the Belgians, have there?'

'No, sir. I've been keeping an eye on them like you asked. All's quiet. I checked with the Humberside police too, to see whether they've made progress with their investigation.'

'Let me guess at this morning's headline in the *Hull Daily Mail* . . . "Police remain baffled". Right?'

'I don't think it's making headlines any more. They've hit the wall and they know it.'

'They're not the only ones.' He sighed. 'Jack, do you have any feelings just now, anything you can't pin down?'

'Sorry, sir?'

'Ach, it's okay. Call me when Stevie arrives.' He hung up, switched the light outside his door to green, then called McIlhenney. 'Neil,' he exclaimed when the DI picked up, 'it's me and I'm as frustrated as hell.'

'You are, are you? Let me guess. You think there's something up. You see all sorts of threads waving in the breeze, and you're dead certain that they all weave together into a great big tapestry, only you don't know how and you can't work it out for the life of you. Right?'

'Spot fucking on! How did you know?'

'Because I feel exactly the same way.'

'Fat lot of help you are, then,' Skinner grunted. 'Let me know when you work it out.' He hung up again. 'Fuck it!' he shouted to the empty office. 'Why the hell did I talk Andy Martin into going for the DCC's job in Dundee?'

For a moment he was on the point of calling his friend and one-time protégé; instead, he called his own number.

Trish, the nanny, picked up the phone. 'Sarah, please,' he asked her.

'You sound knackered,' she told him. Trish's gift for plain speaking was one of her best points. 'Sarah isn't here. She's gone up town.'

'Carving someone up?'

'She didn't say, but I doubt it. She told me she hoped to be back in time for the boys' lunch. Can I give her a message?'

'Tell her not to wait up for me. I've got a late engagement in town.'

'That'll come as a surprise to her.'

'You push your luck; you know that?'

'Sorry, Bob. I just can't help myself sometimes . . . okay, any time. Say hello to your daughter.'

'Hello, Seonaid.'

There was a squeal from the other end that contained most of the five letters of 'Daddy'.

'Hey,' said Trish. 'She remembers you.'

'Bugger off, girl,' he laughed. 'If you weren't too good to fire . . .'

He stared at the ceiling for a while, thinking about home, thinking about Sarah and, although he tried not to, thinking about Aileen de Marco, and how hard it would be to keep his promise to her and to himself. He did not see Stevie Steele's car as it rolled up the drive, or the woman who emerged from the passenger seat.

When the knock sounded at his door, he recognised it as Dan Pringle's thump rather than Jack McGurk's more circumspect rap. 'Come in,' he shouted. 'Don't make me open the fucking thing for you.'

He was halfway round from behind his desk when the head of CID came into the room. He expected Stevie Steele to be behind him. He did not expect the short, crinkle-haired black woman who was flanked by the two detectives.

Skinner grinned, in surprise as much as anything else. 'Special Agent Merle Gower,' he exclaimed. 'How long has it been?'

'Since I was last in Edinburgh?' she replied. 'Since the former president's visit, as I recall, although the Secret Service was so thick around him that day you probably never saw me.'

Merle Gower was the official resident presence in London of the FBI, although Skinner suspected that she had links in addition with the secretive National Security Agency. She had succeeded his late friend Joe Doherty, on his recall to Washington by the previous administration; at first she had been cocky and abrasive, but she had learned quickly and had won the trust of her British contacts.

'Do you have decent coffee here, Bob?' she asked him.

'No.' He walked across to the filter machine on his side table and poured her a mug. 'But you can try this crap if you like.'

'As long as it has caffeine, I suppose it'll be okay.'

He poured another for himself, and brought them over to the coffee table, leaving his colleagues to fend for themselves. 'This is a big surprise,' he said, as they sat on the low leather couches.

'For me too.' She took a sip from her mug. 'Hey, this isn't bad. What is it?'

'Fair trade coffee. My wife buys it from a Nicaraguan importer. It means that the growers get a fair price, as opposed to being screwed by the bulk buyers. I'll give you the address if you like.'

'You wanna get me fired? I thought you liked me.' She turned as Pringle lowered his bulk on to the seat beside her.

As Steele joined Skinner on his couch, the DCC leaned towards him, his eyes narrowed slightly. 'Congratulations,' he murmured, as Special Agent Gower shuffled sideways to give herself more room.

'You know?'

'I always know. You be good for her, hear me.'

'Do I hear "or else", sir?'

'You better.'

'No worries.'

The exchange was quick and whispered. Neither of their companions heard them, as they completed their seating arrangements. 'Okay,' Skinner barked, 'take me through the reason for this intrusion into the most important day of this force's year.'

Pringle gulped and began. 'It's DI Steele's story, boss. It has to do with a bank fraud.'

'The guy that Sarah autopsied last week?'

'That's the one. I'll let Stevie talk you through it.'

The young inspector nodded and leaned back, half turning so that he faced both Skinner and Gower. Quickly, he talked them through the investigation and the twists and turns it had taken, although he skipped over Sarah's misplaced enthusiasm when she had found the shoulder dislocation. 'Whetstone was solidly in the frame, no doubt about it, until Monday,' he said.

'What happened on Monday?' asked the DCC.

'Aurelia Middlemass disappeared; so did her supposed husband. They left his car at the airport and caught an easyJet flight to London, then on to God knows where. As far as we're concerned they vanished into thin air. So I set to work, looking into her background. That led me to a bank in Dubai, where her CV said she worked before coming to Edinburgh. What her CV didn't say was that she was dead. The real Aurelia was killed in an accident, just before our version came to join the Scottish Farmers Bank.'

'So all of a sudden your locked-up investigation's stood on its head. She did it, and maybe killed Whetstone as well.'

Steele nodded. 'Just so, sir. That led me to get in touch with the police in Dubai, but instead of getting someone from their Traffic department, I wound up speaking to a brigadier general, no less, who's your opposite number.'

'I must ask for a promotion,' Skinner grunted.

'That's where I come in,' said Merle Gower. 'We, the US, that is, as opposed to the FBI, had a strong interest in that so-called accident. This was not because of Ms Middlemass, however; she was a South African national. You see, she was not alone in the vehicle, and she was not the only fatality. Her companion was a US citizen, Mr Wayne Morrison; an attaché on station at our embassy in the United Arab Emirates. They were a couple, and had been for a year or so.'

'I take it he was CIA?'

She looked Skinner in the eye, answering him with her silence. 'The vehicle was rigged; there was a bomb, concealed above the exhaust. It was detonated remotely by someone with a radio transmitter, who probably watched them and picked the moment. Morrison and Ms Middlemass were in the habit of going driving in the desert every weekend, the sort of routine that someone in his position should have known better than to establish.'

'Suspects?'

'We have one. He was attached to a technical college in Dubai as a research chemist. He had an Egyptian passport under the name of Anwar Baradi, but that was, of course, false. Eventually the CIA came up with another name for him, and a photograph, found in a house in Kabul, after the liberation. They believe that he's an Algerian, called Hasid Bourgiba, but relations with that country are not exactly brilliant, so that hasn't been verified. What we do know for sure was that he was a member of a terrorist group that wasn't part of, but had links with, al Qaeda.'

'How about the woman?'

'Bourgiba had no known female associates in Dubai. However, there was a woman who disappeared on the very same day that he did. She lived in a rented apartment in the city, had a part-time job in a library, and her passport showed her as a Zimbabwean author, Polly Pride.'

'Photographs?'

Merle Gower nodded. 'I brought them.'

'It's her, boss,' said Steele. 'I've seen them and I'm absolutely certain. The Bourgiba photograph could be anyone. It's years old and in it the guy has a real Taliban beard, but Superintendent Chambers is on her way out to Heriot-Watt with it now, to show it to the people in the chemistry department.'

The DCC frowned. 'So connect me into this, please. Would two terrorist operatives go to all that bother just to set up a bank sting, albeit for a million? Is the network running short of money?'

'Maybe,' Gower murmured, 'but . . .'

'They didn't do it,' Steele announced. He opened his briefcase, took out two clear plastic evidence envelopes. 'These turned up this morning, out of the blue.'

Skinner read Ivor Whetstone's letter to his son. When he was finished, he removed the bank book and flicked through it. 'So it was him all along. The man was dying and he decided to look out for his lad . . . and maybe set him a test too. If that was in his mind, he'd be glad to know that he passed.'

'So why did they run off?' Dan Pringle asked. 'If they'd sat tight . . .'

The big DCC's blue eyes fixed him. 'So why were they here in the first place, Dan? That's the really big question.'

He looked up at the ceiling of his office once more, gazing at nothing as the seconds grew into minutes.

'What is it, boss?' Steele asked at last.

Skinner smiled. 'It's a tapestry, Stevie, starting to weave itself. I can't make out all the pattern yet, but it's forming.'

Suddenly he leaned forward, his shoulders hunching. 'I've no idea why they did a runner, people,' he exclaimed. 'But I'll bet you the million Whetstone nicked on this: they are coming back!'

He shot to his feet, pounding his big right fist into his left palm. 'And you know what it means, don't you?' he continued, speaking to himself rather than to his companions. 'The security briefing I've just attended is now out of date, hours before the ball starts rolling. We do now have a specific threat!'

Seventy-eight

Brian Mackie had never been more tense. The summons to the DCC's office had come as a complete surprise to him, and the message that he had been given there, by Skinner, with a grim-faced Willie Haggerty looking on, had brought his worst dreams of the previous few weeks to the edge of reality.

New intelligence information. Not obtained from the security services, but as a by-product of a criminal investigation within Edinburgh itself. Two terrorist sleepers, moved to his city from an assassination in the Middle East, but hidden among the professional classes, not among the ethnic communities, where previous real or would-be terrorists had invariably been found.

Mackie shuddered as he thought of the implications of this new tactic, and as he watched the chartered Alitalia Airbus make its gentle approach to the runway at Edinburgh airport, escorted by two fighter jets, one on either side. As the Pope's plane landed, they veered off and headed back to RAF Leuchars. The same procedure had been followed when the Prime Minister had arrived an hour earlier. Nobody had told the chief superintendent, but he had guessed that the two aircraft were there to intercept any ground-to-air missile that might have been launched.

He watched from his position on a viewing gallery on the roof that was off limits to the travelling public. He scanned to his left and right, checking that all the snipers were in position, then looked down at the airport's concourse as the big jet taxied in. The reception committee was waiting, headed by the Lord Provost, both as the capital's leading citizen and as its Lord Lieutenant, the personal representative of the Queen. After Lord Provost Maxwell there stood, in order, the Prime Minister, his familiar quiff blowing in the breeze, the much shorter figure of the red-haired Tommy Murtagh, MSP, Scotland's First Minister and clear loser of the precedence argument between Holyrood and Whitehall, Sir James Proud, imperious as ever in his heavily adorned uniform, and last of the five, in richly embroidered vestments, Archbishop James Gainer.

Mackie had suggested moving the formal greeting indoors, but Skinner had decided against the idea since that would have meant explaining the last-minute change to the television crews and rota photographer who were being allowed to cover the first event of John the Twenty-fifth's brief visit. Whatever story they had invented, media speculation would have been inevitable, and some of it might have been uncomfortably close to the truth. However, he had decreed that to minimise the period that the Pope spent in the open, there would be no wives in the line. This message had been conveyed to the protection officers, who had accepted it without argument, and possibly, in one case, with relish.

And so the chief superintendent held his breath as the plane came to a halt, the steps were put in place, and finally the door of the Airbus was opened. He felt his heart pound as the white-robed figure stepped out and made his way down the staircase and on to the red carpet, then knelt to kiss the ground, rising with great agility for a man of his age. Mackie looked around, almost frantically, as the Pope made his way along the receiving line, checking the snipers again, picking out the uniformed officers and those in plain clothes, with the tell-tale gold badges glinting on their lapels, his eyes searching all the time for anyone or anything that should not have been there.

It seemed to take an age, although only two minutes elapsed between the emergence of His Holiness from the aircraft and his entering the familiar vehicle with its canopy of bullet-proof glass and its ton and a half of armour plating, hidden and unsuspected under the gleaming white coachwork.

As the convoy, led and tailed by two police vehicles and flanked by eight motorcycle outriders, headed off for the City Chambers, Brian Mackie allowed himself a very small sigh of relief.

Seventy-nine

There were no smiles around the table in the room that normally seated dinner parties in Bute House, the First Minister's residence. Bob Skinner knew it well enough, having been there on several occasions during his term of office as security adviser to the secretary of state for Scotland, the official occupant of the fine Georgian terrace before his eviction by the creation of the Scottish parliament, but for the other six it was a first-time visit.

Brian Mackie had come straight from the airport, with Giovanni Rossi, Jack Russell, the Prime Minister's senior protection officer, and Adam Arrow, who had flown north with him. Skinner himself, Neil McIlhenney, and Special Agent Merle Gower had headed there from Fettes. The DCC had chosen the venue for its discretion, since there were no watching eyes or wagging tongues in Charlotte Square.

'Thanks for coming, Adam,' he said, after he had explained the day's developments, 'and thanks for not asking why I wanted you here.'

'No problem.' The little major's accent was the one he reserved for serious business, not his customary Derbyshire twang.

'Now that you're all up to speed on this new situation, let's try to analyse the threat. Why are Alsina and Middlemass here? What's their mission? I don't think there's any coincidence about it. I do not believe that two international terrorists would park themselves in Scotland, with almost foolproof and effective new identities, just to be out of the way. I believe they are here to pull something, and until I'm proved wrong, I'm going to assume that it's connected with this visit.'

'Why so sure?' asked Russell. 'Couldn't one of the naval bases, Faslane or Rosyth, be a target?'

'Rosyth's a dockyard,' said Adam Arrow. 'I don't see them attacking an empty vessel. As for Faslane, it's a nuclear bunker. It's the most secure facility in this country.'

'What about one of the nuclear power stations? Hunterston or Torness?'

'That would have to be another September Eleven,' McIlhenney told him. 'And even then, it wouldn't work. They're built to withstand aircraft impact.'

'Something from within, then. He's a chemist, isn't he?'

'That's right; and not a nuclear physicist. Anyway, they're also built to withstand earthquakes and they have all sorts of emergency shut-down mechanisms.'

'What about a gas attack?' asked Brian Mackie.

'Gas is non-specific,' Merle Gower pointed out, 'a random weapon. These two people have been here for eighteen months. If that's what they were here to do they'd have done it already.'

'I have thought about it, though, Brian,' said Skinner. 'In the five or so hours since I found out about this, I've had people crawling all over their home, and over Alsina's work areas at Heriot-Watt looking for traces of anything that might relate to the manufacture of ricin, or sarin, or XV. There's absolutely nothing in their house, and a facility for producing a nerve agent in a university would attract attention, I reckon.'

He pointed at Russell. 'To answer your original point, Jack, it's the timeline that makes me think their presence is related to this visit. I'm going to make some assumptions here; one of them is that these two people were in Dubai for the specific purpose of taking out an American intelligence operative, a counter-strike in the war on terror. Would you go with that, Merle?'

Special Agent Gower nodded. 'Yeah, we know that they both arrived and left there at the same time.'

'During the period they were there, Pope John the Twenty-fourth died, and Gilbert White, Cardinal Archbishop of Edinburgh, was elected as his successor. We're in an era of non-Italian popes now; the last one was French. What do they do, invariably, within the first couple of years of their reign?'

'They go home,' Arrow said 'to let their own people see them in their new exalted state.'

'Exactly. I believe that the people running Middlemass and Alsina, or Polly Price and Anwar Baradi, or whoever, anticipated this, and sent them here to settle down, find work that would fit their experience, keeping them as far away from potential surveillance as possible . . . a South African banker and a Spanish doctorate student are pretty good cover, we have to admit . . . and wait for the moment; this moment. That's what I see so far. The bits I can't see yet are why they ran or what they're planning to do, but does anyone disagree with my assessment so far?'

Nobody contradicted him.

'So what do we do about it?' asked Russell. 'Call the Murrayfield rally off?'

'If that's what the Pope wants, yes. Gio?'

'What's the risk to the public?'

'There's no evidence of a potential gas attack. The place is completely swept for explosives on a daily basis. We've even searched inside the scaffolding poles that make up the platform on the pitch. If there's a threat, it's likely to be personal.'

'Then there's not a chance he'll pull out.'

'What about the mass this evening?'

'Admission is by ticket only; had to be, because of the numbers.'

'I want officers at all entrances to the cathedral all the same, with mugshots of the pair. We've done some alternative images from the Kabul photo.'

'Then go ahead and station them.'

'Thanks,' Skinner acknowledged. 'The Royal Infirmary visit tomorrow's easy: we can lock that up tight. That leaves the rally as our real problem, our point of potential weakness. What do we do about it? We catch them if we can. But if we can't, then at the very least we try to guess what they're planning and make sure they can't carry it out. For example, nobody gets near the Pope who shouldn't be there.'

He looked at Gower. 'We've all got our part to play in this. Merle, forget which agency pays your salary. I want the CIA to put its resources into finding out who this woman really is, and to create some potential attack scenarios for us, based on what's happened elsewhere.'

'That's already happening, Bob.'

'Good.' He turned to Arrow. 'Adam, do we need more soldiers?'

'We could use them to set up a wider security perimeter around the ground and let no vehicles through. That would prevent a mortar attack. I can do that.'

'Do it.'

'Where do the public's cars go?' asked McIlhenney.

'Saughtonhall sports fields,' said Mackie. 'We divert them there. The buses can go on the back pitches, as planned.'

'Anything else we need do?'

'There's already a no-fly zone in place, Bob,' Arrow replied. 'Any light aircraft heading anywhere near Murrayfield will be seen off.'

Skinner looked back across the table at Russell. 'Jack, I'd be happier if there was only one potential high-tariff target on that platform. Could you persuade him to pull out?'

'That would run counter to the basic principle of not letting terror be seen to gain the smallest victory,' said the protection officer. 'Sometimes I reckon that "martyr" is the word, above all others, that my man would like carved on his tombstone.'

Eighty

Mario was gazing out of the window when the buzzer sounded. He liked the view across the water, even at night when all he could see were the lights of the docks and of Ocean Terminal beyond. When his Aunt Sophia had decided that she could live there no longer after his Uncle Beppe's death, he had seized the chance to move into the family-owned penthouse, and had not regretted the decision.

As he picked up the handset that connected him to the main entrance he knew who would be waiting below. 'Hi,' said the quiet voice he knew so well, the one he had expected to hear.

'Come on up.' He pressed the button that opened the door, holding his finger on it till he heard her shout, 'Okay!' then walked out of the apartment to wait beside the lift.

'Hiya,' he greeted Maggie as she emerged, kissing her lightly on the cheek. He held the door open for her, and watched her as she stepped inside. She was dressed casually, as she had always dressed, yet there seemed to be something different about her, about her manner, about her bearing.

'Are you not seeing Paula tonight?' she asked him. There

was no animosity in her tone; indeed, there had been none between them since they had split.

'She's at the theatre with her mum,' he told her. 'They've got tickets for the musical at the Playhouse; afterwards they're going to Ferri's for supper. They had to take a taxi, though. I warned Paulie off trying to drive there: with the papal mass in the cathedral just across Picardy Place, the traffic'll be hellish.'

'So you're on your lonesome.'

'Yup.'

'Are you still upset about Colin Mawhinney?'

'What do you think? I reckon Neil's got a lead, though. He hasn't said, but he was closeted with an American the other day, and then they went off to see the Big Man.'

'How about you? Does the uniform still fit? Are those badges on your shoulders wearing you down yet?'

'Not one bit.'

He walked over to the bar set in a corner of the big open living space. 'You want a drink?'

'What do you have open? No. Wait. Let me guess. Chianti?'

He laughed. 'What else?' He filled a glass for Maggie and topped up his own. 'So what's up?' he asked, as he handed her the dark red wine. 'Why the official visit?'

'There's something I have to tell you to your face,' she answered. 'I've moved in with Stevie.'

She watched his eyes as he digested what she had told him; they gave nothing away. 'I see,' he murmured. 'You mean move in as in share a flat, or move in as in . . .'

'Why would I want a flat-share when I have a perfectly nice house? I've moved in with him, Mario, period.'

'And it's okay?'

She nodded. 'It's okay. In fact it's better than that; it's like I never thought it could be.'

'Does he know? Have you told him? About your father, the abuse?'

'No.'

'Will you?'

'I don't think so.'

'Good. Where is he anyway?'

'Downstairs, in the car. He'd have come up, but I preferred it this way.'

'Well, bring him up, for fuck's sake!' exclaimed Mario. 'I won't eat the guy. Far from it; I owe him a drink.'

'Why?'

'For taking you off my conscience, okay?'

'I'll drink to that too.' She took out her cell phone and called Stevie on his. 'Come on up,' she said, when he answered. 'The bear's friendly.' She pressed the button when the buzzer sounded a few seconds later, then opened the front door.

As he stepped into the room, Mario glared at him; and then a grin spread over his face and he reached out and shook his hand. 'Good luck, mate,' he said.

'As in, he'll need it?' Maggie challenged, as she poured her partner a glass of Chianti.

'Cheers,' said Stevie. 'Before you say anything, Mario, I promise I'll look after her.'

'I wasn't going to, but it's good to hear. How widely is this known?'

'Mary Chambers and that's it,' Maggie replied.

'And Bob Skinner,' Stevie grunted.

'How? God, what's the point in asking!'

Stevie smiled. 'It's okay. I promised him I'd look after you too.' He leaned against the bar and sipped from his glass. 'Nice place this,' he exclaimed, looking around. He wandered across the room to the glass-topped dining table that stood in the opposite corner, strewn with papers and other items.

'Mario,' Maggie began, 'about the house . . .'

He held up a hand to cut her off. 'It's yours. We agreed that, and nothing's changed.'

'Do you mind if I rent it out?'

'Mags, I don't mind if you . . .'

'Excuse me!' There was a strange urgency about Steele's voice as he cut into their conversation. They turned together to see him staring at something on the table. 'What is this?' he murmured.

Mario walked over to join him, to see what had caught his eye, and held it. 'Those are Colin Mawhinney's personal things,' he said. 'I'm looking after them until his colleagues collect them. What you're looking at is a photograph of his wife, Margery. She was killed in the World Trade Center.'

As he looked at Stevie, he saw that his face was chalk white. 'Then either it's her twin sister who's just disappeared from the Scottish Farmers Bank,' he whispered, 'or else she's risen from the ruins.'

Eighty-one

'Neil,' Skinner barked into the phone, 'I want you to pick up your witness Spoons, the guy who knows a Land Rover when he sees one, and I want you to show him a picture of a Mitsubishi Pajero. Ask him if he can really tell the fucking difference. You'll find that he can't. While your guys are finding him, I want you to get hold of the two NYPD officers and have them come to Fettes. Finally, do you know where Merle Gower is? I've tried her cell phone, but it's not responding.'

'She's at the consul's residence. I dropped her there after the meeting in Bute House. Huggins and Donegan are in the Ellersley House Hotel; that's not far away so they should . . .' McIlhenney paused. 'Am I right in assuming that a very big balloon has just gone up?'

'Nah, mate, that would be easy. I'd just shoot it down. This is more like the Martians dropping in for cocktails. I've just found out who really killed Mawhinney.'

'You what?'

'Yes. It was his wife.'

'His what?'

'DI Steele will explain. Between you, you know the whole story; apologies to Lou, but I'd like you back in my office to help tie all the ends of this together. Stevie, Maggie and Mario are here now. We only really need Steele, but the other two might as well stick around. The chief and I are having supper with the Pope and Jim Gainer this evening, but I'll come back to Fettes afterwards.' Skinner's mind was racing; he applied the brakes. 'Listen, forget the Americans. I'll phone Huggins, and Merle; you get here to catch any information they bring back.'

He hung up. 'Stevie,' he snapped. 'I want you to dig up Arthur Dorward, and get him, with his best team, back out to the Middlemass and Alsina house. They've to look for any forensic traces that confirm Mawhinney's presence there. Likewise they should turn their car inside out if they have to.' He turned to Rose. 'Mags, do you want to do something useful, if wholly beneath your exalted rank?'

'Of course.'

'You know your way around this floor. I'd like you to find the guest list for the reception that the chief was hosting for Inspector Mawhinney, and see who was due to represent the Scottish Farmers Bank.'

Rose looked at Steele. 'I don't need to find it,' she said. 'Vernon Easterson told us. He and Proctor Fraser, the chief executive, were invited. But they both had prior engagements, so Aurelia Middlemass was nominated to represent them.'

'And wouldn't that have been a surprise for poor Colin?'

'Remember the press coverage?' McGuire murmured,

drawing a frown from the DCC. 'Colin told John Hunter that he'd be on Brian Mackie's team for the Pope's visit; that must have been reported.'

'But was it?'

'It's a fair assumption.'

'This is no time for them. Check it out. They must plan to be close tomorrow,' Skinner exclaimed. 'The woman could simply have developed tactical flu and missed the reception, but if they read that Mawhinney was going to be in the police team for the visit, in the heart of the action . . . I reckon they decided that he had to be taken out.' He looked back at McGuire. 'Did Colin ever mention to you where his wife worked in the WTC?'

'Yes, he did. She was with a firm with a funny name. Wait a minute . . .' He frowned and scratched his black, curly head, as if it would speed his thought process. 'Garamond and Stretch,' he announced at last, with a note of triumph.

The DCC picked up one of his telephones and punched through to the switchboard operator. 'Sir!' came the sharp reply.

'I want you to get Lieutenant Eli Huggins of the NYPD,' he said. 'He's stopping in the Ellersley House Hotel.'

He slammed the phone back into its cradle, then looked through his personal contact book until he located the number of the US consulate's official residence. He dialled it on his direct line; it was answered, eventually, by a man. 'Barton Taylforth. Can I help you?'

'Bob Skinner here, at Fettes. I need to speak to Merle Gower.'

'Maybe for security she should call you,' the consulate's principal officer replied.

'I don't have time to burn. Put her on.'

'Bob?' Special Agent Gower came on the line within seconds. 'Has something happened?'

'Yes, it surely has. I've got another identity for Aurelia Middlemass. Before she went to Dubai and became Polly Price, she was Mrs Margery Mawhinney, the wife of the New York cop we pulled out of the docks on Monday morning. She was an employee of a company called Garamond and Stretch, in the World Trade Center, and she was killed on September Eleven . . . only she wasn't.'

'I'll patch that through to the CIA. It may help them.' The other phone rang as she spoke; he motioned to Steele to pick it up. 'I'll get back to you,' she said.

Skinner laid down one phone and took the other. 'Lieutenant Huggins?'

'Sir.'

'I've got some news for you. I reckon your people Salvona and Falcone were in Florida after all. Someone else killed Mawhinney. Eli, how well did you know the man?'

'I didn't, sir. The inspector was promoted out of the IAB well before I was posted there. Inspector Donegan and he were close, though.'

'Is he there?'

'He's in the next room.'

'Get him.'

'Sir, you won't discuss Salvona with him, will you?'

'That's irrelevant. Get him.'

He waited, fretting, until Nolan Donegan came on line. 'Inspector,' he said, with no preamble, although he had never met the second American, 'did you know Colin Mawhinney socially, as well as professionally?'

'Yes, sir; for years.'

'Okay. Don't ask questions, just answer them. What can you tell me about his wife?'

He heard Donegan take in a breath. 'Margery? She was the best thing that ever happened to him. I was there when they met.'

'When was that?'

'Colin and I were in a bar on Wall Street one night, out of uniform, when she came in, with a guy. They came up and sat on the stools next to us; she asked Colin for a light and they got talking. It was just simple conversation. I remember he asked what she did, and she told him that she'd just joined Garamond and Stretch, and that her name was Margery Walls; I remember she made a joke of it. "Like two streets," she said. Colin said hello to the guy and asked if was a colleague, and he leaned over and said, "No, now why don't you fuck off?" The friendly sort.'

'Can you remember his accent?'

'Definitely not American or British, and not Hispanic-American either.'

'Did she call him by name at any point?'

'Yeah, she did. I remember that. When he said what he did, she turned to him and said, "Franco, that's not necessary." Then he grabbed her, roughly, by the arm and tried to turn her towards him. She tried to push him off, but he held on to

481

her until Colin showed him his badge, and told him quietly but firmly . . . that was his style . . . that it would be best if he took his own advice. The guy looked at Margery and said, "Ah, fuck you, then," and turned and left.'

'Did you ever see him again?'

'Never.'

'Can you describe him?'

'Dark hair, glasses, heavy set, little moustache, maybe late thirties; that's it.'

'So what happened with Colin and Margery after that?'

'She stayed, he saw her home, and that was that. Three months later they flew to Vegas and got married, and a little over six months after that, she was killed.'

'She wasn't,' said Skinner, quietly.

'Excuse me?'

'Margery Walls walked out of the WTC before the second plane hit. She went to Dubai, with a Zimbabwean passport that identified her as Polly Price. From there, she moved to Edinburgh using the name Aurelia Middlemass, which she'd acquired from a South African woman who was killed when her American diplomat boyfriend's jeep was blown up.'

'This cannot be true.'

'Get over here, Inspector. Have Huggins bring you to my office and ask for Neil McIlhenney. He and his colleague DI Steele will ask you to look at a couple of photographs. Then you'll see whether it's true or not.'

He hung up and redialled the consular residence. This time Special Agent Gower answered. 'Merle, I have a name for you. Franco. That's all, just Franco; but if he isn't one and the same guy as Hasid Bourgiba, and Anwar Baradi, and Jose-Maria Alsina, then it's time for me to make my wife a happy woman by taking early retirement.'

Eighty-two

As he sat in the Archbishop's residence, Deputy Chief Constable Robert Morgan Skinner felt that his life had become the stuff of fantasy. It was as if he existed on three planes, in three contrasting worlds.

There was the one in which he had become embroiled in Fettes, one of mystery, death, and danger. He had stepped out of it for a while, but he knew that he would have to go back, to try to solve the many unanswered questions that still seemed to be pointing him in a certain inevitable direction. There was his crumbling home life. He had called Sarah from the car that had taken him, and the chief constable, to their supper engagement, to explain that he would not be home at all that night. She had been cold and distant; their brief flickering of understanding a few days earlier had disappeared. He found himself in a huge dilemma, aching for his children, yet knowing that a reunion with them would bring a confrontation with his wife. And third, but not least, there was the world into which he had stepped that night.

He had expected others to have been invited for supper: di Matteo, Rossi and Angelo Collins, certainly, and possibly the

Lord Provost and his wife. Yet when they had arrived there had been only four places set: theirs, the Archbishop's and the last, at the head of the table, for the Pope himself.

The conversation had been largely as promised. Pope John the Twenty-fifth was a hopeless football addict, and had been since boyhood, he revealed. He had played the game in his teens at a decent level; he had played in the Boys Guild, like Gainer, he had turned out as an amateur for Albion Rovers and, like Skinner, he had played for Glasgow University.

The DCC looked at him, as they sat in the Archbishop's drawing room, supper over and with brandy goblets in their hands. Cardinal Gilbert White had been a familiar figure in Edinburgh, a hugely popular man who had bridged the religious and political chasms that existed across central Scotland. He had been a giant of the city, and it was difficult to conceive that he could have evolved into something even greater.

And yet he had. He wore simple garments, more of a tunic than a suit, and he sat comfortably back in his chair, yet his presence seemed to fill the spacious room. In his career Skinner had stood close to monarchs and princes, prime ministers and presidents, yet until that evening he had never experienced the feeling of being in the presence of true greatness. With it there came a peacefulness that settled on him as a blanket, making him realise how weary he was.

'So, Jimmy,' said the Pope to the chief, 'you've been sitting quiet all night listening to Robert and me and the other James here, kicking the ball around. Tell me, how much longer will it take for them to prise you out of that uniform and introduce you to the delights of tending your garden?'

Skinner looked at Proud; it was a question he had never asked himself. He assumed, as did his colleagues, that he would carry on to the last day allowed by law. 'Not long now,' he replied. 'I'd go tomorrow if I thought that this man here would step into my shoes, but he's showing a marked reluctance to commit himself to that.'

'What's this, Bob? Are you denying Lady Proud the pleasure of having her husband around all day?'

The DCC sipped his Amaretto, then scratched his nose, until to his surprise he found himself voicing his thoughts in a way he never had before. 'You make me aware of my own selfishness, Your Holiness. I confess that I welcome Jimmy's continuing presence in that office of his, because every day he spends there delays the moment when I have to make what will probably be my last career decision. I'm not so arrogant that I assume his job is mine for the asking, but I know of his ambitions for me, and it would make me feel bad if I had to deny them.'

'Are you saying you might not apply for the chief's job when it becomes vacant?'

'Possibly. Would you have me apply for it if it went against my instincts and my conscience?'

'I would never have anyone deny his conscience, but that's just a word you're throwing around. You're using it to mask your resistance to change. I know this because I've been there myself. I didn't seek the office I now hold . . . you don't apply for this job, son. When it was put to me, I thought at first, I can't do this. I'm a pastor, a priest among priests, not above them. But then it came to me that the College of Cardinals hasn't made too many mistakes in recent centuries, and that my brethren calling to me with such unanimity were in a way the collective voice of God. I'm not bestowing divinity on Jimmy, here, but he's a wise man and if he feels you're his natural successor, don't you owe it to him and to yourself and to your city to listen to him?'

'But, Your Holiness, we're completely different sorts of policeman. I could never do his job the way he's done it over the years.'

'Then do it your way,' said the Pope, quietly. 'He's had you as his deputy. So what's to stop you finding a deputy like him?'

Skinner laughed. 'He's a one-off.'

'So are you. Bob, I'm not simply arguing my friend Jimmy's case here, I'm arguing my own,' he nodded to his left, 'and that of Archbishop Gainer. We love this city and we want to see it in the safest possible hands.'

'Your Holiness . . .'

'Think about it, that's all I ask . . . Well, that and one other thing. I won't say that I don't feel more holy in my exalted state, for it would be impossible not to, looking down on all those thousands in St Peter's Square, but that title is an awful mouthful for evenings like this. Since my first days as a priest, my closest friends have called me Father Gibb. Please join them.'

'Thank you, Father, for that honour,' said the DCC. 'In fact I heard that name for the first time a few days ago.'

'Yes, and from my old friend Auguste, I believe.'

'That's right.'

Father Gibb frowned. 'Angelo told me of the tragedies that befell his colleagues. Do they relate to me, do you think?'

'They make me uncomfortable, but they don't, not that I can see. To be truthful I don't know what's behind them.'

'But there is a threat to me. Tell me, Bob, I can sense it anyway.'

It was impossible to dissemble before the man, to hold anything back. 'Yes, there is,' Skinner replied. 'Two people. We believe they were planted here by al Qaeda, or by the greater network of which it's a part, to await your visit. We know who they are, although not where they are or what they're planning. Whatever it is, they're long odds against now we can put faces to them. If I may say so, you don't seem surprised.'

'I have felt the presence of a threat since my coronation,' said the pontiff. 'And I have felt also that it would be at its greatest when I was among those closest to me.' He gave a twinkling smile. 'Without giving myself any more airs and graces, there's a precedent for that, you know.' He reached across and touched Skinner on the arm. 'Try to do them no harm, please.'

'Our first duty is to protect, Father Gibb, but we'll try to shed no blood, I promise.' He looked across at the chief, who nodded in support.

'Going back to Malou,' said Skinner, 'we're protecting him now also, and his bandsmen. Is there anything you can tell me that might help us identify the killers of Hanno and Lebeau?'

For the first time that night, John the Twenty-fifth looked

his age; he frowned and closed his eyes, as if he was in prayer. Eventually he turned back to the DCC. 'I can't tell you all I know about Auguste Malou, because much of it came to me in the confessional.

'He was a soldier when we met, a young officer. It was over forty years ago, but he was carrying a burden even then. Although he was absolved of his guilt, the letters we have exchanged over the years tell me that he bears it to this day.'

'Have you seen him since your time in Belgium?'

'No.' He shot a bright glance across at Skinner. 'But what makes you think I met him there?'

'If not, where?'

'During my time as a curate at Saint-Gudule, I joined a mercy mission to the civil war in Africa, in which the Belgian army was embroiled. Malou was a young lieutenant then. We met in the Congo.'

Eighty-three

Neil McIlhenney was waiting in his office when the car dropped Skinner back at Fettes at ten minutes before one. 'The New Yorkers?' he asked.

'Been and gone. When I showed Donegan the photograph of Aurelia Middlemass, the poor guy broke down in tears.'

'How about the other one?'

'Progress. I showed him the Kabul picture and the photofit treatments that we'd produced from it. He sparked on one, so I pulled in an operator and we worked up one that he reckoned was pretty much spot on for the version he met in New York. I sent that to Merle Gower on her e-mail; she was going to pass it straight on to her people at Quantico. She said that when she told them about the Franco link, they got quite excited. She called me back about half an hour ago, wondering where she could contact you. She's expecting a preliminary briefing from them through the secure fax at the consulate and she wants you to see it ASAP. I told her that when it comes through she should bring it here.'

'Nothing for me to do but wait, then. You should go home now, though.'

'I'll stick it out.'

The DCC shook his head. 'No, you will not; I'm grateful to you as it is. That wife of yours is a very precious lady, even more so now. You go home and keep her warm, my friend.'

McIlhenney grinned and picked up his jacket. 'That's an order I can't refuse. Once Gower's been with this report, you should do the same.'

'I can't, Neil. I'm too wrapped up in this. Plus I've had a good slug of Jim Gainer's Amaretto.'

'What more can you do? It's going to be all right, man. We've had a huge stroke of luck. The Pope's going into a virtual fortress, we've identified the people who posed the threat to him and we've got the manpower to guard against anything they can throw at him. That's if they come back at all; if they've got any sense they're thousands of miles away by now.'

Skinner shook his head firmly. 'I'm telling you, they're coming back. That's why they killed Mawhinney: to eliminate the risk of him spotting his dead wife in the stadium. And, incidentally, his huge stroke of luck wasn't so good, was it?' He pointed a finger at McIlhenney. 'Has Dorward reported back yet?'

'Give him a chance. Arthur will get results if they're to be had, but he has to do it at his own pace.'

'I suppose so,' said the DCC, morosely. 'I just feel so fucking helpless, Neil. I know all the answers, save one; we know where, we know when, and we know who. But I don't know what they're planning to do . . . and until I know that, then I am dead certain the life of a very brave and very great man will be at risk.'

'I know something else. The more exhausted you get, the less likely it is to come to you.' Lights in the drive made him glance out of the window. 'That's Merle Gower now. Once we've heard what she's got to say, you're for my spare room again . . . and no arguments.'

The big man's sigh sounded desperately weary. 'If you say so,' he exclaimed. 'There's no point arguing, I suppose, since you're one of the few guys in this force I can't shout down.'

The internal phone rang. McIlhenney picked it up and spoke to Night Security. A minute later there was a knock on the door and Merle Gower was shown in. She looked at the inspector doubtfully. 'He stays,' said Skinner. 'He's cleared.'

'I know, but this is . . .'

'He stays.'

'Okay,' she conceded. She took a document from her bag. 'I let you see this and then it goes in the shredder. Is it okay in here?'

'You mean is it bugged? Do me a bloody favour, woman. I say things in here that I don't even want to hear myself.' She grinned weakly. 'Do you feel out of your depth, Merle?' Skinner asked her.

'I'm a strong swimmer,' she replied. 'I've just never been in this deep before.'

'It makes no difference; you just keep going. What have you got?'

'Just this. The name you gave me, Franco. It squares with a reported casualty, Franco Gattuso, who worked in the first tower . . . on one of the floors that took the impact of the first plane.'

'Fuck. But it isn't just that, though, is it?'

She shook her head. 'No. And this is what must be shredded, because our knowledge of it has never been revealed. The aircraft strikes didn't just rely on the skill of the pilots alone. The planes actually homed in on beacons that had been planted in each tower. When the agencies examined the air-traffic recordings, they picked up two signals. They were puzzled for a while, but eventually they determined that they were from homing devices. We believe that the mission of Gattuso and Margery Mawhinney was to conceal them somewhere on their floors, and activate them. The assumption was that the people who planted the beacons had perished also, but now it seems that was wrong.'

'They lived to kill another day,' Skinner whispered. 'And now they're here.'

'There is one last thing,' said Gower. 'The timing of the attacks has always concerned the investigating agencies. The gap between the two strikes was enough to allow a full Fire Department response to the first to have been made when the second hit. It's always been suspected that this was based on inside information; thanks to your discovery, we believe we know how it might have been obtained.'

'That's going to stay secret, I hope,' McIlhenney growled.

'That will only be possible if there is a certain outcome to all this.'

'What the hell do you mean by that?'

'She means, Neil,' said Skinner, 'that when we catch them, we'll charge them with the murder of Colin Mawhinney. Everything we now know about them will become public in the course of a trial here. That's if there is a trial here. As soon as we lock them up, the First Minister and the Lord Advocate will come under huge political pressure from the American government to hand them over. If they have the bottle to refuse . . . which I doubt . . . we could have an internal constitutional crisis, with Whitehall trying to stare down Holyrood. But if they're sent to the US, they'll be at the centre of the biggest show trial the world has seen since Nuremberg, one that will expose the failures of the FBI and the personal indiscretion of a New York policeman.' He stopped. 'What Merle is saying is that it'll be best if we don't capture them; not breathing at any rate. Isn't that right?'

'You get the picture I've been told to paint. I've even been instructed to offer you expert assistance if you wish.'

Skinner glared at Special Agent Gower. 'That's a step too far, lady. I will have none of your fucking gunslingers on my turf, and you can pass that on to whoever needs to hear it.'

'I will. But what else do I tell them?'

The DCC winked at her. 'Tell them I'll do as I've been asked.'

Eighty-four

Sarah Grace Skinner had always taken pride in her self-control. She had known some difficult moments in her otherwise sunny and privileged life, but she had come through them all with a toughness she was sure she had inherited from her father.

So, as she had felt it ebb away over days, weeks and then months, she had grown more and more frightened. Her loss of her sense of place and her self-confidence was starting to show in her work. That stupid rush to an unsupportable conclusion in the autopsy of the banker suicide was something that she would never have done before.

And now she was doing something else that in the past would have been alien to her. She was running away. She had risen from a sleepless night, not for the first time spent alone, had dressed quickly and had seen to her children. She had said nothing to them other than the usual, 'Be good today,' and then she had left them to Trish, with a lame excuse about an early appointment, and had carried on with her own preparations.

She had slung her case into the back of her car when the

nanny was occupied in the nursery, and had driven off without a backward glance, her view of the road slightly blurred by the tears in her eyes.

She was unsure how she would be welcomed, or even whether she would be welcomed, but it was a chance she was prepared to take. Before, she had always weighed the consequences of her actions; at that moment she found, for the first time in her life, that she did not care.

The traffic was building up as she drove towards Edinburgh. She was no fan of rush-hours and had managed to avoid them for most of her working life. She was no fan of city living either but, in the right circumstances, she reckoned she could grow used to it.

As she approached the turn-off to Fort Kinnaird and Craigmillar beyond, she switched on the radio. By one of those random chances that always come up when least wanted, the Beatles were singing 'All You Need Is Love', on Forth Two. She switched it off again, at once.

The traffic slowed through Craigmillar. Edinburgh's traffic planners did not like motorists and went out of their way to make life difficult for them, laying down bus lanes and narrowing roads at every opportunity. By the time she reached Peffermill, she feared that she would arrive too late, but at the Cameron Toll roundabouts, it speeded up. When she turned into Gordon Terrace, it was ten past eight.

She parked across the street from the house and took her case from the car. Slowly she walked up the driveway to his door, as if she was considering every irrevocable step. Just once, she hesitated, thought about turning back; but she kept on, until she stood on his front step. She rang the bell and waited.

She waited for a while; remembering the lay-out of the house, she thought that he might be upstairs, in the shower, so she rang again, keeping her finger on the button for a few seconds.

She had barely taken it away before the door opened. 'Can I . . .' she began, before the question died in her mouth.

A woman stood there, staring at her. She wore a long T-shirt that came almost to her knees, her red hair was tousled and she wore no makeup. The look in her eyes was one of pure, undiluted hostility.

'Maggie,' Sarah gasped.

'Right,' she hissed. 'Now get the fuck off my man's step, and out of his life.'

The big green door was slammed in her face.

Eighty-five

Bob Skinner was beginning to hate his office. He felt trapped in it, a prisoner behind a desk, when all his instincts told him he should be out there doing something, joining his officers in combing the city for any trace of the two people who posed such a threat to its most famous son.

Every one of them, and every officer in the neighbouring Strathclyde force, had been given the Aurelia Middlemass photograph and a copy of the photofit of her partner's most recent image, drawn up by his lab assistant at the university. It was something that had to be done, but the DCC knew within himself that it would be useless. Experienced, resourceful people like these would have changed their appearance for their return to Edinburgh. They would have a plan for gaining admission to Murrayfield, one that did not involve the stupid risk of climbing fences. For all that was being done, for all his desire to help in its doing, he knew within himself that they would have to be taken in or at the stadium.

He had grabbed some badly needed sleep in McIlhenney's spare bedroom, six hours of it before Neil had wakened him at eight, an hour later than he had asked. Once he was dressed he had called home. Sarah had gone, Trish had told him, off to an early job in Edinburgh, but he had spoken to Mark and James Andrew, promising both boys that his whole weekend would be theirs, doubting that their mother would want any of it.

He looked out of his window. The weather forecasters had been correct: the day was mild and sunny, out of place for November, but welcome for the events it would see.

The telephone rang to interrupt his brooding; his direct line, Sarah perhaps, calling to roast him. He picked it up with that expectation. 'Hello, Bob.' Aileen de Marco's sunny voice shone some welcome light into his morning.

'Hi, Minister,' he replied. 'Ready for the big event?'

'My brother is. Forty-two years old and he's like a kid. He phoned me ten minutes ago; I've never heard him so excited. Is everything okay?'

'Work-wise or home-wise?'

'Both, although the second's none of my business.'

'As it happens, things have been better on both fronts. The investigation of the New York policeman's murder has taken a nasty turn that I can't discuss over the phone. As for the other, Sarah and I are barely speaking now. Somehow we seem to have lost contact with each other.'

'Can't you just sit down and talk about it?' asked Aileen, sympathetically.

His sigh was almost a moan. 'That would involve both of us listening as well. I don't know if either of us is capable of that any more. We may have hurt each other too much in the past year or so. We've both had crises in our lives, but hers was worse than mine, and I have to admit to getting my priorities wrong when it came to supporting her.'

'How about just saying "sorry"? I don't believe you'd ever deliberately hurt someone you love. Your wife must know that too, in her heart.'

She heard him hesitate. 'It may go a little deeper than that,' he told her.

'You mean you . . .'

'No.'

'Ahh, you mean she . . .'

'We've neither of us been paragons, Aileen.'

'Did she say anything when you got home on Wednesday night . . . or yesterday morning, rather?'

'I slept in the spare room. It seems that's what I do these days.'

'You could have slept with me.'

'To tell you the God's truth I wish I had.'

'The bad part of me agrees with you. The good part reckons you did the right thing.'

'No, we did,' he chuckled, 'or didn't, as the case may be. Tabloids be damned, I couldn't have a casual thing with you, Aileen.'

'You couldn't with anyone; you're too serious a guy.'

'A bit like you?'

'I suppose. There's something there, though, isn't there? Between you and me?'

'Don't doubt it.' He paused, then his tone turned brisk. 'But I have to put it all aside for now. I've got a lot of thinking to do, love, and maybe a lot of decisions to make, but before any of that I have to focus on the present. My personal problems are irrelevant beside the task of getting our VIPs through today in one piece.'

'Does that include me?' she asked.

Suddenly he felt himself shudder. 'I find it odd to think of you in that context, but you're right; it does.'

'Make sure you do, then. Will I see you at Murrayfield?'

'I'll be there. You concentrate on enjoying the day, and I'll concentrate on making sure that you can. 'Bye.'

He put down the direct phone and buzzed McGurk on his intercom. 'Jack,' he said. 'Give me ten minutes, son, then come on in. I want to do some brainstorming.'

He spun his chair down and turned to his computer. There had been no personal e-mails that morning, but he had left it switched on. He hit the search button on his keyboard and entered one word on the bar: 'Congo'. He found himself offered a series of options, but they were all fairly recent history; even the CIA World Factbook, one of his favourite source websites, told him nothing about the events of forty years before. Finally he turned to Encarta, an encyclopedia that he had bought and installed but rarely used. The entry was comprehensive: the Democratic Republic of the Congo, formerly the Republic of Zaïre, and before that, a Belgian colony. The names were from his boyhood, Tshombe, Lumumba and Kasavubu, although Mobutu had a more familiar ring. There had been independence, there had been chaos, there had been civil war, there had been assassinations; but there was little or no information about Belgian involvement.

He buzzed McGurk again. 'Jack, before you come in, I want you to get someone on the blower for me: Lieutenant Colonel Pierre Winters of Belgian military security. Ask him to call me on my secure line.'

He went back to his computer and began keying names into the search engine. Moise Tshombe, the leader of the breakaway province of Katanga immediately after independence and later prime minister of the reunited country, had eventually fled, and had died, or been murdered, in jail in Algiers after being taken from a hijacked aircraft. Joseph Kasavubu had been a puppet president for the first five years of the country's existence until Mobutu had decided to oust him. Patrice Lumumba, the first prime minister of the new Congo, Marxist hero of the independence movement, had been betrayed, overthrown and eventually handed over to Tshombe and his enemies in Katanga, where he had been assassinated. Skinner was reading an account of his death with growing interest when his secure telephone rang.

'What can I do for you, Mr Skinner?' asked Pierre Winters, with an air of weary tolerance.

'Auguste Malou was a young officer in the Congo in the early 1960s,' he said.

Instantly, the Belgian was rattled. 'Who told you that? Not Malou, I'll bet.'

'Why so sure? Is he still under active orders not to talk about it?'

'You are still wasting your time and mine, sir. These are internal Belgian matters, and I will not discuss them. If you persist . . .'

The DCC's temper was triggered. 'If I persist, pal, you'll wish I hadn't.' Sheer instinct made him fire a name at Winters. 'Patrice Lumumba,' he barked.

The phone in Brussels was slammed down so fast that it was as if it had become red-hot in the lieutenant colonel's hand. Skinner smiled in satisfaction. 'Gotcha,' he muttered. 'But,' he added aloud, 'what the fuck does it have to do with this situation?'

He called McGurk into his office and poured them both coffee. 'Brainstorming, boss?' the sergeant asked.

'Like you've never known it.' He waved McGurk into the seat on the other side of his desk and checked his watch: it was nineteen minutes before ten. 'The Pope arrives in Murrayfield in just under two hours,' he said. 'We've got two al Qaeda terrorists out there trying to crash the party. Willie Haggerty, Brian, Neil, and a small army are there trying to keep them out; their chances of getting through are about one in ten, but these are bright, resourceful and determined people. Let's assume the worst, that they manage it. What are they going to do?'

'Shoot the Pope? Or the Prime Minister? Or both?'

Skinner raised an eyebrow. 'Funny that nobody ever talks about shooting Tommy Murtagh. Our First Minister would probably be very indignant if he realised that. No, Jack, if they were going to shoot anyone they'd have to use arrows. They won't get a firearm in there, and they won't get explosives in either.'

'Could they have planted them at Sunday's international?'

'The place has been swept five times since then; if they'd

503

planted a toothpick it would have been found.'

Skinner pulled Pringle's folder across to him. 'We've got two unsolved mysteries on our hands, Sergeant: that one,' he slapped it, 'and this one. There is no sign that they're connected, but a quarter of a century as a copper tells me that they are. If I'm right, the answer's in here; we're so fucking stretched at the moment just doing the protection job, that you and I are the only guys left to try and find it.' He split the pile of papers into two and handed half across the desk. 'Let's get to it.'

'What are we looking for, boss?'

'If I knew that I'd point you at it. We're looking for something that's wrong. We're looking for something that's out of place. We're looking for something that proves that Hanno wasn't just killed by a drunk driver, and that Lebeau wasn't an unlucky victim of a random lunatic who gets it off by spiking toothpaste tubes with poison. We're looking for a lie.'

He picked up the first paper from his half of the folder's contents. It was an interview with the bus driver, Maurice Roger, conducted in Haddington, after the police team had become aware of Hanno's death. He reckoned that he had probably been the only sober man in the club when Hanno was killed. He remembered that the veteran bandsman had been on top of his form, entranced by the range of ales on offer and determined to try every one . . . at least once . . . but he had not seen him leave.

It was the first of ten almost identical statements that he read in succession. A common theme ran through them; until his death, Philippe Hanno had been having the time of his life. He had been seen in conversation with Lebeau, with young Roelants, with Willi Schmidt, and, animatedly, with the barmaid . . . Philippe still travelled in hope, his colleagues agreed, even if his days of expectation were behind him.

He turned to a series of statements sent up from Hull by the investigating officers there. The second was by the barmaid in question, Mrs Doreen Silk, aged fifty-three, of nineteen Clarindel Drive, Kingston upon Hull. 'He was a nice man,' she had recalled. 'He had that look in his eye, too, as if he fancied himself a bit. I've seen worse, I have to admit.' Who knows? thought Skinner. If Philippe had lived . . . The last time she had spoken to him that evening, he had asked her for cigarettes. 'Gauloises,' he had specified. 'You know, the blue packet.' She had told him that they only sold British fags; he had shrugged his shoulders and turned away. She remembered that he had gone over to the bus driver, spoken to him briefly and headed for the door.

'Wait a minute,' said Skinner, aloud.

'You got something, boss?' asked McGurk.

'The bus driver. He said he never saw Hanno leave . . .'

'That's right. I interviewed him.'

'Describe him.'

'Thirty-something, dark-skinned; could have been North African origin, or Asian.'

'Did you see the bus?'

'Eh?'

'Have you ever seen the Belgians' bus?'

McGurk frowned for a moment, then his eyes brightened. 'Yes, I have; I'm sure of it. When we went to Haddington to interview them there was a bus there. A big brown thing with "Autotours Duvalier de Bruxelles" written up the side.'

'Shit. Who've we got available?' The DCC thought for a moment, then dialled Ruth Pye. 'You busy?' he asked.

'It doesn't sound like it,' his secretary replied. 'What is it?'

'I want you to trace a company for me.' He repeated the name on the bus, checking the spelling with the sergeant. 'How's your French, Ruthie, if you have to use it?'

'*Parfait.*'

'*C'est bon.* Call them and tell them you want the details of the driver who's with the Bastogne Drummers. Spin them a story; tell them that he's been reported for speeding by a punter and we need to check him out.'

He left her to her task and went back into the interviews. 'Okay,' he said. 'He's out of fags, he can't get his brand in the bar, so he gets the keys off the driver and goes across to get some. That's what Malou told Dan Pringle. So why's the driver coy about it?'

'He's out of what?' exclaimed McGurk. He took a slim folder from his pile and thrust it at Skinner. 'Read this.'

The DCC took it from him: it was labelled 'Post-mortem Report; M. Philippe Hanno', and dated. He looked at the opening paragraphs.

The subject is a male in his early sixties, reportedly struck and killed by a speeding vehicle. The body showed multiple signs of trauma, notably to the legs, the cervical vertebrae and the skull, all of which were fractured.

At the time of his death, the subject was in generally

fair physical condition. He was overweight, although not obese, and the liver was slightly enlarged. However, the heart was healthy and normal and the lungs were in exceptionally good condition for a man of this age, with no sign whatsoever of damage. Clearly, as was confirmed by an examination of his fingers, the subject was a non-smoker.

Skinner's eyes widened. 'He was a non-smoker? Yet Malou said he went across to the bus for fags! Fuck!' he shouted. 'Jack, have you got the Hull police report there?'

McGurk flicked though his documents. 'Yes, boss.'

'Is his property listed? Contents of his pockets?'

He scanned his eyes down the single sheet. 'Forty Gauloises; crushed but recognisable.'

'Malou smokes bloody Gauloises! I see it now; he sent him for them. He set him up to be killed, and I'll bet you the driver was in on it. And if he set up Hanno, he did the same to Lebeau. Someone gave him the poisoned toothpaste, and he put it in with his kit. Or . . .'

His eyes fixed on McGurk. 'Who else was billeted at the farmhouse besides Malou and Lebeau? It was a big place. There were more than two people there, I know.'

Before the sergeant could answer, Skinner's direct line rang. He seemed to rip it out of its cradle. 'Yes?'

'Bob . . .' His wife's voice sounded strained.

'Not now, Sarah; later, but not now!' As he hung up on her, his internal phone buzzed. He took a deep breath then pressed the hands-free button. 'Ruth,' he said calmly.

'I spoke to them, sir. The driver's name is Albert Berenger, he's fifty-one and his wife is really pissed off with him because he hasn't called her since he left. They've sent him three text messages telling him to phone her and get her off their backs, but he still hasn't. They ask if we can make sure he does . . . please.'

Skinner whistled. 'I think she's going to have a long wait on her hands, Ruthie. Thanks.' He switched off the phone.

'He's a phoney,' he said to McGurk, 'and I can see the tie-up.' He recalled his secretary. 'Get me Lieutenant Colonel Winters in Brussels back. You'll find his number on Jack's desk. On this line, I've got no more time for fannying about.'

'The bus driver, sir,' the sergeant murmured, once he had Skinner's attention. 'He and three of the musketeers were billeted there with Malou and Lebeau.'

The silence between them as they waited was the kind that seemed to magnify every other noise in the room. The quiet hiss of the coffee filter sounded like a steam whistle. The background buzz of the traffic outside became a military convoy passing beneath the window. When McGurk sucked his teeth, Skinner glared at him. And then the phone rang like a klaxon.

'Sir,' Winters's voice was as icy as his name, 'I am growing tired.'

'Listen to me, please,' said the Scot. 'I don't care what great state secret Malou's mixed up in that you can't let slip. I don't think this has anything to do with that. I need your co-operation or two very famous lives could be at risk. I want you to get me

508

some answers, more or less instantly. First, what are Malou's present family circumstances?'

'I can tell you that myself. When you asked about him I had his file updated. He is widowed, and he has a daughter. She is divorced, and has two daughters. They live with him in a suburb of Brussels.'

'What age are the kids?'

'Six and nine.'

'Oh, shit! Right, find this out, at once. Have the children been at school since the Drummers left for Scotland? If the answer is no, then pick half a dozen of your best undercover police or special troops and get them to his house as fast as you can. You will have to be very careful about what you do there, though. The strongest man's weakest point is his family, and it could be that Malou's is under threat.'

'Under threat from whom?'

'Al Qaeda, or a linked organisation. There are two of them on the loose here, after the Pope and our prime minister.'

'Then say no more,' the soldier told him, 'but stay by your telephone. I will check on the children and take it from there.'

'There's one other thing I need to know. Did the band of the First Guides Regiment provide replacements for Hanno and Lebeau?'

'Okay, I'll find that out.'

'Thanks, Colonel. I have to go to deal with this, but my assistant, Jack McGurk, will wait by the phone. You can tell him everything. He has my complete trust.'

As he ended the call, he rose to his feet. 'What if the kids are okay, boss?' asked the sergeant.

'In that case I assume that Malou's a terrorist, and he goes the same way as the rest. But they won't be okay.'

'Then what if they've been taken somewhere else?'

'That could be tragic, but they'll be at home, held prisoner. Why take the risk of moving them and having someone see it?'

'But what are they planning to do? We still don't know that.'

Bob Skinner laughed; he actually laughed. 'I do. It's fucking obvious, when you weave all the threads together. We're a couple of days off the date, Jack, but . . . remember, remember, the fifth of November.' He headed for the door. 'Get me on my mobile when Winters calls back, and ask him to contact me direct with any news about Malou's family.'

'I'll do all that. Anything else?'

'Keep your fingers crossed. I'm still short of one piece of inspiration.'

He rushed downstairs to his car, turned on the engine and slotted his cell phone into the hands-free holder. As he moved off he dialled McIlhenney. 'What's happening there, Neil?' he asked.

'The crowd are all in place, but there's no sign of our two.'

'Where are the Belgians?'

'In the entertainers' marquee, as far as I know.'

'Make sure. Count them. Then find their bus driver, wherever he is. He's a plant.'

'What do I do with him when I spot him?'

'Who have you got there you can trust?'

'Stevie's here, like you asked, and Maggie, as the two of our people who've actually seen the woman.'

'Keep them looking out for her, then. Ask Adam to lend you one of his plain-clothes soldiers. Are you armed?'

'Yup.'

'Then arrest the bus driver as soon as you locate him, but without letting Malou see you, or any of the band for that matter. And, most important, don't let him communicate with anyone.'

'If he's a plant, why not let him run and hope he leads us to them?'

'Too risky. I want him out of the way. When's the papal convoy due there?'

'Fifteen minutes, maybe a bit more; they've just left the infirmary. The VIPs take the stand in ten and the bands march in as soon as the Pope's in the arena.'

'If I'm not there in time, stop the Belgians. In the meantime, I know the army has a bomb team there just in case. Have them gather outside the tent.'

'Repeat?'

'Don't let the Belgians out of the marquee. Bomb squad to wait outside.'

Skinner hit the red button on the phone and put his foot down; he roared up towards Queensferry Road, swung into it on an orange light and headed past Stewart's-Melville College. He had just turned left at the roundabout when a call came in. 'Sir?' McGurk's raised voice filled the car.

'Speak, Jack.'

'Colonel Malou's daughter phoned their school the day after the band left for Scotland. She said that both girls had chickenpox. No other kids have it. As for the bandsmen, neither the First Guides band nor any other military unit sent replacements for Hanno and Lebeau.'

A smile crossed Skinner's face. 'Thank you, son. Has Winters got my number?'

'Yes. He said to tell you that an anti-terrorist squad will be at Malou's apartment block within ten minutes. They'll be dressed as firemen and the cover story will be that there's a gas leak. It's a ploy they've rehearsed but never used.'

'Let's hope they get it right first time.' He turned right at a set of traffic lights and raced along Ravelston Dykes Road. Suddenly the traffic was heavy; the diversions put in place for the rally were taking their toll. He overtook a line of traffic, blind, and swept down Murrayfield Terrace, waving his warrant card as he approached the barrier at the foot. The officers on duty recognised him instantly and waved him through.

He drove as fast as he dared along the approach road to the stadium until he drew to a halt on the grass, in front of a big tent that had been set up behind the north grandstand. At its entrance, he saw Neil McIlhenney waiting, beside two soldiers in uniform. One was an officer; Skinner recognised him as Major 'Gammy' Legge, a bomb-disposal veteran of Ireland, the Gulf and other less famous conflicts.

'Bob,' the soldier exclaimed, as he approached, 'what's the panic?'

'No panic. Just stick around and you'll see.' He turned to McIlhenney. 'Have you got the driver?'

'No problem. We went to his bus, and found him taking a knapsack out of the boot. He was getting ready to run.'

'Did he give you any trouble?'

'Nothing that having a Glock pointed at him didn't sort out fast. There's a secure room at the back of the west stand, not far from the shop. It's a cell, really, but the SRU doesn't like the word. The soldier who helped me lift him is standing guard at the door.'

'Does Adam Arrow know he's there?'

'Yes.'

'Willie Haggerty?'

'Him too. We didn't make a fuss, though.'

'That's fine.' He saw Legge's eyebrows rise at the mention of the first name; he knew who Arrow was. 'Come, then,' he said. 'Let's talk to the bandleader.' The soldiers made to follow but he stopped them. 'Not you guys, not yet. I'll give you a shout.'

As he led McIlhenney into the marquee, he was aware of a commotion behind him and of the sound of growing excitement in the stadium, and he guessed that the Pope's approaching convoy had been picked up by the television cameras and was being shown on the giant screens inside the ground. The great assembly of kilted pipers near the entrance had come to the same conclusion; they were stirring themselves as the two policemen pressed through their ranks.

Skinner was smiling as he approached Malou. It was forced, for he read the look on the old colonel's face, the mixture of uncertainty and fear that he had seen on so many guilty men before. The bandsmen and the scarlet-clad musketeers were getting to their feet behind him, readying themselves to play. The DCC knew the two replacements instinctively. They held bass drum and side-drum respectively. They were younger, fitter-looking, their blue uniforms were newer and they stood slightly apart from the rest. They, too, had a strange look in their eyes. Yes, it was fear, but there was something else, something he had not seen before and could not describe even to himself.

Still he made sure. 'Those two?' he asked, still smiling.

The old man was trembling, but he gave a tiny nod.

'Neil,' Skinner murmured, 'show.'

The inspector's hand slipped inside his jacket, and reappeared holding a pistol.

'Even if you don't speak English,' the DCC exclaimed, as they stepped up to the pair, 'you'll understand gun, I take it. Face down, arms stretched out.' One of them understood exactly; he did as he had been told. The other looked around wildly, then leaped at Skinner. He jumped into a short right-handed punch to the temple, and dropped like a stone.

The big policeman looked round towards the entrance. The Belgians and the pipers were staring at the scene, many of them open-mouthed. 'Panic over,' he shouted. 'You guys near the door: there are two soldiers outside. Tell them they can come in.' He turned back to Malou. The old man seemed to have shrunk into his uniform, his hands were covering his face, and his shoulders were heaving.

Skinner stepped close and put his hands on his shoulders. 'I know what you did,' he said, 'and why. They gave you a choice; your old friend or all your family. I don't blame you, and neither will he.'

'But my children,' Malou wailed, as forty thousand young voices cheered the arrival of Pope John the Twenty-fifth in the great Murrayfield bowl, 'they're as good as dead. You've killed them.'

'Have patience, Colonel. And have faith too. Nobody's going to die today.'

'What the hell is going on, Bob?' Major Legge's voice boomed over his shoulder.

Skinner smiled and pointed to the discarded drums of the two men on the ground. 'Your guys have swept this place every day for a week. There's not a chance of anyone getting any modern high explosive in here. But what about the old-fashioned stuff, if you could get enough in?' He glanced at the musketeer platoon, and their antique weapons. 'What makes those things go bang?'

'Gunpowder?' Legge exclaimed. 'They were planning to use gunpowder?' He took a big red knife from his pocket, knelt beside the side-drum, slashed a great X across its skin, then peeled it apart. It was full of a black, sulphurous material. 'They were planning to use gunpowder!'

'That's right. And we more or less helped them bring it in. I would empty those pretty quickly if I were you. I reckon you'll find a couple of incendiary triggers inside, ready to be detonated remotely whenever the Pope and the Prime Minister were close enough to the carriers.'

'Stand back, then,' said the soldier, 'and don't light any matches.' He upended the side-drum, and lifted it up, pouring the black powder on to the ground. He repeated the process with the much larger bass drum, then sifted through the residue with his gloved hands until he emerged, triumphantly, with two small packages wrapped in brown paper. 'I wish they were all that simple,' he exclaimed. He handed them to his assistant. 'Take these away and do something to them, Corporal,' he ordered, 'then get one of the lads in here with a water-based fire extinguisher to damp this lot down. It's useless when it's wet,' he explained. 'The drums are waterproof, of course, which makes it such a bloody good idea.'

'Enough to do the job?' asked Skinner.

'That amount? Anyone within yards, old boy. This was a real suicide mission, no mistake.'

As he spoke, the DCC's cell phone sounded. Legge winced. 'Take it away from the powder, please, Bob. Just in case.'

Skinner walked to the other end of the tent before he answered the call. 'This is Winters,' said a voice in his ear. 'The children and their mother are safe; the terrorists who held them prisoner are dead. Three of them. How about your end?'

'I've got three live ones; there are still two to go.'

'How is Malou?'

'Terrified. I'll put him out of his misery in a moment.'

He thanked Winters, then called Willie Haggerty. 'Where are you?' he asked.

'In the command centre.'

'Brian?'

'He's outside. Where are you?'

'In the band marquee.'

'Where are the fucking bands?' the Glaswegian demanded. 'The Pope's here. They should be marching in.'

'Relax. They will be. I want two armed officers here now to take two prisoners into custody. They've to cuff them, strip them, and put them with the other bloke. But quietly, Willie. The threat's over, but I want the other two.'

He turned to the pipe-major; the man was highly agitated. 'Okay,' he told him quietly. 'Line them up, and march them in.'

'Sah,' the man barked, with huge relief.

'But one thing,' Skinner added. 'None of your guys saw anything in here. You're all military; anyone who leaks anything about this will be court-martialled and that is a promise you can rely on.'

He walked to the back of the tent. McIlhenney stood, motionless, his gun on the two men on the ground. The thirty-four remaining bandsmen and musketeers stood in bewildered groups, while their leader sat disconsolately on the remains of the booby-trapped side-drum. He looked up as Skinner approached. 'What now?' he asked, weakly.

'Your daughter and her children are safe, Colonel.' He saw the old man's face light up, and the tears spring to his eyes once more. 'So go and do what you were invited here to do. You can tell me the whole story afterwards, but now, you go and play for Father Gibb.'

He left Malou to organise his men; they were stunned, but they were stolid and they would play and march as best they could. He returned to McIlhenney and waited until the armed escorts arrived to take the prisoners away, watching as two soldiers turned the black pile on the ground to sludge. 'So what . . .' the DI began, but he was interrupted as Skinner's phone sounded again.

'Boss?' It was Mario McGuire and he sounded anxious. 'Am I on time?'

'So far.'

'It's taken a while, but I've got a result. First, no newspaper, website or broadcast station anywhere reported the fact that Colin Mawhinney was staying in the Malmaison. Second, I've been through the list of all the journalists that Alan Royston's accredited for this visit. As you can imagine, there's quite a bunch with the telly people and everything, but there are two of them who stand out; a photographer called Geoffrey Bailey, and a news reporter called Verena Cookson. They're listed as working out of the London office of a news agency with its head office in Venezuela. That's an accommodation address, but the thing that makes them really different is that three years ago Bailey and Cookson were working for a South African newspaper on a story in Angola when they stepped not just on one landmine but on a cluster of three strapped together. If that's them, they've been reassembled.'

'Photographs?'

'He's bearded with glasses, and I can place him. He was the photographer at the press briefing who asked Colin at the beginning where he was staying. You couldn't tell her from Eve, though . . . or maybe even from Adam. She looks weird: she's got short silver jaggy hair, no eyebrows at all, wears blue glasses, has studs through both nostrils and her bottom lip, and three or four rings in each ear.'

'In other words she doesn't look a bit like a corporate banker?'

'Not like any I've ever seen.'

'Thank you, Superintendent. Your late friend Colin owes you one.'

Skinner clicked an end to the call, then found the media-relations manager's number in his phonebook. 'Alan, it's Bob Skinner. Where are the press at this moment?'

'Telly's on the fixed platform, up in the stand, with two free cameras out on the ground. The photographers are in rows just to the side of the tunnel and the reporters are behind them. I can see them now.'

'Two names: Bailey and Cookson. Are they there?'

'Yes. She's sat directly behind him, in fact; they're in the seats next to the aisle. He's got the usual enormous camera and she's got a pocket recorder, for all the good that'll do her. She won't get that close. Bob,' Royston asked, 'do you know when the action's going to start? Everyone's getting fidgety.'

'Tell them one of the pipers fainted with the excitement, but that he's okay now. Neil and I are on our way there. One thing; whatever happens, you do not let anyone leave. Who's the nearest senior officer?'

'Brian. He's ten yards away.'

'Good. Tell him. Nobody leaves.' He replaced his phone and turned to McIlhenney. 'Come on.' He led him, running, out of the tent.

The massed bands were in their ranks outside, inflating their pipes, almost ready to march. Skinner raced up to the lead pipe-major. 'Two more minutes,' he said. 'Then go. It's important. Wait two minutes.'

Leaving them behind, the two policemen ran from the gateway to the ground, round the curve where north stand became west. 'This way,' said Skinner, still breathing easily as he led the way up a flight of stairs to the first level. He looked along towards the centre of the stand and saw Maggie Rose in her uniform, standing by an entrance door, looking out into the ground. Somewhere in the background he heard the skirl of pipes, and the buzz of forty thousand children turn once more to cheers. He ran towards her. 'Press? Where?' he called out, his breath coming harder now.

She pointed to her right. 'Next stairway and down.' Skinner and McIlhenney sprinted on, the DCC wishing that he had asked for an extra minute.

He saw her as soon as he turned into the entrance, her back to him, silver hair, spiked up, seated to the left of the aisle, in the second row from the front, behind a burly man. He paused, gathering himself, and allowing McIlhenney a few seconds to recover. 'I'll take him,' he gasped, 'you take her. Get the recorder, I'll get his camera; pound to a pinch of pig-shit that's where they've hidden the transmitters to detonate the bombs. I don't want those triggers going off in any soldier's hands, and when they see their boys are missing . . .'

'Christ, no,' the inspector muttered. 'But I'll take him. He's bigger and I've got the gun.'

'Deal.'

They slipped quietly down the stairway as the last of the long parade of pipers made their way into the stadium. They reached their targets just as the first flash of blue appeared in the gateway, as the colonel, diminutive in the distance, but marching straight-backed, led the Bastogne Drummers into the stadium.

Skinner was close enough to hear her exclamation as she realised that the front rank was two men short. He slipped down beside her and snatched the small device from her hand. The man in front turned, in time to look into the barrel of the Glock, as McIlhenney grabbed his camera with his free left hand.

'Show's over,' Skinner exclaimed, above the noise. He yanked the woman quickly out of her seat and pulled her towards the stairway, as McIlhenney motioned her companion to follow. He was glancing behind when she slammed a stiletto heel into the instep of his right foot. The pain was momentary but intense, loosening his grip for long enough for her to twist free and run up the stairs.

Maggie Rose seemed to step out of the shadows, to catch her in the doorway, spin her round and slam her, face first, into the wall, as hard as she could. The DCC whistled. 'Who the hell's been annoying you this morning?' he asked, as he limped up the stairs.

The incident was barely noticed, so intent was the crowd on the scene outside. McIlhenney held Bailey's arm twisted up behind his back, as Rose restrained the woman who had been Cookson for the day; together they forced them out on to the concourse. As they did so, Chief Superintendent Mackie appeared, with Alan Royston by his side.

'The last two for the lock-up,' said Skinner, 'but keep them separate from the rest. They're very special.'

'There's another holding cell,' Mackie told him. 'Beside the command centre. I'll put them in there.'

'You do that. Strip-search them, put them in restraints, then lock them up. Put a police officer on the door, armed but with weapon concealed.' He looked at Royston. 'Alan, if anyone asks you about this, tell them, for now, that we thought she looked odd, and that we were concerned that they'd slipped in among the press contingent, so we had them out of there as a precaution. When they've been questioned and charged, we'll release a full statement.' He turned away. 'Okay, get on with it; I'll see you after.'

'After what?' asked Rose.

'After the rally, of course. This is a uniform-section show; officially, I'm not on duty here. I'm going to watch.'

And watch Bob Skinner did, as the pipers piped, the dancers danced, the singers sang, as the Bastogne Drummers played and marched their finest, as the musketeers fired their ear-splitting gunpowder salute and as Auguste Malou came face to face with his old friend Father Gibb, for the first time in forty years.

He listened too, as Pope John the Twenty-fifth preached reconciliation and peace to a gathering of forty thousand, of many faiths and of none, to a generation with the youth and optimism, Skinner found himself hoping, to hear what he was saying and to put his teaching into practice.

And then it was over. The white-robed figure said his goodbyes to the Prime Minister and his wife, to the First Minister and Mrs Murtagh, and to the Lord and Lady Provost, then climbed back inside his bullet-proof, armour-plated bubble for the journey back to Rome. The DCC caught Gio Rossi's eye as he climbed into the car behind; he gave him a large thumbs-up sign, both hands clenched together in the gesture. Jack Russell saw it too, as he shepherded the prime ministerial couple into their Jaguar, and returned it with a smile and a quick wave.

As the convoy pulled out, Skinner made his way down to the ground, intercepting Aileen de Marco as she and her brother walked from the field.

'Is all well, then,' she asked, once she had introduced the two men, 'here at least?'

He smiled. 'Here at least.'

'You look really pleased with yourself,' she exclaimed. 'Is there something the Justice Minister should know?'

Why not? he thought, and 'Why not?' he said. 'Do you want to come for a walk?'

'Sounds intriguing. How can I refuse?' She turned to her brother. 'Peter, you follow Tommy and his wife, the LP, the chief constable and everybody into the reception; we'll be along in a minute. Where to?' she asked Skinner.

'Up to the top level. I'll show you the command centre, and let you look through a peephole at a couple of special guests of ours. I think they're going to become very famous in the months to come . . . if they can ever figure out what to call them.'

'My God, you've made arrests?'

'Let's not talk here. Come on.' He led her inside and up the first of several flights of stairs. The last of the young people and their escorts were leaving the stadium; they passed them and kept on climbing until they reached the highest point of the west stand, the command centre from which everything could be seen, either through binoculars or on a series of monitors, each showing feed from a different security camera.

He opened the door and ushered her inside: Willie Haggerty, Brian Mackie, Maggie Rose and Neil McIlhenney all turned as they entered. She greeted the three men, whom she had met before, and smiled at Rose as the DCC introduced them. As she shook her hand she noticed that her knuckles were grazed.

'Where's Royston?' Skinner asked McIlhenney, as Haggerty began to explain the working of the centre to the minister.

'Down in the press room. There have been no questions that I know of, and I asked him to let me know if any came up. I guess all the hacks must have been watching the parade when we lifted them.'

'Sounds like it.' The DCC grinned. 'Were they not the slickest four arrests you've ever made?'

'I have to say that you cut it a bit fine, boss, but apart from that, yes, they were pretty smooth. If only we could tell people.'

'Right enough.' He glanced at his watch. 'We'd better go. I have to take Aileen down to the SRU reception, and I promised her a look at the rogues' gallery.'

'Mmm,' McIlhenney murmured. 'Aileen, is it?'

'Knock it off,' said Skinner. There was a hint of sharpness in his voice that took his friend by surprise. 'Where's the holding cell?'

'Round the corner to your left.'

'Thanks.' He paused. 'Indeed, thanks for everything, mate.' He called to the minister, prising her away from ACC Haggerty, who was being more solicitous than he had ever seen him, and leading her outside and to the left, as McIlhenney had directed.

They turned the corner, and saw a man, a few yards away. He was in plain clothes, with a small golden eagle lapel badge, and he was smoking. Behind him, a door lay ajar. His mouth dropped open as he recognised Skinner, and he came to attention when he saw the look on his face, crushing his cigarette underfoot.

'What the hell's going on here, Sergeant?' the DCC barked. 'And where the hell are the prisoners?'

'Major Arrow took them, sir,' the man stammered, 'about five minutes ago. He said you wanted them all together, ready for the van to take them to Saughton Prison.'

Skinner took in a quick breath. 'Did he indeed? Then you go and find DI McIlhenney. He's in the command centre. Don't speak to anyone else, just him, but tell him I want both of you outside the cell downstairs in three minutes, tops. And tell him this . . .' He leaned over and whispered in the man's ear.

As he headed for the stairs, he was aware that the minister was on his heels. 'Aileen, please go back in there and ask Maggie to show you where the reception is.'

'Not a chance. I want to know what's happening here.'

He was about to order her back to the command centre, when he paused. 'Maybe you should, at that,' he exclaimed. 'Come on.'

He led her down the stairs as fast as she could go in her high heels. Half way down she stopped, ripped off her shoes, then ran after him carrying them.

The corridor leading to the tunnel was deserted as they turned into it, save for one man, standing impassively in front of a solid door, with a small peep-hole but no handle. He seemed to broaden out as Skinner and the minister stopped in front of him, as if he was trying to fill as much of the doorway as he could. He wore twill slacks and a roomy sports jacket; it was unbuttoned.

'You can't go in there, sir,' he said, in clipped tones that spoke of an authority other than the police.

The DCC held up his warrant card. 'I'm going in there, soldier, I promise you.'

'No, sir.' He flicked his shoulder so that his jacket opened a little, showing the pistol holstered beneath it.

Skinner moved faster than Aileen could have imagined, so fast that it was over before her involuntary gasp escaped her. The fingers of his left hand stabbed stiff and straight into the man's stomach, and then, in the same movement, his left forearm came up and under his throat, slamming him back against the door. When his right hand came into view it was holding the gun, and its barrel was jammed against the soldier's temple.

'Adam!' he called out. 'Open this fucking door or I'll use this guy's skull to batter it down. And don't do anything in there.'

He waited. 'No kidding, Adam,' he called out again, banging the soldier's head lightly against the black-painted steel to emphasise the point.

Finally, the door opened. As it did, Skinner hurled his prisoner inside, sending him tumbling into a corner, where he lay, still winded by the earlier blow, then he and the minister followed him into the cell. He kicked the door closed behind them.

The DCC breathed a loud sigh of relief. Five figures, four men and a woman, were on the floor, with their backs to him. They were in their underwear and they were handcuffed, but they were all on their knees and they were all still alive. He looked at Arrow, and saw the silenced pistol in his hand. Then he glanced down at the gun he held, and dropped it on the floor.

'No,' he said quietly.

'Bob,' said the major, 'I've got orders. I have to.'

'You have to execute five people?'

'Do you know what'll happen if they make it to court?'

'Yes, and it's my job to get them there.'

'And my orders are to see that they don't . . . at any cost.'

Skinner smiled. 'Man, how long have we been friends?'

'Ages.'

'So are you saying you'd shoot me too, and this lady here, who happens to be the Scottish Justice Minister, just to make these disappear? If you do, then as soon as you open that door you'll go down yourself. McIlhenney'll be outside by now and he has his orders too. If you walk out before me, it'll be the last step you take.'

'Then they'll say I was an al Qaeda plant myself,' Arrow replied, 'and that my job was to make sure nobody talked. Bob, please get out of here.'

Skinner shook his head. 'I can't do it.'

'But why not? Fuck me, you've dropped people yourself; we both know that.'

'I made a promise, Adam, that nobody would be harmed today.'

'Who did you promise?'

'Father Gibb.'

'Who the hell's Father Gibb?'

'A billion or so people know him as Pope John the Twenty-fifth.'

As Arrow stared up at him, Skinner felt Aileen take his hand and squeeze it. He felt her body tremble as she moved close behind him.

And then the little soldier smiled. He unscrewed the silencer from his pistol, slipped it into his pocket and reholstered the weapon.

'I guess his orders outrank mine,' he whispered, and blessed himself with the sign of the cross.

Eighty-six

'When you took me in there you did know that he wouldn't have shot me, didn't you?' Aileen asked him.

'No,' Bob replied cheerfully. 'But I was ninety per cent certain that he wouldn't have shot me.'

'Thanks very much.' She snorted.

She sat beside him on his office settee. He grinned as he reached out and touched her hand. 'I'm kidding, love, honest. Adam's done some terrible black things in his army life, and he would have carried out his orders if we hadn't stopped him, but he'd have seen himself as a one-man execution squad.' He shook his head. 'He couldn't shoot a friend, though; not ever.'

'But if we hadn't stopped him, what would have happened to the bodies? It couldn't have been covered up, surely.'

'Now it's you that's kidding yourself,' he told her grimly. 'Black van at midnight, hole in the ground somewhere or up the chimney at Mortonhall Crematorium in the middle of the night. Welcome to the dark side, Minister.'

'These things can't happen. I won't believe it.'

'You won't believe your own eyes? If we'd been a couple of minutes later, you'd have seen the aftermath, the blood and the grey sticky stuff.'

Once more, he felt her tremble against him. 'You know what came to me afterwards?' she murmured. 'All that time, none of the people on the floor said or did anything.'

'They were expecting it. The drummers didn't expect to live through the afternoon, remember. They thought they'd be blown to bits the moment Father Gibb and the PM got close to them at the inspection of the bands. As for the others, well, for two of them at least, it would have been a mercy killing. Bailey and Cookson, to use the names they took today, they will be sent to America . . . that's unless Tommy Murtagh vetoes it, only the PM won't let him. They'll be tried here for Mawhinney's murder, I'll make sure of that, but then, in a few months, they'll be extradited to the US. There'll be a huge legal process, but ultimately, after a couple of years of thinking about it, they'll both be strapped to tables and filled full of lethal injection. The Americans might even televise it. The former mayor of New York said he wants to push the button himself. For me, all that's a sight more horrible than letting Adam put one behind their ears.'

'Yet you stopped him?'

'You know why. It's up to Father Gibb to stop the rest of it, but I don't think even he'll be able to do that.'

Aileen sipped her wine; the table before them was strewn with the remains of the pizza they had bought from the takeaway in Comely Bank.

'What about the rest of it? Will the old colonel be tried?'

'No. He's made a full statement, and he'll be a witness in the trials of the bus driver and the drummers, and maybe the other two as well ... that's unless they all plead guilty, which they might. They're all proud of themselves, you know.'

'What did Malou do, exactly?' she asked him.

'He sent Hanno, a non-smoker, across to fetch his cigarettes from the bus. You know, he made a point of telling me a few days ago that he smoked old-fashioned Gauloises, the brand Hanno had on him when he died. They were holding his daughter and her kids, and threatening them with death, so that was as close as the old man dared get to crying for help. As for Lebeau, he nominated him; that was all. Roger, the bus driver, told him that he had to get rid of two drummers. He didn't tell him why, only that if he didn't there would be three boxes waiting for him in Belgium, each with a head in it. Poor old guy. He says he didn't know what the replacement drummers were going to do, and he didn't know about the extra gunpowder on the bus.'

'Who spiked the toothpaste? Who drove the hit-and-run car?'

'Bailey ... when he was Alsina, that is. He was a chemist, so he knew how to handle cyanide. As for the other, they'll match Hanno's injuries to the bull-bars on his Pajero, you can bet on that. And that, my dear, is just about the whole story.'

'Not quite. Why did Malou choose Hanno and Lebeau to die?'

'Because neither had any family, and also because they

were his old army buddies. He tried to make himself look on it as sending men over the top in a war, to face the enemy fire.'

He did not tell her Malou's last secret. He did not tell her that Hanno and Lebeau, and a third man long dead, had made up the firing squad that had executed Patrice Lumumba, or that young Lieutenant Malou had given the order to fire, or that Malou had confessed his guilt to a young priest, who, fearing for their lives in Africa, had used his bishop's influence to have them returned to Belgium to safe secure postings in which to see out their army careers. Winters had been prepared to sacrifice the Pope to hide that national disgrace: let him live with it, the Scot told himself.

'So what did you think of the Holy Father?' he asked her. 'Are you still an atheist?'

'Yes,' Aileen confessed, 'I am. But I believe in him.'

'Me too. He's a good foundation.'

'To build what? What will you do now? About your other crisis, I mean.'

He peered into his glass. 'I have lots of thinking to do,' he said. 'The food for some of it was provided last night, by Father Gibb. About my marriage . . . When I checked my e-mails after we got here, there was one from Sarah. She says that our problems are going to take more than a night in Gleneagles to solve. She's booked a flight to Florida, and a hotel. She's gone out there this evening; left the kids and a ticket for me with the nanny. She says that if I'm interested in a serious rescue mission, I should join her there.'

'And will you?'

'That's my first big decision.'

She lifted up his hand and kissed it. 'Do you have to make it tonight?'

In spite of all the worries bearing down on him, Bob Skinner smiled. 'No,' he murmured. 'That's for tomorrow.'